MW00781729

Promises of Love

David Selby

Publisher Page
an imprint of Headline Books, Inc.
Terra Alta, WV

Promises of Love

By David Selby

copyright ©2015 David Selby

All rights reserved. This book is a work of fiction. Names, characters, places and incidents, except where noted otherwise, are products of the author's imagination or are used fictitiously. Any other resemblance to actual people, places or events is entirely coincidental. No part of this publication may be reproduced or transmitted in any other form or for any means, electronic or mechanical, including photocopy, recording or any information storage system, without written permission from Publisher Page.

Publisher Page
P.O. Box 52, Terra Alta, WV 26764
www.PublisherPage.com

Tel/Fax: 800-570-5951
Email: mybook@headlinebooks.com
www.HeadlineBooks.com

Publisher Page is an imprint of Headline Books, Inc.

ISBN 978-0-938467-77-9

Library of Congress Control Number: 2014933452

Selby, David
        Promises of love / David Selby
        p. cm.
        ISBN 978-0-938467-77-9

PRINTED IN THE UNITED STATES OF AMERICA

For my family and especially Chippy,
my editor and encourager.

Aesculapius: The god of healing. He was the son of Apollo and Coronis and was brought up by Chiron the centaur, who instructed him in the art of healing and in hunting. When he was grown, he not only healed the sick, but recalled the dead to life. He was killed by a thunderbolt from Jupiter who feared lest men should, by his aid, escape death altogether. Serpents were sacred to him, and the cock was sacrificed to him.

Dearest Elmira,

"......By the way Sunday night was real busy. I had 4 operations. Intestinal obstruction, which involved the appendix. Had a stab wound of abdomen—one of the large vessels was cut. I opened the abdomen and ligated the bleeder. Then I had a bad compound fracture with extensive hemorrhage. And the fourth case was an extensive scalp wound requiring operative procedures. Got two hours sleep then did two hernias and an appendix. You know I love to do hernias, one man's pain is another man's gain...."

Your pal,
Daniel Friend, M.D.

My Prayers

"As I turn the last page, Lord, and close the chapter, let there be no regrets in remembrance of failure, but regard every mistake a lesson by which I may profit, and go forth with joy into the duties of the new day. Amen."

"I cannot imagine a worst fate than to have a wasted life. What good is life if you can't make it better for yourself and for those you love, and for the world at large. Help me, dear Lord, to go forward, bringing all those who will follow. In your name, Amen."

1

On long, hot, summer days, with the drifting smell of dry weeds that made me sneeze, and not a stir of a breeze, nothing suited me more, despite my sneezing, than stretching out on Goat Hill, my chin resting in my hands, my nose in a book, the same book— "Hail Mary," about a star football player who leaps high into the air at the goal line, manages to get his hands on the ball, juggles it, then pulls it into his chest for the winning touchdown. Besides the Bible, it was the only book I had. I knew it by heart. Better than Mother's Bible. I pulled my eyes away from the page only long enough to watch the seemingly endless coal train suddenly appear far below, around the bend, like the little engine that could. It was slowly worming its way through the thick green blanket of the southern Allegheny Mountains along the Roanoke River. Counting coal cars was as exciting as it got in my young life in rural western Virginia. Nothing happened. *Summer went on and on and so, too, did mothers and fathers,* I thought.

One day, I counted seventy-eight over-loaded coal cars without a blink—a record. I knew all seventy-eight cars would at some point return empty. I read that coal went to make electricity—but how? Electricity, my sister Dee, told me, would let me read at night. I could not imagine anything better. There were no clouds in my future. I could feel the deep contentment, appreciation, the joy, and solace of the warm cushiony ground under me. At the peak of Goat Hill, I could see across to a clearing in the forest. I wanted to hike there, but mother said the clearing was just an apparition. It wasn't real, she said. I wondered what was on the other side of the mountain. My teacher said the far mountain was in Tennessee. Would there be electricity there? Watching the train cars go by, I felt happy. I did not know at that moment how fleeting happiness could be.

"Get yer head outta of your butt," boomed my father's voice, the large shadowed figure suddenly looming spread-eagled over me. I was surprised because the slow moving train had hypnotized me, and Goat Hill was such a long uphill hike I figured it was a safe haven from my father. I could usually hear him yell, as he had a primitive kind of growling that seemed to erupt.

"Thought I wouldn't find ya, didn't ya?" He grabbed my book. "Books," he said, with a disdainful Savonarola snarl. "A waste of time, books! Good riddance," and he flung my book over his shoulder, down the hill.

Father removed his leather belt. Bracing myself for the inevitable, I let out a soft murmur as he yanked me up by my arm like a sack of feed.

"When I yell fer ya, ya come runnin'. The dog comes, ya can come!" He only got madder when I said I didn't hear him. "How many times have I told ya! Yer a shirker, boy. Never goin' to amount to a hill of beans. Think yer too good for the likes of us, yer too big for yer britches." Then he slashed the belt across the back of my legs. "Just like the coal and timber carpet baggin' sons-of-bitches." Another slash. When Father was fuming and whipping me, he would lash out at the corporate world that he felt had lied to him, that he had been robbed of his mineral rights because he had been taken advantage of. "All I got was table scraps! They stripped my hills clean as a whistle. Not only raped me, they stole my clothes and pocketbook, 'n called me "family" while they did it—then asked me to pray with 'em! Ya see a do-gooder in these hills one thing ya know fer sure, he's gonna screw ya." Another slash. "They tell ya yer their buddy. Liars, the great pretenders! In these mountains, things can only git worse. Jis remember, nobody cares about ya, boy. Nothin' matters here. Nothin' ever important goes on here. Don't say I didn't warn ya. Ya'll find out. Mark my word. Coal company owns me and I own ya boy, don't forget it." The belt slashed across my legs half way down the hill. Later, I hiked back up Goat Hill to hunt for my book. I found it and still have it.

And sixty years later I still feel the sting of the belt and the words. The words come and go, ebb and flow, but they persist. You learn to put up with them like an uninvited visitor. And you never forget the whippings. They still sting, mark you. Not that I didn't earn the wrath of my father on occasion. The young years stick like glue, the ashes of my youth. This is the bare truth as far as I could discern it. How does one find out what is uncolored, ultimate truth, indisputable fact as far as the soul is concerned? It is a life's search for meaning. Institutions and people have a hard time holding to a moral core…the lies we tell ourselves. Mother said try and find the goodness. "By goodness, I mean love," she said. Mozart felt love was the soul of genius. I was quite young when I read that, and it made me question whether love would ever be possible.

———————

It was a cold damp cloudy Sunday morning, the kind of chilling morning that made my legs shake. Dee and I stood on our gray, weathered porch looking up at Goat Hill, beyond the faded brown fields and shedding trees along the river. We were watching another endless coal train. Counting coal cars this morning brought a calming but no warmth.

Dee and I slept in the same tiny bedroom, while our older brother Raymond, when he was there, slept in a room off the kitchen, where mother stored her canned peaches, corn, green beans, tomatoes, apple-sauce—along with our coats and hats and boots. This morning all was quiet except for some early crickets and the singing of riverbank frogs. Last night after Mother and Father returned home from a church supper, I awoke Dee when I heard them arguing.

"It's really loud."

We crept out into the kitchen, past the wood stove and wash-tub, and down the hall, putting our ears to our parents' bedroom door. Mother was crying. I opened the door. Mother lay on the bed. Father was bent over her. I jumped on his back.

"Git out," he screamed, and his arm flung me across the room. Dee pulled me out.

"Mother is hurt," I said.

"Quick, Father's coming," Dee said and pulled me back into our room. I listened for a while then hid under my bed.

The next morning, Mother appeared on the porch with a smile as bright as the calico dress she was wearing. I was glad to see her smiling and surprised to see her in the bright print dress. Father did not approve of such dresses, especially when mother wore them to church. Nor did he like it when she let her long auburn hair fall to her shoulders, as it did this morning. Her hair was so pretty. Mother was pretty. She was carrying a small bag that she kept her sewing supplies in.

"Let's not be late for church, children." Her voice lilted like a songbird.

It was a three-mile walk to the little stone Baptist church situated at the fork of the Bannister and Roanoke Rivers where I had been baptized a few years earlier. Choosing salvation out of self-preservation, I had stood up in the water in panic, shaking and coughing, spitting out water after having been held under longer than I could hold my breath. I thought I was drowning.

The white clapboard church had survived hell and damnation since 1801. I sat between my sister and mother on the hard dark oak bench listening to the preacher call on all sinners to stand and repent. Everyone stood. There were a lot of sinners in our little community. Mother stood, her eyes closed tight, as though warding off some great pain. She swayed and prayed as the fire and brimstone preacher's torrent of hard words hailed down on all us sinners, piercing us all so the guilt bent us over our knees. Mother pulled me close against her, enveloping me in her arms, my face in her stomach. The last time I felt safe was that church morning when my mother's arms were wrapped around me.

On this cold Sunday, from beneath her closed eyes, mother sobbed. I asked her why she was so sad.

"They are tears of joy, Daniel, tears for the spirit of the Lord. You can cry, too. Cry, Daniel, cry. You can wash out the darkness and fear."

I closed my eyes tight and tried to cry. I prayed as hard as I could for tears to come, not out of fear of God, but out of love for Mother.

"I love you, Mommy, always, Mommy. I promise."

Mother had delivered four children before her nineteenth birthday and wanted no more children. Then I came along. Two of my brothers would die of typhoid fever. After church that Sunday, I gave mother a cross-shaped stone I had found in the creek bed to hold for me while I went to the outhouse. As I returned, I saw mother kiss Dee. She was holding Dee's shoulders looking straight into her eyes. Her words stopped me.

"I know you understand."

"But, I *don't*," Dee protested.

"We women have to look out for ourselves," Mother said.

The congregation was parading out of the damp church into the light of warming sunshine. Dee was 13, three years older than me. Mother had grown to take Dee into her confidence. Marriage for Mother had been one of convenience, an escape. Love would come, Father had promised her.

"Love grows on you. I promise you," he had told Dee.

I don't think it ever did for Mother. All that came were children, and I later would assume Mother simply saw no way out.

"One day, Dee, you will meet a tall, dark, stranger. But make sure you are in love first because the tall dark stranger will want to seduce you first and then fall in love."

"Seduce?" I said.

"You're too young, Daniel."

"I'm not," I insisted. "Tell me!"

"Men insist on too much—love is spoiled. Men are children, remember that."

"Are you leaving?" I asked, rushing up to her.

"No, Daniel, I will be back in a few days," she said clutching her bag.

"But you are going off with a man?" said Dee. There was a man waiting off to the side. He smiled slightly at us.

"Just for some business I have to attend to," said Mother.

"When are you coming back?" I asked.

I was crying. Mother put her hand on my head.

"I shall always love you Daniel, I promise. I will see you very soon. Make it your duty to look after your little brother, Deidre. He is not as strong as you. Be patient with him. He is a good boy."

The man, a small, red-bearded man in a rumpled suit with his hat pulled down to one side of his head, ushered mother ahead of him. I was sure I had seen the man before, maybe at church. It was the only man I had ever seen in a suit. Dee said she remembered Mother saying once that the man was a doctor. "Doctors must have a neat appearance," Dee recalled her mother saying when she asked her why the man was wearing a suit.

"Maybe it's the suit Mother likes," said Dee.

Mother suddenly turned back to us.

"Love is not a duty, remember that." Then she turned away.

"Not for Mother and Father," said Dee, taking my hand.

"They're our parents."

"Yes."

"So they love each other."

"Love is not required in order to be a parent," said Dee.

"It should be," I said.

"Yes."

"I never see Father and Mother look at each other unless they are mad."

We watched the man and Mother hurry down the path. If she heard me shouting "Mommy," she did not look back, not even for a last glimpse of the boy who had clung to her sides, telling her that he belonged, that he loved her. There was no mean intent when my cries were disregarded. I cried a lot. Whenever Mother left the house, I would plead to go with her and would stand at the window and watch for her return. I started to run after her, but Dee stopped me. I watched until I could see her no more, a cold unsentimental image tattooed for a lifetime. Silence....I stood perplexed. Then I ran as hard as I could to the river. I had seen father put our dead cocker spaniel Taffy in a burlap bag. Then he loaded the bag with stones and dumped it in the river. I wanted to stuff as many stones as I could into my pockets and wade out into the river, but that was rather melodramatic, Dee said, as we walked home.

Was love just pretend? How does a mother just walk away and not look back? Her leaving was so sudden, like an unexpected death.

"Why didn't she take me with her, Dee?"

When I had started to talk, I called my sister "Dee," not being able to say "Deidre." Deidre decided she liked it and announced one day that she wished to be called "Dee."

"Where is she going?"

"I don't know," said Dee. But I suspected she did and was just not telling me. I knew Mother had not gone to the feed store or the confectionery, as she often liked to on Sundays after church, because she always took us along. She would buy us each a piece of penny chocolate, and then together we would pick out the prettiest sacks filled with chicken feed. It was those feed sacks that mother made into beautiful dresses.

"Does Mother really love me?"

"Yes. Why do you ask?"

"Why did she leave?"

"I told you I don't know. You heard her. She has business to attend to."

Mother had been my rock. Now a crevice appeared and would only widen and deepen.

———————

Five days later, in the dead of night, I awoke, hearing howling from outside.

"Sounds like an animal," said Dee.

We opened the door and crept out onto the porch and there in the moonlit field below was our father walking in circles, screaming out in pain, guttural screams and moans coming from somewhere deep in his stomach like a wounded werewolf. We ran down the steps and through the gate. Father was clutching Mother, her head limp over his arm. A horse-drawn wagon was going down the lane.

"The man's a butcher! He cut her like a hog," he wailed. "She can't walk. Bastard!" Screaming into Mother's face, holding her in his outstretched arms as though offering her to God. "God won't have ya! You had no right! No right! The Bible is the final say! I told you! Why wouldn't you listen? Yer mother's a killer! She murdered our baby! She had no right! No right!"

There was a bad smell, and a white-foam was coming out of Mother's mouth.

"Mother…" I cried as I tried to put my arms around her.

"Git back in the house, Daniel," screamed Father, "go away!" He buried his head in Mother's motionless chest. Then I saw that father was covered in…it was blood, as though he had just finished butchering one of our hogs. I could never watch the butchering despite father's demand that I do so.

"You can't face this, how are you gonna become a man?" I'm sure it's why I became a vegetarian. I caught a glimpse of the cross-shaped stone in Mother's outstretched hand that I had given her to hold for me at church that Sunday. Dee pulled me away toward the house.

"What did Father mean?" Dee did not look at me. "He said Mother was a killer…..a baby?"

"Mother was…" She stopped. It was too much. She took my hand and led me inside where she removed my night shirt. Dee heated a pan of water on the wood stove, gathered some rags, and a cake of homemade soap Mother had made and washed Mother's blood from my face, chest and arms. Then she went back outside.

The rest of my life turned the moment I realized my mother was dead. A mother is first of all a mother and across the great abyss there is nothing more soothing than a mother's touch.

A house is just a house when you are alone. Love had been grabbed away, stolen, love split open like an atom. I waited all night for Mother to return. She would be the woman in the bright colored dress with butterflies. She used to call me "Butterfly." "Wake up, Butterfly, it is time to spread your wings."

The next morning, Dee, strangely cheerful, made breakfast for us…scrambled eggs and warm cinnamon toast. I wasn't hungry. It was hard to acknowledge that Mother was truly gone from my life. It was a void that I could not contemplate. The emptiness left me unable to speak. My sobbing would not cease. It was then that I first became aware of time. I would sit and watch Father's round brass alarm clock slowly tick off the minutes. Years later, it would seem but a moment ago that my mother passed.

"What did I tell ya, Daniel? I'd like not to hear ya cryin' all night. I been in the trenches, gassed and shot at and I'm still standing. So stop feelin' sorry for yerself."

"What happened to Mother?" I asked.

"Why should ya care?"

"She's my mother."

"Hardly. What kind of mother does that? Tell me that, boy!"

"Does what?"

"Murders her baby!"

"She was still my mother," I whispered.

For the longest time, Father worked till dark, every day, like some continuous machine. His hands were blistered and bloodied from swinging the scythe hour after hour, day after day. He could not work hard enough—the stain of guilt was not removable. His screams were such that his nose would bleed.

"The closer I tried to get to her, the further she drove me away. There was no way to earn her love.….I hurt all over, girl," he said to Dee, "but no place I can point to."

That was true until one day, I don't remember when, but it was two or three years later, Father swung the scythe into the calf of his leg. Then he knew. "That's what love is, blisters and blood, feel like I've been trampled by a team of horses," he mumbled as he sat in the porch rocker as Dee wrapped a bandage around his leg. I suggested he should avoid the scythe for a while.

"Hold still, Father," said Dee. When she finished with Father's leg, he got up and limped toward the stairs.

"We have nothing but love, Daniel," said Dee, as Father stumbled down the stairs and into the blackest night, "and when we have lost that—as Father has—all is lost."

"A cold patch of nothingness," was Father's answer to my question of why he was pitching a tent made of old blankets. I had chased after him as he stomped up Goat Hill. He had given his bed and chest of drawers to the field hand, Charley Zinn. Charley offered to work off the furniture, but Father refused.

"Nope. Ya need a place to lay yer head, and since I can't lay mine on it, yer welcome to it. I want nothin' fer it." It was some time before Father constructed a single bed made of walnut, but he never slept in it. He walled himself in a windowless prison of sad indifference, and there was no way to break through that wall. There was no key in or out. That is what a love gone bad can do, Dee said. Never again, Father vowed, would he take a woman for a wife. In my innocence, I haltingly said, "What about me?"

"Sorry, boy….Couldn't please 'er. Never looked at another woman. That's the Lord's truth! Said I didn't take 'nough time with 'er, love 'er 'nough. What I didn't have 'nough of was money. You git money you can git all the women ya want, boy," he said and straightened up, wiped his mouth with his sleeve. "Love, ha, it ain't what it's cracked up to be. Love doesn't last. Ya get old. Yer mother couldn't handle that. She hated how I looked.

"Never fall in love with a younger woman, boy! Would've lost her anyhow in time. Couldn't figure her. God will punish her! Yer cursed, boy! Ya'll never deliver, boy, the odds are against ya, like a bad mare, got yer Mother's tainted blood! Yer damaged goods! I wasn't the Satan she made me out to be. Clothes don't make the man! Ya think ya put on a nice suit, slick yer hair, strike a pose, Easy!

Smooth! Ya think he's a man of the Bible, a prophet, all-powerful! But it's all a show, not real. Like yer suit of woe, boy, was my love for yer mother! I loved her such, strong, as when I first saw her. Loved her more than she could ever love me, and that ate at me, consumed me, my need for her. I needed her more than she needed me, that's fer sure."

I wondered that if, at one time, Father did know love, what it was like to love and to be loved in return…sort of a partnership. He had not an ounce of love for anyone now, it seemed. Father was tough to be around. I could not see into his heart.

"He has no heart left," said Dee. "His sadness has eaten it away."

"Why did she keep it?" I tearfully asked Dee.

"Keep what?"

"My stone cross."

"It was part of you, Daniel, her connection to you."

Dee took me in her arms and held me tight until my sudden sobbing stopped. But the pain, the pain, crisscrossed my body.

"Did I pester her too much? Did I love her too much?"

"Daniel, stop it."

We had been raised within the bounds of the Old Testament, fearful of a punishing, avenging God. "Repent you sinners!" I knew I must have sinned, if lying on Goat Hill with my book in hand was a sin. I saw the sun come up day after day, and yet did not know what I saw. My ignorance was a sin. *Let me face eternal damnation*, I thought, *I don't care*. I had been made to raise my arms to God and accept God's plan and to never question His judgment, His punishment. It was a mystery. Father would say, as he took his belt to me, "It is God's wish." He believed it, I know. At night I cried myself to sleep talking to God about the hurt and how I wished I could have gone with my mother.

"She was my friend," I explained to God. "Mother smiled at me, she liked music, and she sang funny songs to me. She made friends with my made-up friends, and she didn't know them. I miss her so much, God."

"She's gone, Daniel," said Dee, lying beside me.

Dee's words would not be washed away. They were in my mouth as I lay in bed, the rain beating down making sure her words would never dry, "She's gone, Daniel."

I said, "She's gone to God." I asked God, night after night, why Mother had to die, but I never got an answer. Praying and talking to God about daily events had made me feel better at first. Then I got angry with God for taking my mother away.

"God loves you, Daniel," said Dee.

"I don't care about God." All of heaven had turned black. Twilight was but an illusion.

"I will always love you," she whispered and hugged me tighter.

"Do you promise?"

"I promise," answered Dee.

And sleep came. You do go on, you learn to go on. A dull ache is still there, though, covered by the shadow of years.

———————————

One day when Father did not emerge for dinner, we searched the fields and woods. We called for him. There was no answer. The next morning we hiked up Goat Hill. That is where I would hide to avoid my chores and read my book and daydream about somewhere else. I could not understand why Father chose to pitch his tent on Goat Hill. Dee said he just wanted to be alone. We walked out to the far edge of the hill pointing toward Tennessee where father had pitched his tent. Dee told me to wait while she went and lifted the tent's flap of blanket. She stood, not moving and then kneeled down and crawled into the tent. After a few moments she emerged and motioned for me to come.

"It's not pretty," she said matter-of-factly without looking at me. She held the flap of blanket back so I could see inside. There was Father, face up, what was left of it, his shotgun across his legs.

"He's dead," said Dee, a statement of fact, not surprise. She took me in her arms.

"That's what happens when there is no love," she said. It sounded like a warning.

Unpleasant was not the word. If there was a hell, Dee and I were there. There is no way to forget. I wanted to keep it all a secret. A child has no words. Father wanted to keep Mother's death a secret. He had, at first, refused to attend the church service for Mother, but finally relented.

He did not want people to know what had happened. He tried to keep it all, the ugliness, the pain, inside. That, in the end, killed him. The shotgun blast to the head was just a formality.

2

Father was buried before the church service. The church family had taken care of the simple arrangements. I sat looking through the church window out toward the river, not seeing it.

The preacher read a short passage about time and renewal and then *The Lord is My Shepherd.* He ended with,

"...When I was a child, I spoke like a child, I thought like a child, I reasoned like a child; when I became a man, I gave up childish ways. (For now we see in a mirror dimly, but then face to face. Now I know in part; then I shall understand fully, even as I have been fully understood. So faith, hope, love abide, these three; but the greatest of these is love." 1 Corinthians 13:11-13)

Afterward, we walked over a few yards to the cemetery where our brothers were buried. I could not look at Mother's small stone marker.

"Daniel," Dee called again, "Daniel!"

"I was not a good son to my father," I lamented.

"He wasn't a good father," Dee said.

"You reap what you sow," said Raymond, who had come home from the army to be with us.

"I was a nuisance," I said. "Father shot himself because of me."

"If he hadn't killed himself, someone else probably would've," said Raymond.

"I'm hungry," said Dee. "I'll fix some lunch." We turned and walked home.

In the next weeks, Dee moved into our parents' room. She prayed long and often to God about how she might help me. She stroked my hair, fixed my meals, and washed and ironed my school clothes with the heavy black irons that she heated, like mother once did, on the wood stove.

"May my love be enough," she prayed.

"Do you believe in true love?" I asked.

"Daniel, you are too young to think about such things."

"How do you know if you love someone?"

"Your brain tells you," said Dee.

"What if your brain's not working?"

It would be Dee's mission in life to make my life secure, whether or not I discovered love. I told her of my talks with God and how He had not shed any light on why our parents were dead.

"God has other things to think about."

"What could be more important?"

"You need not fret. God loves you and will always love you."

"I don't care about love. Why love anyone. It's better to just be friends, sort of."

"Love is a mystery," Dee told me when I asked if our parents had loved each other. "Love can make you crazy, like Father was. He was a sick man, detached from everything but his sadness. As long as Mother was here," said Dee, "I suppose Father could hold out hope that she would come around."

"But she didn't."

"And Father could never get out from under that."

"He loved her."

"Yes." He felt like he had been…. punched in the stomach. That is what a lack of love can do, Daniel, what a hard life can do," Dee said.

Our lives afterward revolved around the church. The members were impressed with Dee's mothering of me and in time Dee convinced all, including the preacher, that she alone could take care of me. I was delighted.

It was at church that Dee made a vow to raise me to manhood. The "mommy's boy" had been useless to Father. It was Dee who even at a young age had that inner strength that mountain women have. Dee was the mainstay with her principles. She had defied Father by going off the farm to work. She later managed two jobs, in addition to going to school and taking care of me. Her very early morning job was at a bakery down hollow in the village, a few miles from the farm, where she rolled out the dough for bread, cookies, and donuts. She would always bring me a couple of donuts. Then she would hurry over to the Red Hook Mining Company's boarding house for coal miners where she cleaned, made up the beds, and fixed and packed the miners' lunches. The miners paid her extra when she brought them warm donuts for breakfast.

Old Charley, father's field-hand, continued on working the land. He arranged to rent some of the thirty-three acres for hay and grazing. The hill portion that Father had managed to retain the mineral rights to was leased to a local coal operator. Father had been a coal miner for many years but had hard feelings about what he said was the thievery of his mineral rights to most of his land. Dee proved quite adept at running the land. She was a mature and responsible seventeen year old. I became a member of the church youth choir singing every Sunday. The music was uplifting and transporting. One of the adult choir members asked me if I would like to learn to play the fiddle. Soon I was playing its cousin, the violin, and eventually was asked to play at the church potluck lunch every Sunday. The violin became a sort of therapy.

The church family had been unforgiving of Mother. Divorce was a sin, but what Mother had done was unspeakable. Rumors spread that the baby was not Father's. None of them had ever known or even heard of a woman who had done such a thing. I was confused and questioned Dee as to why people were still talking about Mother in such a way. She told me there were probably other women who wanted to do the same.

"If men had to give birth, there would be no end of abortion," she said.

Some church members were careful not to talk in front of us, but after all the passed time, it was still the talk of the community. I hated the pitying looks and the gossip. It made me feel more alone. By then, I knew loneliness would be my constant companion. Early on, I often asked Dee where Mother was. Was she in heaven? Would we see her again? For years, I insisted on celebrating Mother's birthday. Dee ignored it all, but let me do as I wished.

"It makes me cold to think of it, of Mother being gone."

"We have to be as cold and tough, Daniel."

Some church members blamed Mother for Father's death. "It wasn't the gun that killed your father, it was heartbreak." Perhaps they were right.

"I've decided to forgive God," I announced one morning.

"God will be glad to hear that," Dee replied, delighted. "The angels are rejoicing."

Dee gave me a big hug and told me she would bake sugar cookies when we got home later that day. Sugar cookies had sustained me for several weeks. Dee baked a batch every evening. Several days after Mother had died, Dee baked a batch of peanut butter cookies hoping to cheer me up. Mother had always baked batches of peanut butter cookies, and they were my favorite. But when I ate one of Dee's peanut butter cookies, I thought of Mother and cried. After a bit, I ate another peanut butter cookie and cried again. I decided to give up peanut butter cookies, never eating another. I knew then I could be strong. The next week, I stood up in church and walked down front and was born again. I just did it. Dee was surprised and could not stop laughing when church was over.

"At first the preacher did not know what you wanted."

"I told him I wanted him to tell God that I was sorry I had forsaken him and that I wished to be back in His good graces."

I have always had the feeling that I was being watched over. I had to mind my p's and q's. There is an order to things. I was not sure what the order was but I trusted that I would sense it and abide by it.

3

Four years of working two jobs allowed Dee to save enough money to allow me to enroll for my sophomore year in a small private high school—six rooms, six teachers, and 136 students. She felt the boarding school would give me a chance at an academic scholarship to college. The school, near Lexington, Virginia, was just a hundred miles east of our home, but was in a much more gentrified country than my Clinch Mountain home. There was no transportation, but private housing was provided for many of the students. I did not like the idea of having to wear a school uniform, but Dee was glad because everyone would be dressed the same. She was concerned that the school was coed. The dean assured her that the students living in various houses around the community were chaperoned closely. At first, Dee had to push and cajole me into leaving home, despite the sadness and the unpleasantness.

"We have to do this," she said. "We have to be on our own, make our own lives and not let anyone tell us what we are to be or how we are to live. That is for us to decide. God will guide us on the right path. We will be free, Daniel, from a discouraging home life. You will never have a chance to reach whatever potential you have unless you go. There are possibilities on the other side of the mountain."

"I don't know."

"I believe in you, so you can believe in yourself too."

"You sound like the preacher….'you can do more, be more.'"

"He's right—good, better, best! You can, but not if you stay here. We are on our own, Daniel, no matter what. It is us against the world."

Once Dee was assured I was settled at school, she entered the Roanoke Hospital's school for nursing. I cried because I was so happy for her. She had set her sights on becoming a Florence Nightingale. Dee was able to quit her jobs at the bakery and the miners' quarters because she was going to be paid as a student nurse. For the first time, she said, we were emancipated.

Mr. Goodsell, the dean of my new school, a charming, distinguished man with an air of sophistication, took me under his wing, personally taking me to where I would be staying. We drove there in Mr. Goodsell's Packard, the biggest car I had ever seen. Ocy Chips, a tiny wizened widow, greeted us at the door of a small brown-stained, wood- shingled cottage. It reminded me of our general store's doll house that mother loved, but Dee never showed any interest in.

"It's raining cats and dogs," Ocy wheezed. "My asthma is kicking up. Just ignore it. I do. Best come in before you drown," she said,

She took our coats and told us not to worry about tracking in. "A little water's not going to hurt anything." Her house was like her; nice and warm. We sat in the little drawing room while Ocy fixed us some hot chocolate. The little doilies on the arms of the blue velvety chairs reminded me of mother's knitting. Father had scoffed at such "dainties," as he called them.

"Daniel," said the dean, "is not only a good student, but he is also a good violinist, Ocy. I know you will be impressed."

"I'm sure I will be. The dean tells me, Daniel, you are a very hard worker."

"Daniel is willing to do anything he is asked to do, right, Daniel?" I nodded and smiled.

"My husband said, 'Life is labor and labor is life.' A good dose of discipline will go a long way, Daniel," said Ocy. "I always give myself a good talking to if I have not done something productive in the day." Just then a small calico cat appeared and rubbed her head on my leg. "That's Sophie. That's a good sign. She likes productive people. Sophie is very particular about who she befriends. She is named after a character in a Bernard Shaw play, *You Never Can Tell.* And you know, I find that to be very true, you just never know, do you?"

I had no idea who Shaw was, but I smiled and gave Sophie a pat on the head.

"Daniel does not have his own violin, but I told him that you may be able to come up with one for him."

"I believe I can, Daniel," said Ocy.

"Thank you. That would be wonderful."

Ocy left the room and returned a few moments later carrying a violin case. She opened it up, and there was the most beautiful violin. Aside from Mother and Dee, I thought Ocy must be the kindest woman in the world.

"If you practice every day, the violin is yours to keep. It belonged to my husband. He was a doctor. Musicians and doctors have similar souls."

I thanked her profusely. *Kindness is love*, I thought. Love is a violin that I would play for Ocy one day. That would be the only way I could possibly thank her for this gift.

Dean Goodsell became a mentor. He was aware of my dire financial situation.

"There are many students here who have financial troubles. That's what we do, Daniel, help those who can't help themselves."

The dean would later teach me how to drive a car, his Packard. He also came up with a job for me as a janitor to help offset expenses.

———————

After the first months of my sophomore year, I had come to the conclusion that student government was the best way to influence school policy—which, I thought, could certainly be improved. Serving in office might also help my scholarship chances. Looking at past student office holders, I decided that in order to be elected to school office, it helped to be on the football team, but my dream of catching the winning touchdown and running for school office went up in flames when I didn't make the team.

"Students worship the football team," I complained to Dee during Thanksgiving. "The players are like gods, and I don't know why. They've won four games in three seasons, and they haven't won a game so far this season."

"It does seem that team could use some new blood," said Dee.

"Yes, any blood, even mine. It does say something that these girls think football players are the 'be all and end all.'"

"You must be careful not to concern yourself with girls," said Dee. "That is not why you are there. Girls can be a distraction."

Despite no football practice to attend, my various jobs, mostly scrubbing floors and doing odd jobs for the teachers, and my homework and violin lessons left me little time to complain. But I did complain, especially about the rule that lights be off by 10:00 p.m. The thrill of having electricity was dimmed.

"If you can't read my writing," I wrote Dee, "it's because of school policy that all lights must be off at 10, and Mrs. Chips is tough as nails about that rule. I am forced to write in the dark. I might as well be back at home with no electricity. You are my light, dear Sister. This school is absolutely gray, like the uniform I am forced to wear everyday."

———————————

Easter holiday could not come too soon, but Dee had no patience for my complaints.

"You must remove that dark cloud floating over your head, Daniel."

"I've just had my fill of school for a few months. It is hard to sit up all night and study my head off for the Latin test and then have the teacher take a nap while everyone else looks up the answers in their books!"

"Oh, my heavens! It is their loss, not yours. Concentrate on what you are doing."

"It's wrong! These kids think they know everything. They don't know anything. I don't either, but at least I know I don't."

"You are right, Daniel, to feel as you do—in the end you will come out ahead."

"May God bless the day when the teacher tells everyone to turn in their homework. I am going to be in my great glory because no one else does their homework!"

"God will say Hallelujah!"

"Here's hoping you're right."

The violin was my savior. I practiced faithfully, and after a year had gone by, I got up the courage to play a piece of Bach for Ocy. She said I was so good that the violin was mine to keep.

"My husband would be so pleased that his violin is in such talented hands. There are a number of orchestras that can use a good violinist. You are lucky, Daniel. There are not that many orchestra jobs for an oboist."

I was so excited that I gave her a big hug. It was the first time I had hugged anyone besides Dee since that day in church when Mother wrapped me in her arms. Ocy hugged me back, and I cried. I told her they were tears of joy. She asked me about Mother, and I told her. It was good, I suppose, that I could talk about Mother without crying. She asked about Father, and at first I could not tell her. Later when I was in bed, and Ocy was doing her nightly bed check, I told her about Father. She gave me a pat on my head and told me that I had a great future and would not be surprised that one day I would land at Harvard University. Her husband had been a student there.

"It was at Harvard where ministers first became students of the Bible and then helped make New England people the most literate in the world. Now say your prayers. Good night, Daniel."

I cannot explain how important Ocy's "goodnight" was to me. My prayers always included asking God to please look out for Dee. And I told Him how grateful I was for His bringing Ocy into my life.

By the beginning of my senior year, I had, covertly, finally, discovered girls. Dee had made it perfectly clear that I should not be wasting my time thinking about girls.

"There will be plenty of time for that, I assure you," she wrote.

I had been having trouble with two girls who kept tagging after me. It wouldn't have been so bad if they had been anything to look at, but they weren't. Dee wrote that I was right to resist having anything to do with such girls, but to remember that we are all God's children.

Well, I did not tell her that one of God's children wanted me to tell her how much I was in love with her and how she drove me out of my mind. She certainly did. She followed me all over the place at school and would wait for me after school. She talked in this squeaky voice like one of the seven dwarfs. I expected her to break out in song any minute. She was no angel. My innocence was gone, had been shattered. It would have made even Dee's hair curl. Her brown hair was as straight as a redwood. The girl was right about one thing—she was driving me mad. The other girl had more definite plans, which I was too embarrassed to tell Dee. Let's just say she was none too shy with what she wanted me to do with her. She gave me un-wanted lessons on terminology for the different parts of the female anatomy. I must say my vocabulary grew. She gave new meaning to the word aggressive.

Nursing school had acquainted Dee with the feminine wiles.

"If the girls you described," wrote Dee, in reply to my watered down saga of the two girls, "pursued their studies as thoroughly as they seem to pursue you, they wouldn't have to look up the answers every time your teacher leaves the room. In my nursing class, we are told that girls mature faster than boys. It is God's plan because boys are hopeless."

For Christmas of my Junior year, I received a new Bible from Dee. I assured her I would treasure it. But the Bible was no match for the girls.

"Read your Bible, Daniel!"

"Love for girls must be a short-term affair," I wrote. "These girls don't have a clue about love—of course neither do I. I trust I'll know it when it happens. The girls at school, the couple I am aware of, think they know everything. If that's the case, Sister, how will they learn anything? Not from reading the books they give us. I don't know how we lost the war when the Confederate troops won all the battles! I pointed this out to Mr. Goodsell and he agreed. He said the South was inferior in matters of education, that it was too easy to blame the Negro. He told me I would have to leave Dixie in order to find a good college education."

I did find myself in agreement with the girls over the school policy forbidding students to dance. I discovered I loved dancing. I danced in my room. I sang to myself. It made me feel good. Dancing did wonders for that social desert, and I found myself warming to the advances of the two rather persistent girls.

"Dancing could also help my inhibitions. I would like to dance, just not with any of the 'loose' girls," I wrote Dee, fudging the truth just a bit. They did seem overly concerned about their own self-gratification which was so immature and superficial.

One girl told me we were all going to die anyway so we might as well enjoy ourselves. That was too fatalistic. All I could think about was Mother and Father. I told one girl why not try and make yourself a little better. I think that is all Mother was trying to do. I thought if I did nothing to make the world a better place, my life will have been a failure.

One spring weekend Dee arrived back at her student-nursing dorm to find me sitting on the front stoop.

"Daniel, what are you doing here? How did you get here?"

"Mrs. Chips lent me bus money for a round-trip ticket. I've got some distressing news. I couldn't bear to tell you in a letter. Harvard has rejected me."

"Oh, Daniel. I'm sorry, so sorry. I know how much you were counting on that."

"Harvard was made for me! I don't understand!"

"When did you hear?"

"I got the notice a week ago but did not have the heart to tell you. I cried so hard. Poor Mrs. Chips, she's so worried about me. I told her not to leave any knifes around. I was kidding, sort of."

"Not getting into Harvard is not the end of the world."

"To my world it is. I'm miserable. Not since Mother… have I cried so long and hard. I have been in a deep fog. I pray a lot."

"You must be hungry. Come in. We can go in the kitchen, and I'll fix you a sandwich."

"Don't know how I can continue. My fairy tale won't come true. I pray nobody knows of my rejection. Of course those in the school office know. They sent my records to Harvard with my application. Dean Goodsell tried to console me. He said he didn't understand either. I'm full of self-pity. I just don't understand—my grades were near perfect. I'm sorry to put this doom and gloom on you. I guess it's just as well I'm not going to Harvard. If campus life is anything like what Fitzgerald wrote, I wouldn't have fit in anyway. Maybe Harvard knew that."

"It's Harvard's loss, not yours," said Dee.

I spent the night in a fitful sleep, in my jacket, on a make-shift bed of pillow and blanket. *Like Father's tent,* I thought. That night Father appeared to me, as a ghost.

"Harvard laughed at ya, boy. Oh they're nice to people like us. But who do ya think stole our land, boy? Where'd they learn their evil swindlin' ways? The Harvards of this world, that's where, that's who runs this country. That's who dug the hole this country's in. Commerce! Don't fool yourself. Ya listen to yer father, not some high falutin' teacher, professor.

The Harvards don't care about our kind, boy, no matter how low ya scrape 'n bow or how long ya keep your nose to the grindstone. Ya git nothin' to show fer it. The colored know."

The next morning, I told Dee of my dream about Father.

"Like Hamlet's ghost, Father won't go quietly. We are studying Hamlet in class and maybe that is why Father won't leave me alone."

"I don't know why you should remember him, Daniel."

"He won't let me forget. I've thought about how long he had been lying there. He hadn't come down to the house, had he?"

"I don't remember, Daniel. Of course he did. He got hungry."

"But he didn't eat with us, not supper."

"He must have come down before we got out of bed. Enough. Father is far better off where he is."

"Heaven?"

"I don't know, Daniel. But as in life, I'm sure he is a mean ghost."

One night I was thinking of Mother and suddenly I could not remember her face. It scared me. But the next morning she was back wearing the bright yellow butterfly dress she had on that morning.

———————

When I got back to school, there was a letter waiting for me. It was another rejection letter, this time from the University of Virginia. I immediately wrote to Dee.

"It's beyond my imagination I didn't get in there. Harvard is one thing but UVA?? Harvard hurt, but this is just embarrassing. I am staying far away from all knives and guns. Mrs. Chips has me under 24-hour watch."

"Now Daniel," Dee answered, "I know you are disappointed, but you must let it go, let all your disappointment lead you to a path on which to travel to something great. Besides it is not so bad you didn't get into Harvard because a doctor here complained that Harvard did not offer courses like anatomy and pathology. And about UVA, rich boys cost more than they're worth. If we had money, you can bet every red cent of it the University of Virginia, la de dah, would've welcomed you with open arms. It's nothing but a finishing school for rich kids."

I had just finished reading Dos Passos' *Streets of Night*—oh my God. Who would want to spend time with those people anyway? Guess I should have been glad our father never made much money—

not that I wouldn't have taken it, ha. I decided if I was ever to find a girl or a school to accept me, I had better find some money or get used to starving.

I was slightly mollified when I won first place in the school's Latin rallies.

"The trophy is nothing to look at," I wrote Dee. "It really eats me that there is a huge trophy case for sports. The only trophy for football is for sportsmanship. I am proud of the Latin trophy and most grateful for the partial scholarship that goes with it."

It wasn't long before I could exclaim with joy, "Hurray! Hurray! It's off to college I go."

I thanked everyone for believing in me, and I thanked the University of Alabama for accepting me.

"I am not deluding myself," I wrote Dee. "Alabama is not nearly the level of Harvard. Mr. Goodsell is encouraging me though. He says Alabama is pointing the way to educational leadership. Said there are some good teachers there though they are not paid near what schools in the North pay."

"I'm sure he is right, not that I know anything. You have a good brain, Daniel, I know that, and I'm sure Alabama will give you the opportunity to distinguish yourself. Alabama won't be sorry," Dee wrote.

There were but a few first-class schools and, I felt, it was a shame I had not gotten into Harvard. Mrs. Chips said Thoreau thought Harvard was a bore. Maybe I would have thought so, too, but I would have liked finding out for myself. I was asked to join the college orchestra. The man who came to listen to me play said I had a lot of potential.

"You have an abundance of potential," said Ocy.

4

Only when I was playing the violin did I feel somewhat composed. Music, like dancing, was transforming. Music made it easier for life to go on. The outside world was just that—outside. There was no need to venture out except for class. I was grateful for having been taught to sight read music. I felt removed from the Roaring Twenties because, though I liked almost all music, my favorite music was written before I was born.

Mother's eyes glistened over whenever she sang in church. I never heard Father sing, or laugh for that matter. I went to chapel at Alabama mainly to hear the music. Church music was wonderful, comforting, especially during Christmas. I once went to hear an unusual program of chants, later, funnily, discovering there is no end to chants.

All in all, I had a good time at Alabama. I sensed that the South would rise again and for the better. Life could be good, even fun. It was at Alabama that I became familiar with a dance called the tarantella, a wonderful, lively dance that derived its name from a superstition that the bite of a tarantula spider required dancing madly to prevent death from "tarantism." It was great fun for the dancers to suddenly yell out, 'You've been bit by the tarantula,' and a frenzied dance then ensued.

Football at Alabama was a serious venture, and I admit, it was nice to be part of a winning program for a change. I was excited about Alabama's being national champions again and grateful to be able to lose myself in the joy of football—winning football. I joined a fraternal group at Alabama, but waited a month to tell Dee.

"One of the better ones I'm told—highly moral, not a watering hole—so don't worry, Sister."

I quickly discovered that I had been sentenced to making beds with clean linen but I had to wash the linen first and then clean and straighten up the member's room and shine his shoes—with mahogany shoe polish no less.

"I'm no more than a man-servant," I wrote to Dee, "and like the slaves, am looking forward to emancipation. It is a frivolous thing, but it is spirited, and I am making light friendships with other slaves."

Dee was worried, but glad I was making friends. I assured her that I was keeping up with my studies. At Alabama, I carried a light class load at first, not wanting to get in over my head, but I assured, Sister, I was inspired to aspire. The library had thousands of good books on nearly all subjects of the day. And I suspected those books were every bit as good as Harvard's. Hard feelings remained about the Civil War around there. The campus had been burned. A few buildings survived including the one in the picture that I enclosed in a letter to Dee.

"The girl on my right was trying to pinch my leg. We were having such a good time. I cannot remember ever laughing so hard. But rest assured, she is just a friend. I hope, Sister, you can laugh like that someday."

"Daniel," Dee wrote in her no nonsense way, "you have always been my first concern. You must know that. You should not leave your life to chance. Keep your eye on the ball, Daniel. Do not be diverted by the girls!"

"Don't worry," I assured her, "I am not tempted. You are a wonderful care-giver, like Mother was. You are better. You have been mother and father to me. I am lucky to have a sister like you. I do think my well-being is not only because of your care, but also Mother's nurturing when I was still crawling around on all fours. Whenever Mother held my hand, I felt protected. Perhaps Mother and Father never had anyone to hold their hand, to love them. I know it's not an excuse but Mother and Father were trapped by circumstances."

"Circumstance is in the devil, Daniel," said Dee unsympathetically.

"By the holes of life, I mean. People feel things are going to be bad, no matter, so you might as well not fight it. Perhaps Father was not able, to pull himself out of a hole, to get up and dust himself off."

"But we have a choice, Daniel," Dee wrote. "As much as we may have wanted to stay put, we knew we had to go forward."

I knew Dee was right. We had to leave home. There was nothing to keep us there, nobody to miss us. It is hard to be happy, but I was trying and would always do so.

Dee wanted to make sure I was not detoured from a profession that would provide me with a good life. By then, with her encouragement and with the realization that symphony jobs were hard to come by and hearing that doctors were still as scarce as a two-dollar bill, it made practical sense to consider medicine. It was something I had thought about secretly to myself since Ocy Chips had told me that her husband had been a doctor.

"As a nurse, Daniel, I must warn you that becoming a doctor means a lot of work and study, and I'm afraid that would preclude any laughing times with the ladies."

"Oh, yes, I understand," I wrote. In truth, I had no desire or wish to fall in love. There was another moment when I couldn't remember Mother's face. It was just for a moment, but it scared me. The harder I tried, the fainter her features became. There was no photo of her. I dreamt that I saw mother, but I could not touch her. I could not reach her. Dee was the only one I could reach out to. I was grateful. A child needs someone to go to. I promised myself that someday I would make up all the love Dee had given me so unselfishly.

"I think a lot of who we are," I told Dee, "was in our mother. She is gone. So who am I? That is a hard question. Is it not? Who are we? Well, it is enough to be your little brother. Maybe when I 'grow up,' I will be able to talk about death and love. And I'm thinking of becoming a doctor!"

"Doctor" had a nice ring to it. It could also be, as Dee reminded me, a good financial move. *It did seem that doctors were highly regarded; they must receive many strokes of love for their deeds,* I thought.

"In time you will learn to be as creative with the scalpel as you have been with the bow of your violin," Dee said.

"I trust you're right, Sister. Like a trained surgeon, the classical violinist usually doesn't have much room to improvise. The scalpel and the bow must move with exactness, precision."

One of my professors told me if I kept my grades up he would be able to arrange admittance to medical school for me. His offer made me feel pretty proud. Working summers and part time during the school year, with no feminine distractions, I still managed to graduate in microbiology with high honors. I would forever cherish the sequestered life at the University of Alabama. "Sweet are the dreams of campus life," one of my professors said to me.

At a time when so many did not know where they were going, I felt blessed to know where I would be spending the next few years. Now if I could just stay the course. I never wanted to disappoint Sister.

5

It took me time to acclimate to the city life of New Orleans. But the living was good, and food was cheap. The city was poor, and the Depression meant stagnation for the city during most of the 1930s. The French Quarter was grand, and I never felt unsafe. It was a pretty innocent place back then with no tourists to speak of. I recalled dancing to Phil Harris.

Dee thought I might be enjoying myself a little too much. She told me that the disciple Paul was a man of the city, but he had a conversion that took him out to the country to spread his message.

"When you become a doctor, perhaps you will have a conversion."

I hoped she was teasing.

"Paul must have enjoyed that," I said. "Especially if it was this hot. I can hardly breathe. I'm sure I'll lose weight just in sweat alone. The other day, I nearly fainted. I feel like I'm wet all the time."

"You are in the city to learn how to be a doctor. Then you can return to the country, if you like."

Audubon Park was only five short blocks from the Louisiana State University campus. Tulane, with its beautiful campus was just across from the park. The story goes that Tulane denied Huey Long a law degree so he built the LSU Medical School in revenge. Long hated New Orleans and his political rivals there. But someone hated Huey enough to assassinate him not long after I arrived in New Orleans. I was not a supporter of his, but I hated to see him go out that way. A few weeks before, I had sat stunned, listening to the funeral services for the much beloved Will Rogers who died in a plane crash up in Alaska. Times were hard, and Will made you feel good. There was no one to equal him. His death affected the nation like no other. The aviator, Wiley Post, pilot of the plane, also was lost.

Audubon Park's beauty was impressive. There were so many extremely pleasing attractions, including a beautiful golf course. I decided I would take up golf. It seemed a very social kind of game—all you had to do, as far as I could determine, was hit the ball, then chat with whomever you were playing with until you found your ball. Then hit it again and chat some more. Very civil it was.

One day while waiting for the manager of a restaurant to interview me, I observed huddled couples at most of the tables. I was struck by how intensely involved they were—as though they were absorbing each other.

Each couple seemed as one. But I wondered which was the more loving. They were alone with their own conversations, their duets, to the exclusion of similar conversations and duets at nearby tables. They were cooing, talking like mice, fussing with each others hair. A few of the couples were silent. I surmised that they were simply lost in each other and could only hear the beating of their own hearts. Their longing for each other was so admirable, so much so that I desired to have that kind of longing one day. I noticed one couple, their mouths close, when suddenly the girl extended her tongue—on the end of which was what appeared to be a wad of chewing-gum. The man took the chewing-gum into his mouth. So consuming, enveloping—and nauseating—I surmised, must be the promise of love. But what about the pain of love and its loss, of death, not to mention—germs!?

I studied internal medicine and operative procedures for the first few months—then rotated to psychiatry, which I supposed some people needed, but it escaped me as to why. Why can't people just write a letter? And if it is too angry, then don't send it, but the writing may have taken the edge off. l looked askance at some interns who were quick to masquerade as doctors but, like myself, were still medical students, at best student doctors. *Pity the patient*, I thought. I would not consider myself to be a full-fledged doctor until I completed my residency.

It was a full year and more before I was confronted with what I dreaded the most—dissecting my first cadaver. The experience made me squeamish, sick to my stomach. I had to steel myself before entering the lab with the human cadavers, but it was necessary. I was afraid to admit, "I will get used to it….or maybe not." A doctor needed to understand how the body works. During the dissection, I recall hearing laughter, but did not look up. I had been upset over the joking manner of some classmates, but it was probably just a cover. Before making an incision, I looked uneasily on the cadaver. I had to step away. We were told we had to treat the cadaver as an object of study and nothing else. *What about respect and caring? What about love? What about the soul…where sits desire and betrayal? Someone had loved this cadaver*, I thought. I reasoned it was good that the cadaver had no history, at least none I knew. I could approach it with cold, hard reasoning. Love of a fellow human being did not come into play. The cadaver was an object of study. I understood the necessity of such things. It was how you learned as doctors. I even struggled with the dogs. There was a pen of dogs, the unlucky ones having been picked up wandering the streets probably. They were put down and then dissected. I thought of the dog that followed me home one day. He was a sorry sight. I gave him some water and a piece of meat. The next morning he was gone. I wonder what became of him.

Basically, aside from facing a cadaver down, things had gone smoothly in medical school. I received the "Outstanding Medical School Student Award." All in all, I had been impressed with the quality of patient care and the education I received. Later the next year when a woman was brought in a car to the hospital, as the intern on emergency call, I went to assist bringing her in. She was in such trauma that I had to carry her into the hospital. Before I could lay her on the gurney, she died in my arms. My medical coat was covered in blood. As I knew, having seen several such cases, the woman's self-induced abortion had gone terribly wrong. I doubted that she could have been saved even if she had gotten to the hospital sooner.

I had seen several such women die. *Most were like my mother,* I thought, *desperate women with no money and no rights.* Ordinary people, ruled by prurience and hypocrisy. I thought of the girls in my boarding school days and how a few had the courage, as I now saw it, to rebel in their innocent way against the fundamentalist mores. I knew now that my mother had been in shock that night in father's arms, from a sloppy abortion, probably using some kind of non-sterilized instrument. Her body must have been severely infected. I held the dead nameless woman in my arms. I bent my face to hers and kissed her cheek. You could not rationalize her suffering.

When l thought about it, as I would my whole life, I could only think of Mother. Like the woman in my arms, she saw no other choice.

They had no one to turn to. *That is what love could come to,* I thought. *Pain.* Love could deceive, it could hurt, bring on toxic loneliness, as it had to my father. But love could never erase the bond that I shared with my mother, a fusion of our lives. I cried as hard that night as I had the night Mother died.

After completing my internship, I was one of nine admitted to the resident program at Charity Hospital in Shreveport. Charity had been expanded to 400 beds out on Texas Avenue after a devastating fire had practically wiped out the old hospital. My residency was a rigorous program leaving me little free time. Despite my nearly 24-7 schedule, and being somewhat guarded and contained, I managed to squeeze in some social life. A few of the nurses at Charity Hospital in Shreveport would tease me, called me "dashing" in my white linen suit and matching tie that I had bought with savings from my restaurant job the year before. I had taken a year off from school in order to save some money. "Dapper Dan," the nurses teased. I did not mind at all. On the contrary, I found I was a bit of an actor. The role of a doctor fit me like a good suit, a white linen suit. I thought it would be nice to attract a lot of adoring fans, especially nurses, because with fans there was no seriousness, no chance of pain, just nice relationships like on the golf course…just hit the ball, chat a little, find your ball and hit it again.

I quietly disapproved of doctors and nurses who were as sloppy in their dress as they were with their flirtations—flirtations that turned serious for some and a good time for others, hopping in and out of beds. I was critical of certain nurses and doctors whose behavior I considered to be unprofessional, telling patients, for instance, what their problem was without taking the time to hear the patients out. As a resident, I made a point to listen attentively as patients would ask all sorts of questions having nothing to do with their illnesses. They would confide in me, ask my advice about their children, their jobs. I found myself offering considered suggestions, gratefully received, and hearing,

"Oh, thank you, Doctor. You are so kind."

I was not kind. I was considerate, I think. I had flaws in my character, but you get lucky, people watch out for you, you have certain gifts, like music. You are recognized, awarded, patients say nice things, but it doesn't matter. The mold was set too many years ago.

I would smile warmly feeling the press of a patient's hand on mine and know there was no reason to doubt the career path I had chosen. I often tried to leave my patients' bedsides with a joke. "Not only is kissing likely to make you lose your teeth, according to a Boston health expert, but it quite likely will make you lose your head and heart."

"Physician while taking case history asks, 'Are you married? 'No,' the patient says, 'the reason I look this way is because I'm sick.'"

No one enjoyed my jokes more than I did.

————————————

"Sound the fireworks," I wrote Sister, after completing my three-year residency. I was now officially introduced, for real, as 'Doctor.' After receiving an appointment as surgeon at Charity Hospital, I went right out and ordered some stationary imprinted with 'Daniel Friend,

M.D.' I was looking forward to getting a real paycheck— "Won't know how to spend all the money," I laughed. The first thing I did was send Dee some money.

Being a doctor, a surgeon, defined who I was. I was Doctor Friend! The amount of time I would spend as a doctor, time that could never be replaced, would be transforming. My self-consciousness was no longer drowning me. For the rest of my life, I would rarely, of my choosing, be out of my hospital greens. It was a uniform I was proud to wear. I recalled, or my body remembered, the oneness felt with my mother. That feeling would sustain me. But it would be medicine, doctoring, care-giving, and my care-giver sister that I would use to replace a mother's bond and a father's angry indifference.

The passion, the emotion that I felt, the love I came to feel for my profession and my patients was somewhat of a surprise. This contradicted my training. Only by being disengaged, I had been taught, could I care effectively for my patients. After Mother's death and then Father's, I knew I had become increasingly self-absorbed, preoccupied. I had no other way to go on. My personality and manner kept people, including my sister, at times, at bay, but I had an empathy with patients, their pain, that I could not suppress. *This was the very thing*, I thought, *that would make me a good doctor—if not an 'up and coming star' in the hospital corridors.* "Definite mating material, you are, Doctor Friend," the nurses teased—excepting one dark-haired beauty with a wait-and-see attitude. She could only roll her brown eyes.

"What do you think?" I said to her.

"All new doctors think they are God's gift to women," she replied. "You look nice. New suit, Doctor Friend?"

"You know my name?"

"It's on your name tag."

I could not help but notice the confidence in her intelligence. She did not play stupid. The skeptical nurse with the knowing glint in her eye bothered me every time I passed her station with her seeming benign indifference. The more indifferent she was, the more insecure

I became. I stammered in her presence. I shifted from one leg to the other. Why doesn't she at least acknowledge my existence? Did I say the wrong thing? I had been…oh, what is the word… smitten…yes, smitten the first time I laid eyes on her. I felt a sensation I had never felt. *Why her*, I thought. There were probably twenty nurses on the floor at any one time, and she won't even speak to me. My attraction to her was totally uncontrollable, as though I had no choice in the matter. I had no idea if she even liked me or not. I thought she probably didn't. She had yet to smile at me. That only made her even more attractive. I only knew that I thought about her a lot. That had to count for something. Was it a prelude to love? Or was it love?

One evening I took a bag of popcorn up to her station, and all the nurses but Elmira took a handful. Every evening, popcorn in hand, I passed her station only to have her ignore me.

"Give him a smile, Elmira," I heard another nurse say.

Elmira would barely give me the time of day, let alone a smile. She would hardly look at me when I requested a patient's room number. She was the recipient of many date offers, I was told by one of the other doctors.

"Elmira is quite the social butterfly and has no end of suitors. Her dance card is always full."

Undeterred, I kept dropping by station 103, popcorn in hand, while making my rounds. I tried a joke. "This intern said his ambition was to be a great doctor. 'I want to become a bone specialist.' 'Well,' said the nurse, 'you have a good head for it.'"

"I agree," Elmira said.

When I first met Elmira, I was awkward, oblivious, I admit, with little or no social agility. The gossip among the nurses was that I was "inexperienced." Some teased me about being afraid to join their parties. I liked to have a good time, but it seemed to me that there was too much partying between doctors and nurses. It wasn't proper. After a couple of months, seeing me stop at Elmira's station and offering her some of my popcorn, it became a bit of a joke among the other nurses as to when I would finally ask her for a date. When I did, she turned me down.

"Maybe next time," I said, undeterred, but dejected. "Don't underestimate me. A glance from your eyes, a touch of your hand, and the gates of paradise would swing wide for me." I thought she would never stop laughing. "It wasn't a joke," I said.

"I know, I know. You are so serious, Doctor Friend. Lighten up."

"Is there a flicker of hope," I asked. She looked annoyed. "Don't forget me," I said.

Leaving the operating room one morning after Elmira had assisted me on an operation, I removed my surgical mask and gloves, smiled, and said "nice job." *The nurse's pristine white uniform looked quite splendid on her,* I thought, watching her walk away. I smiled at the way her white cap set back on her head like a sailor's. I wrote Dee about the pretty, intelligent nurse. I neglected to mention her nice figure and her "swivel hips." I had observed that male patients loved to watch her "swivel" out of their rooms.

A few months later when Elmira was about to visit her mother, I asked her to write me and let me know she had arrived safely.

"It is a three-hour train ride, and I don't believe I am kidnapping material."

"Oh, I don't know about that."

"Dr. Friend, Made it alive," Elmira wrote on reaching her destination, "thanks to a tall handsome stranger. Elmira."

"Haven't heard from you since you wrote me that you had arrived home. The tall dark handsome stranger must be keeping you very busy." No response.

"We are very, very busy here now. The new nurse is quite efficient, and I overheard one of the doctor's describe her as being rather voluptuous. Not sure how he knows. Curious. She is good on the eyes. Hoping you continue to enjoy your stay at home." That letter garnered a quick response.

"The nurse you mentioned is a hit on the second floor section 6, very loosey-goosey, I understand. You should check her out."

"No thank you. Those girls act like fools and drink like rips, the worst collection of girls. Don't swap hours with rotten Murphy. She is a crook, and if you have anything to do with her you may be gossiped about, too. She's slippery as butter, the truth's not in her, and she's mean and most all know it. Hope Nurse Smith slides off Dr. Hastings. Nothing but 5 and one-half years of hard work for her and 5 and one-half years older and a name much worse, is all she has to show for it. Isn't that a petty way to spend 5 and one-half years?"

Elmira finally returned to her nursing duties and I redoubled my efforts in pursuit of the girl at station 103. It was as though I had no choice in the matter. One evening, I stopped by station 103 sans popcorn.

"Where's the popcorn?" asked Elmira, with a bit of a smile.

"I think maybe she likes me after all," I wrote Dee. But I wondered if her little flirtation was just that. Maybe she was just happy for some reason, and it spilled over to me. Oh well, take what you can.

The patients on Elmira's floor continued to receive my utmost attention. Elmira would later tell me that I was like an actor who worked too hard, too earnest, is what she said. She also informed me that she could not trust a man who wasn't married by a certain age. I was about to turn thirty-four and was self-conscious and thus secretive about my age. Why should she care? So how did she know my age, I finally asked her.

"Observation, Doctor Friend. A doctor's age is the first thing nurses check if he has no ring on his finger. So you are probably a confirmed bachelor. I am twenty-two, Doctor Friend, and have no desire to waste time with a bachelor's flirtations."

"Who says you would be wasting your time?"

"I say."

"I have been misdiagnosed, I dare say."

"Nurses, especially the young ones, have cloying smiles and sharp claws," Dee wrote. "Beware," she told me. "Being a nurse, I am certainly familiar with such predators."

6

Right after our first kiss, which was sublime, I was transfixed. Elmira's lips were so soft, but, having no subtlety, I told her while in an amorous clutch that a couple could do well if they pooled their resources.

"Yes?" Her eyebrows raised.

"If they had a fondness for each other."

"Yes? Go on."

"If they had similar interests, if their morals were alike."

"I see."

"I want a good practice and a good comfortable home, and two boys and a girl and a sweet wife and some finances for support and also a good name."

"Slow down."

"Sugar, you would make a real good private nurse. You are the type that would be liked and could be depended upon. I like your personality a lot, too. You are quiet, mind your own business and that means everything in private work. Some are snoopy and the nosier, the louder, the better."

"Daniel? Whoa! I hardly know you."

"Our brains know us. Your brain knows me."

"It does?"

"Yes! And my brain knows you. It tells me you are someone I can love. Someone I can trust."

"Your brain tells you that?"

"Yes."

"My brain is a little slow."

"Not at all."

"Yes, and I'm stuck with it."

"You can re-wire it. I've re-wired mine a few times."

"Have you now."

"You have influenced my brain, ten-fold. You introduced me to black-eyed peas, to gumbo, to Louisiana politics, the bayou, so many things."

"I'm so glad."

"So am I, and my brain is glad. My brain is delighted because it has borrowed your goodness, your mind, your strength."

"Daniel... talking about your brain is hardly romantic. It is not helping my impulses. I'm afraid the moment has passed."

"I know I sound crazy but…..I've been sweet on other girls, but….the truth is I've never had a relationship with any girl to speak of."

"What are you trying to say?"

"Well, just that nothing ever really serious developed with other girls, women," I said.

"Are you," Elmira motioned for me to come closer—she whispered, "a virgin, Daniel?"

"Well…," I groped for a proper answer. "If I was, is there something wrong with that?"

"You are! Oh my God. A thirty-four year old virgin? And a surgeon at that. You are a rare bird. Lucky me. How could any self-respecting man get through the Roaring Twenties and still be a virgin?"

"Wasn't easy," I stammered, proudly. "There were possibilities."

"There still are." She smiled up at me. "I mean the warehouse district flashes red lights. Or just go down to the bottom floor nursing stations, the basement, we call it."

My romance was the most intensely glorious time for me. It was one of high heat, and I had not felt so safe since feeling the warmth of mother's arms around me. Elmira was a spring awakening for my body and my brain. I was consumed with her, by her touches, by her softly telling me of her day. All my electrodes were flashing, my brain was screaming, especially from Elmira's physical intimacy. My skin of formality washed away when she gently stroked me, teasing, softly asking me, "Why are you standing there with your clothes on?" She drew me close and offered up her tender mouth and made me a man.

Dee had been very concerned when, on a visit to her, I hinted at marriage. She had no time or patience to hear my exhortations about the nurse from Shreveport. She had little need to listen to men and their problems—the man she had hinted about seeing, I gathered, was no longer on the scene. When I asked her if she had anyone special in her life, she said,

"Why, of course, you, Daniel. Except for you, I have had it with men. The less said, the better. I'm glad for the experience, but I may very well get myself to a nunnery," she laughed. "I expect too much from a man. Common love for us, Daniel, will always be a struggle. It will inevitably go quiet. Only then will you realize that it was a mistake. Remember how your sister warned you."

I was half listening and was shamelessly happy thinking of Elmira. My love would never go quiet. My marriage would not fail. It would go on through the years. Love was making me lonely now, anxious.

"I do believe a job opening here at the hospital has your name on it," Dee offered.

She was well established and very respected as a nurse and had no trouble arranging an interview at the Roanoke Hospital for me. I telegraphed Elmira of the possible job. She telegraphed back: "Wish you well."

After the interview, Dee treated me to dinner. I confided to her that Elmira was somewhat aloof, kept things to herself, did not feel the need to open herself up to other people. Dee offered no encouragement. I shared with her a few things Elmira had told me about herself, but was careful not to mention how she had given herself to me. I realized, for the first time, there were things I could never tell my sister.

"Elmira's stepfather drank up all the money her mother had saved for her college education. Her mother married the hard drinking lumberjack after her husband died in the diphtheria epidemic in 1918. It also took the life of one of Elmira's sisters."

"That is what killed our two older brothers."

"Yes. Elmira did whatever she could to make money and bide her time until the moment came when she saw a way out. She read about the nursing program at Charity Hospital that had scholarships to offer. She sent away for the application. When she was accepted, she simply announced she was going to nursing school."

"And now she has announced her intention to marry you."

"I don't know. I haven't asked her."

"We know what Saint Paul thought of marriage," said Dee. "'I say therefore to the unmarried and widows, it is good for them if they abide even as I.'"

"Dad would agree with Paul," I said.

"Yes, beware! So do I," replied Dee. "I shall never get involved again. You must think twice about this marriage business. Have you ever…this is very difficult…have you had a relationship with a woman?"

"Well, none to speak of, no, but…"

"Have you ever known a woman, Daniel, in the biblical sense?"

"Well, no," I lied. I had never lied to her. My guilt was such that I was sure my face was red. I put my hands over my cheeks.

"Thank God. That is such a relief. It's not all that some make it out to be."

"I dare say Elmira would meet Paul's approval. I have read Corinthians 7 and Paul understands each man has his proper gift of God. Do not fret, Sister, marriage is a long way off, and Elmira has no idea I will ask her."

"It's just that we, you and I, have no good experience with marriage. How could we? We didn't have a good example to go by.

And it does not sound, from what you have told me, that this woman has had much better. That is not a good combination. I only have your interests at heart. You don't want to make the same mistakes our parents made."

"No."

"What do you know about love?"

"I just know it's like nothing I've ever felt."

"You hardly know your thoughts, your feelings. How could you? You have no experience in such matters."

"I just know I need her."

"That is not a reason to marry. You need a lot of things!"

"Meeting her, stumbling into bliss, feeling what I feel, it's a miracle. We both like the same things," I finally, weakly protested. It seemed to me that one had to climb the ladder of love and jump off.

"A marriage of convenience is not a marriage made in heaven, Daniel. Love is not a duty. That was the last thing our mother said to us. It is all chemistry, Daniel. It has nothing to do with everlasting love. There is so much back-biting in certain female circles. Only a precious few females are worth anything at all and would do a man much more harm than good in a home or at his work."

It was fruitless to talk to Dee about marriage, I decided, and how could I possibly talk to her about lust. It was lust I felt for the girl at station 103. I wanted her, night and day, all day, all night. That is what my brain was telling me. *Love may not be a duty, should not be,* I thought. My love was freely given. There was no way she would understand my wanting a passionate married life. It did not matter if it was right or wrong or if God approved, it was a wonderful feeling— to be in love. No matter Dee's words, I had fallen in love. I knew what I wanted, and there was no shame or guilt. I could scarcely contain myself, but I had no one else to talk to but my sister.

———————

I went back to Shreveport to tell Elmira about my visit with Dee and about Roanoke Hospital and the job offer. I pleaded my case extolling the virtues of Roanoke. Elmira did not seem impressed. Certainly, she did not let on as to being the slightest bit interested in what I was talking about. She told me that she had absolutely no wish to ever leave the deep South. My heart sank. My eyes clouded over.

"We have not forgotten that man."

"Man. What man?"

"Lincoln!! We left him at the altar."

"Oh."

"But we are still on our knees because of him. Because we have had to eat all of the guilt."

Persistence and prudence were traits I had nurtured. I bore them like a shield.

"Roanoke is certainly not the North, not by any means. Richmond, Virginia, was the capitol of the Confederacy."

"Virginia is not Louisiana," she said.

"Both places were put upon, made to give up a way of life. The whole affair wasn't your fault, Elmira. You certainly weren't to blame. You didn't take up the sword of death and misery. There is plenty of blame to go around for …"

"For what?"

"Slavery, I suppose."

"Yes, but don't you understand it is we who had to swallow all the guilt, all the shame, all the blame. It affects you like a virus."

"It is regrettable, but it has nothing to do with us. Everything up there…

"Up where?"

"Virginia."

"It's so far Daniel."

"The air is very pure. I do not perspire any in comparison to here. It is so clean there and free from dust, and the weather is just grand. You will enjoy it. You won't have to endure any Yankees or any noise or odor from the oil well pumps. It is quiet there, no noise, and the air is fresh."

"Yes, it's very pure."

"You know!"

"You just told me, silly."

"I did. Oh goodness. Well, it is wonderful, a very…ah… unique place. You know what I mean?"

"No."

"It makes a good impression."

"You seem easily impressed."

"You, Elmira, have certainly impressed me. I gave the hospital director your name. There are some positions open in Roanoke for qualified nurses. I told Sister if I had a chance to recommend a real nurse of ability and possessing real qualities of a nurse, I surely would recommend you. I could recommend you to the Mayo Clinic or Johns Hopkins. Darling, your ability and tactics are to be admired. Of course I will let you know of any opportunities that may come up. One must do these things, Elmira. Face to face contact is very important. It would do you good to see another part of the country…not north, no, no…..I don't think I can let this job go by."

Two weeks later, I was packed to leave the next morning.

"May I see you tonight?"

"Yes," said Elmira.

That night I went out on the limb of love. I could not leave without declaring my love, my promise of love, to cherish her and always look out for her, care for her.

"I'm a nurse, Daniel, not a invalid. I can care for myself."

We were seated in the reception foyer of the nurses' home. General Robert E. Lee hung on the wall behind us.

"I would love for you to be with me. You and I have talked around the subject of marriage."

"You have done the talking, Daniel. I have listened, as I do now along with the General, our chaperone. He's watching your every move."

"Well Mr. Lee—rather, General Lee, I have thought greatly about Elmira's concern that a good team in the operating room doesn't necessarily mean a good marriage team, just as a good general in his office does not necessarily make a good general in the field. But, I do believe our love will last. We will be good pals."

"Pals?"

"Well, I mean, don't you agree? We are good dancing partners. You must agree to that."

"I follow your lead."

"Very well… I wanted to, well…" I dropped to my knees. Elmira glanced up at the General and then down at me on my bended knees. I stammered about how much I thought of her, how much I missed her when apart. "Please know my prospects are good, more than good, excellent I would say."

I then asked for her hand in marriage. Elmira told me that she would think about my proposal. With that she got up, kissed me on the cheek and excused herself, leaving me feeling lost and frustrated.

The next morning at Charity Hospital, I made sure to stop by Elmira's station. I carried a bag of popcorn.

"Wanted to leave you something."

"A bag of popcorn?"

"You left me in the lurch. I was so…frustrated, I made a gallon of popcorn, but I ate all but a handful. This is all that's left. You won't forget me, will you?"

"Not possible. Popcorn is the way to my heart."

I loitered around until it was time for me to make my rounds for the last time. Trying hard to keep my game face on, I smiled weakly as I offered Elmira the last bit of popcorn. She slowly took a handful. As she was about to put it in her mouth, she noticed something shiny among the kernels. It was a ring. Elmira started to laugh.

"Guess I'm lucky I didn't swallow this."

The ring had one main fair-sized diamond with one small diamond on either side.

"It makes a beautiful engagement ring, doesn't it?"

"Yes."

"It is white gold. Do you like it?"

"Yes. How much was it?"

"What does it matter? You like it. That's what matters. I didn't win it at the carnival. I thought you might appreciate a nice diamond ring, more than anything else I could get you. It's already paid for so even if you don't want it, you can keep it." I stopped talking when I saw Elmira put the ring on her finger.

"It fits. I feel like Alice and the glass slipper. I guess it's finder's-keeper's. You know what this means?"

"What?"

"I'm engaged," she smiled.

From behind me, there were whoops and clapping by a couple of doctors and nurses. I let out a whoop of my own. Elmira gave a little bow. I did a little shuffle with my feet then blurted out to the whole hospital wing how happy Elmira had just made me. There could not have been a better going-away gift. I was leaving on the noon train for Roanoke and my new job. It was a joyful, tearful moment. I hated to part from her. The nurses and doctors were soon joined by a few strolling patients and visitors, all applauding the promise of love.

"You will soon be greeted with the new residents," I told Elmira. "Hope they are a better crew than the last set. I got my fill of the last bunch," I announced to a chorus of laughter. "Keep sweet, darling, and keep up with all the news about here so you can pass it on to me when you get time. Oh, God, I can't leave." Again there was laughter, but there were also tears—including Elmira's. She took my arm and walked me down the hall.

"Your patients are waiting to say goodbye."

"I've told practically the whole bunch good-bye (and some, good riddance). I even said good-bye to my old room. Elaine was one I shall miss and I didn't see her, so tell her I said good-bye. She is a sweet girl."

"She was just caught on the operating table with Dr. Mackey."

"What?"

"Yes. She better let the young doctors alone and get some good old bachelor out in town—love him to death."

"Well, I am surprised. You never can tell. I'm sure glad I never had a date with her."

That morning, when I made the rounds with Elmira, I tried to put on a brave face but each bed I passed, I knew I was nearer to the end of the last ward visit at Charity with her. I knew I had to make my way in the world. I so needed her to be with me. I needed her courage. I had wooed and won the hand of an operating room nurse, a strong-willed, opinionated, dark-haired Louisiana beauty. It would still be a challenge for this new doctor to convince his wife-to-be to relocate. I guessed that would be the test of our love. Elmira might decide not to move to Roanoke even if she were offered a better paying job. She might simply remove the ring and return to sender. I thought her mild interest had developed into a curiosity, then to a more definite interest, which eventually led her to accept my proposal of marriage. I knew, for her, it had not been love at first sight, not love from 'across a crowded room'. She had never felt that certain tingling sensation. Her brain was built differently, and the right person had not come along. But on that evening sitting with me under General Lee's portrait, I thought the romantic portion of her brain was triggered and that she knew that here was a love that could last.

But now I was asking her to forego her friends, job, and family and go to a part of the country where, she joked,

"Rum running is the popular sport. I read where Appalachia is worse off than Mississippi," she said.

"Roanoke is a world class city," I assured her.

"I'm sure. Maybe I'll have to visit. After all, I'm a world class kind of girl."

7

The loneliness of the train whistle echoed what I was feeling. There is always a futility in leaving, but a finality lurks. I yearned to be kissing Elmira good night and giving her some popcorn or ice cream. I was thankful for the way she told me yes. And the way she said good-bye. She seemed vulnerable for the first time.

"I don't know why I'm crying."

"You are grieving."

"You're not dead."

"No. Well, I would rather see you cry than laugh at my leaving. Keep sweet. A few more pounds wouldn't hurt. Hope you will be weighing 130 pounds. When I see you next."

"Daniel, go."

"Write me long, newsy, sweet letters. Don't forget your prayers. Your tears make me realize you love me more."

In truth, her tears pierced my heart with a spear. When I got half way across the street to the train station that mid-day, my heart was breaking. I cried all the way to the Virginia border! Tears of joy, and yet, tears of sadness. I could not choke away the sobs. I was miserable, but also the happiest I had ever been. That was one of the worst days I've ever spent and one of the best.

The train was clean and thankfully fast. I did sleep some. My hotel room was grand, and being in Virginia and only a few miles from home made me feel, strangely, just fine, too. Work at the Roanoke Hospital was light in comparison to Charity Hospital. In the first months, I did a few major operations myself and assisted in several others. At Roanoke, they operated on all ruptured appendices and not only drained the cavity, but removed the old ruptured appendix at the same operation. Surgery there was a work of art. The hospital was the most up-to-date and cleanest hospital I'd seen. The library was beautiful, and the lawn in front was marvelous. I knew then I wanted to get a hospital of my own someday. I was doing good work for others and felt sure I could do the same for myself.

My room with private bath and telephone, regular $7.50 a day, was more than fine. Elmira was so far away and I missed her so much. Movies were my escape. Saw *Roberta* with Fred Astaire. He had the ease I longed for. I would go back to my room and try a few dance steps. Elmira and I had seen *Gay Divorcee* on Thanksgiving Day. We danced to *Night and Day* in the nurses' social room. She was good. She said she was faking it. Our chemistry in the operating room was as wonderful as Fred Astaire and Ginger Rogers on the dance floor. I wrote her often and would tease her about eating too many hot-tamales and hamburgers. I sent plenty of love along too with pleasant dreams.

"I am keeping my promise ... am turning down all date-seekers," I wrote. "I trust you are doing the same. Hope you don't have to work much at night. Many ridiculous things go on about that messy hole at night. I'm through with that bunch and place. Any one there can do well with the large amount of cases to work with, but there are more there that don't care a whoop about anything except some old vulgar sexual acts or old rotten debasing amusements that will fade out before they are 35 or 40 years old, and then they will be holding an empty bag with such a record behind them that they will blush to have their attention called to it. What they call wit, is merely sarcasm and bitchiness at others expense. I frequently get disgusted with the entire situation everywhere. Things are so different to what some claim—people posing as real men and women and are anything but. What will they say when they approach God? If only they had the kind of love we have."

My ranting was such that I tore the letter up. Who was I to have such thoughts, say such things? Mother would not have thought them proper to be uttered. The fact was, I had no idea what kind of man I was, what kind of husband I would make. Like my father? I was afraid—afraid that I would be following the footsteps of my parents. I could hear father's cold laughter. I had pursued Elmira unrelentingly but now I was fighting to keep myself together, to allow myself to seize the moment and not let my fear rob me of her magic. Desperate for her not to doubt my intentions which were nothing but honorable, I was writing to Elmira every other day.

I was jealous and could not contain my suspiciousness. I knew a few things about Dr. Pigeon at Charity that I thought were not so good—if I had some fine relatives there, I would not like for them to go to him. He was quite vulgar at times and was always on the prowl. I'd seen the lustful way he looked at Elmira. She would just be another conquest. He just wanted to see what he could get out of a girl, like an old cat. "I want you to have my baby." What a load of bull! That bunch of doctors should be ostracized. Most of them are too rotten to hang together.

I trusted Elmira was wearing her engagement ring, and letting as many see it without just coming out and asking them to look at it. Guess that would have not been too classy. I wanted her to show it to some of that bunch that thought I had quit on her. I wanted Dr. Pigeon and old Edna to see the ring shining on Elmira's finger. We'd show them where to get off. How could anyone work with that putrid Edna Moses? She was so filthy, relatively speaking, that you could almost smell her up in Roanoke –and those who admired her and employed her were as rotten as she was. At first she appeared clean—then she took her shoes off and she was anything but clean! I was glad to be away from that trashy bunch. I worried that my father's low view of life had infected me. Perhaps I feared I would end up as arrogant and narcissistic as those I loathed. My work was my refuge from my mad thoughts—work. I performed on the average of one hysterectomy and two appendectomies every other day.

"I trust no one gets hold of my letters," I wrote Elmira. My father's suspicious nature reared its head. "If they did, they would get a good sample of love, would they not? The atmosphere in Roanoke is much better morally than at Charity. I hear a radio over in a nearby building—wish you and I were dancing, Sweetheart. Love is great when it works well. Isn't it precious? I've been thinking of having you come up here as soon as I can arrange it and also keep down suspicion of our romance. You can join the nursing society and get on the list here in town—and at the hospital just as soon as an opening arises. They pay $65 per month with a chance of making more. My sister is making some more than that. You can do the same. I have mentioned this to Sister, and she is warming. I don't want you working long anyway. I just want you around. This is just a scheme of mine. Tell me how you like it. We could be here and love each other and marry at our convenience. From now on send my mail to Roanoke, Va. Box 1905. By doing this the hospital authorities will not see our out-going and in-coming mail. If they don't know of our deep love affair, you stand a better chance of coming. Box 1905 is mine, and everything is absolutely private this way.

The big cheese, Dr. Sturgess, gave me a few words of encouragement, told me my work was highly satisfactory. He liked the way I handle the patients. He gave me a raise in salary. When the operating room supervisor quit, the position was given to Dee. Dr. Sturgess said he would keep you in mind the next time. I think you and I together here could coin a fairly good check each month."

It was not long before I was put in complete charge of obstetrics. Of course I wrote Elmira boasting of my promotion. I was doing faster and better all-round surgery. Did an appendectomy in around 22 minutes. Had never done one that fast before.

As always, music was good therapy for hard bottom truths. Music allowed me a place to store my grief. It made me a better doctor. There was a common bond in making music and healing people. I think understanding music helped me hear my patients. I hoped and prayed that Elmira would hear me. I began to wonder if Elmira might change her mind. I bought two pieces of music, "Isle of

Capri" and "Nothing Lives Longer Than Love." I had given Elmira
little music lessons. How I wanted to dance with her. Had I known
how bad it was going to be so far away from my loved one, I probably would have lived my life there somewhat different. I didn't know
whether I could wait until things completely materialized for Elmira's
coming until I saw her. My responsibilities at the hospital did not
allow enough time for me to get to Shreveport. I wrote and asked
Elmira if she would if she would see fit to come by train to Roanoke.
I would pay all her expenses. Thought we could meet in Chatta-
nooga and spend a couple of days together. I used to have 25 to 30
dates with her each month, and now nothing. I began to understand
Father's angst.

8

Finally, after telegraphing Elmira and pleading with her to visit me, she wired back that she would.

"I will send you finances. Come on bus or train. Am afraid you will be on the train or bus with some old rotten bums and drunks. Watch those dirty mugs, Hon. I think it is nice of you to come so far to see me. I must hold my job so we can get our little love nest arranged. Tell your mama you are coming back, but I am coming after you a little later. Assure her not to worry, Darling, that you will return this time, but emphatically state you will not return a little later. I have not quite enough finances yet to care for us comfortably. I'll see you late Friday night or Saturday morning. I have a room already reserved at Ponce de Leon Hotel. It is in my name. Get a taxi to take you there. Register under my name—you understand what I mean. Upon finishing work, I'll come directly to the hotel."

My whole being was thrilled. There was only one problem—I had neglected to tell Dee that Elmira was coming.

"It is so nice to meet you," said Dee. "This is a surprise. Daniel did not tell me you were visiting."

"I thought I had told you, Sister, that Elmira was coming for a visit. I guess I've been so busy, it escaped me."

"Yes, well….no matter. Daniel has spoken of you."

"Has he? That is nice to hear," said an amused Elmira. "I hope he had something good to say."

"Oh yes, very good, it was all good. Daniel, have you arranged a place for this poor girl to stay?"

"We haven't…"

"I'm staying with Daniel at the Ponce de Leon Hotel." Elmira said, quickly, with a smile, and she put her hand on my leg. I swallowed hard.

She laughed. I thought Elmira announced this almost as a challenge.

"Oh, I see," said Dee. "I understand it is rather expensive. So you are already settled?"

"Quite comfortably," said Elmira. "The bed is quite soft and really big enough for two—if Daniel finds the couch not to his liking."

"The hospital administrator might not find that appropriate."

"He doesn't have to know," I said, "does he?"

"Well, perhaps not. It is too bad, Elmira, that your visit is so short….I know you have your nursing duties to get back to."

Elmira and Dee locked eyes.

The weekend was wonderful, aside from Dee and Elmira facing off with each other. It almost killed me to part from Elmira. I knew I could not do that again. Everything got dark, sad. I was a stray dog, wandering aimlessly through life. As a doctor, I took care of those in need. In truth, I was the most needy.

———————

"Not now! Not yet! Too young, too young. Too soon, too soon," said Dee when I told her of my marriage plans.

"I'm thirty-five years old!"

"Still a young man. You are not ready. You owe me the respect to listen to my advice. You told me that you wanted to go forward. This, I believe, would be a step backwards. Your possibilities are unlimited, as will be your opportunities. I urge you not to tie yourself down. In time you will make a wonderful husband," Dee reasoned. "You are kind and respectful. You will not be a philanderer. And because you are a very good doctor, you will be a good provider.

Isn't that what every wife wants? If this young woman is as fond of you as she seems, I'm sure she won't mind waiting a few years."

"A few years?"

"How do you know that she is the right one for you?"

Despite Dee's misgivings, Elmira and I announced our engagement. However, I kept delaying marriage. "Delay, delay, delay" was Elmira's reply to my asking her to be patient. I told myself that I wanted to wait until I felt secure in my job, but I wondered if I would make a good husband.

"I'm running out of patience," said Elmira. "I have been too patient."

"If I had had a half a chance to bring you with me, I'm telling you, you would be with me now. I am working every possible scheme to get with you at the very earliest possible time. I am sure things will be good for you here. It is not because I want to shun you, but because I love you and want to have something to bring my sweetheart to. It is so sad to recall our good times knowing I can't be with you for a few weeks yet. It is awful to desire something, to have the promise of something and not have it. I guess that's what love is. Are you still as sweet as you were, Darling? Remember, Dear, I still rave about you, and love you just a tremendous lot. I never could hope to love anyone more than you. I told you many times, while there, I loved you, but many times you would doubt me it seemed. I'm always loving you, Dear, and always missing you. Darling, I do believe we can be real happy together, don't you? You have proven you could be a great help to me and your love and companionship would mean so much to me. As soon as I can possibly get things straightened out, I want you –oh, do I want you, and you already know that. You haven't made a mistake. Please understand. Wish I could do better. I want you to be happy—and I want to be the type and grade of man you will respect and be proud of—you deserve a good man— a man who is as affectionate and loving as you."

What I did not mention to Elmira was that Dee was blowing a cold wind on our marriage plans.

On my birthday, one of the nurses in the operating room played a joke on me by going into the doctor's dressing room and sewing up my shirt. It was quite funny. Dee had been the instigator telling everyone it was my birthday. Elmira sent me a tie clasp and belt buckle for my birthday. And Sister surprised me by presenting me with a nice Philco Radio. She had it put in my room without my knowing it. First song I heard on it was "Keep On the Sunny Side" by the dear Carter family. They used to hold sing-alongs on the front porch of their home on Clinch Mountain during the early days of the Depression because they could not get much for their singing during the hard times. Sara Carter had walked out on her husband. Dee said there must be something in the water.

For my birthday, Dee suggested we make a side trip to Abingdon, Virginia, and the Barter Theater to see a play. The theater put on plays for the community in exchange for food. At the particular play we attended, I was struck, mesmerized, by the quiet poise a certain tall young actor possessed. The actor had such assurance and presence. He appeared so natural, he didn't seem to be working. I made note of his name—Gregory Peck. I was so taken with Peck's bearing and ease, that's all I could talk about on the bus ride back home. I had suggested that we pay a visit to our home-place, but Dee would not hear of it. It was just sitting there. It was 1940, and Dee felt with the threat of war looming, we should wait.

The quiet confidence the young Mr. Peck had conveyed on stage was the kind of confidence I aspired to, not only as a surgeon but also as a man. When I was in surgery or at a patient's bedside, I was secure. I knew what I was doing. It was out in the world where I was uncomfortable. I did not know what was expected of me.

"Clark Gable could be your image," said Dee. I laughed. "Why not? You loved *It Happened One Night, Mutiny On The Bounty, Gone With The Wind.* Besides, this Peck fellow may be an up and comer, but Gable is already a star. You look like him…. brown eyes and full, bushy, very expressive eyebrows."

"I'm not good-looking like Clark Gable."

"Who is?" Dee had said.

"He is a matinee idol."

"So are you. Certainly your intended thinks you are the be-all. If you look the part, you are the part," Dee told me.

Then one day, back at the Roanoke Hospital, as if it was pre-ordained, a nurse commented to me, "You remind me of Clark Gable."

"Thank you, thank you very much," I effused trying not to be too delighted, trying to maintain some sense of decorum, dignity. The truth was, as Dee knew, nothing, absolutely nothing, could have pleased me more than the nurse's compliment. In fact, nothing ever had. Well, except for Elmira saying yes to my proposal of marriage.

"Daniel, all the nurses think you are handsome. There are plenty of nurses out there who would say yes."

It occurred to me that it was somewhat coincidental that the nurse had mentioned me and Clark Gable in the same breath. I walked on air for a week, but soon Dee was disappointed to finally realize that I was helplessly in love. Life was wonderful! And if Elmira should have decided not to reciprocate, I would still have my love. I would feel the lightness in my walk, the joy in my heart, and this had made me feel good about myself.

I continued writing letters non-stop to Elmira, sometimes two a day. When I was courting Elmira, I had told her, hoping to persuade her to marry me, that I was a good "level-headed" man, "a sure man who will take care of you, always." I would make a good father, I assured her. I knew she was tired of my postponing marriage. A couple of doctors at Charity told me she was still wearing the ring. Missing her so much, I kept busy. I saw *"On Borrowed Time,"* but the young child being orphaned hit too close to home. I made my rounds, read the newspaper—the funny papers—Pop-eye. The radio was good company. The Russian music was a little fast to dance to, but I kept trim practicing up. I wore out the rug practicing dancing (by myself in my room).

The war situation in North Africa was worrisome. I had not thought the U.S. would become involved, but Dee disagreed. The prospect of war was another reason, she said, to delay my marriage.

"The President has said we will all have to make some sacrifices."

National security was at the forefront. I stood to get on the first call if they should draft men, but I was thinking things would clear up. If all the men stayed home, Dee said, there would be no war. Germany had seemed very confident. Goering said with enough planes, he would be master of Europe in a week. Never underestimate your enemy—whether in war or on the football field. As it turned out, I was not called because doctors were needed in the community. I wished another film like *Top Hat* with Fred Astaire and Ginger Rogers would come along. *Top Hat* had been good medicine for me, and the times. It helped soften the blow of losing Will Rogers.

Winters were cold in Roanoke. My overcoat felt good. But it did not protect me from my anxieties. Still, I was doing my best work. Had done about 67 major operations since I arrived in Roanoke—much better than I ever expected to do. I would do over 200 major operations a year there. Had no trouble getting my Fellow of the American College of Surgeons degree. Kept dreaming of a fine home with awnings over a porch.

Bell Telephone put on an interesting program. The electronic devices were very accurate. A man on the stage talked directly to another man in London. Their voices were magnified and the relays were two-fold from Roanoke to New York to an English port by radio, then from the English port to the main office in London by telephone. The conversation was just as plain as if you were in the room with them. No lapse at all for time in transit. The lights were switched off, and a machine arranged a graphic picture of the conversation between the men in London and the men on the stage. It was magical, one of the most interesting things I had ever heard and seen. Not so long ago, I had wondered what was on the other side of the mountain. Something grand I had imagined.

It had been nearly two weeks since I had heard from Elmira. I was worried and anxious. I had asked her to write when she got time. "But your correspondence should not interfere with work," I wrote. "Work before pleasure is an old proverb."

Amos and Andy were going strong on the radio. They seemed to be visiting the Kingfish. Later the radio was playing "I'm in the Mood for Love." I certainly was. I wired Elmira:

"It has been twenty days. Don't write until you feel like it—because I don't want anyone to write me when it is the least bit tiresome." I had to trust that I could put Elmira's inattentiveness on hold long enough so my hand did not shake during surgery.

"You know, Elmira," I finally wrote, "You have been dear to me and I hate to quit, but will be compelled to if this continues very little longer. It strikes me our romance is about over. You have been sweet to me, and in return I've tried to be nice and appreciative of you. You know I could not stand for what is taking place in Charity's corridors of sin. I was shocked when you told me that Elaine had been found on an operating table in a compromising position with Doctor Pigeon. I would not even try to put up with a past that was my future. Am sorry if I appear to be too independent, but as I stated long ago to you I shall always be more independent than I once was. I've found it pays, and people in general respect you more. You know there are a very few decent men still left. If you care to write at your leisure, do so. I'll be glad to hear from you. It is easy to remember, but so hard to forget."

At last I heard from her.

"You seem to be asking for something I cannot provide. Are the number of letters I write the measure of my love? I think not. If I wrote a thousand letters, would you be convinced of my love? I am not deceiving you. Nor should I feel the need to flatter you. My love is uncomplicated and rather elementary in its simplicity. Trust it. It may not be the love you are looking for. You may feel it is not commensurate with yours. I have told you time and again that I love you. I said yes to your two-year old proposal and my promise of love still waits that happy day, but my patience is wearing thin. I must warn you; if we are ever to be joined in Holy Matrimony, it is imperative that your sister remain at arm's length if not in another state!"

Elmira's letter struck at my heart. I pleaded with her to forgive my weak neediness. It was an illness as lethal as cancer. I would get better, I told her. All my cavalier talk about love went out the window when Elmira's justified behavior had about destroyed me. "I saved myself for such a woman as you and I promise we will soon be husband and wife. It is you who makes me strong, gives me courage to go on." It was only the country's entrance into WWII that delayed our marriage another two months, but it was Roosevelt's earlier, "We have nothing to fear but fear itself" that I had repeated to myself many times over the past years. A man's fortitude would carry him through.

On the morning of our wedding, I arose early and put on a suit and tie. Not bad, I thought catching my reflection in the mirror. Father was suddenly there, a ghost, but ever more real.

"Ya been passed a terrible bane, boy. Like yer mother, ya'll never be capable of love. Ya had your chance to git away, but here ya are makin' a fool of yerself. Ya think she loves ya?! She's just like yer mother! The great pretender. Yer mother was never happy. Take a tip from yer ole man, a suit and tie is just a costume. Ya think if ya put on a nice suit, slick yer hair, strike a pose, people'll think yer Cassanova. Easy. Smooth. But it's all a show. I wasn't as bad as yer mother made me out to be. She would have liked that actor. Women trust him, yeah, ya probably like him too but he's nothin' but a low class actor, dime a dozen, not real, but ya think he's a prophet, all powerful. What's that big word ya like?"

"Omnificent," I said, turning toward the door and away from Father.

"That one, yeah. The great pretender, boy. That's what ya are. That's what women love .....for awhile. Trust me, boy. I know."

"I know, Father, life is hopeless, and somebody out there is sure to get you so don't try to make something of yourself."

"That's the nail on the head, boy."

"Don't hope for anything 'cause you're apt to be disappointed. A dead-end, I know. What's the point of living if that is how you feel? Everything I do has a purpose, a moral purpose, but I know how to have some fun, something you never had. I can dance, Father, dance to my heart's content." I started crying. Tears, it seemed, were always on the cusp. I just could not let go. Why?

"Yer out-smartin' yerself, whistlin' in the wind. Had to see it with my own eyes, a bigger fool there never was. Ya listenin'? No, 'course not. Got yer'self hitched. Yer set yer'self up fer a fall. Ya think you can trust her any more than I could trust yer mother? Never could figure her out."

"She wanted more, Father."

"Good luck."

I did not want to be like my father, a man who kept going over what he should have done, a man who felt misled, cheated, lied to. He was always suspicious. Someone was out to get him…..He was afraid of love, afraid to be foolish. I did a last check in the mirror. "I can love, Father. I will not be afraid to hear the sweet music of love in my heart! And I have somebody to love and dance with!" Father was gone.

Fritz Kriesler's "Love's Joy and Love's Sorrow" came to mind. I recalled that he had studied medicine.

I memorized the wedding vows.

9

A few years after we married, I arrived home, happily telling Elmira that the actor who had so impressed me at the Barter Theater was in the movies.

"It is Gregory Peck's first film, *Days of Glory*. It is showing in the theater here!"

I arranged to exchange my on-call duty with another doctor so Elmira and I could attend. After the movie, I insisted we stay to see the second showing, too. Later, sharing a banana split, I asked Elmira what she thought of Peck the actor.

"He was good. The film was a little long-winded—all the talk about freedom and sacrifice."

"But Peck was tough and caring."

"Like you, dear."

"You mean it?" I was delighted.

"I wouldn't have said it."

"I'm not still working too hard, am I?"

"You and Mr. Peck could relax a little."

I slid down in my chair and felt my shoulders sag.

"Yes, I suppose you're right."

"But I don't want you too relaxed, like an old tired tom-cat."

"You will always keep me on my toes. Gregory Peck is going to be a big star, mark my word," I said. "I want to hang my star on his."

I decided then and there that Gregory Peck would be my role model. I turned my profile to the soda fountain mirror, this way and that. *It wasn't bad*, I thought.

"There is a likeness to Peck. Don't you think?"

"I'm sure you both will become big stars, dear."

I struck a pose as I imagined the actor posed in front of a mirror preparing for a dramatic scene. Elmira laughed.

"I like to see you laugh," I said.

———————————

On May 7, 1947, our daughter Elly was born. I slept in Elmira's hospital room. Watching mother and child, I knew this was love. This was the miracle of love, the triumph of love. We smiled at her little sounds of grace. I held my daughter as my mother had surely held me, unwanted though I may have been. There was a mother's undeniable love. Despite all, I could still feel the warmth of mother's hand holding mine as we ran through the yellow field of hay. Elly, I thought, looked like my mother. Elly's presence in the world was luminous, I told Elmira. She was worth all the pain, the broken heart of having love taken away. Suddenly a love was there that had not been there before. All my life I would feel her love bundled in my arms, but I knew I would have to earn it.

The war was over. All the churches were open throughout the day. The stores closed to celebrate. Of course I still had babies to deliver, and hernias to repair. I was the chief cook and bottle washer of doctors, a one-stop shop. But I found time to make it to church and pray for our new-born and give thanks that earth, sea, and sky were safe again—the guns were silent. I could not quite believe the war was over because there was still action in the Pacific. When Japan finally surrendered a few months later, my heart soared. I dedicated the victory to God's love and glory.

I was overjoyed that my prediction came true when Gregory Peck's next movie, *The Keys To The Kingdom,* won him an Oscar nomination. It was Peck's resolute and unyielding strength, his gentle and quiet understanding of people that was inspirational. My fondness for the actor grew after I saw his honest portrayal of a warm and affectionate farmer in *The Yearling*. After I discovered Peck had considered being a doctor, I felt my attraction to him had been fated. It was an omen when I learned that Peck's father was a pharmacist whose nickname was "Doc." I began to comb my hair like Peck's, and I searched for just the right suit, a dark-gray flannel suit. I chose the right hats, brown and gray fedoras—very Gregory Peck.

"Clothes make the man," I told Dee, grinning. "And I'm the proof," only half joking.

It seemed my whole demeanor was more relaxed. Thank God for the movies. They had brought me such joy, such escape, and most importantly, Gregory Peck, who became my image for sheer polish and confident poise, for a sense of fairness. *You can adopt these things, make them mine*, I thought. *Why not?*

———————

Our older brother, Raymond, turned up one day at the Roanoke Hospital. He and Dee had been writing to each other. There was a happy reunion. He had been a navigator in World War II, had been shot down three times but managed to survive. Raymond had bought a piece of land at the bottom of the Alleghenies, near the old home place.

"Don't have much of a job, only giving me two weeks out of each month, just $60.00 a month. Stand to lose everything."

I looked at Dee who smiled and said, "...if your brother becomes poor, and cannot maintain himself with you, you shall maintain him...You shall not lend him your money at interest, nor give him your food for profit."

"It would be my pleasure to loan you some money, Raymond, to carry you over," I said.

———————

Dee had not been in favor of my returning so close to the home-place, where we had never visited since leaving.

"You can go wherever you want, Daniel—Houston, Mayo, John Hopkins, Columbia. I did not work tooth and nail to see you back in that unkind, dark, forbidding place. It is haunted, and I never wish to return. I did what I had to do," Dee said, "to free us of that place and now you want to go back?"

"Ya had yer chance but ya came back to the mountains." Is that what Father would have said? "I knew ya'd come back with yer tail 'tween yer legs."

"He would have laughed because you would be back in hell with him."

"The mountain people need a surgeon."

"More's the pity," she said with hardness.

It was a land of poverty, bad diets, and coal mining accidents. Father would have said "Nothing ever goes right around here." That was still true. There was also a scarcity of doctors. So, despite Dee's misgivings, the family settled in a small coal town on the border of Kentucky, West Virginia, and Virginia. Equipment for an operating room cost about $3,000, the building $50,000, bedding, etc., about $20,000. The mountain road, a dusty, rutted, dirt road hardly wider than my car and with no guardrails, was nearly a two-hour drive from our new home. Three years after Elly was born, came baby brother, Danny Jr.

As the Fifties came around, optimism was high, even in the southern Appalachians. World War II had brought little new industry to the forgotten hills, but demand for coal and timber were at peak levels. The mountains had limited accessibility, and the people had little money. Rotarians were the power players in the Appalachian highland town. The Rotary Club was philanthropic, and I was impressed with business leaders who I felt were intelligent and had money, though the two, I knew, did not necessarily go hand in hand. I was especially proud of being elected president of the Rotary Club. Elmira, despite my assurance that the southern Appalachians were not part of the north, was not convinced. She considered the area northern territory, and Rotarians the kind of, "Eastern establishment men who make decisions about when and where to go to war."

"That is not me," I said.

"Guilt by association."

She was also not pleased when I told her that I had asked Dee to join me at the hospital.

"I promised Dee that we would be in practice together one day. I owe her so much."

"She seems to be a wonderful nurse."

"As were you. It would help if you gave Dee a call and told her that you were looking forward to her moving up here. You seem to get on quite well with her."

"We have a truce. Perhaps Dee and I can team up against the doctor in the house."

I hoped she was kidding, but was delighted that she agreed to talk to Dee.

When first locating to the area, Dee lived with us, but soon Elmira put her foot down, and Dee got her own place, not wanting to be "underfoot." Her own place was not forty yards behind ours. She adorned her house with everything from jeweled crosses to statues of Mary. Dee was most proud of the brass prayer hands prominently displayed on a shelf in her living-room—all gifts from Reverend Parker for her generosity. Dee didn't care about money. She gave what she had to Reverend Parker's ministry. She was a believer and a soft touch.

For years, I had been trying to persuade her to renovate her little house. I thought the right addition would set her house off nicely and would add substantially to the property. She had recently made an off-handed remark to me that perhaps her house could stand a little updating. I took it in stride, but I was delighted. Sometimes it takes a seed a long time to germinate and flower.

I think I was the reason Dee continued to work, going and coming with me almost every day, spending far more time with me than Elmira did. Dee was always aware that I had a family. God may be first in her life, she once told me, "but you stand next to God." I was afraid I had fallen behind. There was a halo of serenity about Dee that carried over to those around her....except perhaps for

Elmira. Dee's calmness had been a requisite for her job as supervising nurse of the operating room.

Dee had the vision of what I could become. Everything was open for me—everything was possible…. "but Harvard," I replied. She worried that perhaps she had led me astray with all her praise and encouragement, making me believe that all things were possible. Saving a patient's life was possible but not always doable, no matter how hard I tried.

At the hospital we were each busy with our own duties. Dee would often assist on one of my operations, and we would eat together in the hospital cafeteria most every day, but it was the drive to and from the hospital that was precious to both of us. Brother and sister loved talking with each other, and in the car there were no distractions. It was our time together, "quality time," Dee called it. Our conversations were about patients, about our worries that the hospital would be taken over. We rarely talked about our mother and father anymore. The home place was still there on the side of a hill in western Virginia. We simply never got around to selling the old place.

Right after the hospital had opened for business, I bought a new car, a Packard. *If only Mother could see me now,* I thought.

"Wonder what she would think of her son the doctor," I asked Dee.

"She would be proud. Very proud."

"But she will never know. I guess there are no answers. It's just as well."

Dee put her hand on mine.

"Maybe we could go to one of Gregory Peck's premieres in the Packard."

"He loved me in his way," Daniel said to the night.

"Gregory Peck," asked Dee, laughing?

"Father. So why don't I just accept that and move on?"

"That highway doesn't end, Daniel."

——— ———

I was grateful for what I had, marriage and children, though I knew it was all temporary. Time would have its way. I fretted I could never do enough for my family. I feared for their health, I worried for their safety. I hated to be apart from Elmira. She was my rock. I took the family along on my trips to medical meetings. We saw the New York Yankees and the Chicago Cubs play. I bought scrapbooks for the children and encouraged them to keep the ticket stubs and programs of the baseball games they had seen, the postcards of the cities we visited and hotels where we stayed: the Palmer House in Chicago, the Waldorf in New York, the Ritz in Boston. It was nice to have a taste of the high life. This is what families are supposed to do. These things make up the 'this and that' of love.

While in Boston, I arranged for a tour of Harvard University, including the Medical School and Museum. There was a touch of sadness of what might have been as I walked through Harvard Square. *But then*, I thought, *I would not have met Elmira and that had made all the difference.*

I admired the old family homes where generations of families would return year after year, where everything had a history. Things that were passed down from family to family, the same relationships. I wanted to create such a home, a family's rich history for my children. I told the children they could return to their scrapbooks year after year to see the history of their lives, and their children and grandchildren would be able to see that history. I wanted to create a home that our children and grandchildren would want to return to year after year.

I was relieved and thankful that my own star was rising, as well as Gregory Peck's. I had been profiled in the local paper as "a treasured resource for the community's health and welfare." I carried the clipping in my wallet, noting to Elmira that Lincoln kept a good write-up of his war effort in his wallet. Elmira was not impressed.

"Typical insecure man who wants nothing more than to be forgiven and remembered. Can't have it both ways, Daniel."

As years progressed, l attained my house, car, and community standing, only to realize I did not really need such adornments. The decoration of my life concealed nothing, certainly not grief and not unhappiness. The accumulations had nothing to do with love. The clouds of self-consciousness shadowing me were, thankfully, drifting further away, but still hazy. The days of wanting a bigger house, a bigger car, a more important honor, a more connected friend, those days, like a freed prisoner's shackles, were fading. But like the freed slave, I wasn't sure how to behave. There was the adopted cloak of Gregory Peck's personality. It followed me, always, like a shadow, watching over me, making sure I did not get too lost when I was in a place I did not recognize or with a person I did not know. It was Gregory Peck who reminded me, looking into the mirror, that the person I did not know was myself. *How funny*, I thought. *Who am I?* I suspected that whatever the answer, it would not please me.

My need to make a good impression stubbornly hung on, but I saw nothing particularly wrong in that except to find the need irritating at times. Years before, I found it hard to acknowledge that who I was, where I came from, was enough; because it wasn't enough. I needed embellishment. Nothing wrong with that. You act the part— you become the part. Isn't that what Dee had said? I had become a very good actor, a polite actor.

"A good impression," I repeated over and over to my children, "is something to strive for if it is honest and true. Nothing wrong with vanity if you can look at yourself in the mirror and be satisfied with who is looking back at you."

Of course I was not pleased with my reflection…I tried to whitewash it and became boring. Mr. Peck was my veneer. With Elmira I had the freedom to be whatever I was. That I was becoming more comfortable with that person was largely because of her. She offered her hand, and once I took it, she was my moral core, my idol.

There was something else selfishly driving me, and I knew what it was the moment I first held my daughter, my golden child, the apple of my eye. This something, this revelation, came like an apparition. The ultimate release, would only come, I had told Dee, when my children were admitted to Harvard University. It would complete my journey. To this end, this child of God pushed and pulled and willed myself and my family.

10

So it came to pass, when Elly reached an age, that I filled out an application to Harvard on her behalf, even writing the required essay. In the essay, I emphasized Elly's Appalachian background and how President Kennedy had been an inspiration for her. No politician could match up to Jack Kennedy in my eyes. I had also followed Joe Kennedy, the father of the president. If Joe Kennedy had his boys to groom for power, I had Elly. I was impressed by how Joe Kennedy had nurtured his children, especially his sons, to be leaders. This country needed leaders who had courage, the courage to speak up, the courage to be, as the theologian Paul Tillich had written. I had no doubt Elly would fit the Kennedy mold—the thought that she was a woman never entered my mind.

Along with the application, essay, and Elly's transcript, I decided to send along a copy of my own old boarding school transcript. I was a man remembering and hoping that Harvard would see its long ago mistake. *This could be revenge*, I thought, *delightfully Machiavellian.* The best was yet to come.

"Yes," I said aloud, looking at my old transcript, "my grades were good enough!" I wanted to show that despite my rejection, I had been well qualified to attend Harvard—I had belonged. That was the fight—to prove that I belonged. I wasn't just a mountain boy that nobody cared about, one of the forgotten, one of the "others."

Elly gave me the chance for redemption. It was just the opportunity I needed. I also inquired as to whether someone in the admission's office might locate my own application in the school's records. I closed by saying I hoped my daughter's application would be viewed in a positive manner.

The Harvard registrar wrote back almost immediately.

"Yes, we have it—your daughter's application."

But, alas, the registrar told me he was sorry, but records from that far back, when I had applied, were not kept. He promised they would give Elly's application careful consideration. "Careful consideration." I reread those words over and over. I would save the letter. I saved everything. History mattered. I had none, no memory of grandmothers and grandfathers, no aunts or uncles.

When Elly told me she had decided to go to the state college, I was forced to tell her that I had applied to Harvard on her behalf.

"You never asked where I wanted to go."

"I couldn't see the point," I said. It had never occurred to me that Elly would be upset. "How are you supposed to know? Trust me, Elly, I have given it a great deal of thought. Harvard will be lucky to have you. You'll be lucky to have each other. You'll see. I didn't want to bother you and so I just jotted down a few words and sent them along."

"A few words about what?"

"It was an essay."

"What essay?"

"Oh…it was required and I knew you didn't have time."

"So you wrote it?"

"Yes."

"How dare you," torched Elmira, overhearing from the hallway.

"Please, Elmira."

"Don't 'please' me!"

At an early age, Elly had been eager to please me because it made me happy and I would shower her with love and buy her whatever she desired….though she never desired anything but my love.

"You must reach higher than the state school. You must strive for the best, Elly."

"How embarrassing," said Elly. "It is an insult!"

She then gave me a no-holds barred piece of her mind, demanding to read the essay. Under duress, I went to my room and returned with a draft of what I had written. Elly sat and read it.

"You're trying to shame Harvard into admitting me?"

"No, not shame."

"I would be ashamed to show my face on that campus. Oh my God. Even if I had wanted to go to Harvard, I could never go now."

"It will work, Elly."

"I don't need their sympathy, 'A hill child?' And this stuff about spending too much money on courthouses and highways—that was mother's complaint, not mine and certainly not yours!"

"I hope you at least gave me credit," said Elmira.

"I took a little liberty there," I stammered.

"You took a lot of liberties, Daddy," fumed Elly. "'Deserved the opportunity to uphold the Kennedy legacy of service to her country?' How could you, Daddy?"

"You read *Profiles In Courage.*"

"So what?"

"It was a big influence on you. I remember how touched you were. I just told them the book gave you hope and confidence for the future, Elly."

"Those were Robert Kennedy's words!"

"What words?"

"Hope and confidence! They're in the foreword to his brother's book. Oh, Daddy."

"I didn't mean to upset you. Forgive me…. Please, Elly," I pleaded.

"……And if I don't get in?"

"You will," I said.

"But if I don't?"

"You can go to the state school and re-apply next year."

———————

When college notification time rolled around, I was on pins and needles as I once was with first bloom of Elmira's love. I considered myself a reasonable man, a moderate man, intelligent, a prudent man. But now I was anxious. Everything I had worked for was on the line. It was all or nothing—Harvard or the state school, which was not even listed in the top one-hundred colleges. I feared the great disappointment of my young life would return when Harvard held my life out on a limb and then let it go with a few cold words, the hard-bottom truth. I conjured up the blackness of that moment. I called home from the hospital every day asking if Elly's anticipated acceptance letter from Harvard had arrived in the mail.

"No, Daddy, not today," was Elly's can't-wait-till-this-is-over reply.

When Elly did not hear right away, I could sense her disappointment, not so much about not being admitted but having to tell me. When the eagerly awaited letter did arrive, I was in Chicago for an International College of Surgeons meeting. Elmira knew I would hate not being there for this moment.

"Hi, Daddy."

"Elly," I answered.

"How's Chicago?"

"Ah, it's fine."

Elly started laughing. She could not keep up the ruse knowing how I would respond to her good news.

"I got the letter."

"…Yes?"

I knew Elly could hear the anxiousness in my voice.

"Do you know where Cambridge is?"

"You're in?"

"Yes!"

"I knew it."

I began to sob—my voice was choking. "My knees are weak. Oh, Elly, I'm so happy for you."

"I'm happy for both of us, Daddy."

I told her I could not speak, I was too emotional, too relieved. Elly had seemed to forgive me. Elmira would not have done what I did. I never knew when to stop. Still, I was glad I had sent in Elly's application to Harvard. I do not believe she would have considered applying, out of the doubt that she would get in. I had some doubt. As a doctor, it was my job to doubt, to question. With no doubt, could there be faith? I told Elly I would pack my suitcase and be home on the first flight I could get.

"You can shout to everyone at the medical meeting that your daughter is going to Harvard."

"I can tell the world," I said through my tears.

I arrived home in the midst of a celebration party with just the family, including Dee. Elly was playing the piano and singing.

"Sing a song of college days, tell me where to go.
Texas for her sunshine, Wisconsin for her snow.
Harvard for her ivy halls is the only place I know."

"Great song!" I said and jumped right into the joy. Nothing was hard. This was family. Everything was perfect. l was rather astonished that it had all worked out. "They've got some good football, too. A great time for us, Mama."

"A great time for you," deadpanned Elmira.

"A great time for all of us. Our girl is going to Harvard."

"Hip, hip, hurrah!" shouted Elly's brother, Danny, who had taken the train in from Front Royal, Virginia, where he was in military school.

I gave thanks to John F. Kennedy, Harvard alum. He, I reminded the family, had kicked off his presidential campaign in the heart of Appalachia.

"Didn't you meet him, Daddy?"

"I did, Elly. Had the good fortune to shake his hand. He was speaking at the State House. It was raining hard that day. After he finished speaking, he dashed down the steps and mingled with the crowd. The people loved him, adored him. He shook a lot of hands. Fine man."

"Fine, fine man," said Danny.

"Fine" was one of my favorite words. My children loved to tease me. I loved words. Words helped. They could sooth a missing mother's soothing touches. I grew to depend on words. I was a collector of words. This had started early and then during my first year of medical school, I came across the word—etiology—meaning to investigate the causes and origins of diseases, the origins of hurt, of pain. "Etiology" was included on a list of vocabulary words that I would occasionally hand out to my children and then quiz them.

"The weather's fine." "It was a fine sermon." "But nothing's finer, even the state of Carolina, than Elly being admitted to Harvard," said Danny.

"Harvard appreciated your Appalachian background, Elly. I knew they would," I said.

"Poor little ole me wouldn't know how to put shoes on even if I had them."

They all laughed, including me, who laughed the hardest. I thought of the girl beside the library at Alabama and how we had laughed. She was one of the ghosts, like those spirited and fresh high school girls, like kind and loving Ocy and dear Mr. Goodsell, who I had learned when I was at Alabama, had found second love with Ocy, and they officially became a couple.

"I guess if you live here, people are supposed to feel sorry for our underprivileged background, Elly," remarked Dee.

"If people want to believe that Appalachian nonsense let them," I said, beaming with pride and joy. "It doesn't matter if you've got a shoe on or not, Elly. You've got your foot in the door. You have been admitted to the greatest school in the world, and you deserve it. You have the opportunity to uphold the Kennedy legacy of service to your country."

"Did you vote for Kennedy, Daddy?"

"Yes, Elly. I believe I voted."

"Mother always tells you whom to vote for," laughed Elly.

"That's true, Daniel," said Dee.

"JFK was made out to be the end-all of presidents," said Elmira. "He was Elvis. We voted for him. I thought the people around here never won anything, and it would be the same old story. JFK would lose and so would the people, as usual. But he won, and, I think if he had not been assassinated, things would be a lot better than they are. I felt he really cared, and it was not just about a bunch of boring statistics."

"You're right, Mama. Something needs to be done and it's going to take someone like Elly to do it, to lead the way!" I was waving Elly's acceptance letter to Harvard over my head. "I'm going to get it framed right away."

"Let's hear it, everyone," said Danny. "Three cheers for Sis. Speech, speech."

"Everyone I know is going to college. It's not a big deal," said Elly, trying to diffuse the excitement.

"They're not going to Harvard, Elly."

"It's Radcliffe, Daddy."

"Your diploma will be stamped with the Harvard seal! Your classes will be at Harvard! Believe me, I checked into that."

"We believe you, Daddy," Elly said, laughing.

Elly knew I did believe in her, a belief I carried in my heart, the promise of love fulfilled before my eyes.

"Bless you, Elly."

My hope for her was a burden that she would not admit to me. The other side of my hope was expectation. I expected Elly to do well at Harvard. Perhaps she knew I was counting on her to make my life better, richer, fuller. And I knew she would try her best to make my dream come true.

"To be on that campus with all the history and culture," I said in reverie.

"Dad's going with you, Sis."

"I'm just thrilled, Elly. You'll have the kind of education only Harvard offers. While in Chicago, I bought you a little something at one of the finer stores," I said and handed her a rather large box. Elly opened it. It was a dark green floor length dress. Elmira, most always, made Elly's dresses for special occasions, but I decided to chance it. Elly held the dress up in front of her tall frame. *The dress was very nice, beautiful really,* I thought.

"I know you have your prom coming up….You like it?"

"It's beautiful, Daddy."

"You really think so?"

"Yes," said Elly.

Elly would never tell me otherwise. When she was much younger, I had bought her a dress to wear for Easter and she refused to wear it. She did not like it. Elmira told her that my feelings were hurt. Of course Elly had no idea that my feelings were hurt, but she had, I felt, censored herself ever since. She had, however, remained gracious in accepting my gifts, though her first two-wheeler had been a boy's bike, her first car a boat-sized fire-engine red-hardtop Oldsmobile, that she was too embarrassed to drive, and her luggage for going away to college—Harvard—that I had already purchased, was actually men's luggage. I justified all as "good and strong."

"It's green, stunningly green," said Danny, trying not to laugh.

"It would have been nice if she could have seen the dress before you bought it. It may be too sophisticated for your prom, Elly," Elmira said, tactfully.

"Well…yes, but she couldn't. It's a fine store, one of the best, Marshall Field's."

"It is beautiful," said Dee.

"Yes, it is," replied Elly.

"I know it was expensive, too. You'll be the queen of the prom," assured Dee.

"I'm certainly green with envy," said Danny barely able to suppress his laughter.

"Don't pay any attention to him, Daddy," said Elly, "I'll try it on." She put her arm around me.

"You're really going to wear that dress?"

"Danny!" Elly had little patience for Danny's remark. She then went upstairs to her room to put the dress on.

"Let your sister be an inspiration, boy, and in a couple of years we'll be celebrating again."

"Do I get a dress, too?"

"You get into Harvard, you can have two dresses," I said. Everyone laughed. "And just remember, you're as good as the…"

… "the next man," Danny chimed in.

"Better! Your sister's admittance to Harvard makes you a legacy, son. Military school is good training. You will improve, gain confidence, discipline, independence, respect, and most important, perseverance—fortitude."

"An all-American boy," said Dee and smiled, warmly, putting her arm around her nephew.

"That's right, boy. Harvard will welcome you with open arms."

"Danny just made sergeant," said Elmira with a big smile. "He insisted on taking the train from the Academy for this celebration."

"Wouldn't miss it," said Danny.

A few years back, Elmira and I had been disappointed with Danny's lack of motivation in school, and when Danny, then too young for a driver's license, was arrested for participating in an illegal drag race, we felt we had to do something.

"How do you tell a boy he is not a boy anymore," Elmira had wondered aloud one late night. That reminded me of Gregory Peck again in *The Yearling*. It was Peck, the warm and gentle, loving, father in *The Yearling* who reminded his son that a boy is only a boy for so long. I thought of Peck as Frank Savage in *Twelve O'clock High*. "We've got to fight," Savage told his men. Excitedly, I told this to Elmira.

"What about military school? Gregory Peck attended four years at a military academy and was pleased with the discipline and structure it gave him."

Elmira was not convinced but in the end, she decided to pack Danny off to the Staunton Military Academy, where the structure and discipline had seemed to be good for him. He was doing very well, was decorated, sang in the glee club, and was on track to graduate with honors.

Later, there was even talk of West Point, but Danny never applied and warned me not to apply for him.

"The General's orders are out?" I asked.

"Yes, sir," said Danny.

"Come on then, show off your moves, son."

Danny proceeded to show off his sergeant stripes and then executed a few sharp military moves to an appreciative audience. We all cheered. I saluted Danny and told him how proud I was of his work and his attitude.

"Highly satisfactory, son." I put my arm around Danny and drew him close.

"I can't wait to show Sonny," said Danny knowing how much his dear friend would love the uniform and the sergeant's stripes.

Elmira clapped her hands and said, "We have two wonderful things to celebrate."

"That's right, Mom," said Elly, coming down the stairs holding up the bottom of her gown while exchanging, I sensed, a knowing glance with her mother. These glances between Elmira and Elly had become rather routine especially when I would be going on about things that the family should be doing.

"Wow," I said, "you are beautiful!"

"Yes," all agreed and applauded. The gown fit perfectly.

"You are so lucky," said Elmira. "You can wear a dress right off the rack. That's what a tall, thin, body allows. Alas, I shall never know that delight."

Elly hugged her mother and gave her brother a big kiss.

"Congratulations on your promotion," Elly said to Danny.

I knew she was sorry that all the attention was back on her and the gown. Elly knew she could do nothing wrong in my eyes. There were no clouds in her future. She had always been aware of being the big sister, making sure to compensate for my inclination to treat her as the chosen one, the favorite. I could not help it.

"Danny has entertained us with his expertly performed drill maneuvers," I said, "and I have been trying to get my legs to remember some dance steps. Been practicing my moves, keeping trim."

There was the time of country club dances when big bands from New York would play, and Dee would watch the children while Elmira and I dressed to the nines and danced every dance all night long. "Remember, Elmira?"

"Oh, yes."

"I think I must have been a dancer in my other life." Along with Gregory Peck movies, Fred Astaire movies were required watching.

"You can learn a lot about style and class watching Fred Astaire," I was fond of saying.

"I bet Astaire didn't wear seersucker suits," laughed Elmira.

"Gregory Peck wore this exact one," I said, laughing. I put my hands on the lapels of my suit coat.

"Atticus Finch wore seersucker, didn't he, not the real man," said Dee.

"That's right, Dee. Peck would not be caught dead in a seersucker," said Elmira.

"He wore a gray flannel one," I said, remembering the haunted Tom Rath character that made me uncomfortable. "It's just a movie." I could hear Peck's reasoning voice.

As a little girl, Elly delighted in having me put a Benny Goodman record on and perform my dance moves for her. I was never self-conscious about dancing.

"Dancing is a mirror to the soul," I would tell her. Dancing was a discipline for me, a form of exercise, a release.

It had been several years since Elmira and I had danced together. At one point, I had practiced the dances from the Astaire – Rogers film *Swing Time* and then taught them to Elmira.

"You two were the country club's Astaire and Rodgers," said Dee. "The children made me promise to get them up when you two would come home exhausted from your country club dance. Elly and Danny would jump out of bed and want to hear all about your night of dancing."

"You children should have been in bed," said Elmira.

"You're right, Mama," I said with a wink. Elmira would laugh and fix scrambled eggs, and we would regale Elly, Danny, and Dee, of our exploits on the dancing floor while enjoying our midnight snack. Somewhere along the line, I stopped eating eggs, but I never stopped dancing. Gregory Peck was my hero, but when it came to dancing, there was no one comparable to Fred Astaire for sheer grace, elegance, and agility.

"Your daddy always said if he could have the ease and perfection in the operating room that Astaire has on the dance floor, he would be the world's best surgeon," said Elmira.

"And you are, Daddy," said Elly.

When Elly's favorite dancer, Gene Kelly, came along, there was a bit of fun competition between father and daughter. I was appreciative of the new dimension Kelly brought to dancing with his athletic prowess. Elly could do a fair imitation of Kelly's puddle-splashing dancing in *Singin' in the Rain.* Then I would do a little Fred Astaire.

Our reminiscence of times past motivated Elly to dig out some old records from my collection and put them on to play.

"No, Elly, this is your celebration. We should play your music."

"We don't have a record of Harvard's fight song," said Danny.

"I doubt if it's good dancing music," replied Elly, placing Astaire's *The Way You Look Tonight* on the player.

"Well, Fred, Ginger waits," said Elly, holding up her mother's hand.

"Come on, precious, let's dance." I took Elmira's hand and pulled her into my arms. Danny and Elly and Dee cheered.

We were very good dancers. Elmira followed my lead without missing a step, as we glided back and forth across the porch recapturing our youth, taking us back.

"All the nurses used to flirt with the new doctors, especially those who were good dancers," said Elmira.

"You didn't flirt back, Daddy?" asked Elly.

"Only with your mother."

"Good answer," said Elly.

"I saved all my dances for my sweetheart," I said, pulling Elmira closer. "She didn't chase after every new intern like a lot of nurses. Your mother was the only one out of that entire bunch who didn't let you kiss them on the first date."

"How would you know," teased Elly. "Did you sample all the nurses?"

"No, no. There was a lot of scuttlebutt among the doctors about the other nurses, but none about your mother. I only had eyes for you, Mama."

"And lips," laughed Danny.

"Remember, Mama, how we used to dance, and I would steal a few good kisses?"

"You sure I was the only one you were stealing them from?"

"Steal one now, Daddy," said Danny. And I did and all laughed.

"Ginger has nothing on you, Mom," said Elly, as she watched me twirl her mother an arm's length away, step into her, then spin her the length of the room. We were as one, as we must have been in the beginning, so fluid in our moves, seamless. After a few more spins, Elmira was ready to rest her feet.

"Come on, Elly, take a spin with your daddy," said Elmira. "Let's see how the gown sweeps the floor."

"All right, if Daddy doesn't mind getting his feet stepped on."

"It will be my privilege to have my feet stepped on by a Harvard girl," I said, and we danced around the room "Like your mother's, Elly, your dance card will always be full."

11

"Fight fiercely, Harvard, fight, fight, fight
Impress them with our prowess, do.
Aw, fellas, do not let the Crimson down.
Be of stout heart and true.
Come on chaps, fight for Harvard's glorious name
Won't it be peachy if we win the game
Oh, goody, let's not try to injure them
But, fight, fight, fight."

I was still in my hospital greens. Hearing the singing, I opened
my eyes, thinking I had been dreaming I was hearing the Harvard
fight song. Elly and Danny had just pulled up to the curb in Danny's
1957 Chevy convertible, top down.

"Is this a vision, or are you really here?" I asked as Danny and
Elly came up the porch stairs.

"Did we wake you, Daddy, with our singing?"

"We may not be on key, but we are loud," said Danny.

"No, no. Good song, Go Crimson," I said. "Just rocking here
on the porch, getting some good fresh air, resting my eyes…awhile,
you know how I do."

"Yes, the only person who can sleep standing up straight."

"I suppose you're right, Elly. What a nice surprise, didn't know you were coming. You drove?"

"No, I flew."

"Flew, you flew. Good for you. Had I known, I would have met your plane."

"Danny met me."

"Remember me?"

"Could hardly forget you, boy. Looking sharp." Danny was in military dress. I got up out of my rocker, and Elly gave me a big hug.

"You let your hair grow long, Elly. Wish your mother would let her hair get longer."

It was Easter break and both Elly and Danny, who was on leave from the Staunton Military Academy where he was a senior, were glad to be home from college. I was not surprised that Elly was feeling at ease in the world beyond the hills. The Harvard campus with its red-brick Georgian look was comforting. Though at first Elly felt unprepared for academic life and was initially at a loss when asked to express an opinion on a subject in course papers, she soon warmed to the notion as I knew she would. She was doing quite well in her junior year. She had told me that outside the classroom, Harvard was not particularly interested in an undergraduate's thoughts, especially if the undergraduate was a woman.

"She will buckle down and do the work," I had told Elmira.

During Elly's freshman year, girls had not even been allowed to eat on the main campus. Elmira was livid. Elly lived in a dorm on the Radcliffe yard, and a couple of her classes were only taught at the Radcliffe campus.

But before her sophomore year, she and her four roommates were moved to the Lowell building on the Harvard campus, where they were tolerated. They lived next to five male students who, according to Elly, were mostly cordial. Apparently there were a few male students who did not appreciate women on "their" campus and in "their" classrooms, and they were not subtle in their disapproval.

"The important thing is you're at Harvard and doing superbly," I said, "as I knew you would."

"My Andover and Exeter classmates probably think I got in because I'm from some shanty town in Appalachia where my father's an unemployed coal miner," said Elly, teasing me. "The red carpet is not laid down for women. Being a woman at Harvard," said Elly, "is sort of like being a second-class citizen."

"That's just ignorance. Harvard is a little slow evolving."

For now, brother and sister were home, and I wanted them to enjoy themselves.

"All work and no play...,"

"Well, we played tonight, didn't we, Sis?"

"Danny took me to Gene's."

"We were carousing, Daddy," said Danny, standing in the doorway, I knew, because he wanted to make a quick exit.

"Sorry to hear that, boy. Fore-warned is fore-armed, I suppose."

"Orgies and debauchery," laughed Danny.

"You want to watch who you cater with there. It would please me if you children did not frequent that establishment. That place is not on a high moral ground, Elly. You don't want to be gossiped about. You'd do well to avoid that hole." Thoughts of my days at Charity raced.

"The Devil was working overtime tonight at Gene's, right, Sis?"

"Disappointed in you, boy, for taking your sister there, and you in uniform. Rotten drunks and dirty mugs."

"Lucky we weren't arrested, Sis."

Elly and Danny smiled at each other listening to me waxing on about the evil dispositions of the patrons of the local watering hole. I never learned. Why couldn't I keep quiet? I was always grave, referencing the underside of life. Like father, like son—the same patterns. I was a bad actor playing another role, the same role my father played. It was a role I detested but seemed destined to play. I would struggle my whole life on how to play the good father.

"None of us are pure and righteous citizens, Daddy."

"I suppose not, Elly."

I never discussed morals or sex with my children, but they knew where I stood. They also knew I took my religion seriously. I had counseled Elly before she left for college about attending church, telling her when I had been a student I tried to attend church as often as my studies allowed.

It was at church I learned of the Devil's temptations, and of the value of prayer. *Prayer*, I thought, *could help guide me to a truth.*

My moral stand was rigid, uncompromising and unforgiving— none more so than for myself. I would frequently pass moral judgment on even minor indiscretions I had no real first-hand knowledge of. Nothing put a bigger scowl on my face than the mere mention of Gene's.

"You know better, boy, than to frequent that place, especially when you have your uniform on. You are representing your country. Show some respect. Soldiers have died in that uniform."

"I'm not in the military, Daddy."

"It's a military school."

"It's a prep school."

"Still, you must be respectful."

"All the girls loved Danny in his uniform, Daddy."

"Many ridiculous things go on about that messy hole at night."

"That's what nights are for, Daddy," said Danny.

"You should not subject your sister to such going-ons."

"Miss Goody Two-Shoes here was having a pretty good time," said Danny. "It's good for her. Give a little edge to that Harvard-girl refinement. No one offered you drugs, did they, Sis?"

"No drugs," she said.

"No one talked nasty and nobody fornicated on the floor, right?"

"That's far enough, boy."

"The *Crimson* wouldn't be interested in that, would they Sis?"

"The *Harvard Lampoon*, maybe."

"How do you know what's going on out there anyway, Daddy?" asked Danny. "You holding out on us?"

I felt my eyes roll. Something censored me, thankfully. I knew it was imperative that I get away from myself, and lose the cloak of

Gregory Peck. Until I did, the truth would be evasive. I asked if they had brought their books home.

"It's Easter break," said Elly.

"This will be a good rest for you, Elly. Don't want to neglect your studies during this time—brief though it is."

"You just can't help yourself, can you, Daddy?"

"I guess not, Elly. But a penny-nail can develop rust over night. You want to be quick on the uptake. Goes for you, too, boy. Harvard's looking at your grades, so you can't slack up. You're in the home-stretch. I've talked with the provost. He's flagged your application. It's the least they can do for my munificence."

"I'm pretty magnificent, too," said Danny.

"Yes you are…..Glad you're home, Elly. Good to see you here, you too, son, hear your voices in the house. Brings me great pleasure. Glad you can spend some time together, too, just not at that watering hole, please."

"Have you ever been there, Daddy?"

"No Elly, can't say I have."

"Then you don't know what really goes on there."

"You hear things."

"You wouldn't operate on someone because you heard from someone else they were sick."

"No," I said, laughing. "You're right, Elly."

"As usual," said Danny, smiling because Elly was always right as far as I was concerned. They may all have the same set of facts but it was Elly's opinion of those facts that mattered most to me. I plead guilty.

"Togetherness," I said, putting my arms around my children. "That's why we have this house."

"A good house," said Danny and Elly in unison. They laughed. I laughed, too. I looked up at the half moon. *It wasn't as dark as it used to be*, I thought.

"What you work for, boy, this house. Hard work got us here. I was on call last night."

"How unusual," smiled Elly.

"Busy time of year. All our beds are occupied."

"All but yours," said Danny, in an aside to Elly but he knew I heard.

"You're right, boy." I sat back down in the rocker. Finally, I said, "It's so nice on the porch, I just might camp out here tonight."

Danny once asked when he was much younger if "mother and you were…"

"What?"

"I don't know…together. You have different bedrooms?"

Elmira and I had not been intimate in ages.

"I sometimes wonder how I was….," said Danny. He never finished, and I had changed subjects. There is not much, if any, privacy in a family. Perhaps I was old school, too reserved. Could you be in love and not have sex? My parents had sex but no love and no fun.

It had been a number of years since Elmira and I slept in the same bed or the same room for that matter. Our lives had drifted. Love had been a struggle. We had forgotten that sex could be a good time. How that could have happened was beyond me. Truth was, Elmira had long tired of my coming in late at night from the hospital and waking her up and telling her about the operations I had performed that day.

"I have a devil of a time getting to sleep, and then you clomp in and wake me up. I think you do it on purpose."

In the interest of preserving marital harmony, I had decided it best if I took the spare room. Besides I liked to read in bed before closing my eyes. I was not fearful of the solitude but I felt, and was physically, isolated. Not that being alone in bed is shameful. Sex is not the be-all and end-all of a happy marriage. Perhaps Elmira and I needed a rest from sex.

"What time were you out of your bed this morning, boy?"

"Break of dawn, sir," said Danny saluting.

"Good. Each day is a gift. Don't waste it! Starts at dawn, ends at night."

"Not at Gene's," said Danny.

"You sound like Jean Paul Sarte, Daddy," said Elly.

"Heard of him. Life doesn't slow down, it only bids farewell. This is a country of workers! Put your head down and go. Love and work."

"Yes, Daddy," came the chorus of brother and sister.

I talked in platitudes. That was how I dispensed fatherly advice. I disgusted myself.

"Your eyes are a little red, Elly. Make sure you rest them. I know you study a lot. Need your eyes. Don't waste them on television. Goes especially for you, boy."

"We're not allowed television except on weekends," said Danny.

"Good rule. Glad you're wearing contact lenses, Elly. You look better."

"Better to see you with, Daddy."

"I'm still fighting trim, 185. Would like to be 190. Your weight been falling, Elly?" I looked over Elly as I would a patient. "You look like you could use six or seven pounds. That would be my wish."

"That's not my wish."

"Would please me so much."

"Drop it, Daddy. This Harvard girl needs her beauty rest."

"Love you, Elly."

"I love you, Daddy. Good night."

"Night."

"Think I'll turn in, too," said Danny, as he started inside behind Elly.

"I want to talk to you, boy." Danny turned back.

"What about?"

"Your future."

"What about it?"

"Your direction, where you're going."

"I'm going upstairs."

"Yes, you are. You're going 'upstairs' to Harvard." There was a long pause.

"I don't want to go to Harvard," Danny finally said.

"Can you give me one good reason?"

"Harvard will put me in the loony bin."

I was stunned, astounded. But the choice was not Danny's to make. I had long since sent his application to Harvard, guessing correctly that the Appalachia application would be given priority status in the Harvard admissions pipeline.

"You have a leg up, son. Your sister has paved the way. She has set the table for you. Degree from Harvard is worth its weight in gold. Believe me, son, I know. Harvard's a great school. *The* school. You understand? It stands apart, head and shoulders above all other schools. You've done it, son. You're into Harvard. You earned your spot. Don't get complacent. Step it up, son, put it into another gear. There's never a down time. There's always something new to learn. People are always evaluating you. Believe me. Everything you do gets a mark. You hear me, boy? You're in a wonderful place. You're a blank space on the map of knowledge."

"Good thing I'm not the sensitive type."

"I'm just saying you have an unburdened mind."

"Daddy, please."

"You're raw, that's all. Like I was, but you have the chance to fill that space with the best education you can get, and come out a man, strong like a steel curtain. What a wonderful thing. They can take everything else away, but they can't take away your knowledge."

"Daddy, I know it's important to you, I guess I understand, but sometimes I think school's a waste of time. It's just a big hype to keep kids occupied doing nothing."

"You think I could have learned my life's work, how to treat people and operate on them, give lectures and write papers without going to school?"

"I know."

"If you have the opportunity to go to Harvard, you grab it, that's what you do. There's no decision. It won't be easy but you'll do it, one step at a time. You can be the salvation for these hills, do your share to improve things, you and your sister—Harvard graduates."

"It's just not what I'm interested in, not want I want."

"Please don't say that, boy; you're going to give me a heart attack. What do you want?"

"Something real."

"Any day now you will get official word of your acceptance to Harvard for the fall," I said, spreading my arms to heaven. "That's real. I'm real, your mother's real, your sister, your aunt, they're real…flesh and blood real, but there's nothing more real than a Harvard education. I'm trying to light a fire under you so you can light the world on fire. With a good education, you can do whatever you want, son. You think positive, good things will happen. I worked part-time while I was in medical school selling fried onions. Ask me."

"Ask you for what?"

"Fried onions."

"I don't like fried onions."

"That's the point! People coming into the restaurant had no notion of getting fried onions on their steaks. But I was right there with a big spoonful of 'em, big smile on my face. "Fried onions, ma'am? Some of these good fried onions, sir?"

"No, thank you," Danny said.

"If the customer said 'no,' I'd say, 'Good for what ails you,' or 'These fried onions will put hair on your chest.' Course, I wouldn't say that to the women. I'd give them a sample taste, and many times they'd change their minds."

"I'll remember that."

"I hope you will. You see, fried onions cost an extra fifteen cents. I had to make those people think they couldn't do without them. That's positive."

"That's larceny."

"That's determination."

"That's crazy."

"May be, but you combine determination with a Harvard education, and the world will be your cupcake."

"Oyster, Daddy."

"Daniel, what are you running on about?" Elmira was standing at the screen door in her housecoat.

"Life! I want you to know, boy, I sold so many pies they called me the 'dough man.' Get it? Money, see?"

"Yes, dear, we see," said Elmira, opening the door for Danny. She watched Danny start up the stairs and then turned back. I saw her book in hand, *Dearest Child*. "My book is Queen Victoria's letters to her daughter. The queen was positively silly. She had tried to instill her doctrines and thoughts about government into her daughter so the daughter could change things in Germany. Many Germans did not feel the same way, and this led to a great deal of resentment. Why can't parents leave well enough alone? I resented my mother's power attempt to decide how I should live my life. I escaped the first chance I got. Be careful, Daniel, you may drive Danny away."

I greatly enjoyed having the children at home, hearing their conversations, their laughter. Sunday dinners were the best times for stories and laughter and all was right with the world. It was the atmosphere I appreciated in the hospital, civilized, relaxed. I was known around the hospital for sedate, but corny jokes. "The doctor tells a patient…I don't like to mention it, but that check you gave me has come back. The patient tells the doctor…well that sure is funny, doc, so did my lumbago." As always, I laughed at my own joke, not a robust laugh but a refined, polite laugh. I did not think of myself as a stuffy man. Dee and I talked about my operations over Sunday dinners at home, many times my only dinner at home. The more gruesome I could make the Sunday dinner war stories, blood spurting here and there, the better. Comparing body parts to various foods—sausages and intestines, eggs and the reproductive system—was a favorite pastime.

One day to the surprise of the family, Dee, who always had Sunday dinner with our family, broached the delicate subject of a male patient's particular problem. Elmira looked at me wondering what Dee was about to tell us. To illustrate the male patient's problem, Dee held up a piece of asparagus that drooped as she held it out. It took a moment for the family to realize the joke. Elmira starting laughing and could not stop. She choked on an aforementioned piece of asparagus. She had to briefly leave the table. We were all, most of all, me, pleased, or rather surprised, I think, that Dee thought of sexual matters.

Elly and Danny had been in high school then. They had giggled non-stop at Dee's show and tell. They would forever see their Aunt Dee in a new and more appreciative light. I had always delighted at any mirth my stories created, but none would ever match the laughter that Dee's story, with illustration, had caused. Dee, covering her face with her napkin, seemed very pleased that her story had met with such laughter.

"You're blushing, Aunt Dee," said Elly.

"No, no."

"Nurses are lusty creatures," said Elmira. "But I do wonder what the Reverend Parker would think."

"Oh," said Dee, "I imagine he has heard much more risqué things." Asparagus was never served again at family dinners without convulsions of laughter.

———————

Using Gregory Peck as my image, I had cultivated a gentle low-profile kind of man, but among mountain people, I was "Doctor Dan"—not just a regular Joe. I wanted my modesty and profession-alism to have a quiet elegance. My hair was still curly, but graying, so I had "touched it up" to complement what I considered my still fairly young face, wanting my patients, especially those going under the knife, not to have any thoughts about my age, which I carefully guarded from all, especially my fellow doctors and the nurses. I never dis-cussed age, especially mine. Who cares how old you are. Of course there was the speculation. But only Dee and Elmira knew my age. Even the children were unsure of my age. I did not, would not, cel-ebrate birthdays, refused to acknowledge them. What was the point? Esteemed, appreciated, and loved, I became, gratefully, the go-to doctor. The people, it seemed, needed me.

"You are more beloved than Luke," said Dee. That brought a howl of laughter from Elmira.

The people became my patients and in time they did come to, if not love me, appreciate me. No one called me by my name, except Elmira and Dee. Elly and Danny called me "Daddy." Everyone else called me "Doctor." I found "Doc," too familiar, undignified, almost condescending, certainly disrespectful. Did I have an ego? What good surgeon doesn't, I wondered.

For a man who never liked to be aware of time, as a young surgeon I would clock my surgeries attempting to better previous surgery times—and when I did lower my time, I was proud of my expertise. But those self–conscious glory days had long past. Time was the ever unbeatable enemy, and putting a stopwatch to life was not productive or healthy. One day I quit clock-watching cold turkey. When the hall clock stopped working, I didn't want it fixed. I wanted to remove all the clocks from our home. Elmira protested. I did put away my watch, and had all clocks removed from my office and examining rooms, and instructed the nurses not to remind me that I was taking too long with a patient. As a result, patients-in-waiting were lined out the door. They knew to bring a snack and something to entertain themselves while waiting for the people's doctor. My nurse had replaced a cushioned chair in my office with a more austere straight back wooden one in the hope that patients would become so uncomfortable as not to linger.

"Don't know where the day went," I would say upon entering our house.

"That's because you enjoy what you do so much, Daddy," Elly had once replied.

Holidays had no meaning. My body seemed to know, like some primitive instinct, when Wednesday noon rolled around. That was when Rotary met. The same instinct along with church bells beckoned me to the 10 a.m. church service on Sundays.

I dreaded when the time came for Elly and Daniel to return to school after their holiday. I offered heartfelt advice through a flood of tears, telling them how I dreaded all the hard work they had ahead of them, but they were both good students, and I knew they would be just fine— "more than fine." I would stand at the train depot and could not resist some last words of advice.

"Your mother and I look forward to your visits home. Keep up the good work. Always stand up for what is right and work hard, and you will always win. I hate to see you both leave home, but to get a good education it is necessary. Take care of yourselves and remember to say your prayers. May our good God bless you both again this year."

By this time I was sobbing. Elmira and I would go back to our house. We missed the children so. The big house was deader than a confederate dollar bill. Seemed like a tomb. I prayed for my children night and morning.

12

Danny, like Elly before him, did very well on the standardized test and was admitted to Harvard. His first term went well, with the exception of his being charged with procuring a prostitute during his first week there. At first, I thought it was a joke when Elmira told me. But according to the police report, Danny had just come out of a fast food establishment with a milkshake along with a couple of his Harvard classmates. They walked past a girl dressed in a white cowgirl outfit complete with hat and boots. One of the boys, from New York City and thus perhaps more aware of such things, said the girl was a hooker.

"A hooker?"

"A prostitute, Daniel," said Elmira.

"How did he know?"

"The girl was dressed like an Indian princess, the skirt barely covered her ass."

"Elmira!"

"You wanted all the details. Danny thought she was a cowgirl. All that was missing was her six-shooter. They told Danny to ask her if she's working."

"Who told Danny?"

"His friends."

"Not the kind of friends he should be making," I said.

"They go to Harvard! They are his classmates."

"Why would they care if she was working?"

Elmira looked at me and started laughing. "I knew you were a virgin, but really, Daniel. Danny was not prepared for all that Harvard has to offer."

"That's for sure," I said.

"His friends said he was a hick from the sticks. Anyway, Danny asked the cowgirl if she was working. 'What do you have in mind?' The cowgirl asked. Danny said she was very sweet. Danny was at a loss as to what to do so he conferred with his friends. 'Ask her for a blow job,' one of them said."

"Elmira, I think I have heard enough," I said.

"This happened on Harvard Square! As soon as Danny got the words out, two plain-clothes cops lifted him by both arms from behind, dumped his milkshake in a trashcan, and deposited him in the backseat of a police car!"

"I'm confused," I said.

"The prostitute, Daniel, turned out to be an undercover police officer."

One week at Harvard, and Danny had been in trouble. He had called Elly, and she had arranged bail and later accompanied him to his court date where the court-appointed attorney pleaded no contest on Danny's behalf. Danny was fined. It was only afterward that Elly and Danny learned he had been mistakenly charged with procuring in a men's rest room. Again my ignorance showed, and Elmira had to explain to me what procuring in a men's room meant. My face blushed bright red.

"Where did you learn this kind of rubbish?"

"Life, Daniel. I read the police report in the newspaper every Tuesday. You would be surprised what goes on around here."

Elmira rightly expected I would see no humor in the situation. I later learned that Elly saw little humor in her brother's escapade and insisted he pay back the fine-money she had advanced him for his hooker debacle.

"You're blackmailing me," Danny had said to Elly, but later, Elmira told me, Danny showed up at Elly's Lowell building living quarters and gave her the first installment of the money he owed her—explaining he would get the rest to her when Elmira sent him his spending money at the end of the month. All, at first, had conspired to keep me in the dark. But the school sent me a full report with the warning that another episode could result in Danny's being suspended from school.

Of course, I was appalled by the false charge, but Elmira had insisted it wasn't worth fighting. At first, she decided it was better for me not to know certain things. She was right, but the dean's report sent to me required her to come clean. That all of this happened at Harvard left me rather dumb-founded. "What did I tell ya 'bout Harvard," I could hear Father say.

———

At my request, Elly had served as Danny's personal tutor, hand holder, and motivator. She had been so concerned her brother get off to a good start at Harvard that she was exhausted, worried about her own grades, and had no personal life. The policewoman posed as a call girl episode was a test of Elly's love. She had enjoyed spending time with Danny and felt rewarded when Danny passed all his first year courses. I was relieved. It had been years since sister and brother had spent so much time together. Occasionally at Harvard Elly said they would meet for dinner, and a movie. Brother and sister were close, though not the kind of closeness I shared with their Aunt Dee.

Danny felt Elly could do no wrong. She was a "goody two-shoes," he'd tell her, a "Daddy's girl." He was right, but Elly was strong, like her mother. And Danny, I knew, could be weak and im-pulsive. He was proud of his sister and was always pointing her out to his classmates.

"The guys are surprised such a beautiful girl could be so smart."

"Maybe," Elmira said, "women at Harvard is not a bad idea after all."

When the children were small, Elmira would let Elly and Danny make bread with her. I can still smell the freshly baked golden loafs.

Danny was always chasing Elly around the house, his fingers sticky with bread dough, ice cream, or play dough, or later on with car grease. Once, after one morning of baby-sitting her littler brother, Elly wrote her mother a note, which Elmira kept in a frame on her kitchen desk.

> He hit me with the sugar bowl top.
> Ate his breakfast in the living room.
> Wouldn't answer the phone when I was busy.
> Wouldn't take his bowl to the kitchen.
> Took my pen and I still don't have it.
> Took some of my papers and tore them up
> Took my test I was supposed to hand in today.
> Talked nasty and said he was going to make up a pack of dirty lies to tell on me. Wanted to fight with me and called me a chicken.......
> All this before 7:30 a.m.
> He was very good after that….

Near the end of Danny's second term at Harvard, he again was summoned to the dean's office. This time my presence was requested. The dean came right to the point.

"There are a series of recent rule infractions on your record, young man. One, soliciting in a men's room," I lowered my head in embarrassment, "two, drinking beer in the dorm—three, playing loud music—and most recently, installing a pin-ball machine in your room."

Listening in disbelief, since I had not been forewarned, I was dismayed, to say the least.

"What do you have to say for yourself, son?"

"No true southern boy can feel welcomed without his beer and pin-ball machine."

Neither the dean nor I appreciated the joke.

"Is West Virginia considered the South?" asked the Dean.

"It's a border state…."

"Mother says you always told her West Virginia was the South," said Danny. "She said she hates the North."

"That's not so."

The meeting ended with Danny escaping with a mild reprimand with the understanding that the pin-ball machine would be removed from his room. Danny finished out the year with no other incidents.

During the fall term of her senior year, Elly had been invited to apply to Harvard's graduate school in English literature, a rare invitation handed out to a woman. Elly had grown appreciative of Harvard and was glad to be there, not just enduring but flourishing. She had arrived as a naïve young woman from southern Appalachia. She hadn't admitted it to me, but I sensed she was glad I had insisted on her going to Harvard. I thought Elly had forgiven me for writing the essay. It was in her smile, the way she hugged me. She had thrived at Harvard, as I had no doubt she would—as I knew I would have if I had been given the opportunity. And Danny… well, making it through his freshman and sophomore years, despite all, had put me on cloud nine.

13

There was no way I could have foreseen that the years 1968, and especially 1969, would be very tumultuous for my family, not to mention America. In fact 1968, turned out to be the most challenging year for most of America's families since 1939 when the world was fighting for its soul, or 1929, when I was entering medical school.

Since the end of WWII, I had never kept up much with the news of the day. Watching television was something I rarely did. Watching it made me feel, strangely, a little like a voyeur. Seeing the race riots made me squeamish, made me turn away from what I had seen. I found man's inhumanity unsettling, my stomach churned, recalling the stray dogs I saw in the medical labs, the skeptic look in the dogs' eyes akin to the look in a patient's eyes when turned away due to a lack of funds. At Charity the wards were full of old chronics and everything else. I had wanted to root out about half of them, at least those that needed no more hospital care. At my hospital, I had long vowed never to turn a patient away who was seriously ill. As far as I knew, I hadn't.

Seeing something called the Tet offensive in Viet Nam, Martin Luther King's and Robert Kennedy's assassinations, the riots at the Democratic National Convention in Chicago, all brought vividly, and uninvited into our home, I felt assaulted, ashamed. And yet I wasn't sure why. I was a patriot. There must be something in man, a gene, I thought, that causes him to beat other men. Watching people being pounded, fire-hosed as if they were beasts, the scenes of horror, the image of my mother's bloody body would sweep over me and drive me to my room. In the midst of Vietnam and the turmoil in myself and in American, I pondered the future. Would it be the forlorn future of my parents? I prayed for my country just as I had when the Nazis surrendered over two decades before.

By late spring 1968, Elly had graduated with highest honors from Harvard-Radcliffe—her diploma signed by both the president of Harvard and the president of Radcliffe, thus delighting me. She stayed on at Harvard working toward her Master's Degree and teaching two classes of first year English as an instructor.

"Elly has been hired as a "professor" at Harvard," I told everyone.

"Dad, I am a lowly instructor," said Elly.

"I did some research. It was not too many years ago when if a woman taught a course, it had to be under the name of a man. You've made your father very proud."

As the year progressed, Danny, somewhat to my chagrin, was cementing his hard-earned reputation as one of Harvard's more ardent and imaginative anti-war demonstrators. On one occasion he decorated a motorboat as a gunboat with a huge sign, "The Harvard Destroyer," and ran it up and down the Charles River shouting anti-war slogans through a bullhorn and playing the Phil Ochs anti-war song, "I Ain't Marching Anymore.*"* He had discovered the song in his last year at Staunton Military Academy. A fellow classmate told Danny that a folk singer named Phil Ochs had attended the academy several years before. Danny had never heard of him, and I certainly had not. Authorities at the Academy, apparently, had not gone out of their way to publicize that Ochs was an alum. Danny could find none of Mr. Ochs' music in the area or hear it on the radio, but a classmate brought an Ochs record to campus, and Danny was hooked. He brought the record home and played it for me. I was enticed to listen to it several times, and each time my appreciation rose.

Danny was a lost soul, and I knew the territory. I was praying that a first rate education would lead him out of the forest, the torment. Ochs' music spoke to him and in time, surprisingly, to me. The songs expressed a defiance Danny felt but couldn't articulate. Later, with Ochs—along with a couple of Danny's Staunton classmates who lost their lives in Vietnam—as his inspiration, Danny had a cause. Though I questioned the tactics, I understood his protesting at Harvard. It was foreign to me but inspiring. My father, thinking back to the coal miner's protests, would have loved it, knowing how much he hated the "Harvards" of the world. *Some were offended that protests had come to the Harvard campus, but that is where they should be,* I thought to myself.

The election was looming, and things were heating up on the Harvard campus. Danny, in contrast to Elly, who was putting her studies and teaching first, was ardently in the middle of all the protest mayhem—when he wasn't in the dean's office.

"We might as well be war grunts," Danny told Elly. He let drop to her that he was thinking of planting a bomb in the administration building.

"Gonna bring the war home."

Elly called me immediately and told me what Danny had told her, telling me, in no uncertain terms, that Danny needed psychiatric help. I had the same regard for psychiatrists that I had for faith healers and herbal medicines. I called Danny and encouraged him to study his English and Bible—told him it would pay off in the end. "Read the 23rd psalm, over and over, son. And Daniel 9. While he prayed for knowledge to serve the prisoners see what Gabriel said to him in verses 21, 22 and 23." I believe my suggestions went unheeded. Ironically, Danny's grades, despite his busy protesting, improved. School was becoming easy.

"You understand the honeymoon is over?" asked the dean, not realizing that Harvard's own long honeymoon was about to come crashing down.

Danny was silent. I answered for him.

"I think he does, Dean."

I had always acknowledged those in authority. I was impressed by them, sometimes foolishly so as I was with Huey Long. I assumed they were usually right, that their years had taught them the difference between right and wrong. It wasn't that I felt Danny's protesting was silly or childish, but I did disagree with him on intellectual grounds, and Elly's concern was enough for me to notify the dean and request a meeting.

"The junior year, as your father will remember, is a pivotal one. We are barely a month into the fall term, and you have already missed several classes, young man—not an auspicious start. I presume your absence without leave was due to your extracurricular activities?"

"It's possible," said Danny.

The dean was referring to Danny's position as a fervent leader of the on-campus anti-war movement.

"Need I remind you that Harvard is not Berkeley. We believe in compromise and deliberation. We do not appreciate grandstanding or threats. We do have a tradition to uphold, you know. We have a respect for manners," cautioned the dean. "How do you feel about school?"

"I don't know," Danny shrugged.

"Like a bad job?"

"Yeah," Danny replied, laughing, "something like that."

"How bad?"

"Real bad. Like your job, Dean."

"Not a bed of roses, my job."

"Especially with students like me taking up space in your office. If it's up to me, your job is about to get thornier."

"Danny, the dean has enough problems."

"You running low on fuel?" asked the dean.

"No. I'm full up, on frustration, on political energy, you know. King and Kennedy getting assassinated gave me a boost. JFK was very popular in our family. Right, Dad?"

"Yes."

"I wasn't aware of that," said the dean.

"I'm a political animal, I guess you could say," Danny said.

"And the reason you have been missing classes?"

"I was kidnapped."

"Danny!" Being kidnapped was what Danny had told me after the dean told me about Danny's missing several classes. Danny said he gave the kidnappers all the money he had and that they had dumped him on the road, telling him to never show his face in Cambridge again.

In the dean's office, my anger had been quiet, sullen, hesitating to say anything I might regret. Don't be foolish. Don't let your anger show.

"You are fortunate to have such a caring family. Your sister has been her brother's keeper, and a very good one, I may add, but you must assume responsibility for your actions. My advice would be to take time off from school. Decide if you want to return the next term."

I thanked the dean for his understanding and very much agreed with his advice. This was exactly what Elly had been telling me. Why could I not leave well enough alone? Elly's handholding duties were over as far as she was concerned. She felt Danny needed help—the kind of help she could not provide. Danny was getting more withdrawn and depressed. He seemed to mirror the times.

"You get brushed back, you get up and dust yourself off and get ready to hit again."

Danny laughed. My little life lessons drove Danny nuts.

"I was lousy at baseball."

"No, you simply did not apply yourself."

"I was afraid of the damn ball."

"Your language, son."

"White flour, that's Harvard. I'd liked to bring that war right to Harvard Square."

14

Late March is not September when thousands of people need no reason to visit New England other than to chase the fall colors in their full glory. However, I had the greatest possible reason to visit New England, in March. Elly had invited the family to sit in on one of the classes she was teaching. Her invitation was for the spring, but I could not wait. Also, Danny was still a student, for which I was thankful.

"We'll be celebrities, Mama. Elly has arranged a special tour for us. Won't that be wonderful!"

"Indeed."

"Have invited Sister to accompany us. She is looking forward to it."

"Indeed, I bet she is," said Elmira, with a straight face.

"It will be Sister's first time to see Harvard."

On arriving in Cambridge, Harvard Square seemed more crowded with undesirables than during my previous visits. Elly told me not to worry. The campus was perfectly safe. The weather was cold, but there was no snow. We cheered the Harvard basketball team to victory. The highlight, of course, was sitting in the back of Elly's classroom watching her conduct her class. Elly introduced us to the class. I was speechless, and very shy, and, oh, so proud. Afterward, in the academic serenity of Harvard Yard, I silently cried my mother's tears of joy.

"You sure you don't want to enroll?" Elmira teased. She had no idea I had once applied to Harvard and had been turned down. I had never told her—never told anyone except Dee, and she had kept my secret about the disappointment of not being admitted.

Elmira was right about my wanting to enroll. Walking the campus, Elmira remarked, with my Harvard children at my side was the happiest she had ever seen me.

"Your father is in hog-heaven."

We proudly wore our Harvard buttons, including Dee. Elly and Danny escorted us to where Danny was living. Danny sat quietly on his bed waiting for his mother to return from the bathroom. When Elmira arrived back to Danny's room, she was laughing.

"I didn't expect to see a young man enter a stall next to where I was. He didn't say anything, but I started laughing."

"They are still not used to us, Mother," said Elly.

"Used to you? What is a male student doing in the bathroom?"

"It's a coed building, Daddy," said Elly.

"Coed?"

"Yes."

"Surely not the bathrooms."

"Yes."

"Well, I'm not sure about that."

"I can't imagine John Harvard would have approved," said Dee.

"I don't think he cares," Danny smiled.

"Surely the boys are polite and stay to themselves—the boys in their rooms and the girls in theirs?" I asked.

"There's no sex at Harvard, Daddy—if that's what you mean. It's not permitted, right, Sis?"

"Yes, right."

"Just like the nurses you told us about, Mom."

I gave a little uncomfortable laugh and saw Elly give Danny a look of keep your mouth shut.

"Just kidding," Danny said. Dee pretended she didn't hear.

"Elly wanted to spare you knowing several rooms in her building had been integrated, so to speak," said Elmira.

"Sex has only recently been invented here at Harvard," said Danny. "Birth control pills have been a boom to free sex, Daddy."

I was not sure what to make of Danny's comment. I had prescribed such pills for some patients. I had reservations about doing so, but if it would help women avoid later abortions because of unwanted pregnancies, I thought that was a good thing.

"It was in her living quarters where Elly met her beau," said Danny.

"Shut up, Danny," said Elly.

"Beau?" I asked upon hearing this news for the first time.

"Yes. After dating for a few months, Elly joined him under a blanket at an all-night "love-in" demonstration against the Viet Nam War."

"It was all very tame, Daddy," replied Elly, with a look to Danny that could kill.

"It was Sis's coming out, going against the status-quo. Make love—not war' is the chant," said Danny. "It's now in the official rulebook."

"Why don't we change the subject," Elmira suggested.

"I'm leaving school," Danny suddenly said.

Silence—dead silence.

"I thought you wanted to change the subject," said Danny.

"Where are you going?" I asked, catching my breath.

"I'm quitting."

"You mean taking a leave of absence?"

"No, Dad. I'm quitting."

"But you're in Harvard, boy." I was confused. "You don't quit Harvard. You can't quit."

"Daniel, please," said Elmira.

"You don't resign from Harvard. You know how many would like to be in your place? How many are lined up behind you waiting for the chance?"

"Well, a spot just opened up."

"A spot has not opened up!"

"It's already done."

"Listen to me, you've worked hard to get here. Is that all for nothing?"

Needless to say, Danny's news of quitting school put a pall on the weekend. Despite the academic trials and tribulations of Danny's first two years and the inauspicious start to his junior year, he had managed to stay in Harvard.

"Danny, you never told me this," said Elly.

"Why? You'd just say what Dad is saying."

"Danny, I know how you feel about Harvard, but none of us want to see you waste the work you've put in," I said.

"No," came the chorus.

"There are other circumstances," said Danny.

We waited for him to continue but Danny did not elaborate.

"What circumstances?" I asked. Danny did not answer. "You're in Cambridge, son. I left a dark, hard, ruthless, abusive world a long time ago. There was no play-acting for me. I was ignorant as a pile of dirt. Look at your sister."

"Please don't," said an embarrassed Elly.

"Not only does she have a diploma stamped with the Harvard seal, she is earning a master's degree."

"Daddy, please."

"No, Elly, We're very proud."

"Isn't this fun," said Danny.

"I wanted to go to Harvard, but I wasn't admitted. You were, son," I blurted out.

Dee broke the silence, "I desperately wanted to marry Clark Gable," as though admitting something nefarious.

"You wanted to go to Harvard, Daddy?" asked Elly.

"Ah…. well, yes, very much," I stammered.

"Your father was a very good student, excellent, but the school he attended did not have the status of some New England prep schools," said Dee.

"Harvard's rejection of me was a severe blow at the time. I've worked hard, saved my money so you and Danny could come here to Harvard. Having you both here … I can't explain the feeling." I was breathing hard, almost gasping for breath. "It was a dream to see you graduate. To watch you both is a joy, but it's been…a relief too, I felt the chains were off—I've felt free for the first time in my life. Don't be afraid to live," I pleaded. "Don't throw your life away, son."

"I'll get a job."

"Doing what?"

"I don't know. The circus."

"Circus?!"

"Yeah, thought I'd go to clown school."

"Did you know about this?" Elmira ignored my question.

"It's a joke, Daddy," said Elly. "Isn't it, Danny?"

Danny shrugged off Elly's look. "I'll work on cars."

"Is that a joke?" I asked.

"No. A mechanic."

"You've got to reach higher, son."

"A good mechanic's hard to find," said Elmira.

"I'll open a auto repair shop." Danny rose from his chair.

"You won't be able to open a can of beans without a degree," I said.

Elly urged Danny to sit back down. "Please." Danny did.

"I'm getting married," said Danny, nonchalantly.

"Stop joking. Quit school now, you'll regret it the rest of your life. You'll wake up one day and be holding an empty bag."

"I'm not joking, Dad. I'm getting married."

"What are you talking about?"

"I'm getting married."

"You have no business getting married. Don't be foolish about romantic love."

"Like your father was," said Elmira.

"We waited till I got established."

"I don't think Danny wants to wait that long," said Elmira, remembering the delays before we married.

"You've got to be resolute when things are against you, son. The structure and discipline you're learning here will pay big dividends. When you finish up, you'll be a man. You work and are thrifty, in a short time you'll be independent, self sufficient. With a Harvard degree, you won't be beholden to anybody. It will pay dividends. People will respect you more. Once you're in the club, you get established, then you can think about someone, a pal, someone from a good family who will be a good companion, a good friend."

"Someone like your mother," said Dee, smiling.

"Thank you Dee," said an unsmiling Elmira.

"We have to…" Suddenly all eyes were on Danny as though he was about to confess to some blood curdling crime.

"What?" asked Elly.

All eyes were on Danny.…

"Speak up, son," I said.

"Get married," said Danny, tiredly, in a half-whisper.

"Oh," said Dee, as though the wind had been knocked out of her.

"Did I hear you correctly, son?"

"I have to get married!"

"But why?" I asked innocently.

"Because her father will kill me if I don't."

There was a heavy silence.

"I don't think this is an appropriate place for such a conversation," said Elmira. "Besides, if we don't get a move on, we are going to be late for our dinner reservations."

Discussion of where Danny's revelation was about to lead was put off until everyone had finished desert. Shortly thereafter, the family was back in the closure of Harvard Yard. Leaning against the statue of John Harvard, Danny half mumbled,

"Joan's going to have a …baby."

"What?" I seemed not to hear.

"Joan..." Danny's arm movement looked like he was in a game of charades.

"Who?"

"The girl Danny's seeing," explained Elmira, impatiently.

"She's in high school still, isn't she?" asked Dee.

"What Danny is saying is that Joan, his girlfriend, is pregnant," said Elly. "Isn't that so, Danny?"

"Yes," Danny said, hardly audible.

"This is a fine how-do-you-do. Your aunt comes up for her first visit to the campus beaming with pride over her nephew, and this is your greeting. This is beyond my comprehension."

"This is not about Dee!"

"No, it is not. You're right, Elmira," said Dee.

The statue of John Harvard was as stoned face as I was. My mind was racing. "Who else knows?"

"Joan's mother for sure," said Danny. "She didn't want me to tell you."

"This is making my head swim. You took her word for it?…How did this happen? Someone tell me this is a joke."

"You don't see us laughing, do you?" said Elmira.

"How do you know the baby is yours?"

"She told me."

"The only reason the girl got pregnant is to make you quit school!"

"I don't think she wanted to get pregnant."

"Did you take no precaution?"

"It's getting late," said Elmira.

"It's all this sex education," I said, looking up at Mr. Harvard.

"I believe sex education is supposed to prevent pregnancy," said Elly.

"That girl knew what she was doing. She used sex to entice you, boy."

"She didn't," Danny protested.

"It wasn't her mind you were interested in."

"I should be with her."

"No, no, no." I was trying to keep what was left of my composure. "Best thing you can do for her is stay in school. Don't worry about this girl. We'll take care of her."

"Lift your head to the mountain, Danny, and you'll find the way," was Dee's advice.

Danny looked at Elly and started laughing. He strode across the square singing, "Climb every mountain, search high and low—Follow every by-way, every path you know." His voice echoed loudly. "Climb every mountain…" Danny continued the song, his voice getting louder with each phrase until he was shouting. Then quiet.

"What do you mean, we'll take care of her?" Elmira asked. I did not know what I meant. I just shook my head and turned back to Mr. Harvard and the school that had spurned me. "Danny wants to go home," said Elmira.

"He's in Harvard, for God's sake! What do you think I'm working for, running up debts? That girl is no good for him. She doesn't care if he doesn't amount to a hill of beans!" I stopped, realizing that was what father had told me.

"We're going back to the hotel," said Elmira.

"He's not going to waste his life!" I walked out toward the middle of the square and looked around thinking what I wouldn't have given to be at Harvard.

15

"Please, come in."

The woman softly closed my office door. I stood and motioned for her to sit. "Please." Confrontations, despite outward appearances, made me uncomfortable. Taking a few quick deep breaths helped me relax—breath in for four beats, hold your breath for seven beats, and let the breath out for eight beats. Repeat five times. I did this religiously before facing something I did not relish. She turned to catch me exhaling.

"Yes, I understand," she said.

I moved away from the door revealing an autographed picture of Gregory Peck that hung on the wall.

"Oh, I see you're a fan of Gregory Peck."

"Yes."

"So am I."

Peck had been a good icebreaker more than once.

"Looks like a comfortable chair," she said, indicating with a slight gesture to my desk chair.

"It is, yes. Please sit."

The leather chair had been issued to me at my first job in the Roanoke, Virginia, hospital where I had gone to work after medical school and my residency at Charity Hospital in Shreveport.

"The hospital is much different than when I was here."

"Yes. It was just a cinderblock building then, but we met all the licensing requirements, and today we have the latest in medical machinery. I'll have to take you on a tour. Of course my chair," I grasped the back of it, "has been with me since I started practice. My wife thinks I should get it reupholstered."

"It has character," the woman said.

What I did not say was what else Elmira had said. "You dye your hair but won't recover that awful chair."

"You're a member of the Rod and Gun Club?" The woman was looking at the certificate on the wall in front of her.

"Yes."

"I find that surprising."

"So did my wife," I said, holding tighter to the back of my chair. "To be a true accepted mountaineer, I felt I should buy a hunting and fishing license though I've never hunted or fished in my life. I grew up not far from here."

"Not everyone who lives around here hunts and fishes, Doctor," she said. "I'm more impressed by your medical diploma."

"That's good," I replied, sensing that she was trying to put me at ease. "My wife won a good-natured dollar bet with me that I would never use the thing, the hunting and fishing license." I pointed to the certificate on the wall.

"But you want your patients to see it."

"Yes, I suppose, like the Rod and Gun Club. Pure bunk. You've caught me up."

I slowly came from behind my chair and sat. My hands sat folded on my desk as I leaned slightly forward, moving a pile of charts to one side as I did, then moving them back. My soft shoes, cushioning my standing for long hours over the operating table, now seemed to squeeze my feet.

"Our children have their whole lives ahead of them," I said without looking up—moving the charts again and rearranging the pencils and pens. I spoke evenly, deliberately, with a doctor's quiet authority. I was, after all, on my home turf. Why should I be so nervous?

Inhaling deeply, I calmly told the mother that I did not feel our children were ready to be parents, that it would be best for them to stay in school. The mother nodded as though she agreed, but she was silent, sitting stoically, looking uncomfortable.

"You brought our Joan into the world," the mother said, almost in a whisper.

She smiled, warmly, with the fond memory and shyly thanked me for having taken such good care of her during her pregnancy. I try to make each mother feel totally at ease and confident that all will be well with their pregnancy. The mother assumed I remembered her, and I did – the memory jogged by the chart in front of me. But this was not the usual patient-doctor routine. This woman was the mother of a child I had long ago delivered. That baby was now a teenage girl who was pregnant with my son's baby. But it had been sixteen years since I had seen this mother. She reached across the desk and put her hand on mine. I nodded, recalling that Danny had dated other girls named Joan, or Joanne, or was it Jonelle? Surely I knew the name of the girl my son had impregnated. But I couldn't come up with it. Truth was I didn't have a clue. I had reminded myself to ask Elmira the night before, but I had gotten home too late, and she was already in bed. I couldn't remember any of Danny's girlfriends. There was always another girlfriend. None of them appealed to me.

The small heavy-set woman had a little red pill-box hat perched on her head that reminded me of the kind Jacqueline Kennedy wore. We made small talk about the weather and how wonderfully toasty my office felt. A late season snow for most of the day had welcomed in Spring.

"I'm sorry you had to make the drive in such bad weather."

"The road is clear," she assured me. "The cinder truck was out early. It was no problem," she said in her bird-like voice. "My husband is with the county road department, a supervisor. He knew the road was open."

"It's odd, isn't it?" I said.

"What?"

"Life. Life is odd, sometimes."

"That we are here with this… problem?"

There were other doctors. How ironic, it was I, who had delivered the girl now carrying my son's baby. A coincidence? Why not? Or was there some more intricate plan? Though religious, I did not believe in fate. God had a plan for Danny, but surely this could not be it. I was always disturbed when hearing someone say something was God's plan. Or that God was on their side. Whose side? The ones with the most money, who go to the biggest churches?

"This is a most trying time for our children—and us, as parents. It is awkward. I wanted to call you as soon as my son told me."

"Joan doesn't know what to do. We just found out. She does not want a baby, but she's frantic, frightened. So am I."

"Have you and your daughter discussed, considered … terminating the pregnancy?"

"Terminating the pregnancy? You mean an abortion."

The word, abortion, sounded dirty. I had thought about what I would say, how I would say it. Those words, "terminating the pregnancy," had fallen, almost casually, out of my mouth before I could stop them, as though on the spur of the moment. Of course the words were anything but casual. But, still, the words just hung there in a black pool of silence over two lowered heads. For a second I had not realized what I had said. During the last rationalizing moments of the tortuous previous week of sleepless nights, I had told Elmira that perhaps the girl could just go away… somewhere…have the baby and put it up for adoption.

"Wouldn't that be convenient," said Elmira.

"Who would know?"

"All her friends, that's all."

"Yes," I said. "Perhaps the girl does not want the baby."

"Perhaps she does," said Elmira. "Sometimes a baby gives a girl something other girls do not have."

"A medical procedure," I said to the mother, espousing a relatively new terminology for abortion I had read about in one of the medical journals, "is no longer dangerous, in the main because it is being done well by physicians."

"We talked about it, but we are not, as you can understand, educated about the medical procedure."

"Certainly."

"How dangerous would it be for her?"

"Whatever trouble may arise usually comes from self-induced procedures. In the first months the fetus is like a piece of tissue. You evacuate the uterus."

The mother made a face as though that part of her anatomy was an unmentionable.

"Like a vacuum cleaner?"

She had not asked this in any sarcastic way. It was simply a question. Her imagery was surprisingly fitting.

"It is not a real person," I heard myself assuring her, and me. "If the abortion"…that word… "if the procedure is timed right, all will be fine." I did not suggest otherwise to the mother.

"It would have been nice, I suppose, if this would not have to be…." She did not finish.

The only thing, I had decided, never really contemplating otherwise—was for Danny to be…at Harvard. My every day had been and was still dedicated to one dream: my son and daughter would both be Harvard graduates. That would be vindication enough for all of Father's, "yer livin' in a dream world, boy, like yer mother, and ya know where she is. In hell, that's where. Wake up." It was hard, as a young boy, not to have an encourager.

"But you do, Daniel, me," I could hear Dee say.

"My daughter is concerned she will be thrown out of school if the word gets out."

"There is that. It's unfair. The procedure, for confidential reasons, would need to be done elsewhere."

"I need to discuss this with my daughter and husband."

"The procedure should commence as soon as possible. A late term pregnancy would make terminating the pregnancy more difficult. Girls the age of your daughter have small tightly closed cervixes so the doctor has to be very careful when he dilates the cervix."

"Would you perform the "procedure" on Joan?"

"We do not provide that particular *procedure*." It wasn't the stigma I was concerned about, what the public or my colleagues would think if they knew I had performed an abortion, which many surgeons had. As an intern, I had been tormented seeing women die with infections from attempting self-inflicted abortions with sticks or wires, or with pouring Lysol into their cervix. I had seen young women die when an abortion could have saved their lives. Later, as a doctor, when a woman's life was in peril because of pregnancy, I would do a quiet abortion knowing it was necessary and justified. I did not doubt the personal toll on those who performed abortions.

In my personal medical journal, I could recall no mention having been made that human life began at conception. What was the right decision? Abortion had been the lament of many of my Bible study groups.

"Men's Bible study groups," Elmira pointed out.

I had delivered thousands of babies over the years and had lost precious few. My job was to save lives, not take them.

16

My hand moved with the assuredness that comes from being totally absorbed in the only thing I ever wanted to do, to be the best surgeon I could possibly be. Medicine, surgery, was my passion, my obsession, the only place where I fully rejoiced. I took pride in self-denial with an uncommon discipline to abstain from anything I considered harmful, anything that would take me away from "doctoring." Even my love of music had taken a back seat to medicine. I had long given up my youthful habit of devouring any football or baseball statistic. There were no activities, aside from church, watching Gregory Peck movies, and attending the local Rotary Club luncheons. I slept, operated, and talked medicine. I read nothing but medical journals and the occasional cursory glance of the sports page, but nothing else of the morning paper. I was tireless in keeping up with the latest medical advances, studying relentlessly, never letting myself go into the operating room without knowing I was as prepared as humanly possible. It was essential that my life be devoted to being a good surgeon. I was doing what I wanted to do. My childhood had receded. Fortune had smiled on me. My fellow doctors maintained that if anyone of them had to go under the knife, it was "Doctor Dan" they wanted wielding it.

In my world a clanking of an instrument on a tray was a clap of thunder to others, but I seldom seemed to notice. An artist with the scalpel, no broad strokes, but exacting lines was what I aspired for.

My concentration, no facial expression, was such that the nurse would not dare disturb, only softly placing the instrument in my out-stretched hand. There was the soft purr of air-conditioning and the faint calming note of Beethoven in otherwise stillness. Outside the operating room, I was contained within myself. One would think me aloof, not wishing to be bothered. If one had troubled to question the man behind the surgical mask, he would find a contented, indeed, happy doctor…that is until the mask came off. It is hard to be contented.

When a surgery goes right, it is a thing of beauty. I feel a burst of pleasure. I have witnessed operating rooms run as a tyrant might run a country, and though I demand fastidiousness in the operating room, I am always open to a better way, to not postpone doing things until being forced to do them. I challenge my fellow doctors and nurses to question whether what we are doing is in the best interests of the patient.

"Can we do it better?"

The time I take with my surgeries was to the chagrin of some of my colleagues. Most would try to avoid being called in to assist on a surgery I was performing. In the end they had no choice for I owned the hospital.

———————

Leaning close to the patient, I hesitated, catching my sister's eye looking up at me from where, as the head nurse, she was administering the anesthetic to the patient. I then made a precise, small, delicate, two-inch incision in the right lower quadrant of the patient's abdomen. Removing a patient's appendix was a routine operation, one I had performed thousands of times—but never approached as routine. Life was the price of such folly, I lectured when counseling young nurses and doctors. Every surgery is the first surgery was my mantra, even a relatively simple appendectomy. Taking a moment to inspect my work, satisfied, I continued, removing the inflamed appendix, careful to make sure the area was clean and ready to be sewed up.

Doctor Hays, the restless assisting surgeon, standing opposite, was the kind of doctor I detested. I had taken a dislike to the man, thinking that it had been a mistake to hire him, but at the time I could not be choosy about surgeons. I tried not to be judgmental but couldn't help myself. Doctor Hays was far too heavy, and he was slovenly. It was all I could do to look at him. How do people go out in public like that? Worse, Hays reminded me of Father, overweight, overbearing, who thought women were inferior, dependent, subservient, had been created to serve him and have babies. The laws had been changed from the time when a man controlled all the earnings of his wife and children. In the mountains however you could pass all the laws you wanted. Customs were not so easily changed.

Doctor Hays was breathing heavily, sighing, when the day was still young. There were many such men shuffling the halls of the hospital, not caring or even noticing the clean walls and floors that I took pride in. It wasn't just that Hays needed to lose 75 pounds. I saw overweight patients on a regular basis. Occasionally, after referring to a patient's chart, I would tell the patient, "Since your last visit, I see you have gained some weight." One such patient had once reached out and tapped my belly, suggesting I had done the same.

"Look who's talkin', Doc."

It had been the first time in my life to have a little roll around my middle and the first time to have anyone call attention to it. Despite being offended by the patient's effrontery, I thanked him. It wasn't that I was overweight. With a suit coat on, no one could tell. No one had been so bold before as to suggest that I, a doctor, could lose a few pounds. I was, admittedly, a vain man and I was upset by my lack of discipline—something I had always prided myself on. After some soul-searching, I took the autographed picture of a standing Gregory Peck that Dee had given me and posted it on the back of my office door. It was the inspiration I needed. Along with Mr. Peck and a vegetarian diet, combined with a daily lunch-time walk, my roll was gone within three months, never to reappear.

As I was about to sew up the patient, I heard a tap, tap, tap. Doctor Hays was tapping his foot.

"Do you need to go to the bathroom, Dr. Hays?"

"No."

I could not abide sloppy dress in the operating room, an untucked shirt, a surgical mask sitting crooked on a face, idle chatter, all things I frowned upon, and all things Dr. Hays was guilty of. He nearly always had an excuse why he couldn't be on call. Oh well, let it go, let it go. Judge not for thou will be judged. The man is a doctor. It was hard to attract good American surgeons to southern Appalachia. When I could, I hired better doctors from the far-east who welcomed coming to the United States. And they did not mind the remote mountains or feel superior to the southern Appalachian people they were serving.

It was wonderful to be doing the work I loved. I would do it as long as I could, equating retirement with death. *How many surgeons were still operating,* I wondered*, when they could be collecting social-security?* It was a blessing to be able to help people, a blessing to put off death as long as I could for as many as I could. Death was a constant companion in the mountains. Hardly a month went by when some coal miner did not lose his life. Life was at times treated carelessly in the mountains, taken for granted, especially by those outside the mountains who enjoyed the convenience of electricity without having to consider the great risks that miners took to dig the coal that provided that electricity. Just like many did not know where their bread came from, most did not know where electricity came from. Many homes were lit up with the work of dead coal miners.

As I commenced to sew up the patient with the care, Dee said, "of an expert seamstress," Father's voice ambushed me from the dead.

"What's takin' ya so long? Ya fall in, boy? The hole's too big fer yer scrawny butt." Father's words and laughter mocked my fear as a young boy of falling into the dark, smelly abyss of the outhouse. "That hole goes straight down to hell. That's where boys like ya end up—in hell."

Dee glanced up again as another nurse laid a sterilized, surgical instrument into my out-held hand. The surgical instrument, gleamed under the hot lights, sat in my still open palm, like an uninvited guest. The operating nurse and I had made the surgical instrument pass many times, like a finely tuned relay team passing the baton. Dee knew I hated anything that distracted me, like the feet shuffling Doctor Hays. Dee knew my every nuance. Any hesitation, however slight, in my…what I liked to think… fluid, efficient work would catch her eye. Any change in my demeanor was a red flag in her eyes. I took the instrument without looking up.

"What's ya doin' in there, boy. Ya can't hide from me. I'm gonna count to ten and if yer not outta there, I'm gonna knock the door down and skin ya alive. Ya hear me?"

Hearing Father's voice brought home, that the young years, say before the age of ten, go far in defining who we are. This was a battle I had fought all my life, leaving me resigned to the notion that we are all stamped for life by the age of ten.

"The mold is set, and any discussion about the past is foolish and futile. What's gone is gone." This I had told to God.

Again, I sensed Dee's searching eyes looking up at me and I heard her voice echoing back to a past I had never understood. "Besides what can you do about it? You go on, Daniel, you have to. There is no choice if you wish to make something of your life. Look straight ahead at what you have—your wife and children."

"And you, Sister. I have you."

I stared at the instrument in my hand and went back to work sewing up the cavity.

Outside the operating room, Dee and the other nurse welcomed the warm air blowing up through the floor register. I insisted the operating room be kept on the chilly side. I preferred cold winter days, so the nurses usually made sure to layer clothing under their uniforms. Doctor Hays sneezed loudly as he went hurriedly by. I untied and removed my surgical mask.

"Are you all right?" asked Dee, seeing me glance up at the clock on the wall.

"Yes. Why do you ask?"

"You looked at the time."

"I did?"

"You seem ...bothered."

"Our esteemed Doctor Hays is a bothering man."

I knew with every fiber of my being that it would be a terrible miscalculation to ever compromise Dee in any way. I owed her that. But it was too late. Sister and I, with a detour for my marriage, had traveled on the same road, but now that was not possible. She would have forbidden me, implored me not to go down this road.

Could I afford to turn away from God? If, in the end, l recanted and gave my life over to God, would not that be enough? Would God overlook what I had done? Hesitating a moment, I then turned away from Dee and hurried down the hall to my office, not offering my normal smile to any I passed, knowing that Dee was watching me. Inside my office, I leaned against the door for support. I removed my operating gown and cap. I was sweating all over. All would be well, I told myself. I sat down at the desk, cupping my face in my hands. Nothing is wrong because nothing is wrong. I buzzed the station nurse to ask if the call I was expecting had come in. It hadn't.

My next operation was not scheduled until late afternoon. I did not like operations scheduled close together, preferring to do no more than three operations on any given day. There was nothing good to say about doctors who scheduled as many operations as they could squeeze into a day. It was all about money. I operated two days a week unless there was an emergency such as the ruptured appendix I had just removed.

After a few minutes, I stepped out of the tiny bathroom. I put on a clean shirt and my woolen sport coat. I bought my clothes from the men's store in town. At times Elmira would shop for me in the nearest city, a hundred miles away. I buttoned the middle button of my coat and put a smile on my face, then frowned. No, no, better to keep the operating coat on, more professional. I changed coats again and wiped the sweat from my brow with the always-pressed white handkerchief and called the station nurse again.

"No call?....What time is it?......Oh, all right." If any man needed God...

At last, after another hour, the phone rang. It was the girl's mother. She told me that after talking it over with her daughter, they had decided it would be best to have the procedure.

"Could you arrange the procedure and share in the expense?"

"Yes. I will pay the entire bill. Your daughter will need to stay a few days to allow for the doctor to examine her before the procedure and then to make sure there is no infection. You and your daughter have thought about it all?"

"Yes, it is her right. It just can't be. That's all there is to it. Joan wants to graduate and go to nursing school."

"The nearest provider is out-of-state, three hundred and fifty miles away in Washington, D.C."

"That is better. Joan does not want anyone to know, including her father. He doesn't know she's pregnant. I have not told him, you understand. I simply think it best. Joan is not going to tell your son about the procedure. She says Danny would not want her to do it. It had been a mistake, she said, to tell Danny that she was pregnant. She says he wants to marry her. Your boy seems very passionate, Doctor."

"He is."

"Joan and I have talked it over and she thinks it would be best if she tells your son that she had a miscarriage. You do understand?"

"Yes. Of course.

"I will tell my husband that I am taking Joan to Washington for a few days to see the sights. That will work for school as well because Easter is next week."

"Yes," I said, glancing at my desk calendar, which still had February up. "April sixth. The doctor in Washington is quite good. He will try to do no scraping and only use a suction process, which he has told me he finds much better because it is clean with little blood and it is quick. He was a classmate of mine at medical school. He has been doing this work for a long time. You don't want any kind of place that would be dangerous for your daughter. You could take your daughter out of the country, but that is not necessary."

There was a trembling, choking sob in the mother's voice. I told myself that I was thinking about Danny's welfare or was it only about me. A gray cloud hovered.

"We could say you and I are in this together, Doctor Friend."

"Yes."

On the wall were my framed degrees along with the doctor's Hippocratic Oath, a modern version of the oath, which I had been given a few years back by the American Medical Association as an exemplary physician. I lowered my eyes from the Hippocratic Oath.

"You know, doctor, the baby would have been our grandchild."

The phone went dead.

We shared a bane neither of us would ever forget.

17

It was well after dark, and the winding mountain road was hazardous, snow piled high on both sides. My slow, deliberate driving, my fingers habitually pulsing the steering wheel, drove Elmira to distraction, but did not seem to bother Dee. The silence between us made the commute even longer. Finally, an hour and fifty-five-minutes later, I inched the old dark blue Buick down the short narrow cinder alley marked with snow-covered evergreens on one side and leafless maple trees on the other. The sliver of a moon barely backlit the trees' bare branches, not that I noticed them even in full sunlight. For that matter, I never noticed the neighbors up the street.

"Haven't seen them lately."

"The reason might be, they moved last year," Elmira had replied.

The trees outlined the large dark, foreboding, stone house, my pride and joy—not bad for a poor country boy. The door-less garage was so close to the narrow alley that a direct turn into it was impossible. It took several tries to maneuver the car in. Dee and I sat silently in the dark. Finally, she spoke.

"As a man of God, as a doctor, it was not your decision to make."

She suspected why I had been at sixes and sevens for the last couple of weeks.

"It is not my decision. Can't you understand?"

"I understand you will have to live with this for the rest of your life, Daniel."

"The girl does not want the baby. The mother came to me for my help, my advice. I told her what I thought. Danny is the father of her daughter's baby! Never in my wildest nightmare did I imagine this scenario back in medical school. Everything seemed so clear then… What am I to do?"

"Nothing. Are you paying for it?"

"Dee, I don't believe abortion to be wrong under certain circumstances."

"As a nurse, I have always understood those circumstances and have always supported your decisions. This was not one of those cases."

"I could not put the girl in harm's way."

"In an abortion, Daniel, someone always dies. In our case, two people died. I loved our mother," said Dee, "but she should not have killed her baby."

"She had no choice."

"You always have a choice."

"She made a desperate choice."

"Yes, I know," said Dee. "But it was still the wrong choice. Not only did we lose a brother or sister but we also lost our mother….Are you paying for the girl's abortion?"

My silence confirmed her fears. She shook her head, gathered her purse, and opened the car door, not bothering to fasten the large safety pins that had long ago replaced the buttons on her coat.

"How could this be wrong?" I asked, reaching for her arm.

"Oh, Daniel. It has always been wrong, believe me. It will always be wrong," she said with a quiet, uncompromising finality.

I was glad I couldn't see what I knew was a pained expression on her face.

"Surely you can understand, Dee. Think of where we came from. It was only because of your love that I wasn't left behind like a stray dog! I had no idea what was in store for me, was going nowhere. I was so afraid I would never know if there was a life on the other side of the mountain. The dreams you had for me, Sister, I have fought and worked to make them come true! I could do no less for my son. I can dream for him!"

"But he is the one who has to fight and work to make that dream come true!"

"I know."

"It will be nice for you to say 'My son is a Harvard graduate,' but it must be his dream too, Daniel."

"Yes, yes, I know…it was my dream to be a doctor so…." I did not finish.

"Medicine was right for you. But I'm very concerned about Harvard being right for Danny. I'm not sure it is. You are pushing too hard."

"I know how you feel."

"You don't. You can't. But it's not how I feel, it is God you must answer to. It is God you must look to for salvation."

"I know."

"What you have done, I'm afraid, is a sin, a blemish on your soul, Daniel, that may very well keep you out of heaven."

"Right now it's this life I'm worried about, not the next."

"I didn't mean that. I'm sorry."

We sat quietly, staring straight ahead at nothing. I was pondering heaven and wondering about Dee's love, which I had never before doubted.

"I will always love you, Daniel," she said, as though knowing my thoughts.

"Thank you, Sister," I said, pressing my hand into hers. "The girl is barely sixteen years old. She has her whole life ahead of her. Letting her go to a bad doctor would be a sin. It is not my job to tell them what to do, but I cannot stand by and do nothing. Then the girl might try to abort herself."

"The girl, Joan, will never forget this, Daniel. It is a loss that cannot be replaced. This I know."

"Sister, are you trying to tell me something?"

She opened the car door and swung her legs around to the ground, sitting half in and half out of the car.

"Some things, you think, should remain in shadow," she said, her back to me. "This all takes me back. You once asked me if there was a man in my life. There had been briefly, but long enough. I could not tell you then."

"And now?...You can tell me anything," I said.

"I was with child. The man asked me to abort it, demanded me to. He was a doctor at the Roanoke Hospital. So I did so, not wishing to bring a child into a forlorn relationship. I could only think about Mother. How could it possibly have happened to me, I wondered? And now, with Danny and Joan, it is like it's happening all over yet again. Afterward, I went back to my quarters. Actually, I ran back, though the doctor who had performed my abortion told me to take it easy. That day I cleaned every inch of the place. When night fell, I did not turn on a light. I just sat there and thought about the things that I had wanted to buy for the baby. I had made a list. I was several weeks into the pregnancy before I told the man. It all came crashing down. I was devastated upon hearing his reaction. I was too innocent about such matters of the heart. I told him, fine, I would have an abortion, but only if he agreed to leave the hospital. Otherwise, I told him, I was going to tell the hospital administrators. So he left."

"Who was the doctor?"

"You never met him. He was long gone by the time you arrived. His leaving had created an opening for a surgeon."

Dee turned her head a bit toward me and the moonlight caught her eyes.

"Me?"

"Yes.....One door closes and another opens."

Dee's voice had a lilt to it like the chirp of a small bird. It was a soft voice, and when she was disturbed, it got even softer, finally fading to nothing. Then she would make a graceful exit as if a soft breeze had lofted her away on the wisp of a cloud.

"I fear it will be a curse for you. It is in no way a similar burden to carry. I know the weight of such a burden, and I worry for the girl and for Danny," said Dee, getting out of the car.

Best to let it go, I decided. I would have a talk with Danny. "Watch your step, Sister......Sure you don't want to come in—see your mail?"

"It will wait," she said, closing the car door and turning on her pocket flashlight. She made her way out of the dark garage down the snow covered stone steps toward the path leading to her little house situated behind ours.

Whatever it was I wanted, perhaps I wanted it too much, pushing too hard. Perhaps I was too driven. How far is a man willing to go? I had stepped over the moral line—a line, which seemed to be moving, depending on where people needed it to be. But parents should pave the way for their children. It was common sense, a duty no less. That was the promise of love I had made to myself when my children came into the world. They would never have to tread my bramble path. That was what love was about. Life should be better for your children. My path for my children led to Harvard. I knew Harvard would give them more of everything, more to offer, more to give. Was God really against that? My children would know that I fought for them. Their father tried. I laid my head back against the car seat, exhausted. In the rear view mirror, I could see the moonlight cast a faint long shadow across the back alley of my life.

"My dear Father, please forgive me for I know not what I do. I am a good man who is susceptible to ambition's poison. My failures are mine and mine alone. Thank you, Father, I am yours."

Waking up, still in the car, not knowing how long I had been asleep, I retrieved my briefcase and suit bag from the car's back seat and then remembered the plaque of the Hippocratic Oath, which I had removed from my office wall a few hours before. I knew those words by heart, especially the portion that read,

"….If it is given to me to save a life, all thanks. But it may also be within my power to take a life; this awesome responsibility must be faced with great humbleness and awareness of my own frailty. Above all, I must not play at God."

The house looked as lonely as I felt. There was a Lincoln saying I was fond of, "Broken eggs cannot be mended." My decision had set things in motion, the stream was flowing on and on, and there would be no rock big enough to stop the flow from its inevitable destination. Inside the house, I wrapped the oath in the day's newspaper and carried it upstairs.

Lowering the attic stairs, I half expected Elmira to come out of her bedroom having heard me, she being such a light sleeper. Thankfully, she didn't. I removed my shoes and climbed the six narrow stairs up to the attic. My medals and awards, my certificates of appreciation and honorary degrees, my hundreds upon hundreds of patient thank you cards, and gifts—dozens of fountain pens, brass book-ends, framed photos of patients, including newborns named after me, my treasured collection of Gregory Peck memorabilia—all were stored in the repository of memories, the attic.

Turning the bare light bulb on, I tiptoed across the wooden planks to an old steamer trunk—the same trunk I had taken to boarding school and college. It was full of clothes and a couple of scrapbooks along with some keepsakes, mostly little things like the cross-shaped stone that Dee had taken from Mother's hand and given back to me. There was also one of Mother's pretty ribbons that she would tie in her hair. And there is where I buried the Hippocratic Oath, under some old newspapers, one of which had a picture of Huey

Long's wife and his son Russell. I remembered Russell from the LSU days. "Fine man," some echo of the past. The Longs were royalty in the South, and Huey was the dictator of Louisiana—the state run by his political machine until his assassination. Other newspapers detailed the woes of the Depression and the end of WWII with the surrender of Germany and Japan. Father had fought in WWI and I had thought I would be called for duty in WWII until told by the War Department that my doctoring was needed at home.

Just then an owl hooted its lonely call. The hooting always made me reflective, despondent, especially when I was exhausted. Late at night, I would often hear the owl's call to the dark. I turned the attic light out and made my way down the attic stairs. I took a lengthy shower, then stopped in the kitchen for my nightly slice of bread topped with applesauce while standing at the counter, glancing at the day's newspaper. Elmira would circle the articles she wanted me to read. She had circled in red where Gregory Peck was to be in a new movie, *Mackenna's Gold.*

Picking up the *Bible* that Dee had given me so many years before, I looked at the inscription she had written, "God loves you, He forgives you."

I repeated those words to myself, then got down on my knees.

"All I can do is my best. Be the best I can be. Help my children be the best they can be. I want to leave the world a better place than the one I grew up in. What do you want, God? Give me a sign, God."

I opened to Psalm 22.

My God, my God, why hast thou forsaken me?
Why art thou so far from helping me, from the words of my groaning?
O my God. I cry by day, but thou dost not answer: and by night, but find no rest.

18

"Thank you, Doctor," I said, relieved. It was a courtesy call from one doctor to another. Joan was doing fine. The procedure was done. There had been no complications. There was no mention of a baby. I fell back in my chair and cried. I thought about what Mother must have asked herself. What else could she do? Asked for God's forgiveness, I supposed. What could He say? I lowered my head and prayed, for Joan, for her mother, and for Danny and myself. Not long after the doctor's call, Elmira called me at the hospital.

"Danny called me early this morning," said Elmira, "and told me Joan has had a miscarriage."

"Oh," I said... at a loss to say anything else.

"Daniel? Did you hear me?"

"Yes, I just.... Danny is staying in school?" I asked after a moment.

"I assume so," said Elmira.

The picture on my desk of my two Harvard smiling children wearing their Harvard sweatshirts, standing in front of the statue of John Harvard, beamed up at me, piercing my heart. Did not their smiles confirm that I had done the right thing?

Eminence and achievement do not come easily. There would be those who criticize. But yes, there could be no question. It was the right decision. Then why had I just sat there in my chair going over and over in my mind, had I done the... right thing? It was too easy to rationalize away the shame that I felt. I could not look in the mirror. It was my faith I struggled with and had long privately questioned, since my intern days. I had made sure the mother's daughter, Danny's girlfriend, got the best care she could. I had seen too many patients with botched abortions carried out by untrained practitioners.

Opening my file cabinet, I found a folder marked "Harvard." Inside was the essay I had written for Elly as part of her application to Harvard. The fraudulent essay was my first transgression in striving for the best. I read the essay.

> "Our family admires the Kennedys and how they have dedicated themselves to the public good. President Kennedy, a Harvard alum, kicked off his presidential campaign, as you may know, in the hills of Appalachia. He never forgot West Virginia and said if he became President, he would do something to try and reduce the amount of poverty he had seen. He kept his promise. He helped many poor West Virginians. Unfortunately, and not his fault, too much money was put into highways and public buildings and new courthouses at the expense of the real cause of poverty. Education. He was one politician who gave hope and did not take it away. Because of President Kennedy, children from poor families could go to school and have something to eat. I was enamored of President Kennedy not only because he loved West Virginia, but also because he was a true inspirational leader. Like millions of young people, I became interested in politics because of my love of the President. I dared to hope, to trust the goodness in me because of President Kennedy. I so admired the President that my father bought me a rocking chair like the President's. [I was getting quite creative—

and had worried if I was going too far. But I had thought about this essay, long and hard] The rocker was made of solid oak with a high back and wide arms, just like the President's rocker. [In truth, I had bought the rocker for Elly after the President was assassinated]

After President Kennedy's assassination, I would sit in the rocker every evening after dinner. It made me feel close to the President. I read where he said that that the children of West Virginia could hope to follow in his footsteps and be President one day. I truly believed I could become whatever I wanted to be. I do not know if the country will ever be ready for a woman president, but I hope Harvard will consider this young woman's application. Nothing would make me prouder than to walk the halls of my hero's school. In President Kennedy's honor, I am, Elly Friend.

After finishing reading the essay, I read it again, wondering why I hadn't written an essay as good for myself when I had applied to Harvard.

It was the spring of 1969, and Danny had recently joined his fellow "revolutionaries" in commandeering Harvard's Administration Building. It was Danny's continued protesting of the Vietnam War. It was his stated wish "to make Harvard suffer like those in the war were suffering." The president of Harvard called the state and local police to clear the building. Elly agreed with Harvard's president that freedom within the university was at stake, but felt that school officials had over-reacted.

"You can't allow the university to be held as a hostage, no matter how we feel about the war," Elly told me after meeting Danny at the jail where he and others were being released. Danny, I suspected, wanted to be expelled and was very disappointed when he wasn't; none of the offending students were. Elly herself later joined a protest on campus against racial exclusion.

The next week after a class, "Instructor Friend" was asked to report to the department chairman's office. Elly was preparing herself for the bread line—or at least an early departure for Berkeley where she had been admitted to the Ph. D. program—assuming the chairman had discovered he made a mistake, thinking that he had hired a male instructor. After her meeting, Elly called her mother, and told her that Danny was in the hospital with a broken leg.

Apparently in the dead of night, as Elly related the story to Elmira, Danny raced a car through the quad, tearing up the sod and damaging some trees before ramming the car into the statue of founder John Harvard. Elly's solemnity was not lost on Elmira.

"You'll have to send them a check," Elmira warned. "It won't be a small one."

"Well, he only has a year left and he will graduate," I said and then seeing the look on her face…. "What?"

"Elly told me Danny has been dismissed."

"Suspended?"

"No. He will not be allowed to return."

"That doesn't make sense. He has been doing so well."

"Elly says there is no recourse. I'm sorry, Daniel."

It was quite a blow. I had the same feeling I had those many years ago when Harvard rejected my application.

Elmira and I made a quick trip to Cambridge. Walking through Harvard Square with Elly, we saw that a large portion of the marble base had been violated. Emergency supports had been erected to keep Mr. Harvard afloat.

"As you know, Daddy, the statue is everyone's favorite photo op. Danny's escapade has drawn a lot of attention from the administration."

"Thank goodness no one else was injured," said Elmira.

"Do you have any idea why your brother would do such a thing?"

"Danny needs to be free. He detests authority."

"I will talk to the dean."

"Daddy! It is over. You are lucky if they don't decide to pursue charges against Danny."

Elly was right. The dean was unforgiving of Danny's behavior. His latest adventure was the proverbial straw that broke the camel's back, and my spirit.

"The president is going. It's a good time for both of us to go." Danny was referring to Harvard's president who had just announced his resignation. "I'd like to think I helped drive him out of office," said Danny. "Maybe he's like me; he doesn't know what else to do. If you give a huge chunk of change, Daddy, they'd rename the place after you."

Tough times don't last. Tough people do, I had told myself. I had said that to Danny once when he was in military school.

"You should be in the army," Danny had said.

"Don't let yourself be daunted by the clouds of doubt. Don't give up hope. We all get down, we all have doubts, and we all get depressed. It is part of how we are made, but find the thing that carries you over the hump. When I am operating, I am never depressed." I believed what I told Danny. I still do.

Elly, self-preservation in mind, decided, unbeknownst to me, that it was a fortuitous time for marriage. The prospective husband had been two years ahead of her in school and was from an old Harvard family. His father and grandfather had gone to Harvard. The young man had taken a position with an investment firm in Boston and was a licensed pilot whose family owned their own plane. Elly had trusted him enough to take a couple of Saturday afternoon flights around New England. They had great fun together and became fast friends. Elly had never indicated to me that the relationship was anything more than that—he was just a good friend. The good friends found a justice of the peace who agreed to ride along with them and perform the marriage vows at 15,000 feet.

When Elly called to tell her mother what had transpired, that she had gotten married in the air somewhere over New England, Elmira, not having had a church wedding, said that church weddings were "not all they're cracked up to be."

––––––––––––

I went into mourning. First, Danny had quit Harvard, and now Elly had eloped. I was devastated. How had it come to this? This must be God's punishment, I decided. I fell into the Kennedy rocker on the sun porch, thinking that the rocker had been a fitting present for Elly and a fine piece of furniture for our home. I had modeled our house on the White House… complete with pillars and a flagpole. What did it matter? Elmira had been fond of what once had been a small bungalow—before I started my on-going remodel, enlarging it so many times that now the house dwarfed all the other rather modest houses on James Street. Pretty imposing, but now, as I looked out at the night, our house, like all the other houses, curtains drawn against the cold and dark, must look abandoned, too, as if the nuclear holocaust had finally arrived—and it had. At that moment, I thought I could walk away and never miss the house. How strange. But a house was just a house when no one was in it.

Opening my briefcase, I removed a few of my patient's charts that needed updating, but my eyes kept closing. I finally got up, unable to concentrate and walked through the empty dark rooms slowly, a hiker unsure which path to take, a prisoner pacing his cell. The formal dining room was now rarely used. Before Elly went off to college, Sunday dinners were always in the dining room. The family sat around the table on Sundays laughing and enjoying Elmira's cooking. "Wonderful, Mama." Now the furniture looked unfamiliar to me. I made my way into the library where my collection of medical books, records, and sheet music, helped fill floor to ceiling bookcases. Elmira's history books took up the most space.

Turning on the light, the book *Dearest Child* caught my eye. I remembered Elmira mentioning it. Sitting down in her chair, I opened the book and found it was full of letters between a mother and daughter. How it pleased me to hear Elly and Elmira talk on the phone and know how often they wrote to each other. The book brought to mind the many letters I had written to Elmira so many years before. I certainly wouldn't want those letters found and published.

Putting the book back on the shelf, I noticed a paperback novel, the cover of which showed a skimpily clad reclining sultry dark-haired young woman reaching her arms up to a muscular bare-chested young man who resembled Gregory Peck. There were several stacks of such books. What were these doing in the library? Why did Elmira feel the need to read these books? My attention was diverted by my old violin case leaning in a corner. It had been years since I had played the violin. Opening the case, I removed the purple velvet cloth the instrument was wrapped in. I took out the violin, uncovering a card with Beethoven's picture.

> Dear son,
> Beethoven has a great place in history for his beautiful music. I know you will love his music as much as I do. Hopefully this violin will inspire you to want to play Beethoven's music.
> > With much love,
> > Your father

I had forgotten the note I had written but had not forgotten that Danny's taste in music did not mirror my own. Placing the violin under my chin, I carefully turned the pegs to tune the violin, though one string was missing. No matter. I softly drew the bow across the remembered first notes of a Mozart string quartet. The resulting sound did not enchant and would have offended Mozart. I loved Mozart, especially his religious music, and also because Mozart loved dancing. The violin wasn't an instrument you could just pick up after years of inactivity, any more than you could pick up a surgical instrument, any more than you could resume, unquestioned, an old love. Perhaps I would take the violin to the local music shop and have it restored. I once entertained the idea of starting up a group of older, former musicians. The Prime Time Orchestra could still become a reality. All was not lost. Under the light, inside the violin, I saw the stamped words: 'Stradivarius model.' Would that it were the real thing, I mused.

Putting the violin back in its case, I made my way into the foyer where General Robert E. Lee's portrait hung. I had become "acquainted" with Lee's portrait while at Charity Hospital where the General kept watch over the young women in the nursing quarters. Elmira had once told me to remove my hat before passing General Lee. I was not sure if my bride-to-be was joshing or not. Lincoln was not to be discussed in her company.

The nurses' housemother knew how much Elmira admired the charcoal drawing of Lee and arranged for it to be given to her as a going away gift. The treasured portrait of Lee held a place of honor in our foyer.

The Steinway grand piano I had bought for Elly was prominent in the far corner of the seldom used living room. The piano sat away from the windows so the sun would not fade the finish. An oil painting of thirteen year-old Elly and ten year-old Danny hung over the fireplace. The only reason I ever came into this room was to view the painting. I loved the portrait of my children. I turned on the special light that softly highlighted the painting giving it the softness of youth, the innocence, the promise. I had commissioned an artist to paint the portrait and was unhappy with it when first seeing it at the artist's studio. After three or four visits, I concluded the artist had captured Elly and Danny to my satisfaction. If I had to choose only one object I could have, it would be the portrait of my children. I took one last long look at the painting. One child was my greatest achievement, the other my greatest failure.

19

Elly's hasty marriage was a decision she had regretted. She apologized profusely to her husband of one month for abruptly changing her mind.

"Never marry your best friend," Elly told us. "The flight was longer than the marriage. As it turned out, we were simply different—out of tune with each other. All we had in common was our politeness to each other." I was delighted with the outcome, all the more so when a year or so later after getting divorced, Elly enrolled at the University of California at Berkeley where, after three years, she received her Ph.D. in English literature—with an emphasis in Shakespeare. Elly's divorce and enrollment at Berkeley had been the remedies I needed to bring me out of my long funk. I heartily endorsed Elly's decision to attend Berkeley—despite my concerns about the Berkeley upheavals Elmira had told me about. Gregory Peck had been a Cal Bear graduate. The fact that Peck was also an English major made it easier for me to accept Elly's decision to do the same—rather than becoming the doctor I had wished she would.

"Your mother and I are so happy for you."

However elated I was that Elly was no longer married, I was much more ebullient that a child of mine was out in the world, satisfied that in a small way I had introduced her to the larger world on the other side of the mountains. She would make contacts, but more importantly, she was pursuing higher goals. She would continue to dream, to aspire. Her education had only begun. Elly would never assume that graduation meant the end of striving. She would touch life in as many ways as she could muster. This I knew. My patients were suitably impressed and somewhat bewildered when I would regale them with Elly's latest travels and accomplishments.

Two plus years into her Berkeley doctoral program, Elly suggested that we pay her a visit. The trip was extra special when Elly surprised us, telling us that once she finished her doctorate, she was invited back to Harvard as an assistant professor. Elly was pleased with the invitation, not just because she was not a "big name," but because Harvard had been notoriously slow in adding women to its faculty.

"They appoint a woman about every time we land on the moon," she joked. While her appointment was not something Elly anticipated, I, of course, was not surprised. Though I could only share in Elly's accomplishments vicariously, it did not dilute my elation. I was soaring with excitement.

"I could have told you so," I buoyantly told Elly. "You are fully qualified. You are a trail-blazer. You are history in the making." In my excitement, I went on to tell Elly how fascinated I had been to hear one of the first transatlantic live broadcasts from London. And how excited I had been, contrary to the general American reaction of disappointment and chagrin, when the Russian cosmonaut Yuri Gagarin made the first flight into space with no physical harm.

"Daniel, what does that have to do with the price of eggs?"

"That shows you what man can do, the heights to which man, or <u>woman</u>, can soar."

"I could end up like Icarus," said Elly.

"Who?" I asked.

"It's a Greek myth, Daddy," said Elly. "Icarus flew too close to the sun, and his wings melted. He fell to the sea."

"The man needed a better machine," laughed Elmira.

Like Gagarin soaring into space, Elly with her appointment as assistant professor at Harvard had soared beyond the hills. As taken as I was with the live transatlantic call and Gagarin's flight, they did not rival Elly's accomplishment. Back home, when Elly's appointment had been announced, this exultant father gave Elly's phone number to a local newspaper reporter, and there was a resulting long article about the hometown's "shooting academic star." I bought extra copies and passed them around at the hospital. Then the article was carefully placed in a scrapbook.

Elly's return to Harvard had only accented Danny's floundering state. After Harvard, Danny spent several years on the "inactive list" as he liked to joke, "a near Harvard grad" he would boast after a few beers, knowing the pain that would cross my face. After dropping out of Harvard, he did some mechanic work and raced stock cars. But after too many crashes, he ran out of rides. He had passed the requirements necessary to be an emergency medical technician and segued into a stint as an ambulance driver. He became known for his fast responding time.

But basically Danny was "at liberty," though he had gotten married, in a simple ceremony, no family. Janice had been a high school classmate of Danny's. They had gone to Atlantic City for a weekend of fun and on a whim got married. Unlike Danny's old girlfriend, Joan, who had long since moved away, Janice was not pregnant. In the end though, Janice's love did not seem to be enough. Danny simply walked out of their doublewide one day, said he was going home, telling Janice he needed a few days' break.

The days turned into weeks and weeks into months, then years. At home, Danny had grown more and more distant. At times he claimed he wanted to get into his souped-up Corvette, stick his neck out, let his hide all hang out while screaming, whining, threatening down those new, clean, wide, straight, wonderful interstates to promised destinations. He was, he said, afraid by the time he reached those destinations, it would be too late—everything would be the same, no surprises. Yet he would still be a stranger. I was afraid that Danny had inherited my insecurities, my depression, my… irresolvable flaws.

After Danny had refused to go back to Harvard, I was at a loss as to how to help him. Elmira was concerned that though Danny seemed to be at loose ends, we not go overboard.

"Parents," she said, "will give a child everything at such times if they can. Along the way, we have given him perhaps too much, and this can make life seem cheap."

By this time, Elly, long back at Harvard, had since remarried. Her husband, Darren, was a vice-president of a major advertising firm in Boston. I had gotten my wish, a church wedding for Elly at the Methodist Church, where I was an elder. There was a reception afterward at our home. When Elly first informed us she was getting married again, I was not pleased.

"Darren is a MBA graduate of the Wharton School of Finance, Daddy."

Elly laughed, and told me that Wharton was the premier business school. I was suitably impressed as she knew I would be, not only with Darren's degree, but with Elly's knowledge of Wharton. It was her mother's influence. Elmira had long subscribed to a magazine called *The Economist*. I had seen a copy lying on the table beside her chair one day and browsed through it out of curiosity, noting articles on world news, politics, science, among others. *Some expert knowledge in these pages*, I thought. I asked Elmira about it, saying I had never heard of it.

"It's only been around since 1843," Elmira said, laughing.

The memory of walking Elly down the aisle is with me still, as is Danny's downward spiral that I had no answer for.

"You've been talking about opening a drugstore as long as we've been married," said Elmira.

"Yes?"

"So open one and Danny can run it."

"I don't know. Danny may too soft for business. He should be in school anyway. I mean, he doesn't know anything about business."

"What do you know? Everything you ever tried business-wise has been a disaster," Elmira said in frustration, leveling the dagger straight at my wannabe businessman's heart. My head lowered. "You bought all that bank stock because, if I remember, 'Banks don't fail.'"

"They're not supposed to."

"The Titanic wasn't supposed to sink."

"Banks aren't supposed to fail," I repeated over and over, barely above a whisper, as though I had just lost a patient. I had invested some money in a local bank that went belly-up. "Those people had no conscience, like some of those at Charity. They partied as though there were no tomorrow, as though life were a lark. The extravagance of the Twenties was responsible for the Depression."

"Concentrate on now, Daniel, the present! One sure thing I learned as a nurse," said Elmira, "get a surgeon out of the operating room, and he'll trip over the first curb he comes to. Yet he thinks he can swing oil deals in South America!"

"Broker said it was a good investment, Mama."

"We lost every red cent! No wonder he's called a broker, and I'm not your mama."

"The Rockefellers were big in South America." I said this without any rancor. My voice did, at times, quiver and simmer but never loudly. I could wait for others' revelations to catch up with mine. Like Elmira, I had faced hardships in life, but unlike her I always tried to put a white picket fence around the past where an apple pie was cooling in the window of bad memories. A white picket fence was a popular thing to see in the old movies I loved—where the husband went to work and the wife stayed home and raised the children. I had once wanted to erect such a picket fence around the old home place. Dee said it would be a total waste of money. We need to sell it, she said. For some reason, I could not contemplate doing that.

Elmira's comments about my bad business decisions were like waving a red flag in front of a bull. She knew how to bait my pride.

"Our son doesn't have a suitable personality for business," I insisted.

"What's wrong with his personality?"

"Nothing. I just feel he's got to aim higher. He should be in school."

"He hasn't been in school in a dozen years! You will never get over it, will you?"

Perhaps Elmira was right. There was a sudden sad dark cloud hovering over my head. "It's just a school, Dad," Danny had said. "Harvard is not just a school," I had replied. "It's the oldest school!"

"I want a contract between you and Danny soon, or else I'm leaving," said Elmira.

"You don't mean it," I said.

"Don't test me."

I acquiesced to Elmira's wish.

TO: Daniel Friend, Jr.
FROM: Daniel E. Friend, Sr., M.D.
May, 1982

This is to certify that Daniel Friend, Jr., and Daniel Friend, Sr., do hereby enter into an agreement to pursue an enterprise, we hope, for gain not only in the present but for the future as well. I have spent long hours, as it were, attempting to analyze the local areas, as well as some other areas, to invest in. I would like for the two of us to work for our entire family in a mutual partnership. I am, at present, thinking of establishing with you a drugstore or two or three or possibly a speed auto parts store. Plans to investigate these will begin immediately. You could be the manager of each. We could begin one store right away. I hope you will agree with these decisions. A large amount of money will be necessary for these endeavors. Costs are high, and a hefty loan will be necessary, but I believe I can arrange the financial requirements. These thoughts and endeavors are not for gain of profit for me but for you and your sister and mother. The business will depend on your cooperation with each other for a very fine future. Realizing no one is perfect and many ideas can be improved upon, I will concede to any errors and will be open to constructive criticism. I hope all of the remarks made above will serve to continue every family bond of love I have tried to set forth. I will be glad to participate with you and/or all family-related persons as a silent partner. With great respect and admiration for you, Elly, and Elmira, I remain,

Sincerely,
Your Dad,
Daniel E. Friend, Sr.

I called Elly and insisted that she be a part of the "family business team" being formulated.

"Drugstores sell everything today," Elly told me. "They look like supermarkets, Daddy, like Walmart. What the customer wants most is convenience, more to choose from, and above all—low prices. I'm just saying things have changed. I don't want you or Danny to be disappointed."

"I don't read the Wall Street Journal, maybe I should," I told Elly.

"Me, too," she said. "Darren is so well-informed, and he has schooled me."

"Mrs. Albright had to close her grocery store. You remember her?"

"Yes."

"She knew all her customers and gave them all credit. I stopped by to see her, and the store was closed. I had no idea. Elmira called her to pay our respects, said she seemed fine. Your mother laughed remembering how Danny would lift a cookie or two out of the cookie bin while Mrs. Albright was in the back."

Elly laughed when I first asked her to be president and CEO of the family business.

"Listen, Daddy, I don't know anything about the business world."

"You have a doctorate."

"In English Literature. My business experience is limited to Shylock in *The Merchant of Venice*."

Elly said she thought there might be something simpatico between Shylock and me. I was not Jewish, but as a man from Appalachia I understood the slights one could suffer from other men. "You and Shylock," Elly mused, "are both complicated men who have reasons for the things you do. Shylock was a shrewd businessman and a disgruntled father, and disgruntled is what you will be, Daddy, if I am involved in the family business."

"I want you to be a partner in any such enterprise, Elly. Otherwise I can't do it."

Elly reluctantly agreed, reiterating that she knew nothing about business.

"Your mother said that liability has never stopped me from thinking I am the next Rockefeller."

———————

Before the Pleasant Valley Drugstore got out of the planning stage, Danny suffered a heart attack. It was his good fortune to have been on an ambulance run when it occurred, and his fellow driver had him in the emergency room within minutes.

"He could have died! They said he was blue in the face."

"Danny's heart never stopped," I assured Elmira.

After four days in the hospital, it was determined Danny's heart had not sustained significant damage, but the drugstore's grand opening was postponed, and for the next three months Danny was treated like a celebrity. That Christmas was a joyful one. Danny's barber came to the house and gave him a haircut. Family friends sent baskets of fruit and other assorted gifts. His fellow ambulance and stock car drivers came by to visit. Then there was Sonny, who came to see him everyday. Sonny had been born with Down's Syndrome. His was a moderate case. Danny and Sonny played Shoots and Ladders, Sonny's favorite game. Danny almost always lost, and not intentionally. Their friendship was the purest I had ever witnessed. Danny's wife, Janice, was, I had to admit, a constant care-giver to Danny during those days, even though Danny had left their home.

When Elly returned home for a couple of days after the New Year, she found her recovering brother in his rocking chair smoking a cigarette. He had been feeling so well that he had become rather cavalier about his condition. I hesitated suggesting to Danny that he curtail his destructive behavior.

"I have a doctor," he had reminded me.

"At this rate, you'll live another year if you're lucky," Elly said.

"You trying to scare me?" Danny grinned. "Everybody ought to have a heart attack at least once. It puts a glow on your cheeks, right, Daddy?"

"He always has a lot of junk food around. He's getting a pot-belly. Some sitting up exercises would help," said Elmira, when Elly expressed her concerns.

It had been a "minor" heart attack, "nothing to sweat," Danny told everyone. He had consented to slow down after his heart attack but indulged in the occasional beer along with a good steak... "man's gotta have a little fun." The two things he couldn't seem to cut back on were cigarettes and potato chips—the chips that came in a can. He was a two pack-a-day- and a three-can-a-day-man. He had been given a clean bill of health and told to not smoke or drink and to watch his diet.

"Doctor told me not to smoke,
Drink nothing stronger than a coke.
Ain't even supposed to hear a dirty joke,
For laughin'll strain my heart."

20

Love and companionship did not mean enough if you were not around to give it or receive it. It was the doctor's wife's lament, especially at night.

"A good man is hard to find," I once wrote to her. Elmira's good man was indeed hard to find, those days. I was spending more and more time at the hospital and my moping around when at home got on Elmira's nerves. She wondered why I bothered to come home at all. What was the good of loving someone who wasn't there?

"Doctors!" she said. "Best advice I ever gave Elly was not to marry a doctor! You all think you're omnipotent. Most arrogant of the lot are surgeons!"

"You married one anyway," I reminded her.

"Notorious shot givers, too."

Being a doctor's wife meant cold dinners and, many times, lonely dinners.

"You never appreciated dinner at home with your family anyway," Elmira complained, "Never went to one of Danny's baseball games."

There is no way to make up the lost time. Missed dinners, old photos, old songs, old disappointments, old denials, pages of old letters, snatches of old conversations, old heartaches—bits and pieces come and go, calling out to those no longer reachable from a place ever illusive but still there. Something is still there. My utter devotion to doctoring, ironically, was a defense against a lingering despair, a futility realizing all that I could not fix, make well. Would Elmira have been happier with someone else?

When the children had gone off to school, I would eat supper almost every night at the hospital. Elmira retreated to bed with her books. When she ventured out, which was less and less because she hated getting dressed, she headed straight for the book store. She would load up on books, some of which, she said, were sort of interesting and a couple would be downright dull, but all of which she read. Books became her life. Somehow I hoped to rekindle the physical life we had so enjoyed.

I understood her love of books, but the trashy romance novels left me perplexed. That was not Elmira. Books on politics, especially corrupt politicians, was her milieu. She could have taught a college course on contemporary American history. She could expound on why FDR was not right about certain things, why Johnson was courageous, why Carter was underrated, why Reagan was maybe the most adept politician. Elmira had her books, and I had the hospital. We were two loners with separate addictions and separate bedrooms. "Just an old Victorian couple," Elmira said.

One night Sister and I arrived home to find Elmira, thankfully, still up. Having no key, I knocked on the kitchen door....then again...and again, much louder.

"Who's there!?" Elmira finally said loudly.

"It's us, Mama. Who else are you expecting?"

"Your mama's dead, Daniel. If you don't stop calling me mama, that's what you're going to be!"

"What? Please open the door."

Elmira turned the latch and slowly opened the door, lowering a rolling pin she was holding as she leaned out the door.

"Why didn't you answer me?" she asked.

"Didn't hear you."

"Scare me to death. There has been a rash of burglaries in town. Where are your keys?"

"We must have left the keys in the car," I said to Dee.

"Reckon we might have," said Dee.

"Be sure and wipe your feet," Elmira said. "Since when does the Greyhound Bus deliver passengers to their doors?"

I ignored her casual question, wiped my shoes on the mat. I was dressed in my usual "scrubs."

"Help me, will you, Mama?" Elmira took my briefcase as I made my way to the kitchen counter, setting down a bag of groceries.

Dee, having dutifully wiped her feet, was in her nurse's cap and uniform. Her plain long black coat was open. Her right arm was in a splint. Two weeks prior, she had fallen over a rock while making her nightly trek from our house down to her house, breaking her arm near the wrist joint.

Dee went straight for her mail as though expecting something special. Elmira had placed Dee's mail most every day for the last thirty-five odd years on the small wooden desk near the breakfast table. I saw Elmira look at the smudges of dirt on my "scrubs."

Elmira shuffled away from the doorway back across the kitchen and placed her rolling pin in a drawer. She hit her sore toe on a chair and emitted a howl of pain. It reminded me of father's howl while he held mother's dead body.

Dee turned on the small desk lamp in order to see her mail.

"Close the door," Elmira barked. "It's cold out." I retraced my steps and shut the door.

"It's warm out, Mama. It's August."

"I've been cold all day in this barn." Elmira shuffled over and put her arm across the bag of groceries. "You never answered my question. A Greyhound Bus? Your car stolen?"

"No," I said.

"Left the keys in it again, didn't you?" There was a long silence. "Daniel," said Elmira looking me straight in the eye. "I will stand here till I fall or hell freezes over."

"We don't want to bet on which event occurs first, do we." I did not mean for my attempt at humor to fall so flat. I was, even under the most trying of circumstances, always polite….at least I tried to be. Cold, hard, soothing reason, I had learned, would win me what I wanted. I did keep a detailed memory of all the personal slights. It was a character flaw, but it didn't harm anyone. I tried to always put myself in the position of the underdog.

"Tell me what happened. I mean it," Elmira demanded. There was a long eye to eye pause.

"We slid off the road and got stuck," I said sheepishly.

"You had a wreck!"

"No."

"What would you call it?"

"—An incident."

"Incident my foot. You've had a lot of 'incidents,' lately, Daniel Friend. You had a wreck, didn't you?" Dee was conspicuously silent. "Speak up, Dee. What happened?"

"Nothing really, just an incident," said Dee, looking up from her mail.

I looked straight ahead as if trying to remember whether I had had a wreck or not. There was a demand in Elmira's tone as she nodded her head.

"Uh huh, he had a wreck. Didn't he, Dee?"

"We're fine," said Dee flatly.

"What happened to your arm?" Elmira asked.

"Oh, you know, I broke a bone."

"Your left arm, Dee. There is a bandage there that was not there when you two left this morning."

"It's just a scratch," Dee said and went back to her mail.

"Stop stonewalling! You had a wreck. Admit it."

"I was just backing up."

"You can't back up. You can hardly go forward. You've got that back seat so piled with junk, you can't see out the rear window."

"Oh, Mama, I know that road like the back of my hand."

"If you call me Mama one more time…." She pulled a cutting knife from its holder.

"Now Elmira," I said.

Dee, concerned for me, casually walked over positioning herself between Elmira and me.

"You really don't value your life, do you, Dee?"

"I was just going to help Daniel with the groceries. I have a few things here."

"You ride with a man who cannot drive to save his life, and you interject yourself between a mad woman with a knife and her husband."

"Coal truck ran us off the road," Dee said. I had over-reacted when the on-coming truck seemed to be over the center line as it came around a curve. Dee had been worried about me because I had not been as talkative lately on our commutes to and from the hospital. My habit of drumming the steering wheel with my fingers had gotten more agitated, more pronounced. Dee had seen my leg twitch nervously. She had suggested we spend that night at the hospital since we had been so late getting off because of an emergency operation.

"We rolled down the hill, landed on the railroad tracks," Dee said with some amusement, trying to lighten up the situation.

"Right side up," I said and explained that I had run off the road and when I tried to pull back on, I accidentally hit reverse and the car lurched backward down the hill. When the car settled, it took a moment to realize that we were not injured except for the small cut on Dee's arm. This must have resulted from the broken windshield.

"Thank God for looking out for us," said Dee.

"Thank that old tank of a Buick," said Elmira.

"Don't make cars like they used to."

"No indeed," said Dee.

"Don't make a lot of things like they use to," Elmira said.

"Remember our Packard? Now, that was a car. The Packard would have come through the wreck un-bloodied."

The Buick could in no way replace my beloved Packard, which had been discontinued, so I drove the Packard until it gave out like an elderly patient who simply got tired. I had been very upset, in mourning, when my Packard had to be put to pasture, could not watch when the tow truck came to take it away. Elmira did the deed while I was at the hospital.

"A tour bus driver saw us go over the hill. He came down and got us out."

"We had to crawl out the window," said Dee. "Some of the passengers came down and helped us back up the hill. Driver told me I was lucky I didn't break the other arm. The bus driver wanted to take us to the hospital but we told him there was no need. He got out his first aid kit and bandaged my arm. The tourists insisted the bus driver give us a lift home.

"You came home on a bus? On a Greyhound Special?" asked Elmira.

"The tourists said they were already late and a little detour wouldn't hurt," said Dee. "They were from Iowa—on a tour of the mountains. They were very concerned about us. It was very sweet. They liked the way I talked."

"Said your talk was like music, Sister."

"Wonder they didn't ask me to sing," laughed Dee. "One woman said when they crossed the state line they all cheered. They were delighted to find out that there really was a West Virginia. She said it was like they had discovered the lost city of Atlantis. Bus driver said they were glad they got to meet a couple of genuine hillbillies and said we looked like we could use a little moonshine. That got a big laugh, didn't it Daniel?"

"Yes. They thought we were 'colorful,' Mama."

Dee finally finished unwrapping the big package she had received in the mail. It was a huge Bible with a white cover and gold-leaf edged pages. "This is the Reverend Parker special edition. Beautiful, isn't it? I remember the first Bible I presented to you both. It was a red-letter edition. You remember, Elmira? All the words spoken by our Lord were printed in red."

"I'm sure the Lord liked that. I read where Reverend Parker was arrested for soliciting a prostitute," said Elmira. "I guess he was just spreading his ministry to those who needed it most."

"It's got the big letters, Daniel," said Dee, ignoring Elmira's comment and showing the Bible to me. Dee and Elmira saw my hand shake as I picked up the Bible. I suspected Elmira had noticed my tremor before but had not said anything about it perhaps thinking it was one of those things that would go away on its own. I knew it would not. I was relieved to feel the shaking stop once I grasped the Bible.

"Look at this cover, feel it," I said, rubbing my hand over the cover. "Isn't it grand?"

"Where are my pills?" demanded Elmira.

"Tour bus driver took us by the all-night Convenient Mart," said Dee, attempting to rescue me.

"Bet they loved that," said Elmira, knowing it took Dee an hour to buy six cans of cat food.

"They did love it," I said. "It was an outing with the natives."

"They were a little disappointed not to see any Hatfields or McCoys or fiddle players," said Dee.

"My pills, Daniel?"

"I prepped another Caesarian section today, gave the patient a transfusion. She's a tubercular case with eight months gestation."

"Somewhat anemic," Dee said, nodding her head.

"Quit stalling! Where are my pills?"

"Your pills must have fallen out of my pocket while we were rolling down the hill."

"I have no intention of walking around with headaches! I'm not about to suffer because I'm denied proper medication! My dizziness and hallucinating, my doctor says, are caused by depression."

"What doctor?" Dee was truly perplexed. "There is no other doctor who could possibly be better than Daniel."

"There are other doctors," said Elmira, defiantly.

"Not like Daniel. He knows what's best."

"Your brother is a wonderful doctor, Dee. Good at remembering milk and bread, putting up shelves, but he's very undependable about my pills!" She then turned back to me. "You've never had a headache in your life."

"About to get my first one."

"You certainly are." She retrieved the rolling pin and wagged it at me.

"I'm still pretty agile, Mama and I've got plenty of life insurance, but it's payable only in case of accidental death."

"You don't make out a will, insurance won't do us one bit of good."

"The brain must produce its own remedy," I said.

"My brain needs a little help. So don't tell me. I was a registered nurse for twelve years."

"You were the modern, ideal nurse."

"Not quite, I didn't put out like all your others. I should have."

"What?"

"Put out!" The pain in her leg forced her to sit down.

Dee put a couple pieces of mail under her arm, pulled a flashlight out of her pocketbook and headed for the door.

"Sorry, Sister. I'll walk you down."

"I'll be fine. See you in the morning. Good night," she said and hurried out not wanting to risk further injury.

"Good night." I knew Dee would be careful. Forced to miss two days work hurt her far more than a broken arm. I closed the door as the hall clock struck 1am.

"The clock's working?"

"Just don't look at it."

"I can hear it."

"Oh, for God's sake. I hate to be the one to tell you, but time doesn't stop even though you don't hear it."

"I was teasing you, Sugar."

"If you don't bring my pills tomorrow, I will order a case of the best Tennessee scotch whiskey your money can buy. I need a good stiff drink to numb the pain in my toe."

Years ago, I strongly disapproved of Elmira's having as much as a single cocktail in the evening, which is all she rarely had as far as I knew. I do not drink or smoke and do not like coffee. It was not so much being a puritan as it had just never been part of my life, and being a physician might have played a small part. Elmira's stepfather had been a heavy drinker, and her mother would imbibe to keep him company.

"Just because your life is boring does not mean mine has to be. Since you are rarely home at cocktail time, I happily fix myself a drink, put my feet up, and pick up my book. It is very comforting. It would be nice if you saw fit to join me, but that you never have is fine. I do not hold it against you. However, if you continue to nag me about my nightly cocktail, you will drive me to excessive drink."

"I'll get you some pills, but you want to be careful."

"Don't start…I've about had all I can stand of your wallowing around in self-pity like a pig in slop! Danny is not going back to Harvard. Your hounding him about school was undoubtedly a contributing factor to his heart attack."

"Let me do that," I said, seeing her pull at the bandage on her big toe.

"I know how to change a dressing," she said.

"You were the best nurse I ever worked with."

I went into the pantry to get some gauze and ointment, eyeing the level in the whiskey bottle. Every so often I would make a mental note of the whiskey level, comparing it a few days later. Pulling a chair close to Elmira, I bent down and gently lifted her leg, resting it across mine, and slowly unwrapped the bandage on her toe. This was the most intimate we had been since…well, I could not remember when.

"You didn't mean it, did you?" I asked, softly.

"What?"

"Putting out," I said, shyly, as though tasting something foreign. Elmira's stack of romantic novels flashed in my mind.

"What if I did?" She gave a little smile. "No, I didn't. You were supposed to come home early to change the dressing on my toe. You were also supposed to help me get some packages out to Elly."

"Looks like you have an infection."

"I keep that nail short."

"Looks like you filed into the tissue."

"I can't wear a shoe. It hurts."

"I think it will be better by morning. Are you seeing another doctor?"

"What if I was?"

"That's fine."

"I was bluffing, but I may be forced to check the yellow pages." I looked at her, and she smiled. "I was unable to sleep because my head was throbbing, and my sore throat was worse and my nose was stopped up—sinus trouble, which affects my breathing and forces me to sit up in bed. My left hand hurts, but my right hand is the worst. Dee and I, are a couple. My writing is getting worse and worse all the time. I finally gave up, got out of bed, put on my housecoat and came down here. All these aches and pains make me feel old."

She wore a worn green terrycloth robe and bunny-rabbit slippers. The ear of the right slipper was missing. She had cut open enough room to allow for her injured big toe. I never talked about being old—older, yes, old, no. "You could have your face lifted, nothing wrong with that."

"My face doesn't hurt! What's wrong with my face?"

"Nothing. I am not unhappy with how you look. Don't misunderstand me. You are a beautiful woman. You just want to look as young as your heart, Mama. There's nothing wrong in fixing the external features to match the inner feelings. We're all the same. A little facelift is like the makeup you use. It's just there to help."

"You're getting in deeper and deeper. Stop talking, Daniel!"

Discretion being the better part of valor, I left the room. I tried never to give a bow to age. You simply go forward. My concern was about what you could do to better yourself. "Everything is possible." This was my mantra, and in that I felt very American. To live up to my mantra was a high wire act, and I occasionally fell.

The dimly lit hallway gallery of family photos that I had long ago helped Elmira to frame and hang was a testament to family. A photo of a small shingled house made me stop. Like Elmira, I had liked our old house before I decided to do a massive renovation. It was a huge disruption to the family. But at the time there was a picture in my head of what I wanted my house to look like, and I was determined to make the picture come to life. There was a photo of me as a student standing on my head in front of my alma mater. There were so many photos:

Elmira and Dee receiving nursing degrees
Me in surgeon's apparel
Me standing between the two nurses, Elmira and Dee
A moderately-sized Colonial house
Me holding baby Elly
Elly, with golden curls, playing with a toy John Deere tractor
Four-year old Elly holding her baby brother
Elly as a cheerleader
Danny with his hot-rod
Elly "posing" at the Steinway grand piano
Me in front of the hospital
A huge rambling stone house
Elly, in cap and gown, in front of Harvard
The family at Harvard

21

The Pleasant Valley Drugstore would be reminiscent, inside and out, of earlier times, with a soda fountain and jukebox. Danny had spent practically every day of his three months' recovery planning the store.

"This is not going to be a boring drugstore," he exclaimed. "I'm gonna put this place on the map. The store will be a tourist attraction." I liked hearing Danny's excitement because he was following his heart and intuition. When cleared to resume his life, Danny took a road trip around the tri-state area to visit all the drugstores, taking pictures, having them framed and hung. He visited antique stores to find pharmaceutical supplies and colorful advertising signs. Up in the attic, he found my first doctor's bag from when I used to make house calls. In it was a drug kit that had never been opened. Danny put them all on display along with old prescription books and stethoscopes. It was a museum. Danny joked he would charge admission.

The Pleasant Valley Drugstore was going to be "civil and soulful." He said the town he had grown up in was losing its soul. "Or maybe, I'm just feeling old before my time," he joked.

He wanted the store to be the kind of place where people could spend a whole afternoon. As a child, Danny would sit for hours in Mr. Hooper's store reading comics. So he put a comic book rack in the pharmacy. He had a large collection of his old comics that he put on display under glass. He hoped the local kids would spread the word that they could read comics at his store, eat ice cream, and drink Coca-Cola. He called the corporate offices of Coca-Cola hoping they could help him locate some old-time glasses with Coca-Cola written on them in white lettering. They did arrange for him to buy an old time Cola Cola vending machine.

"Just a sentimental fool. Me and the penny," Danny laughed.

Besides Danny and the druggist, Janice would be the only other employee. The closer the Pleasant Valley Drugstore opening day got, the more Danny wanted to get it right. He said that Mr. Hooper's store had a certain smell, a sweet smell.

"Everything from lipstick, ice cream, and pharmaceuticals—those things you seemingly can't do without—they all make me feel homey, intoxicated." To that end, to help bring back those old comforting, familiar, smells, Danny installed old wooden flooring and found some old wooden cabinets to hang.

But it was getting harder to get the locals to notice these sweet smells. The outside world had intervened. Everyone had a television. There were too many cars whipping by at warp speeds down the interstate with out-of-state license plates. The word "drugstore" was passé and had been for years in parts of the country. At least that is what Elly had told us. But Danny was charging full speed ahead, a race car with no brakes.

———————

It was the end of March, and not surprisingly the month was going out like a lion. The family was standing by, steadfast, bound together yet remote from each other as only members of a family can be, I guess. All were bundled against the cold, collars turned up, arms folded tightly against their chests, freezing, except for me. I was having a wonderful time at the grand opening of the Pleasant Valley Drugstore, a "family business." I wore a suit and tie but no overcoat.

"You catch a cold, I don't want to hear about it."

"Elmira's right, Daniel," said Dee.

"Jack Kennedy never wore an overcoat for such occasions," I reminded Dee when she mentioned I might catch cold.

Danny looked positively splendid. He was dressed appropriately for opening day in a buttoned up black woolen topcoat with a scarf around his neck and earmuffs. He was happy and excited. His heart attack, if not forgotten, was definitely on the back burner. Elly and Darren, with their son Doug, had made the trip. Elmira, Dee, Janice, and Danny's friend Sonny were also in attendance along with a smattering of neighbors, a few of my hospital colleagues, and some former and current patients of mine.

In the middle of my speech, as I was thanking everyone for coming, the "Star-Spangled Banner" was heard.

"What in the world is that racket?" Elmira asked.

"The paper said the high-school band would be performing today at Walmart's opening," offered Dee.

The grander grand opening was across the state line in Kentucky, but within shouting distance of the Pleasant Valley Drugstore's West Virginia location.

"Walmart lined the Kentucky politicians' pockets," Danny said.

"Doesn't surprise me," said Elmira.

"They got all kind of concessions," said Danny. "They put an exit off the interstate that's right by their parking lot. Walmart's doing what the ice did, messing up the earth."

Danny, to my consternation, had protested a few times at the Walmart construction site with all the energy of his old anti-war protesting days at Harvard. The Kentucky state police were not as forgiving as the Harvard administration had been. A state trooper paid Danny a visit and curtly told him to get his butt back across the state line. So Danny bought a bullhorn, like the one he had used up and down the Charles River in Cambridge and announced his protests from safely across the state line.

"That atrocity went up like a weed," he said.

Walmart had not entered my consciousness, being convinced that the family drugstore would be a success, no matter. If our store provided personal service combined with my good name, the customers would come. After all, I had delivered half the town.

"I'm worried," said Danny.

"Walmart will help our business, son."

As the national anthem played, I thought it appropriate that everybody stand at attention.

"Can anybody tell me why <u>we</u> are standing at attention?" The voice belonged to Janice.

"It's our national anthem," said Dee.

"It's Walmart's celebration," said Janice. "Over there—in Kentucky!"

She snapped a military point toward the Walmart camp.

"Doesn't matter. I stand every time I hear it," replied Dee with more than a touch of pride.

"Every time?" Janice smiled at Dee.

"Every time," said Dee returning Janice's smile.

"Your aunt's a regular jack-in-the-box," said Janice to Danny.

"It's Daniel's patriotism, his dedication, desire, tenacity, along with his imperturbability, and his undying faith that make him such a..."

"Pain in the ass," fumed Elmira, interrupting Dee.

"An American, a patriot," said Dee, matter-of-factly.

It was impossible for me to continue with my little welcoming speech. Once the *Star Spangled Banner* ended, there were raucous cheers from across the road.

"Who's bright idea was this?" asked Janice.

"This is Daniel's day," said Dee.

"It's not his day, it's Danny's!" Elmira fumed, turning so abruptly toward Dee she practically knocked Elly off her chair.

"You're right, Elmira, I'm sorry," said Dee. "We big sisters sometimes get overly zealous. Right, Elly?"

"Right, Aunt Dee."

We all wanted the store to work for Danny, that he would be able to make it a go on his own.

"Sam, Sam, Sam!" The God-like voice coming through the loudspeaker came from the other "grander opening." It announced there was "plenty of hot coffee, hot chocolate and fresh donuts." Hearing that, our little crowd got sparser.

"It's Darth Vader," said Danny.

"That's all the people need around here, more donuts," Elmira quipped as a couple of my overweight ex-patients were dodging a coal truck getting across the road to get their free donuts.

"The more donuts, the more patients," said Elly.

"Who's Darth Vader?" Dee wanted to know. Doug explained Star Wars and the dark menace and said he had a Darth Vader doll.

"Ah! Thank you, Douglas," said Dee.

"That loudspeaker voice sounds like James Earl Jones," said Elly.

"He's the actor who played Darth Vader," Doug told Dee. "I saw him in a play in New York."

"Give me a 'W,'" boomed the loudspeaker.

"This is a farce," said Janice.

"There's that old fool, Fred Cooper," said Elmira. "He stands at his window waiting for Daniel to come home so he can sniff out free medical advice."

"It's a great day for our community," I said.

"That free-loader is always telling me how well his boys are doing. Always asks about you," said Elmira to Elly. "He never asks about Danny."

"W" came the roar from the Walmart crowd.

"Louder," came the James Earl Jones' God-like voice via the loudspeaker.

"Louder!" Elmira called out to me.

"Give me an 'A,'" called the loudspeaker while I was trying to be heard, though I wasn't sure why.

"Being a family man..." I tried to raise my voice.

The crowd across the way roared out "A."

"Did you say "family man?"

"Yes, Mama."

The loudspeaker called for an "L," and the crowd responded with gusto.

"Gimmie a squiggly!"

"Oh boy, oh boy, oh boy, oh boy," exclaimed Sonny. "Oh boy" was Sonny's favorite expression. "You do the hoochy-coochy, and you squiggle all around."

"You do the hokey-pokey and you squiggle all about…" Danny corrected him. Elmira told them to cut out the "shenanigans," and gave a sharp look to Dee, who was laughing at Sonny. Danny and Sonny called out in unison,

"That's what it's all about!" Danny put up the palm of his hand, and Sonny gave it a slap.

The loudspeaker called for an "M" "A" "R" "T."

The crowd roared the individual letters in return.

"Now what does that spell?"

"WALMART!" Came the joyous response.

"Public enemy number one," shouted Danny.

"And who's number one?"

I halted my comments to listened for the answer.

"THE CUSTOMER!" yelled the crowd.

"The customer is always right," I said. I went on about how much I appreciated the love of my family and "the support of our friends," though several had deserted ship. I thanked those remaining for coming and explained that the mayor couldn't be there because of a conflict in his schedule.

"He's across the road where all the votes are," said Elmira.

"We look forward to serving our community," I said. "A growing town, rates well, not dirty with crooks and bums."

Once again came the Walmart crowd's boisterous chant, "SAM, SAM, SAM…."

"They are so rude," complained Dee to Elmira.

I remained ever cheerful to the few faithful freezing souls. I regretted that the Pleasant Valley druggist, "a professional with degrees from top universities couldn't be with us today."

"He's probably hung over," said Janice.

"A fine man our druggist, fine personality, peach of a fellow, a real gentleman. Fine wife too… Clean too, fellow Rotarian. Prior owner of a drugstore," I enthused.

"It went bankrupt!" said Janice, just loud enough for me to hear.

"Phil the Pill," as many knew him, was rumored to be a source for buying under-the-counter prescription drugs. Nothing was ever done because, Danny said, "The sheriff was paid off to keep his mouth shut." This had all been mentioned to me, and I tried to find another applicant for the job, but no one else applied. I stopped talking long enough to complain to Elmira about Janice.

"She's an agitator."

"She's your son's wife." At that point Elmira rose from her seat, pushed me aside and told Danny to stand. She then introduced him as the president and manager of the Pleasant Valley Drug Company. The loudspeaker boomed,

"Folks! Sam is talking to me from the other side! Hal-la-lu-ya!"

Danny waited till he thought he could be heard. "I got this thing about drugstores. Any of you remember hanging out at Hooper's Drug?"

The crowd noise of "Sam! Sam! Sam" shut Danny down for a moment.

Sonny yelled, "Danny, Danny, Danny!"

"Reading comics, eating ice cream, real ice cream, out of a dish! Drinking coca-cola out of a glass! The place was civil. It had soul. It was a genteel place."

"Ain't this a handsome building? Downright beautiful. But it's just a building," said Darth Vader.

"That big blue windowless box?!" shouted Danny. "Walmart ought to be arrested for littering, defacing the earth. Annihilation!"

"Walmart's about people and love. Family. Plain- folks. Standing tall, looking each other in the eye, talkin' the straight talk."

"Darth Vader Sam sounds like a good ole shit kickin', hard as nails, hell-raisin' hillbilly, full of fire and brimstone," said Danny, feeling suddenly exhilarated, as though recalling the glory of his Harvard protesting days.

"Do it, try it, fix it. Help people grow and be all they can be is what Walmart's all about. America's store!"

"Listen to 'em. 'We are the world.' They think they're Walt Disney! That sucker's a little greedy, too, and probably just as cheap! Excuse me a minute folks." Danny suddenly left the podium.

"Did you hear that, Mama?" I asked. "Walt Disney?"

"This is Mickey Mouse all right," said Janice!

"There's goes our name." I stood up. "Folks," I said to the few remaining brave souls, "I apologize...we'll be dancing shortly."

"Dancing?" Elmira was incredulous. "Did you say dancing? We are freezing."

"We want to feel good about ourselves, gain confidence in ourselves, keep improving ourselves, proving worthy of your commitment to Walmart!"

There were more shouts of "Sam, Sam, Sam!"

Sonny yelled, "Danny, Danny, Danny" as Danny was back at the podium hoisting his bullhorn. Dee and Janice joined the chorus—"Danny, Danny, Danny!"

"They ought to be arrested for littering," shouted Danny through the bullhorn. "This place's under siege with bullshit! We're drowning in it. Annihilation! How do you like that, Sis? One of your big college words, ain't it? You impressed, Daddy?"

"Words are like scalpels," I said to Elly. "Wonderful instruments, but you've got to know how and when to use them. Philology."

"There can't be a better definition for annihilation than Walmart," said Danny through the bullhorn. "Isn't that right, folks? Even that doesn't do them justice. I'll have to think of a new word."

"Neologism," I said. "That's what it's called."

"What?" asked Dee.

"When you make up a new word," I explained. "Right, Elly?"

"Yes...I believe you're right, Daddy."

"There are six-hundred thousand words in the English language, and thousands more are added every year." I had kept a series of little black books over the years in which I would notate new words that I came upon. But I could not think of a better word for this debacle than Janice's "Farce." *It was unfortunately true*, I thought. It certainly was far away from the questions of life and death that I had faced most days of my professional life. I had tried to do so with some bit of grace. Maybe this was all just a bit of distraction from my intimacy with death. If so, I was grateful.

"I believe I'm adscititious to this life," Danny said as he walked away from the speaker's stand. "Bet there's a word you don't know, Dad."

"Boy's right, I don't know that word. Do you Elly?"

"No, Daddy," said Elly, laughing. "Danny has one-up on you, Daniel," said Dee.

"I will have to look that word up," I said.

"Sam, Sam, Sam."

"Who in God's name is Sam?" asked Elmira.

"Sam Walton," I said.

"You know, John Boy and Grandpa." Dee was referring to a popular television show, *The Waltons*, "Walton's Mountain is just down the road from where the Carter family grew up. There was a lot of creativity on Clinch Mountain."

Janice and Sonny had joined Danny, cheering in unison, "One, two, three, four, we don't want your Walmart store!"

"Walmart. Where another day, and another dollar still means something. You're 'sound as a dollar' at Walmart."

"Since you're on a first name basis with Sam," said Elmira, "why didn't you ask him to reschedule the circus?"

"Because Sam Walton is dead."

"Is John Boy, Sam's boy?" asked Dee.

"No, no," I said, feeling a pinch of exasperation in my voice.

"Together-ness, responsibility, honesty," came the Walmart cry.

Danny, Janice and Sonny countered, "One, two, three, four, we don't want your Walmart store."

"Work, neighborliness, thrift," countered the Walmart chorus.

"This is the battle of Jericho, and the "Wall" will come tumbling down!" yelled Danny through the bullhorn, as he, Janice, and Sonny marched back and forth.

"Determination, discipline, perseverance," continued the Walmart chant.

My grandson, Douglas, was having a ball. He had joined the march and was going full-out on the "one, two, three four, we don't want your Walmart store."

"Independence, respect, courtesy…"

"This is embarrassing," I moaned, cupping my head in my hands.

"I want to invite all of you now to come and join our family, join and be Martinized, be all you can be!"

"Somebody cut the ribbon," said Elly.

"WALMART, From Our Family To Yours-America's Super Store. We sell everything—prescriptions to pet food."

My head lowered in prayer.

"WE SELL FOR LESS, WE SELL FOR LESS."

Danny handed the scissors to Sonny who cut the ribbon while the photographer's camera clicked away. *God Bless America* was being played by the Walmart band. Everyone at both celebrations began singing the song. I sang in full voice. Dee joined me. Danny, Janice, and Sonny were laughing at the absurdity of it all, then started singing themselves, almost unconsciously. Even Elmira joined in, as did Darren, however softly. I saw Elly's eyes take us all in—her husband, son, brother, mother, me, and aunt as we sang. Patriots all, no different than the folks at Walmart's celebration.

I felt a snowflake on my cheek and looked upward. The cold weather had turned what was supposed to be rain on our parade into a light snowfall. This was a good sign, *God's blessing* I thought, as I looked up and smiled at Elmira, thankful for her arm across my shoulders drawing me close. We were both thankful for the love that had produced our two wonderful children. Danny was smiling. The look on his face was one of peace. I remembered what a vulnerable boy he had been and still was. I had wanted to put a warm blanket over him, protect him. When I looked at Danny, I saw the part of myself that I never wanted to see. My behavior, in trying to do everything, had been atrocious, and my love had been selfish. I had not felt with him. I had tried to put him in my shoes.

My heart ached for Danny, knowing how much he wanted the store to work. After the song, Dee suggested we say a prayer. Elmira took the Lord's name in vain as heads were bowed. Janice snapped a photo with her instamatic camera.

22

Walmart was the social event of the season. The local paper hailed Walmart's arrival as an economic boom for the area.

"You'd think it was the second coming," Danny said.

The drugstore managed to co-exist with its monolithic rival, though Walmart's little Thanksgiving morality play, "The First Thanksgiving," performed with deer hunters wearing Pilgrim hats and smiling Indian braves dancing real Appalachian dances to authentic Appalachian folk music was a little too much for Danny's teetering world.

Danny had his own plans for the Walmart Thanksgiving celebration. He had invited a newspaper reporter along to witness what he promised would be a colorful protest. According to the subsequent newspaper article, Danny and Sonny donned Pilgrim hats, and Janice adorned herself in a very sexy and revealing low cut Indian outfit that was sure to draw the attention of everyone including the police. Danny and Sonny constructed a large turkey using chicken wire covered with newspaper for Janice to hide in, â là the Trojan horse. During a lull in the festivities Danny and Sonny wheeled in the turkey, and when it was in place out popped the scantily clad Indian princess. She was an immediate hit.

"How low will the Wal go?" Danny shouted

"They'll rob our graves and steal our corn and beans and spread their diseases!" Janice and Sonny answered.

At this point Danny and Sonny looked at Janice in her sexy, skimpy dress and asked,

"How much is that dress?" And Janice answered,

"Ask the kids in Bangladesh!"

To Danny's amazement most people seemed to love their little show—and booed when the trio was escorted off the property by Walmart security police. There was lots of laughter and applause. Janice was even asked if she would appear in the local Christmas parade in her costume.

Danny was pleased when he saw their little protest not only on the newspaper's front page but also on the late night news with a close-up of Janice. I was not thrilled when informed of the event by the druggist "Phil the Pill," who blamed "the scandalous event" on Janice, "the instigator." The newspaper photo of Janice was like some party girl at the local roadhouse jumping out of a cake. All so undignified.

"That's what you get from her kind," I told Elmira.

Dee tried to calm me and reasoned that all the news coverage would help our business.

———

Danny exhaled slowly, hearing Christmas music courtesy of Walmart. The cold heavy overcast air could not keep the music from penetrating the drugstore. It was Sunday and I had stopped by the store after church. Janice, dressed for her appearance in the annual Christmas parade, entered, carrying a frozen turkey. Danny shut the door on Walmart's *Santa Claus Is Coming To Town.*

"That music's gonna drive me nuts," Danny said, running his hands through his hair.

"Keep your hands outta your hair," said Janice. "You're not supposed to touch the plugs." Danny had recently had a hair transplant.

"You're late, Pocahontas," said Danny, looking at her skimpy Indian princess outfit, that had attracted so much attention in their Thanksgiving ruse at Walmart. Janice said the outfit she wore had been modeled on a cowgirl outfit that Danny had seen on a police-woman posing as a prostitute he had encountered in his first year at Harvard. I remembered only too well.

Danny took a long drag on his cigarette and put a quarter in the jukebox hoping Willie Nelson would soothe his nerves.

"Shouldn't smoke in the store," I said. Danny ignored me, which I thought was probably good.

Inside the drug cage, Janice set the turkey down and removed a key from under the counter to the refrigerator, which housed the perishable drugs. Danny shook his head as she removed the lock and opened the refrigerator.

"What are you doing?"

"What does it look like?" She was bent over making room in the refrigerator for the turkey, her short Indian princess skirt hiked up over her panties.

"I'm sure all the old geezers will like getting an eyeful of your butt on the float," said Danny.

"There'll be a lot of young geezers in the crowd, honey."

"You can't do that," I said, watching Janice about to stuff the turkey into the refrigerator.

"You want salmonella poisoning?"

"Is it quick?" Danny asked.

"Quicker than cigarettes, but the result's the same."

As Janice wiggled the turkey into the refrigerator, something caught her eye, and she reached further in and pulled out a whiskey bottle.

"There's already a turkey in here. Wild Turkey."

"Oh, …my God…. Jesus, oh, no, just great," Danny said, spitting out his cigarette. The health inspector just shows up, unannounced. It will probably be today."

"Well, thank goodness you found this," I said, picking up the whiskey bottle.

"Thank the turkey," Danny said.

"Whose bottle is this," I asked

"Your fine pharmacist's," said Danny.

"Where is our drug pusher?" asked Janice.

"It's Sunday," said Danny.

"People don't take pills on Sunday? Suppose a guy comes in and needs a heart pill?" Janice asked.

"He can go to Wal-Wart," Danny snarled.

"You can bet your butt that's what he'll do."

"This town's getting to me," said Danny, "cheap motels, every fast food joint you ever heard of. Hold-up city." He took a seat on one of the old fashioned spinning stools he had installed for his soda fountain. "Makes me tense." He took a spin and then lit another cigarette.

"Please don't smoke, son."

"You're talkin' to the wind," said Janice, rolling her eyes. Then to Danny, she said, "Have a shot of Wild Turkey while you're at it."

"We gotta get rid of that," Danny said pointing to the whiskey bottle. He took another spin on the stool. "Deck The Halls" was seeping through the walls. Danny got up from the stool and went to the door.

"Turn it down!" He yelled and shut the door. "Jesus. Being vandalized. Walmart mutants. They shouldn't be allowed to breed. Spreading like the plague."

"You want quaint, I'll make you a quilt," Janice deadpanned as she proceeded to get the store ready to open.

Danny knew no one was ever going to describe the town as quaint, what with Jiffy Lube coming to Main Street. Sometimes he agreed with his mother who had never quite forgiven me for moving to this "God-forsaken place," even though she appreciated its raw beauty.

"Beauty, no matter how majestic," I had told her "cannot camouflage the hard life of the people. You can't deny the hardships you see in the people here."

Danny certainly didn't deny them. He understood the expression "getting fucked" in this part of the world. That expression was foreign to me, but it no longer shocked me. What I didn't understand was why Walmart, which hated unions, was so welcomed in a union state.

"Politics honey, politics," said Janice.

Danny looked around the store, appreciating what he had created.

"This is a drugstore, not a superstore," said Danny, sitting back down on the stool. "There must be," he mused aloud, "something in man makes him want to get bigger and bigger."

"It's America's mantra, honey," said Janice. "Stop waxing philosophical and get busy."

"You know what I want?" Danny asked me.

"No, son. What is it you want?"

"I want real," he said. He had said that to me once before when I was trying to convince him to attend Harvard.

"Real is right in front of your eyes," Janice said leaning across the counter, her generous bosom fairly exposed in her Indian princess garb. I turned away. "Real's not living at home with your parents. Sorry, Dr. Friend." She walked around the counter and sat on the stool next to Danny, putting one hand on his shoulder and her other hand on his leg.

"What's wrong?"

"There must be a million different places," Danny said. "We're all selling the same shit. We're all buying the same shit, eating the same shit, watching the same shit. It never ends. One big blur. We're the turkeys. They're going to gobble us up."

"Where did Walmart start?" I asked.

"Where will it end, that's what I want to know," Danny replied.

"Aunt Judy's Uncle Bob is Walmart's "green coordinator.""

"Yeah, he coordinates all the green going from everybody's cash register to Walmart," said Danny.

The Walmart Christmas music could still be heard. Danny dropped another quarter in the jukebox and turned the volume up.

"Walmart's raping the land, America's dream run amok. That predator's crushing everything in its path, country's under siege. It's a stampede. Get out of the way or be trampled! We need action. We got to organize, arm, and eliminate. It's going to be the Hatfields and McCoys all over again."

Danny sounded just like my father and seemed just as lost...the same patterns...father to son to father to son.

"I like it when you get passionate about politics or the hills," said Janice, "but I am concerned how your passion is slipping into something more—rage maybe. You are such a romantic. Don't be paranoid."

"Only the paranoid survive, baby. Even the pigeons have left. The courthouse ain't good enough anymore. Pigeons are hanging out with everybody else at Walmart."

"Too easy to blame Walmart, honey," said Janice. "All that matters is the competition's fierce and half-way fair. After that, it's dog-eat-dog."

"Yeah, but that St. Bernard needs a leash."

Danny put out his cigarette in the Philip Morris antique ashtray. His head was throbbing. It was the same blinding headache he got at times when he was at Harvard. Smoking "grass" was the only sure-fired remedy he had told Elly. The drug was cheap and easy to buy in Kentucky where marijuana was called the state flower. But this was a workday; so three Bayer aspirin chased by a coke would have to do. Danny ran his hand across the red linoleum-like counter top. His star was now the Pleasant Valley Drugstore. He was clinging to its sides like a child to its mother, telling everybody that with all his inse-curities and fears, he belonged. I heard him, and knew his frustra-tions and limitations. Truth was Danny hated all the paperwork, in-surance claims, Medicaid forms and the realization that he could never sell Kleenex as cheaply as Walmart.

"I'm crazy," he said, rubbing his temples.

He had marked down the prices as far as he could, but people could still buy cheaper at Walmart. I blamed myself because I had not foreseen this "David versus Goliath." The questions and uncer-tainty that Danny was voicing reminded me of the Thirties, when people faced such hard times. But the people then, fought and won gains. It seemed the challenges were greater now because of places like Walmart, which, as Elly had told me, imported so much from China and other countries.

When I mentioned the hospital had several empty beds, Danny laughed.

"People around here clean up their acts, I'll be out of business." There was not a chance of that happening. The people were just more desperate, not having insurance or money for a doctor. I saw this every day. It was hard to find something, a little interlude, before the next crisis. The word was, Appalachia was the leader in prescription drug consumption, and Walmart, like all the other drug runners, wanted in on the action. Over-prescribing was an abuse that I warned our doctors about. The hospital saw far too many overdoses. Nine out of ten deaths were because of prescription drug overdoses. Some patients couldn't grasp the concept of why they even needed a prescription for any drug, even morphine. Most drug users got their drugs from family and friends. There had been a rash of drugstore break-ins. One druggist was shot and killed. Danny wanted to install a security screener.

He was delighted, he joked, rather amazed, at the number of pills people in the hills took for every conceivable ailment—especially blood pressure and heart pills. When the coal mines were down, anti-depressants were up. For the drugstore's first couple of years, Danny couldn't keep enough pills on hand. He would go home tired but pleased that the store was holding its own considering Walmart's own pharmacy had been running for a few months.

"It's only a matter of time before we go into free-fall," said Danny. "At least," he told me, "I'm not some airhead writing up phony prescriptions for his friends. Why is it so hard to find a good pharmacist?"

"No pharmacy grads want to come to southern Appalachia," I told him.

"I'm telling you, for all those young buckaroos out there itching to find their way in life, it's pharmaceutical school."

Danny lit up another cigarette and ran his fingers through his new garden patch of hair. He glanced into an old advertising mirror for Burma Shave and checked out the hair plugs above his forehead that Janice had persuaded him to try. He laughed thinking they looked like the little grass plugs his mother had planted in the front yard hoping for a thicker bed of grass. Danny leaned in close to the mirror examining the hair plugs to see if they were taking.

"I think you need to water them," laughed Janice.

"Yeah, a little fertilizer probably wouldn't hurt," said Danny.

We laughed, and then Janice saw me glance back toward the empty drug cage. It was Sunday, and "Phil the pill" did not work on the Lord's day. I could not fault the druggist for not working on Sundays.

"If a patient needs an emergency operation, do you say wait till Monday?"

"That's different," I said.

"What's different about it?"

Danny selected another song on the jukebox. At that moment the first customer of the morning entered and neglected to shut the door, allowing *Joy To The World* to crash the party.

"Lovely day, Mrs. Meyer," said Janice. "Stop in to see your boyfriend?" There was no reaction from Mrs. Meyer. Janice unplugged the jukebox.

"What are you doing?" asked Danny, as he got up and shut the door.

"Sick and old customers don't want to hear it," whispered Janice, pointing to Mrs. Meyer.

"She can't hear it, can't hear anything so stop whispering."

Janice saw Mrs. Meyer down one of the aisles writing on a pad.

"Good day, Mrs. Meyer," Janice said, loudly.

"Every day's a good day if you wake up when you're my age," smiled Mrs. Meyer putting her pad and pencil into her pocketbook. Janice asked if she could help her find anything. Danny got up from his stool and told Janice to leave the customer alone.

"Customers don't like to be bothered."

"I'm just trying to help her, she's our guest," Janice said evenly.

"That's the truth 'cause she never buys anything," Danny said to me as he sat back down. Mrs. Meyer seemed to see Danny for the first time.

"Hello, Danny," said Mrs. Meyer, with a big smile, and pinched Danny's cheek. "Oh, hello, Doctor Friend. I saw you in church this morning. I haven't seen Mrs. Friend at church for a long time. I hope she's feeling good." I smiled and said she was.

"Perhaps I should stop by and give her God's regards."

I should have told her not to bother. Elmira could not abide God's people knocking on her door.

23

The crab apple tree in Elly's front yard was blooming, a fragrant white cloud. The cardinals were eating from the kitchen window feeder. On this spring day, I could feel a bounce in my step, as though I had just come out of the operating room after delivering a healthy set of triplets. But nothing seemed to generate my excitement more than having persuaded a family member to do something that I absolutely knew was for his well-being.

After two years of the kindest cajoling—a confiding whisper was how I conversed when plying my art of persuasion—I had convinced my son-in-law to erect two stone pillars and a gate at the base of their steep pine tree-lined macadam driveway that emptied out onto Foxhill Road. The name "Foxhill" had been a source of inspiration, of imaginative joy, for I made up a story populated with foxes for my young grandson. I had never read or told stories to my own children when they were young. I had, for the most part, not been involved with child rearing at all.

I was rather amazed that Darren spent so much time at home.

"He took the week off," Elly told me.

"Well, he could not have done anything more to make me happier than agreeing to build those stone pillars."

"Darren loves it."

"Your father wanted to fence in our whole property with those white fences like they have down in Lexington."

"Would have set our property off, Mama."

"We're not raising horses. Why do men feel the need to do that, build walls?"

"Daddy likes projects."

"His projects end up being my projects because he never has the time to finish them."

Elly produced a letter from her son's baby book. "I don't think I've ever showed you this." She handed the letter to her mother. "It's from you to Doug, Daddy, right after Doug was born." Elmira took the letter and read it aloud.

Daniel Friend, Grandfather
Jan. 12, 1978

My Dear Grandson,

I understand you have not been eating too well but seem to be making some improvement. I got reports there is some difficulty in getting your covers to stay on. I believe we can blame that on the covers, and not on your moving, squirming, and turning.

You know it might be best for you to eat a little more anyway—whether you actually like it or not, and drink more milk. You want to gain some weight. It would please your grandfather so much. In a few weeks you can take over the rule of the house and tell your dad and mama they have ruled a long time and it could be possible they are tired and would greatly appreciate your help. You need not tell your dad or mama but call your grandmother to one side and break the news to her. I believe she will help you out on that score as I know your grandmother very well.

"You don't know me as well as you think."

I have a lot of suggestions but believe it might be best for me to impart this information privately to you in order to keep your mama and dad off guard!! I can explain this more fully and at considerable length when I see you. You and I together can put our wits to work, and Boom!! Who knows just what might result? All said and done, I can see we have a lot of work cut out for us, and we will have the most wonderful time getting the work done.

"Your father was already planting the seed to work his wiles," said Elmira with a sideways glance at me.

The whole world is now before you. You are born in a great era when so much is being done. Wish I could live a lot of years with you and see you grow and succeed in finding life. There will come some hard gloomy days in your lifetime as come to all lives, but I like to strike adversities head on in order to eventually be able to legitimately and honestly win.

Your life is now in its first chapter. Your time is limited so don't waste it living someone's else's life.

"You had your nerve. You certainly wanted Elly and Danny to live your life." *That was true*, I thought.

Write each chapter and each volume carefully for a great worthwhile ending. I am so thankful and so proud of you and yet have not seen you. I hope to see you in a short time. Here's wishing you a real good night's rest and sleep. Tell your mama, dad, and grandmama—goodnight.

Love,
Your Granddad

When Elmira finished reading the letter, there were tears in my eyes. I had determined long ago that I would not display my emotions in public. There should be some mystery. Though the day Elly had her church wedding, I bawled like a baby when she and Darren left our home as husband and wife.

"Don't be too disappointed," said Elmira, "if Douglas drops a little once in a while. He has to relax and have some fun. Daniel would never let Danny do that...or you either for that matter." She took a piece of toast and started back upstairs. "I can feel a headache coming on."

Elly and Darren had moved to the third floor bedroom so Elmira and I could have their bedroom. Elly had thought that the extra stairs would be too much for Elmira, who tended to spend quite a bit of time in bed.

Before breakfast, I had scoured the steep hillside property for just the right stones for the pillars, not just any stones, but the right stones—the corner stones, the facing stones, the stones that would top each pillar, "like a fine icing on the cake," I told Darren while proudly showing him my treasure of stones. The hillside property reminded me of my old home place in rural western Virginia. Darren had loaned me a pair of garden gloves as I was careful to never let my hands come in contact with any foreign element.

"A surgeon can't be too careful," I explained, "like a pianist. Finding a stone reminded me of when I used to pick blackberries. Some of the best ones, the bigger ones, were down low, hidden. Some of these stones didn't want to be found."

Elly smiled seeing me in my short-sleeved shirt and tie.

"Have located several well-proportioned stones for our pillars, Elly, fine specimens." Elly fixed me my usual breakfast of dry toast with apple sauce. I ate and looked over some drawings Darren was showing me of the prospective stone pillars. "Look at these, Elly," showing her the renderings. "They are going to be grand." I saw her give Darren a glance. He was smiling and dressed appropriately for hard labor.

"Elly, check on your mother in a bit."

"I will Daddy."

"She took some antibiotics before we arrived. I believe she has a sub-acute and chronic sinusitis especially in the right frontal portion. I'm concerned about her taking too much medication."

Attached to the stone pillars would be an automatic hand crafted metal gate, which I had offered as a gift. It would not be just any gate but the right gate, a gate announcing to passers-by that someone of "significance" lives here. A metal artist had been located who proceeded to weld together a finished product, based on my vision of two winged horses and a charioteer.

When we finished breakfast, I said we had better get started gathering the stones I had located. I shot up and headed to the door, causing Darren to laugh.

"Daddy thinks he's won the lottery," said Elly. "He's in a state of pure bliss."

"That's right, Elly. I'm very pleased."

"The Phaedrus," said Elly looking at the plans.

"What?" Darren was puzzled.

"The soul is compared to a pair of winged horses, the noble and the ignoble," laughed Elly, calling back to her minor in philosophy days. "You are the noble horse."

"That's nice," Daniel said, smiling.

"Daddy sees himself as the charioteer."

The price for the finished endeavor was $5,000. This was startling to Darren. "This would not do," he said. How could he possibly accept such an extravagant gift.

"This is outrageous," said Darren. "It's just a gate. $5,000!"

"It's my pleasure, Darren."

"We know, Daddy. Besides it's too late now, the gate is already paid for. What did I tell you? Daddy is very good at the art of persuasion, the soft sell approach. You must always be on guard because when Daddy desires something, irrational though it may be, he will not rest, come hell or high water, until his desire is fulfilled. Now it is. You have been tamed and humbled, dear."

"You make it sound like a jail sentence, Elly. You are going to scare Darren."

Darren had been tamed and humbled the first time he had met Elly. She had finally found time from her teaching schedule, having recently returned from Berkeley to assume an associate professorship at Harvard, to clean her apartment. One morning while dumping her trash, she met her second husband. She literally threw her trash on top of Darren because he was down in the trash bin looking for a client's contract he had accidentally thrown away. When Darren stood up holding his treasure, Elly was shocked and apologized profusely and then started laughing seeing shreds of paper and apple peels on his head and shoulders. Darren, though embarrassed, also started laughing. His office had been on the ground floor of Elly's apartment building. He had joked maybe he would see her again at the trash bin, but then asked her if she would like to have lunch. Darren had told of their first meeting at the rehearsal dinner the night before their wedding.

"Tamed and humbled. Yep, that's me." he smiled flirtatiously, kissing her and giving her a love pat on the rump.

"You have stone pillars to build. You are now under the rein of another charioteer. Save it up. You better go. Daddy has always had a vision of Heaven's Gate. Now you are building it for him."

"The cost is worth it Darren, trust me. I'm thrilled."

"See, Daddy loves it when he converts one of us. He's delighted you have seen the light. A successful surgery for Daddy is very satisfying, but stone pillars and a gate are right up there."

"I suppose, Elly, but nothing can compare with having a Harvard professor for a daughter."

"Don't forget it," Elly teased Darren.

Darren laughed and grabbed the drawings and his gloves.

"I wonder what the neighbors will think of the gate?"

"That we've converted to the Krishna. The road to Damascus."

"Great."

"It's done, enjoy it." Elly put her arms around her husband and kissed him. "Man is mortal. He is not perfect. Go."

"The workers are off to the fields, Elly, to collect what must be at least a hundred stones I have found suitable."

It took a full day to gather the stones and another day to set the re-bar that would support the pillars. The next day, the "fun work" began. "This is not just for the common folks. Stone work is an art, Darren. Working with your hands, like a surgeon. I see the care you take to select each stone, and how you place that stone. Commendable. I am so appreciative. This entrance will make an announcement. You have a splendid place, and the entrance will be the promise of something grand on the other side."

"People might not be too impressed with what's behind the gate. Not very grand," said Darren.

"Don't waste time concerning yourself with what other people think. That has been one of my follies. I have spent far too much time worrying what people might or might not think."

Elly and Darren had bought their home two years after Doug was born. It had been a three acre, one-time chicken and rabbit farm with an old barn and a hundred-plus-year-old house in dire need of repair and paint. Darren had taken me on a tour, pointing out all the work he had performed on the place. The three-story farmhouse had recently undergone a renovation—all done impressively by Darren.

"You've put on the petticoat," I joked, "and now you only need to dress it up a bit. A touch here, a touch there and you will have a fine spread. There is promise, great potential. It's a fine place, a fine place. Little touches like the intercom by the gate will allow you to know who your visitors are. That way you can ward off any intruders, any free-loaders, you know what I mean, riff-raff. Your wife and child will have an added layer of security. You want to think of your family, Darren. Take good care of them. You are somewhat isolated out here."

"Well, yes I suppose, but it is safe, just the occasional M.I.T. ax murderer…I'm just joking, I mean…there is a healthy competition between Harvard and M.I.T, but it is somewhat restrained."

I contemplated the various stones we had wheel-barreled down to the end of the driveway. "Yes, these beautiful stones, when you get done, will make a beautiful sculpture. You are the doctor here. You are doing exceptional masonry work. Be firm, let the stone know you are the doctor," I said, noticing an irregular stone that needed trimming in order to be placed just so. "It is protruding on the side. You may want to make an incision here," I said, pointing out what I felt was an imperfection in the stone and where I thought the incision should be made. "Only prescribe when necessary for discomfort. The stone won't need a pain killer."

Darren worked with the precision of a surgeon as he carefully chiseled away the offending part of the stone.

"Yes, sir, it's how you build a life, Darren, stone by stone."

It was the first time we had spent any time together, just the two of us. We discussed many subjects while erecting the pillars.

"Things just about always seem the same at home," I told him in response to his question about the state of affairs in the Appalachians. "Economy is the big question in the coal fields. Many thousands of coal miners are idle. Several mines have closed. Many families are in bad financial condition. If things don't pick up, the next Christmas holidays will be dull for many families. Coal is the only meal ticket for many of them."

"How's the drugstore doing?"

"I believe it's paying its way even in the poor economy. The future will tell. Fact is, we will probably put up another store in the area."

"Oh?"

"Yes, we'll use the money we make from this one to build the next one. I'd like your input on that, Darren. But from my investigation, I think the area is ripe for another store such as ours."

Darren was non-committal about being included. He said he didn't know a whole lot about the area Elly came from. He had pretty much maintained a hands-off attitude with the drugstore. He related that he and Elly had talked about whether or not the store was a good idea. The trend of going to large stores was a concern Darren said he had voiced to Elly.

"The bubble's right there in the middle," I beamed, having laid a level across a layer of stones to make sure the pillar was going up evenly. "Very good, Darren," laying the level down as I would a medical instrument. "I don't think the election back home will change much of anything, especially the economy."

Darren was ready for another stone. Each stone was deliberated over, placed and replaced, where its home should be in the pillar. With each carefully laid stone, Darren looked for my nodding approval—given only after careful observation.

"It's like pondering the set of a broken arm or the preciseness of a delicate incision. You cannot abide anything done half way. If a nurse does not have the proper tool ready when you need it, well, you have to let her know and rehearse the handing of the instrument."

"At this rate," Elly said, appearing with some lunch, "the first snow will fall before you two finish."

"You may be right, Elly. It's good exercise, especially for Darren. He's doing all the lifting. I'm enjoying it."

"Of course you are," she said, laughingly. "You're getting your way."

"I mentioned to Darren about our expansion plans for the drugstore."

"Next thing you know, you'll be cashing in, Daddy, going *public*," said Elly, laughing.

The camaraderie between Darren and me continued for the next few days. We formed a mutual admiration society. The stories also continued.

"Two sisters owned this land," said Darren, lifting a stone I had selected.

"Don't mean to interrupt your story, Darren, but you want to smooth out the mortar there," and I pointed to a spot where the cement had seeped out between the stones. "Don't want to see the cement. It will give the stones a more natural look. Like sutures, you want the stitches to be such that in time the scar will be virtually invisible."

Darren took his trowel and removed the excess cement and then went on with his story about the two sisters.

"They sold homemade bread and jams, eggs, chickens and rabbits from an old stand. I found some old boards and a sign reading, "Birch Grove Farm." Their best customer was a man who lived in the big house at the end of the road. The story goes he would stop each day in his buggy and buy something. He fancied one of the sisters. One day he stopped and the chosen sister climbed on board to never return. She moved in with the doctor, but she later died in childbirth."

"What happened to the sister who got left behind?"

"The story goes, she stopped selling her goods and for the next forty years was a recluse. When we bought the house, it had been empty for some time. It was run-down, and you sensed there had been a sad story here. It needed a family as much as we needed a house."

"Sad, yes, very sad, but you and Elly have brought it back to life. A house needs people to care for it, to do the little things to make a house a home. I enjoy our visits up here very much. You want to keep this home, Darren."

Nearing dinnertime, Elly and Elmira walked down the driveway to see how the stone pillars were progressing. They stopped a short distance back not wanting to interfere with the work at hand.

"Doesn't look bad," said Elmira as they got closer.

"They're going to look nice," replied Elly.

"I mean… your father's hair. He insists on dying it himself."

"I'll take you to where I get mine done, Daddy. The guy is fabulous."

"Doesn't want people to know how old he is," said Elmira. "You're too old to keep trying to impress people." I laughed, having learned to take my wife's ribbing in stride. She was right. I was vain and had been too concerned with myself, selfishly so. It had taken too long for me to purge myself of such folly. No longer did I mind the ticking of the hall clock. Everything did not have to be in its place.

"It's never too late to be what you might have been, right Daddy?"

That had been one of my sayings that the children were fond of quoting back to me.

"One person can make a difference. Be a leader. Success must be earned."

"That's the nail on the head, Elly. I keep telling your mother that…not to give up on me."

Elly looked at Elmira who seemed far off. There were times she seemed to disappear in an ocean of loneliness, a prisoner of its strange comfort. I suspected Elmira's loneliness was not all harbored in being a doctor's wife. It was sowed years before when her stepfather would invariably come home drunk.

"He'd park his car in the middle of the dirt road in front of our house. Once he actually plowed the car up the wooden steps parking it half-way on the porch." Elmira had told her story with no hint of self-pity. "Mom and Mr. Turley would fight right in front of me. I was a piece of furniture."

Elmira loved her mother, but resented the way she had cow-tailed to her drunken step-father.

"The two pillars and gate will double your investment."

"From your mouth to God's ears, Daddy."

"Why, it will increase the value of your home tremendously. Your children and their children will return here to the family place. This entrance will welcome them and fill them with the warmth of family history."

"I'm sure it will, dear," said Elmira.

"We're getting hungry," said Elly as she and Elmira started back up the driveway.

"We just have some finishing touches to take care of," I said.

"In marketing products, packaging is all-important," said Darren. "You know what a Glad bag is?"

"Glad bag? Can't say I do."

"That's it. People didn't know. They're trash bags. So I had to come up with an advertising campaign for Union Carbide, the company that makes Glad bags, to convince people that they couldn't live without Glad bags."

I thought about my selling fried onions.

"So I came up with an idea where an elephant stepped on a full Glad bag and the bag did not break." This seemed as exciting to Darren as removing a hernia was for me. Darren understood a doctor's passion for his work.

"That's what bought this place—Glad bags! I got to mingle with the stars. They too were looking for a good paycheck. I lounged at the Beverly Hills Hotel dining with certain celebrities in the Polo Lounge in order to convince them to pitch my products. Tom Bosley was a great pitchman for me."

"Don't know him," I said.

"He's an actor."

"Gregory Peck is the only actor I pay much attention to." I could not imagine Mr. Peck hustling Grab bags.

"I once did a campaign for anti-freeze in which a car was submerged in snow and ice for an extended period of time and when uncovered, the car started up immediately!"

"I knew I liked you Darren, right from the get go."

"I won an award for that one. I called them my "little movies." Each one would cost a couple of million." I could only marvel and shake my head at the kind of money Darren was tossing around.

"It's not my money."

"No, Darren, it isn't, but one day…it will be." Darren laughed.

I asked Darren if he, by chance, read *The Economist.*

"Oh, yes, we get it at the office. It's quite good."

This reaffirmed my thinking that Darren really was deserving of Elly. By this time, Elly and Darren had been married nine years. Later at dinner, I decided to discuss with Elly the idea of asking Darren to come on board as a consultant for the drugstore. She quickly shot down that idea.

"As part owner, I veto that."

"I want you to have an input, Elly."

"I just did. Don't mix business and family, especially at dinner. Agreed?"

"Certainly, Elly."

Later, I could not help throwing out the notion to Darren.

"This is strictly confidential, Darren, just between us that is. Perhaps we could one day go into business together. What do you think? I think you would be a tremendous asset. We need to do some advertising at the drug store. Of course not on the scale you are used to, but something along those lines. So what do you think? Just between the two of us."

"It might be a possibility."

"Wonderful. We will just, you know, keep this quiet, our little conversation. Keep it to ourselves."

Apparently, feeling guilty, I guessed that Darren did not keep our little discussion under hat. At breakfast the next morning in Elly's homey country kitchen, I felt a whiff of trouble in the air as I sat down to the table seemingly in the middle of an on-going dispute. Darren looked a little sheepish. I think he surmised that it would be in his best survival interest to play his cards close to the vest.

"You are incorrigible, Daddy," Elly said, before I pulled up to the table. "You just cannot help yourself."

"You cannot control him," said Elmira. "You can only hope to contain him."

"The family business, an oxymoron," said Elly.

"What makes you such an all—fired expert in business, Daniel, is beyond me," said Elmira with a wearisome frustration in her voice.

"Never said I was an expert. Darren is the expert, and I thought his expertise could be valuable."

Darren sort of hemmed and hawed, wanting nothing to do with the subject.

"You keep trying to tell Danny how to run the drugstore," said Elmira. "You gave all those people credit, and most of them have no intention of paying on the bills they've run up, and you won't let Danny collect on them."

"I plead guilty."

"Your pharmacist keeps insisting Danny stock the shelves with things nobody buys," said Elmira, getting her dander up again.

"The pharmacist and Danny have had a little personality clash. Phil says that a salesman must look neat. He says Danny never wears a coat and tie."

"He's not going to church, Daddy."

"He should. Be good for business if the whole family went to church." Elmira and Elly erupted in laughter. Darren lowered his head. I believed he was laughing because his body was shaking.

Elmira had soured on religion after Elly went off to Harvard. Elmira decided she had been brainwashed and stopped attending church cold turkey. This was extremely unsettling for me. I tried to persuade her to rejoin me at church, tried to convince her to get down on her knees with me in prayer, all to no avail. She said she didn't need my prayers.

"I don't need or want your prayers."

I had long nurtured the philosophy that the sun will come up tomorrow, and most things would get better by morning. "If you take care of your health, it will take care of you. Study hard and you will go far. Keep up the good work and you will always win. You're only as old as you feel. And don't forget your prayers."

Anxious to get the breakfast conversation on to any subject not having to do with Danny and the drugstore, I asked,

"Who are we voting for this time, Mama?"

"Not that scoundrel chairman of the finance committee. He and his aide—also his girlfriend—went to Florida to a supposedly very important meeting just when the legislature was trying to wind up the session."

I smiled in relief knowing nothing got Elmira started more than politics.

"The chairman had to give a report before they could finish the budget. The governor had to send the state plane to bring him and his girlfriend back. The gall! The idea! Turns out the chairman and his aide-slash-girlfriend have taken several trips on the state to these little rinky-dink meetings so they can shack-up. He will not get my vote, or yours!" She looked at me with a 'there will be no argument.'

"No, sir, Mama. He won't be getting our votes." Darren laughed now that I was in the hot seat again.

"We either get the government and all the bureaus under control or else face a civil war," said Elmira.

Her political talk was eating into work time, but Darren was finding the discussion illuminating especially when Elmira's attention turned to various presidents. He was surprised to hear her take on her favorite, Jimmy Carter.

"When the hostages were hugging and all in Germany, one of the hostages hid in his room to keep away from Carter. Every time Carter saw him, he started hugging the man and pounding him on the back. I'm sure Carter was sincere, but he overdid it. He really hoped to use that event to put himself back in the White House. It just came too late. Poor leadership. Iran just wanted to embarrass Carter. That's why they waited until Reagan was in office before releasing the rest of the hostages."

"Carter was no Kennedy," I offered.

"Especially when it came to women," Elmira countered. "Carter knew this country was going to be in trouble if it didn't get its house in order."

"Everyone thinks it's easy to be a Kennedy," I said. "Elly knows, right, Elly? If you're a Kennedy, you carry a heavy burden. Always remember the ones who paved the way. Their burden was heavy."

The completed stone pillars were massive at their base, tapering off at the peak of their six-foot height. The gate was installed late on the final afternoon of our stay. I tried to put to rest Darren's fear that the gate might be a little over the top. Though certainly eye-catching, the steeds on one half of the gate and the charioteer on the other looked proportionately true and right at home. Darren and I got into his Pontiac sedan and slowly inched down the driveway. It was a test run. When the car passed over a wire submerged in the driveway, it triggered the opening of Heaven's Gate.

"Magic," said Darren.

"Magnificent," I replied. We drove out onto the main road, turned around and came back to the entrance of the driveway. When Darren pressed his remote, we again sat in wonder at how smoothly and quietly Heaven's Gate had parted.

"Magic," said Darren again in awe.

"Magnificent," I repeated. Darren then re-closed the gate and pushed the intercom button.

"Yes?" came Elly's voice.

"You can hear me," said an excited Darren.

"Loud and clear."

"Push the button that opens the gate." After a beat, the gate slowly opened.

"Did it work?"

"Like a charm."

We drove to the top of the driveway and asked Elly and Elmira to join us so they could admire the gate. They too were suitably impressed, especially with the ease in which the gate seemed to glide open. I explained in detail the work that went into each pillar, far more detail than either Elly or Elmira wanted. Passing the medical exam could not have made me happier, as I enthused how expertly the gate had been engineered. The hydraulics worked flawlessly, allowing the gate great fluidity. I explained how the pillars were supported with metal rebar, relating how Darren and I had gone to a local lumberyard to buy the half-inch metal bars.

"Your father insisted we double the rebar."

"Just to be on the safe side," I said. "Notice how erect the pillars stand, how proportioned, the balance of each, how they taper just so. Each stone was handpicked. Your husband, Elly, has done an outstanding job. These pillars are strong, built for the long haul."

"Yessiree," said Darren, "these pillars will be here ages and ages, for the duration."

"I guess we won't have to go to Stonehenge," smiled Elly to her mother.

"These pillars and gate will announce the property. People will notice," I said with an assured self-satisfied tone upon surveying the finished masonry and iron work with my arms folded proudly across my chest. Indeed people did notice. Cars slowed on the turn as the passengers caught view of the winged gate. A friend of Darren's asked him, "Where's the Tabernacle?"

"He's jealous," I said. Then with a triumphant smile, eyes straight ahead: "Isn't it grand." I might have broken into song. "A grand entrance, a fitting entrance for a Harvard professor." Elly rolled her eyes relating that she would probably have to leave Harvard in order to gain a full professorship.

The first winter after a good snow, the gate failed to open, and Elly slid her station wagon into one of the stone pillars. While trying to extricate the car, she proceeded to slide the tail end into the other pillar. The station wagon came to a rest against the gate, prone between the stone pillars, situated such that Elly was eye to eye with the charioteer. She cursed the pillars.

"But like you, Daddy, they didn't budge."

I insisted on paying for all damages. Darren refused, saying that insurance would cover it. Would that insurance covered all my wrongs.

24

Danny sat on his red leather antique soda bar stool, spinning around and around. The more nostalgic he got, the more shattered and broken his world seemed to get. The ground was moving and changing under him, and I didn't know how to help him.

"You can't stop progress," I said.

"I'm sure as hell trying. But we cut our prices, Walmart cuts theirs, same merchandise. How you figure? We can't cut any further, down to the bone now."

"Aunt Judy said it used to be the other way around," said Janice. "When she lived in Florida, she said cuttin' prices was the only way the little guy could stay in business."

"Aunt Judy should've stayed in Florida," said Danny, exhaling, blowing a smoke-ring. I kept quiet. The store was on life support.

"She wanted to retire back home. She's a Walmart greeter."

"Yeah, well, she's retired then. Those old farts are all retired."

"Aunt Judy's not an old fart."

'Welcome to Walmart, welcome to Walmart,'" mocked Danny. Just then Mrs. Meyer came in.

"Welcome to Pleasant Valley Drugstore, Mrs. Meyer. Lovely day isn't it," I said.

"When you're my age, Doctor Friend, every day is lovely." Mrs. Meyer wheezed and coughed.

"If you need help finding anything, don't hesitate to ask," said Janice. Mrs. Meyer nodded and had another coughing fit.

"Janice?" Danny was rubbing his temples, said his head was throbbing.

Janice glanced at Danny with one of her 'leave me alone' looks. She was concerned about Mrs. Meyer, who was fumbling with something under her coat. Janice asked if she needed help. Mrs. Meyer shook her head.

"Several items are on special."

"Leave her alone," said Danny, a tired resignation in his voice.

"Satisfaction guaranteed or your money back—no questions asked."

"We need to talk," said Danny, taking Janice by the arm. "Excuse us, Mrs. Meyer." Danny put his arm on Janice's back and ushered her to the rear of the store, where I was seated.

"It's good business to talk to the customer," I said. Danny nodded and put out his cigarette.

"Aunt Judy told me how things are done at Walmart."

"She's an old fart greeter, what does she know?"

"She was night manager at a big grocery store for 30 years."

"Good for her."

"Aunt Judy says the customer is a guest."

"She's right," I chipped in.

"Stop it with this 'guest' crap, both of you. Aunt Judy's getting on my nerves," said Danny. "So are both of you." He took a breath and told Janice he was going to have to cut back because of cash flow problems. Janice looked blankly at him. "I have to let you go."

"Excuse me, I believe when you moved out, you let me go." Danny agreed she had a point.

Shortly after Danny recovered from his heart attack, he and Janice started seeing each other again, much to my despair, a reconciliation of sorts. Danny hired her, over my objections, to work in the drugstore.

"I have to lay you off until we get over the hump."

"You mean you're firing me?" Danny did not answer.

"It's necessary," I said.

"I'm his wife. I don't care if we don't live together, you can't fire me," challenged Janice, her hands set determinedly on her hips.

"Did I say that?" asked Danny.

"Who's pulled this store through while you fight with the pill pusher?" Her face was an inch from Danny's nose. "Who does the books? Who mops up? Who opens up every morning and closes every night? Me! Why? Not because I couldn't get another job—like at Walmart."

Danny just shook his head.

"I am being recruited," said Janice.

"By the army?"

"Walmart, smart ass."

"Must have forgot about your Indian princess routine," I said.

"Actually the manager was impressed," Janice snarled at me.

"I bet. Walmart has a great thirst for human blood." Danny was holding his own.

"I have been offered the chance to be a Walmart 'associate!'" Janice was rocking her head back and forth. "Stick that in your pipe and smoke it, buster!"

"Strike up the band," said Danny moving away from her, concerned for his safety. "Better duck for cover, Dad."

"They give you uniforms," said Janice, talking to his back as she followed close on Danny's heels.

"Cheap," said Danny, not turning back to her. "You want to look cheap?"

"They are not flattering," I agreed.

"They're a nice shade of blue," said Janice.

Danny laughed, "Cheap. That's all they care about—cheap."

"What do you care about, huh?" Janice was on fire. I moved off my seat and walked toward the door. "Certainly not your wife. You wanna talk cheap. Walmart pays more than you, honey." She grabbed Danny's arm, spinning him around. "I'm broke, Danny. No health insurance, no pension, no nothing."

"You're right," said Danny. "I don't blame you. Why don't you go?"

"Because…. I'm stupid," said Janice. "Because without me this place would be in the toilet. Who was out here the whole time the sewer backed up, ankle-deep in water, walking around in shit?"

"There's a customer, Janice," I said.

Janice turned around and nearly knocked Mrs. Meyer to the floor. "Excuse me, Mrs. Meyer, fecal matter." Janice turned her attention back to Danny. "Who stuck with you through thick and thin?"

"This is just temporary."

"Tell you what else is going to be temporary," she said, walking behind the counter and pulling out a handgun, pointing it at Danny and inadvertently at Mrs. Meyer. "You, darling."

"I was just joshing you," said Danny.

"Is that what you were doing?"

"I didn't mean it, come on. Jesus, Janice. I just wanted to see if I could get a rise out of you."

"Well, guess what? You did."

"Please, Janice, put the gun down," I pleaded.

Mrs. Meyer was standing beside Danny with her arms in the air.

"Mrs. Meyer is having a 'fun' shopping experience," said Danny. "Right, Mrs. Meyer?" At that point, Mrs. Meyer collapsed. Danny wasn't sure if she had fainted or died. I wasn't either. I bent down to check her pulse.

"Great! Wonderful. Hooray, Janice!" said Danny. "Customer dies in drugstore when a store employee pulls a gun!" He kneeled down beside me and noticed Mrs. Meyer's coat had fallen opened revealing the Walmart blue uniform.

"Jesus. Oh my God. She's works for Walmart! How funny is that?" Danny quickly realized there was nothing funny about it because he and Janice saw Mrs. Meyer had a tape recorder strapped to her waist. "She's wired! She's no damn missionary. Mrs. Meyer is a Walmart plant! Sons-of-bitches! She deserves to die!"

Phil-the- Pill merged from his drug cage in his white smock to see what all the commotion was about. He saw Janice holding the gun and put up his hands.

"Call an ambulance," I told Phil.

"Before or after I call the police?" he said with a tight little smile.

25

After the episode with Janice, the gun, and Mrs. Meyer, who made a speedy recovery, Danny and I headed home—in separate cars. It was before sunset, but our large stone house was situated on the dark side of the mountain. Inside the house, Danny, speeding home much faster than my very deliberate pace, was eating the pizza he had bought on the way home.

"I was reading in the sunroom," said Elmira, "enjoying the last warm rays of the day with my book. You take what you can get."

"Is that a new philosophy?" I asked. Usually the longer winter hung on, the deeper was Elmira's gloom.

"It's just a sign of getting older, maturing. Of course you would not know about getting old."

"Older, not old."

"Oh yes, I forgot. How was your day?"

"Fine," I answered.

"I've got a headache," said Danny, appearing in the kitchen.

Elmira placed her bookmark, closed the book, got up, and limped to the pantry to get her shoebox of drug samples. I would often bring home samples from the hospital that Elmira dispensed when the need arose. I did not like her taking so much headache medicine. Headaches were a state of mind, I had told her, so I finally stopped prescribing any new medicines for her.

"If I can keep my headache down to a small one, nip it in the bud, I can manage," she said sorting through the box of medicine. "All these pills and I can never find the one I need. I made some chicken salad and deviled some eggs."

"I'm not that hungry," said Danny, lifting another slice of pizza from the box.

It bothered Elmira that Danny did not pay attention to his diet. His expanding stomach seemed not to bother him. She had long decided to pick her battles.

"Afraid you've inherited my most brutal affliction, sugar," she said still scavenging the box tossing aside a couple of vials of expired drugs. "I've tried everything but decapitation. Your father thinks my trouble is sinusitis. But my sinus troubles are caused by my breathing problem. Have had it for forty-two years and expect to have it on out. I use all the little things that help. Afrin doesn't do me any good anymore. I don't know what to change to. You tell Janice?"

"I don't want to talk about it, it'll just make my headache worse." He pulled a bottle of beer from the refrigerator.

Elmira dumped the shoebox of drugs on the table.

"Try one of these," she said in a not too hopeful tone while handing Danny a vial of pills. "They don't do me any good anymore." She poured him a glass of water. Ignoring the water, Danny washed the pills down with the beer. "Wouldn't a glass of milk be better?"

Danny didn't answer. He walked out to the sunroom. The wind was howling. Would that it could blow away the cobwebs in my head, the stories of old. Danny sat down in the Kennedy rocker I bought for Elly. Elmira was ever fretful about his heart attack. She joined him in the sunroom.

"Sorry, Mom, I'm in your rocker."

"It is comfortable. I wasn't always comfortable with its namesake.... Danny? Are you all right?"

"Fine, I'm fine, just fine, real fine," said Danny, a little short and with a touch of sarcasm echoing my penchant for over using the word *fine*.

"Did you talk to Doctor…"

"My heart is fine, Mom."

"I didn't mean…I meant…"

"What?" Danny laughed. "My shrink?" He shook his head. "That guy should pay me."

"I would agree," I said.

"Talk…talk, talk. My life's an open book to that guy. He's got a flashlight."

"A flashlight?"

"He shines it in every corner of my head. I'm tired of talking, thinking, thinking about what I'm thinking and then talking about what-the-hell I'm thinking about."

Danny finished off the pizza he had brought out to the sunroom. Elmira asked him if he wanted a piece of cake. He did. She could not bring herself to stop baking the sweet goodies Danny liked so much.

"So I take it things did not go swimmingly today?"

"I don't think I can accurately describe it."

"Try," she said.

"I couldn't do it justice," said Danny, a man on a mission to eat the cake in record time.

"We can't afford Janice," I said.

"It's the pill head I can't afford. Every time I mention getting rid of him, you tell me what a fine man he is. You want to fire Janice, fire her."

"I can't help but feel sorry for her," said Elmira. "She hardly makes enough money to live on. Four hundred dollars a month what with rent and car payment, utilities, groceries and clothes doesn't go far."

"I told her."

"You did?"

"Yeah," Danny half smiled.

"Well, you see, you did it, it's over. Don't you feel relieved?"

"Not particularly."

"I don't want to know what she said because she can go on. I've gotten to where I dread to see her when she comes over," said

Elmira, raising her hands to fend off what she knew must have been an onslaught of unprintable words.

"She didn't say much."

"I don't believe that. That's not the Janice we all know and love."

"Yeah, it was pretty weird, right, Daddy?"

"Well, I'll give her credit," said Elmira, "she took it better than I thought she would."

"She pulled a gun on Danny."

"What?"

"Yeah," said Danny pulling the gun out from under his jacket. Elmira looked warily at the gun. "I told her I had to let her go, just temporary, and she pulled my gun out from behind the counter and pointed it at my head."

"It wasn't pointed at your head, boy."

Elmira was shaking her head, rather astounded. "What did you do?"

"Got real polite, real fast, very courteous, told her I was just kidding. There was a customer in the store, this old lady. I thought she was some missionary. Told her she should be up hollow saving some lost souls. Anyway Janice is wavin' the gun around and the old lady thinks it's a stick-up and passes out, and I see this wire. It was pretty damn funny. The old lady's wired. She was a Walmart plant, company spy! They were checking our prices. The biggest company in the world's checking our prices! Maybe I should've let Janice shoot me. Least my headache would be gone."

"What happened to the Walmart spy?"

"Phil called the ambulance. She was awake before they got there. She refused to let them take her."

"She's fine," I said. "Said she was sorry she had been spying, but she needed the money."

Elmira walked behind Danny and rubbed his temples and forehead. "Mama always said there's nothing more soothing than a mother's touch. Ten minutes later she'd be wailing the daylights out of me."

Danny's head massage over, he got up, took the gun, and retreated downstairs. Elmira and I looked at each other with the resignation that it is risky business to bring a child into a world. I wanted, badly, a father-son bond. So why did I do everything to resist it.

"Leave him alone," Elmira said starting down the hall. "I don't know how much his heart can take."

"Danny gets himself riled up."

"All I know is I was finally asleep on my good ear the other night, and the racket still woke me up."

Elmira was up the stairs and into her bedroom. She shut the door. I sat down on the steps and after a while noticed they had been newly carpeted and wondered when that had occurred. Getting up from the stairs, I walked over to the foyer table where the large white Bible that Dee had given us was setting. Rubbing the cover with my hand, I opened the Bible to Mark12, verses 43 and 44.

"And he sat down opposite the treasury, and watched the multitude putting money into the treasury. Many rich people put in large sums. And a poor widow came, and put in two copper coins, which make a penny. And he called his disciples to him, and said to them, 'Truly, I say to you, this poor widow has put in more than all those who are contributing to the treasury. For they all contributed out of their abundance; but she out of her poverty has put in everything she had, her whole living.'"

The passage illustrated the plight of mountain people. The coal companies kept a boot on their throats. The price for digging coal was sickness with little health insurance, making fewer dollars but paying more taxes. As Father had said, "the colored know." While I was at the University of Alabama, I had heard rumors of coloreds being forced into labor at a coal mine near Birmingham. I wondered how that was possible since slaves had been freed supposedly sixty years before. Of course no one talked about slavery back then. It was like it had never existed, but the scuttlebutt persisted. Then when Elmira's stepfather passed away, she went back home to spend a few days with her mother. During a conversation about the timber camp where Elmira's stepfather was the boss, Elmira's mother said that he used a lot of coloreds. They'd just arrest the coloreds for no reason and then take them to the timber camp. When they needed more, they'd just go arrest as many as they needed.

Looking up, General Lee met my eyes. I recalled only recently hurrying home in order to view a television presentation of "The Blue and the Grey" starring Gregory Peck as Abraham Lincoln. To appease me, Elmira watched it with me, though she felt the South had absorbed all the guilt for slavery when really the entire country was culpable.

"New Englanders had few slaves and were against slavery, at least most of them pretended they were. They weren't too anxious to abolish slavery. They had a growing ship-building industry, and many of those ships carried slaves to the southern states."

"I reckon you have a point, Mama."

"The country's economy was dependent on slavery, and the South was not going to rise again by itself. So these camps like my stepfather's were needed because of money, and the coloreds were easy prey. It was a God-awful thing, and people pretended not to know but Mama knew. If LBJ hadn't signed the Civil Rights Act, it would still be going on."

Elmira had hoped that Jimmy Carter's election would finally bring the country together. "The new South," she had said optimistically.

Having no such optimism that my endeavor would be any more successful than Carter's had been, I clutched the Bible under one arm and made my way out to Elmira's favorite sitting place, the sunroom. I looked out into the full moonlit back garden. The garden was Elmira's domain, her world. It had been my idea to install the post-and-rail fence along the border, thought it was a nice finishing touch. I liked borders, definitions. We all need boundaries, I had counseled the children. I watched the moon shadows slice a soft peaceful cool glow through the garden and noticed the big elm tree, which Elmira said was hollow halfway through. Supposed it could be dangerous, but it was still standing—like me.

Wondering about my soul in relation to death and judgment, heaven and hell as I looked out at the serenity of the moonlight, I told myself I had tried. I had re-settled safely in Appalachia, joined a church, built a home, provided the necessities for my family, supported the local government, and then went about seeing that my children were educated. I caught my ghostly reflection in the window and saw my father.

"This house don't fool anyone, don't impress anybody. Ya took yerself serious. It's jis a game. Nothin's changed. Ya may be gussied up like an actor but underneath ya wear your dirty "hillbilly" underwear jis like the rest of us ignorant curiosities, along with yer hand-me-down moth—eaten coats 'n sweaters that hardly cover yer shoeless feet shuffling,' self effacing,' what can I do for ya helplessness that makes every do-gooder tingle with excitement. Don't be so high-fallutin' 'cause it's all going to bite ya in the ass, mark my word. Yer're a cursed fool. A dead end."

Turning away from the window and my father, I opened the big white Bible again and read aloud a passage:

"He that refuseth instruction despiseth his own soul."

It was hard to unlearn old habits, to listen more, to laugh at myself. Could I make a contribution of sorts, something that would better the community? Would that bring God's kingdom any nearer? No, a pay-off is a pay-off no matter how disguised. There was no deal-making with God. The commandment 'You shall love your neighbor as yourself' came to mind. It takes practice.

"Janice is a challenge, God."

26

Danny's lair was a clutter of junk food: an empty pizza box, potato chips, a slew of empty and full Diet Coke cans, an ashtray full of cigarette butts, and several vials of pills he swallowed to keep the world at bay. All my guilt and misgivings came to bear. There was a gun case with a shotgun and a couple of 22's. A pool table, its soft felt green surface clawed to death by Timmy, Danny's calico cat, took up half the room. The pistol Janice had pulled on Danny was on the table where Danny had apparently set it the night before.

Danny was in his rocking chair.

The television was on, but neither he nor Sonny was paying attention to it. Sonny had dropped in earlier through the basement door, his usual mode of entry. He had his own key. He and Danny had been best friends for 30 years, ever since Sonny's family moved to the area because they wanted a smaller community for Sonny. On this night he was wearing the well-worn jacket of Danny's old military school uniform. It was Sonny's favorite piece of clothing. He loved it, especially the ribbons. He loved wearing it as much as I had loved seeing Danny wear it.

Danny couldn't imagine a more appropriate name for Sonny. Nor could I, because Sonny was "sunny." He was like the song I remembered singing, something about the "sunny side of life." Danny once said he had never seen Sonny sad or even upset. Danny hated anybody's making fun of Sonny. Usually it was some punk kid with squirrel tails hanging from his car antenna, yelling...not nice things, showing off. It never seemed to bother Sonny, for which Danny was grateful.

"I love you, Danny," Sonny would say. I wanted to tell Danny the same thing but it was hard. If I did, Danny would just shrug, a little embarrassed and smile.

Sonny's dancing and singing to Chubby Checkers' *The Twist* was entertaining.

"Around and around... come on, Danny, let's do the twist. Come on, Doctor Friend." Sonny pulled me up from my chair, and we did the "twist." Well, I tried but was afraid I was going to throw my hip out of joint. "We do the hoochy-coochy and twist it all about." Sonny was laughing so hard he fell to the floor but quickly got up and with unabashed, exuberant innocence, he put his arms around Danny.

"You do the hokey-pokey and you shake it all about," Danny corrected.

"Oh boy, oh boy, oh boy, oh boy!" exclaimed Sonny.

"Attention!"

Danny issued this command whenever he felt Sonny was about to become a little too exuberant.

"About face! Present arms."

"Rest," Sonny would say.

"At ease, soldier," Danny would smile.

"What's a hillbilly retard?" Sonny asked out of the blue.

"Redundant," said Danny, dryly. "Never met one, Sonny. You didn't marry your sister did you?"

"No sister."

"You too drunk to fish?"

"What?" said Sonny not understanding Danny's mocking humor about the hills.

"Forget it," said Danny.

"Guess where I'm going," said Sonny excitedly. He changed subjects on a dime.

"I give up. Where?"

"Camp."

Sonny pulled a pamphlet from his pocket and handed it to Danny. He then retrieved his favorite board game, Chutes and Ladders. Danny had once surprised Sonny by buying the game, so Sonny wouldn't have to carry his back and forth from his house.

"Want to finish Chutes and Ladders?"

"We've been playing the same game for a week," said Danny. "Set it up."

"Oh boy, oh boy!"

"A camp?" Danny shook his head while reading the pamphlet.

"Nova Scotia," said Sonny, excitedly. "Far?" asked Sonny.

"Pittsburgh's far, Sonny. Nova Scotia's in another country."

"No-va Sco-tia," said Sonny slowly.

"How you gonna get there?"

"Plane."

"Fly? A plane. No kidding?"

"Danny go?"

"Won't catch me on a plane. Besides I hate camps."

It was true. We had enrolled Danny in a summer camp when he was 10, but he only lasted a few days, and the camp director called us to come and pick him up. Elly, on the other hand, seemed to enjoy her time at camp. Danny looked at the pamphlet.

"It's an island almost. I remember there's a fort up there; withstood fourteen sieges. Piece of useless information left over from my military days. Why do you want to go to Nova Scotia?"

"Because." Because was always Sonny's answer to why.

"I don't know, Sonny. You got to be prepared. It's not for children. Says here you have to do your own housekeeping."

"Hard to find good help," said Sonny.

"Your own cooking! This is a concentration camp, Sonny. Wait till you have to clean the toilets. That won't be fun, trust me. And you don't get used to it. I don't care how much you do it. I don't think you should go."

Sonny's face turned sad.

"No?"

"I didn't mean...no. Just...It will be wonderful. When are you going?"

"Summer."

"Why the rush? That's practically tomorrow. There are a lot of summers."

"How many?"

That was a good question, I thought. Danny, I concluded, didn't like the notion of Sonny being gone for the whole summer. Summer was the time to put the top down on his convertible and whiz around the mountain roads with Sonny, who would raise his arms like he was going downhill on a roller coaster ride. When Danny would go fast over a hill, he said Sonny would squeal, loving the feeling of weightlessness, I suppose. It was crazy. Danny was missing Sonny already. Danny read aloud from Sonny's pamphlet.

"Nova Scotia: a province on the east coast of Canada. Capital—Halifax; population, 92,511."

From the television came a commercial: "Walmart. From our family to yours. Walmart, America's pharmacy, bigger and better than ever. With always low prices."

"Jesus, I bet Walmart's up in Nova Scotia, too," Danny said to me.

"I reckon."

"Down the chute!" Sonny was completely focused on the game board and delighted in Danny's fate in the game. Sonny usually won because Danny would lose patience with how long the game was taking.

"This game could take all night," Danny said as he went down the chute, backward.

"That's life," I said.

"Won-der-ful," said Sonny, smiling. He was on a roll.

"Walmart, America's store, is a great place to shop for the whole family."

Danny got up to turn the sound off on the television. He had the habit, because of his hating to hear the commercials, of muting the sound. It was like watching silent pictures.

"It's Janice!" Sonny exclaimed, excitedly. Danny and I looked over to the television, and indeed it was Janice.

"Janice," Sonny said excitedly, waving at the television. "Janice! She's a star!" Sonny was jumping up and down.

"Fucking carpetbaggers!"

"Please, boy, your language."

"Janice is a star," said Sonny.

"You should eliminate that woman," I said to Danny as he turned the sound up.

"My family shops at Walmart because Walmart sells for less."

"Eliminate. You sound like Al Capone, Daddy....It's that pharmacist I want to eliminate."

"He's a fine man. When you run below plan, you cut back. If you don't react, you can't be successful. Brandishing a gun! She wasn't qualified to work in the store in the first place."

"Job description didn't require a PhD," said Danny, landing once again on the wrong square.

"Down the chute!" Sonny exclaimed.

"You're like a puppy, Sonny. You get so excited, you're going to have a kitten." Sonny laughed. "I never win this game. Need a Ph.D. to play this game."

"Janice doesn't project a good image." A photo of her in the skimpy outfit at the Walmart Thanksgiving celebration had graced the local newspaper, which I failed to see the humor of. I seemed to be fighting predictability. It was my contention that, with her amoral advances, she had seduced our "uncertain, late-maturing, complicated, and abstracted son." That was the Harvard dean's written characterization of Danny, of which I took umbrage—never showing it to Danny. "She's got to go, boy."

"Said she'd smear the family if I let her go."

"She already has. That gun business will be all over town. Woman's too rotten to hang together. You let her bamboozle you!"

"She had a gun to my head."

"She was bluffing. You got to terminate her employment, boy!"

"She'll terminate me."

"Nonsense. Woman's only got one oar in the water."

"I win," announced a pleased Sonny.

"No way," Danny protested. Sonny pointed to where he had reached square 100. He was bouncing up and down because it had been a marathon game.

"I'm terminated," grumbled Danny.

"Son, she'll fuss and fume for awhile, then get another job and pester somebody else. We should have her arrested, carrying a concealed weapon."

"It's my gun," said Danny, referring to the pistol on the table.

"Yours? What in God's name are you doing with a gun in the store?"

"I don't want some crazy stoned-faced, half here, half nowhere, s.o.b. red neck shootin' me because I forgot to say hello."

"Preposterous."

"Son-of-a-bitch who shoots me," said Danny, getting out of his chair and picking up the gun, "better do it right. It'll be my luck some hothead'll jump over the counter and trip over the trigger."

"Put the gun down, boy."

"One of the perils of surviving in a modern world," said Danny, waving the gun. "Don't leave home without it." He then fired a shot, hitting the large white Bible I had placed on top of the television when I entered Danny's domain. Sonny hid under the pool table. Falling back into a chair, I thought I might be shot. The Bible, miraculously, was still upright on top of the television but there was a hole right through the middle of it.

"You put a hole in the Bible! It was a gift from your Aunt Dee. What am I going to tell her?"

"You were saved by the word of God."

"Put the gun down, boy. Have you lost your marbles?"

"Nervous, Daddy? You don't like having a gun pointed at you?"

"Please, son."

"Sonny's nervous. I'm nervous," said Danny.

"I hope that didn't wake your mother."

"Bad way to go, don't you think?"

"Calm yourself."

"If I 'calm myself,' everything's going to be fine?"

"You were not able to cope with school because your emotions went unchecked."

"You're agitating me, Daddy. Relax me. Be a little whimsical. Tell me what a bright boy I am."

"You are."

"If I'm so bright, why don't you let me run the store?" By this point, Danny was pacing the floor, waving the gun.

"It will all work out."

"Just give it time, huh?"

"Your judgment's impaired, boy," I said, my eyes locked on the gun.

"What about your judgment? That leech of a pharmacist is stealing us blind! Charges personal items to the store, overbuys stock, never puts the stock he has on the shelves. Lied about the amount of stock he brought from his store, which went bankrupt, I might add. Claimed he had twice as much stock as he had and most of that was in expired drugs!"

"You're not being rational."

"I know what I'm not!" Danny looked at the television and turned the volume up.

"Turn that thing down, boy. We don't need to hear her again."

Danny proceeded to empty his gun into the television. There was a loud pop and a spark of fire and then the room filled with smoke.

"You shot Janice," said Sonny.

"Yeah, she's terminated, Dad."

Danny tossed the gun into my lap and left. Sonny was right behind him.

Closing my eyes, I lowered my head in prayer and heard my father.

"Ya think the country club set cares? They're too busy feelin' superior. Ya act, ya are, but yer still an imposter. Yer like 'em who go broke 'n try to keep up appearances. Real heart wrenchin.' Ya sold yer soul, son, tryin' to run away. Yer no better than yer old man. Don't ya forgit it."

Danny and Sonny encountered Elmira limping her way down the stairs.

"Can't wait till I go deaf," I heard her say. I had to smile. "What's going on? What did you do?"

"Turned off the television," said Danny.

"Thought I heard gunshots."

"You did."

"Boom! Boom! Shot Janice," I heard Sonny say.

"Where are you going?" asked Elmira of her son.

"Nova Scotia."

"Where? What time is it?"

"Oh boy, oh boy, oh boy."

The side door slammed. Danny and Sonny were gone.

"Nova Scotia? Danny! My God, oh my God. Janice?" Elmira made her way down the smoke filled stairs, encountering me sprawled in the rocker with my eyes closed and the gun in my lap.

"Daniel? Daniel? Are you all right?" She gave me a shake. I wanted to keep my eyes shut.

"Are you dead.?

"Unfortunately not," I said, opening my eyes.

"What happened?"

"Nothing."

"I heard gunshots!"

"Nothing to be concerned about, don't get worked up."

"Don't be so damned condescending."

"Sorry."

Elmira looked around the room through the smoke as though searching for something.

"Where's Janice?"

"What?"

"Janice. Sonny said she was shot."

"No, no, no. She was on television."

"The television?" Elmira looked at the television. Smoke was still coming out of it. She walked closer and was rather dumbfounded. "The television."

"What?"

"It was a good one," she said.

The telephone rang.

"Hello," Elmira answered, abruptly… "Yes, Dee?… Yes, everything is fine. What are you doing up at this hour?… Daniel shot out the television….No, I don't think it can be fixed."

Nor could much else, I thought, as my eyes surveyed the scene—the ugly couch Danny slept on half the time—Elmira hated it. Didn't she say something about buying some material from Sears to recover it? The chairs were so far gone she wanted to get rid of them—the hardly used pool table was going, she said, even if she had to get somebody to saw it in half in order to get it out.

"All right, I'll tell him." She hung up the phone.

"What?"

"Dee says you can go down and watch television with her."

"I didn't shoot the television."

"Who did?"

"Danny."

"You're lucky it was the television he shot!"

"We've got to do something with this gun."

"Give it to me," said Elmira.

Gingerly, I handed her the gun, then got up and retrieved the Bible from the smoldering television and examined the damage.

"Let's get out of here," said Elmira. "I can hardly breath."

We made our way upstairs.

"He shot clean through the Old Testament."

"Who did?"

"Danny."

"The Old Testament's full of holes anyway," said Elmira

"God forgive us."

"He already has. That's his problem. What's yours?"

"What am I going to tell Sister?"

Elmira said she didn't know and didn't care, then—using the gun for emphasis—said,

"You tell your hired help, Phil-the-Pill, to mind his own business, stay in his own department, and show some respect. Danny needs our support. I know he's disappointed you. He doesn't have your degrees, your will. He's frustrated, and I don't blame him. You won't let him be. He's trying but he needs your help Daniel. You're ashamed of him, I know, but he is your son. He is not your employee. You are not his teacher. You are his father and he is your son." She brought the gun closer. "Are you listening to me? And don't you dare say 'Now Mama!'"

"I believe the gun's empty."

"You believe? But you're not sure."

"Be sweet, sugar."

"I'm in a sour mood, Daniel. You and Danny can't talk about the store anymore without getting into a knock- down drag-out. I've tried not to interfere. Mama was so domineering. I've tried my best not to be. She and I were antagonistic to each other from way back. I didn't understand it for a long time. She knew I didn't approve of all she said or did. Mama's idea was that every child should feel exactly like their mother did about everything, especially daughters. She was always ready to physically bring me back in line. She said she could make me quit being afraid of Mr. Turley. She used to make me go over to the beer garden to fetch him for supper. He'd tell me to scram, and I would cry, and he'd give me a dime for an ice-cream cone. Mama sure didn't say anything about Elly and Danny. Dee made up for her.

"Being an old maid didn't stop Dee from thinking she knew everything about raising children. Elly has had to listen to my complaints all her life. You men," she said moving the gun ever so closer, "you always want your women to be soft and smell nice, be there when you need us. I've always felt that way about men! I just hope Elly won't be as disappointed as I have been. Danny is always concentrating on TV. He does keep up with current events fairly well, but we rarely discuss them. I honestly don't believe you know half of what's going on, and what little you do know, I tell you."

"Yes, Mama, I may not hear all you tell me, but what I hear, I remember."

She moved the gun closer to me. I could feel the cold steel of the barrel.

"My insurance, remember, is payable only in case of accidental death or by natural cause."

"Like dropping dead over a patient one day."

"What do you mean?"

"Look at your hand shake."

"You're pointing a gun at me! My hand doesn't shake during surgery. Rock steady with an instrument in my hand. Operated four times today, felt good. Oh, Elmira, you're the only one I ever gave a hoot for." I noticed the ring on her finger, a ring I had given her so many years ago. "A beautiful ring, good grade of diamonds, white gold. Two hundred and twenty dollars, it cost…….Why have you stayed married to me, Elmira?"

"It's a little late in the day to entertain that question, dear. Trying to explain myself would be folly."

"I'm not worth your love."

"At first I wasn't taken with you."

"I remember."

"But you were persistent. After awhile I found myself looking for you when you made your rounds at the hospital. You most always stopped at my station."

"Always. The patients on your floor received extra attention."

"Sometimes I talked to you. Sometimes I ignored you."

"Painful."

"You became even more curious and, you know, curiosity killed the cat. You were adamant I go out with you. By then, my interest was piqued, but still qualified. We went out on several dates. I was intrigued, and soon it was more, much more because I felt I had found the right person, or rather you found me. You were fun. You loved movies and dancing. It was wonderful, but the hospital soon had your undivided attention. That has stood between us, Daniel. You learn to settle in. If you're lucky, love is like a warm fire on a cool night. There has been no betrayal, but you are a doctor first. You couldn't have it any other way. That is what keeps you going. I think you are most alive when performing surgery. You prepare for every surgery like you've never done it, your concentration in the operating room is something to behold. It affects every fiber of your being. It's strange, but no matter how much you try to remove your-self from your patient's sufferings, you can't, never could, even when there is nothing you can do but listen to the inconsolable. You will listen however long to the cries for one who cannot be brought back. You have never been able to emotionally disengage. They never taught that in medical school."

"They tried," I said.

"It has been a lot for you to carry all your professional life. It must be a wonderful thing to be so precise with your medical instruments when fixing an illness. There is nothing arbitrary when you pick up an instrument. I've seen it, the sureness. I've seen the satisfied look on your face after a successful surgery, and that feeling over-comes whatever personal anxieties you carry. It's been my experience that most doctors are dreadful serving their patients, but not you. You return all their calls and answer all their questions. I used to think about other men, nothing much, affection, friendship, but even that felt like betrayal, so I stopped."

"Thank you."

"You're welcome."

"If you ever decide to write a book, Elmira, you'll have some good material."

"I wonder why so many people write about themselves. I guess the books sell, or they wouldn't keep on. I wouldn't waste my time reading one of them. This 'all about me' is just a phase that will hope-fully soon pass."

The fingers on her empty hand were fumbling with a loose but-ton on her housecoat. "Sorry to ramble on."

"Thank you for telling me all this. I love you."

"And I you. But every time you come home early reminds me…. of how lonely I am. That's another thing about getting…older."

"Remember how we used to pick out our basketball teams at the "Y"? You remember? How we would bet on the games. If we could do that again, I would sing, "Happy days are here again." Dropping the Bible, I went to my knees and put my arms around Elmira's legs, clinging to her, crying. "I'm sorry. I've failed our boy. I've failed you. Don't leave me, hon, please. Pray with me." I said a few words to the heavenly father. Elmira cupped her hands around my head. We stayed motionless for a long time.

When my arms fell to my side, Elmira looked down at me for a moment—then left, taking the gun.

Father was standing over me, scolding me for crying.

"Look at ya. Bawlin' like a baby."

Picking up the bullet-ridden Bible, I hugged it to my chest.

———————————

After Danny had rendered the Holy Bible 'holier', and Elmira had again reminded me why I loved her so much, I sat embracing the Bible, grappling with what to do. I couldn't bring myself to dump the Bible in the trash or burn it—finally decided to bury it. I wrapped the Bible in Saran Wrap and found an old metal box in Elmira's sewing room she used to hold her scissors and other tools of a serious seamstress. The box was the perfect size for the Bible. I emptied the contents and then went out to the garage and found one of Elmira's gardening shovels. Putting on a pair of surgical gloves I had retrieved from my medical bag, I took a flashlight and went into the backyard and dug a hole as deep as possible. The ground was still hard, and the digging was slow. Finally, exhausted, I carefully placed the metal box containing the Bible in the hole. After shoveling the dirt back into the Bible's grave, I said a prayer.

Walking into the kitchen, I washed my hands, scrubbing them for several minutes. I did this several times a day, remembering from my medical school days the heart-rending story of the man who fought to convince doctors and nurses to wash their hands. He was scorned because they did not believe the washing of hands would stop the spread of disease. I had so instilled this hand-washing lesson into my children that they could never just wash their hands in a perfunctory manner. After drying my hands, I found an opened jar of applesauce in the refrigerator, pulled a spoon from the drawer and ate from the jar—while admiring the walls and cabinets of the kitchen which were constructed of California redwood. I had gone to the lumberyard and personally selected each board.

Early the next the morning, I phoned Reverend Parker's office explaining that I so admired the special edition Bible with the white cover and big print that I wished to have another right away. A nice contribution to the reverend's coffers was understood.

Later that morning, Dee was on her usual perch waiting for me.

"Reverend Parker's message for the day is "Forget all that lies behind, and with hands outstretched look forward to whatever lies ahead."

"We know what his hands are outstretched for," deadpanned Elmira.

"On Reverend Parker's broadcast this morning, he mentioned how he was thanking God yesterday for His presence ever with us."

"Danny!" Dee was interrupted, momentarily, by Elmira's shouting for Danny. "I know you can hear me, young man."

"Suddenly," Dee continued, "Reverend Parker became so conscious of His presence there was nothing but God. He said the feeling was still with him when he awoke this morning."

"I get the message, Dee. If you wish to be dominated, mesmerized, and flattered, you deserve what you get. Your Reverend Parker is deceived by his own ranting so please do not utter his name in my house again."

There was a lull in the conversation. The happenings of the night before loomed heavily. Finally Dee spoke; "The warm light of God fills everyone and everything this morning." It was meant as a peace offering.

"Why doesn't God's warm light melt the snow?"

"He's made it beautiful," said Dee.

"Ingratiates you one moment and sucker punches you the next."

"You can't ask for more than beautiful."

"If He can manage a virgin birth and resurrect Himself, melting this snow should be a piece of cake."

Elmira was peering out the window. The snow clung to the tree limbs and formed a soft blanket on the ground. Her perennials, those two and three feet tall, were sticking out of the snow and looked fine. The bright sunlight made the shadows starker and beautiful. Elmira's moment of reverie was interrupted.

"The drugstore business has been very trying for Daniel. Isn't that so Daniel?"

"That goes for all of us, Dee," said Elmira. "The drugstore was Daniel's idea in the first place."

"It was you, Elmira, who pushed him so hard for it. He wants to do what's best."

"Then he should stay out of it, and so should you."

It was as though I was not in the room. I tried to act as though it was just another morning.

"I won't be able to get my car out again. Nobody has the time to shovel my car out unless they need it. That barn of a garage has been door-less since the day it was built! You put it so close to the alley, you have to go back and forth fifteen times to get out. When the snowplow goes down there, it pushes all the snow and mud right into the garage, where it is now because Spring is mean."

"Capricious, Mama, spring is ca-pri-cious. Our new Buick is going to be in today. I'll leave early and pick it up on our way home.

"You look like a rag picker in that thing," commented Elmira on the coat I had put on. It was an old one that I used while I buried the Bible.

"It's an antique," I said.

"Only fitting you wear it then," she said. "I can't give that ratty thing to Goodwill."

"Now Mama."

"Take it off. You look like a hobo, a tramp."

"There is a difference, Mama. A hobo wants to work, a tramp sees physical work as something to avoid."

"Gonna ride the rails, are you? Supposing you should run into one of your patients wearing that?"

"They'll just think poor old Dr. Friend is on the ropes," I said, checking myself out in the hallway mirror. "Believe you're right, Mama. Don't think I could walk down Fifth Avenue wearing this coat."

"You couldn't walk down the alley." With that she brought me the one-hundred percent black cashmere top coat that she had bought for me one Christmas.

"There is much more Gregory Peck than mountain man in you. You have evolved into a stylish, contained, firm, gentle man with a warm smile," she said. "If you're going to play the part, you have to dress the part," she said and kissed me. "Keep your eye on the road."

27

Gardening is hard work. It had taken Elmira years to collect plants, and to arrive at a distant point where she started seeing results. When gardening, you can't be impatient. *A mature garden is a step at a time. But the reward is great or it can be like raising children*, I thought.

Looking out the sunroom window, I reminded myself to order a couple of new bird feeders for her as a birthday present. She loves watching the birds and I could not think of anything that would please her more than new bird feeders. The squirrels were always making a mess of them. Elmira complains that the pigeons are always hogging all the food and scaring the finches and cardinals away. But that's what happens. You put up a bird feeder and all the birds and squirrels come. Making Elmira happy was my new goal in life. I bought her a slingshot and several bags of marbles to use on the pigeons, never thinking that she would ever hit one. But she got quite proficient with her aim, actually hitting and knocking unconscious a couple of pigeons and cold-cocking a squirrel. The squirrel stayed down so long, Elmira thought it was dead.

"They are sitting ducks," I said, shaking my head, commiserating with the targets. But Elmira comes first in my love...over-coming pigeons, indeed over-coming all, including children and grandchildren.

"They are predators," she argued about the pigeons. "The birds are helpless, except for the blue-jays. The squirrels don't fool with them. They are feisty." That is a quality Elmira and the blue-jays shared.

The sun had dropped out of sight behind the mountain, leaving our house a little colder. Elmira planted her garden so that it would have a life throughout the year. In the winter, a few plants sufficed. The winter garden is an emotional experience for her, the textures, shapes, and how plants fade and disappear. In the winter garden, quiet is appreciated. She refuses to cut back certain plants because there is a beauty in the faded stalks of gray and brown reaching above the snow especially the grasses she plants. Elmira insisted that there is still beauty after the flowering of youth is gone. We had discovered such in our relationship, the love of old between us. There will come a winter when I will be happy, as I trust she will be, to hold hands and find contentment, much as we will when walking in her winter garden.

"Bare branches can be pleasing," she says. "It is the cycle of life." I have always leaned on her wisdom. Old age is a welcome, a privilege. In old age, one can be satisfied with less just as in the winter garden. But at this time of year, winter has a tendency to hang on past its welcome. Spring would flirt with Elmira, giving and taking at its whim, and she took it personally. She never knew when it was safe to call her yardman to help her with the spring cleanup. She enjoyed getting out, wearing her gardening gloves and knee-pads and digging in the dirt, hours at a time. When she was younger, she would put a ladder up and climb high into the trees, thinning the branches to let more sunlight reach her flowers. The crocus had peeped their heads above the snow. Elmira had made sure to cut back the dead material in order that the three hundred new daffodil bulbs she had planted in the fall would not be disturbed. The daffodils soon would appear with their fresh smiling yellow faces. The sea of yellow always made us both smile.

With the arrival of spring, Elmira found renewed contentment in her garden, romance novels and a guilt-free, overt, nightly cocktail, which I was careful not to say anything about. Dee and I were busy caring for and healing patients and enjoying our commute in the new Buick. Elly stayed "on call" as need presented itself. Sonny enjoyed his garden and continued his winning streak in Chutes and Ladders, and Walmart thrived. By now you couldn't buy a pair of underwear in town unless you bought in bulk. Janice was, to my dismay, still employed, "and still underpaid," she told Danny, "despite my television celebrity bringing in more people than we have seen in this store in weeks."

"Local woman stars in Walmart commercial" was the by-line in the newspaper article about her. It included a picture of Janice. People were coming into the drugstore just to say hello to her.

Danny's heart attack was history. He happily inhaled his pizza and cigarettes, and Elmira and I worried that life was catching up with him. The gun incident had left a residual melodramatic doom and gloom pall over the family, but the glorious warm promise of spring's last rays of sun had not yet disappeared over the mountain. Young birds were chirping their last chirps before bedding down like the neighborhood children's muffled shouts of pure joy before their mothers herded them to bed.

"The songs of spring, Sister."

"New beginnings, Brother," said Dee, patting my arm as I drove. We made eye contact. I was grateful for Sister's touch. "They are hard to resist, the sounds of spring," she said, smiling. "Driving home in spring, I love watching the sun's beautiful light on the mountain of green. It is God's simple way of restoring beauty. I am so thankful. When we ended up in the gorge that time over the hill, it was dark, wasn't it, but you could see fallen trees, trees that had rotted and been hit by lightning. Their leaves were gone, but I was in wonder,

Daniel, that so many trees were standing tall reaching for the light. And there we were a little bruised from our tumble but none the worse, for God restored our shaken bodies with His promise of spring. We too can reach for the light, Daniel. He is a forgiving God."

Spring, like the warm womb, held people on their dark porches, the only light dimmed deep in the houses keeping the moths at bay. I had been anxious for spring, the gift of a new day. Like Dee, I loved this time of year. You could smell the pawpaw trees of our youth and hear the songbirds. As a young man, I had looked forward to reading about spring baseball practice so I could take measure of where my favorite teams stood. Spring's promise heard talk of 20 game winners and 300 batting averages. I would take measure of where I stood in my life. Fulfillment wasn't beyond my reach.

Hurrying through my day at the hospital meant I could get home in time to take an early evening walk with Elmira in the neighborhood. I had promised her I would not be late.

We could hear the soft easy hum of porch conversations, the occasional soft chuckle fronting the houses up and down the streets. It seemed the warm close evening air muted all sounds till there was just the purr of contented silences. A street lamp swarmed with dancing moths and inspired children's cries to play on past their bedtime. I remembered how I had rarely seen my own children playing on the same street, playing the same games, games I knew as a child, Hop-Scotch, Simon Says, Kick the Can, Thirty-Scatter. I was pleased and surprised these games could still bring joy to children. In particular, I noticed a little blond girl prancing about. My eyes literally welled up in a combination of sadness and joy. Elmira smiled and put her hand in mine. I knew she felt my hand shake a bit. It was a struggle to keep my tremor in check. It was, I knew, a mild form of Parkinson's. It was not life threatening, but I could find no cure. So far the tremor was behaving and was not interfering with my surgeries. Elmira thought I was ignoring the obvious. I did not want the children to know.

"You're going to have to plan for this," she said. She knew it was a touchy subject. "We may need to find a place that will be easy for you."

"Nonsense. Operated two times today, felt good. Rock steady." I held my right hand up. "Just the insurance guru under my skin, second guessing what test I can order or not, what procedure I can or can't do. He finds out about my little condition, well… For a man who got his degree from a paper mill, he's pretty magnanimous. Magnan-i-mous." The word swirled around in my mouth like a good wine must to a connoisseur trying to decide if he likes it or not.

"Insurance companies, along with the coal and timber knuckleheads, are the ones making the money," said Elmira.

"Yes," I agreed. "Take a hip replacement—same surgery today and we don't make half what we used to. Wish we could do without insurance companies. I believe I'd be a better doctor without them."

"Not everyone can afford to pay."

"People can't afford insurance, makes medicine too expensive for the common man. If I could cut the insurance out, I could treat some patients for free. That big conglomerate is still knocking on our door."

"The Walmart syndrome."

"I suppose. One of these days we may have to answer the door—or close it."

"You need to hook up with that health care group."

"I will not surrender to that bunch of political crooks and their prostitute supporters. That loathsome gang is repulsive. Might as well be in bed with the Devil."

"You don't have any choice but to get in bed with them. Like it or not, it's a way of life around here."

"I know those doctors. Sellouts!"

"I believe I've heard you say, 'power never takes a back seat—only in the face of more power.' Medicine is a business, Daniel, whether you like it or not. You're partnered with a couple of those 'fine men,' and now they own more shares than you because you saw fit to give those 'upstanding doctors' a few of your shares."

"It was the only way I could get them to come to the hospital. And I didn't give it to them. They paid some money, which has come in handy."

Elmira was right. I just felt I was being undermined because I had been promised the hospital would not be sold unless I agreed, But I had neglected to get the promise in writing. "What a sorry, trashy, vulgar bunch they turned out to be, a din of inequity, in bed with the drug companies. Junkets to Hawaii. Turncoats! No loyalty or decency. They ought to be ostracized and will be if they go back on their word. I gave patients to those doctors, my own patients I had for 25 and 30 years!"

"I'm afraid nobody cares about the patient anymore."

"Patients aren't patients anymore, they're just subscribers."

We walked on in silence. I reminded myself to send Elly some extra cash she could use for little things in general. It was money Elly did not need but she always took it, thanking me profusely as she knew the joy it brought me.

After our walk, Elmira went in to fix some dinner, and I sat down in the porch rocker, papers on my lap, my head falling, chin against my chest, half asleep and half listening to old time radio and the standards I loved. Dee, still in her nurse's uniform, came up the walkway to the porch steps. She stopped and looked out over the rolling lawn greening up from the long winter.

"It is steaming, Daniel," smiled Dee.

"Keep the windows open wide tonight, Sister," I mumbled without opening my eyes.

"I opened up my whole house. The warm breeze felt so good. It must be eighty degrees."

"It does feel good," I said, my head leaning against the back of the rocker. For a moment my mind was free. I liked a high backed rocker.

"I'm glad you're resting."

"This rocker's too comfortable," I said, stretching my arms above my head and then brought my hands down to caress the rocker's wide arms. I looked at my hands as they rested on the arms of the rocker, steady they go I thought.

"Month behind on my charts. Have to see so many more patients now-a-days."

"Everyone wants to see you. You are the best," said Dee, my ever encourager.

"Well, a few less patients would make life easier."

Lifting myself out of the rocker, I walked to the edge of the porch and leaned on the banister. "Who's digging up all that dirt down by the turn-off?"

"Somebody's building themselves a house."

"A big one."

"Not as big as yours," she smiled.

"Remember coal barren Harley's mansion, Sister? He had a porch that wrapped the whole house."

"I remember," Dee said, tilting her head like a bird listening for a worm, "being on Harley's back porch a few times selling blackberries."

"Yes. Never inside."

"Not once. It's too bad old Harley's not around to see your house. I would pay to see his face."

"He'd be surprised, wouldn't he?"

"He'd be jealous, that's what," she said.

"He owned some tobacco farms, didn't he?"

"Oh, yes. South Carolina, I think. When all the commotion started about smoking, he jumped on the tobacco companies' bandwagon, real quick too. He knew which side his bread was buttered. No scruples, just indifference at best and outright greed at worst."

"You're right, Sister."

Elmira nudged open the screen door and stepped out onto the porch wearing her housecoat and carrying a tray with bowls, spoons and napkins. "Have you two solved the country's problems yet?"

"No, we were just talking about our fine little bungalow."

"Bungalow? The carpet cleaners asked today if the President was in," she said, setting the tray on the table.

"All things are possible. Each one of these blue stones was hand-chipped," I said proudly, rubbing the exterior walls of the house. "Our kitchen is all redwood, ceiling, real redwood from the Pacific Coast! This house is what we are."

"Redwood?" Elmira said, laughing.

"Yes, Mama. Our faith, love, sweat, our heart is in this house, Mama!"

"I'm not your mother."

"I know and I'm sorry. It's a habit. It's just an endearment, Mama. Sugar, I mean Sugar. Sugar's better, isn't it?"

"It's sweeter, dear," said Elmira.

"Yes it is, that's good. Like this house, it's good. Thank the Lord. With a home, a couple has more to work for, like Elly and Darren. They can equip their house to suit themselves."

"The refrigerator conked out again. Repairman made an adjustment. He had trouble finding the house. He thought it was an apartment building."

"It's us, Sugar, this house. Enduring, persevering, strong, like our football team, the Bobcats. This house suits us. It's everything I wanted it to be."

"Dusting this house is like painting the Golden Gate Bridge. By the time you finish, you have to start all over again," she said, and went back inside.

The earlier walk in the warm night balmy air had lifted Elmira's spirits. I would not have to forage for food on this night. Earlier in the day Elmira had called me at the hospital saying she felt pretty good, her hands were better than they had been in some time. She was feeling so good she had defrosted the freezer for the first time in…well, she couldn't remember the last time. She found several things in the freezer she had forgotten about. One was a quart of frozen peaches, so, in addition to some soup, she made a peach cobbler. She allowed that she was glad to finish up before the arthritis pain in her shoulder and hips kicked up. She had a zillion things to do, she said, but had lain down a while to let the pain ease off in her shoulder so that she could enjoy our walk.

"You promised you would get home in time, and you did. If you continue on your good behavior, meaning getting in at a half-way decent hour, you can look forward to homemade soup and peach cobbler on a regular basis."

Elmira returned with a crock pot of hot soup and filled the bowls.
"That's plenty for me," said Dee.

Putting a spoonful of soup up to my mouth, I pulled it back, looking suspiciously at it.

"What's in this soup?"

"Arsenic," replied Elmira. "I used a bone and boiling beef and skimmed off the little bit of fat, added a couple of bouillon cubes. You won't drop dead if you find a spec of beef."

"It's tasty, Mama."

"Yes," Dee concurred.

"This soup is wonderful, isn't it, Sister?"

"Even on a warm night," said Dee.

"Good soup, good rocker, high back, wide arms—strong, solid oak. Bought these rockers so you and I could sit out here and watch the sunset, Sugar." I leaned over and put my hand on hers. "Made a good deal for these rockers."

"You haven't made a good deal in your life, Daniel Friend."

"Got you. Best deal I ever made."

"You got that right."

While sipping her soup, Dee was reading the paper, a day late. She was notorious for talking about events days after they had occurred, even her weather reports would be a day or two late.

"It says here poor old Mrs. Hance died."

"Last week, Dee."

"I didn't know she was sick."

"She had surgery two years ago," said Elmira. "She was eighty-six. Remember her, Daniel?"

"I believe I do."

"You should," said Elmira. "You're the one who took out her gall bladder."

"Been a lot of gall bladders. You're right, Sugar. I remember. Mrs. Hance would look at her hands all the time saying how beautiful they used to be. I think she had just realized she was old."

"Well, some people don't like to admit it," said Elmira, pointedly to me, as she looked at her own hands.

"You can tell a lot about people by looking at their hands," I said.

"Didn't know you were a palm reader," said Elmira, and just then we saw a familiar figure across the street. "There's that old fool, Earl. Stands under the street light 'bout every night, waiting for you to come home so he can sniff out free medical advice."

"He's just admiring our house."

"Don't encourage him. You give that poacher more medical attention than you do your own family. He steps on this porch again, I'm going to put him out of his misery. Don't suppose you two would like some peach cobbler?"

"Peach cobbler," I said, with a big smile. "You bet we would."

"Made it today."

"Soup and a good rocker and peach cobbler can spoil a man."

"You were spoiled a long time ago. I believe Dee took care of that." Elmira smiled and went inside.

"I tried to be a good big sister."

"You were very good," I said.

"When's the last time you've had homemade peach cobbler?"

"It's been awhile, Sister. Had an acute gangrenous appendix this morning. Also did a forceps delivery. Then I had a bad thyroid. Woman had a goiter modular."

"You see those mostly in women," said Dee.

"Yes. Variations in ovarian pituitary activity may influence how the thyroid reacts. On this lady, the goiter wasn't interfering with the breathing process, but it was growing a little too quickly, so I removed it. Afraid of a carcinoma….Ah!" Elmira had returned with a pan of cobbler.

"That's a beautiful crust," said Dee.

"Yes, indeed," said Daniel.

"Warmth feels good on the joints," said Dee, spooning up some cobbler.

"It's not doing the pain in my shoulders and hips any good," replied Elmira."It even hurts to sew. I have a pile of mending you won't believe. Whoever took my toolbox better lay low." She said this without looking up. "The sewing room is off limits. When I get it cleaned up, I am going to close the door and put a sign on it to 'stay out.'"

"That's a good idea," I said, looking straight ahead, concentrating on my generous piece of cobbler. Reverend Parker's office had already delivered a new Bible exactly like the one that Danny put a bullet through. I had heard Elmira laugh when she saw it.

"I see the Bible has resurrected! A miracle!" She had asked me what I had done with the evidence. I took the fifth. So discovering that her toolbox was missing had aroused her suspicions.

"You might consider putting a lock on the sewing room door, what with repairmen going in and out," I said. It was one of those delicious shared husband-wife moments.

"What are those flowers springing up by the road?" Dee asked.

"Wild flowers. Spring Beauty and Bird-on-the-Wing," answered Elmira.

"Bird-on-the-Wing," I mused.

Tuning the old Zenith radio to the old time music station, I caught the last refrain of *Stardust*.

> *The nightingale tells his fairy tale*
> *Of paradise where roses grew.*
> *Though I dream in vain, in my heart you will remain*
> *My stardust melody*
> *The memory of love's refrain.*

Could never get enough of *Stardust*, had several renditions of it in my record collection. There had not been a better song written in my opinion. Music and the peach cobbler took my mind away from things I didn't wish to dwell on.

Finishing my cobbler, I called to mind the times when Elmira, Elly, and Dee would, in the 'glory be to God' days, adorn themselves in their new Easter bonnets and corsages and accompany me and Danny to the Methodist Church on Easter Sunday, the day of resurrection. Dee would tell me I was a good man. Everything can become new, she said. I would not get distracted, sidetracked. I would not stop nor quit. Spirituality was my quest, there would lie a truth.

The balmy night air was soothing, good sleeping weather. I closed my eyes and slowly rocked back and forth.

28

It was the end of a long hot summer, and Elly was back home on another damage control mission at the request of her mother and brother. Danny and I were at "loggerheads" over the drugstore. I remember when Mrs. Cordray, Elly's fourth-grade teacher, told her that if she didn't brush her teeth every morning, her little brother, in the second grade, wouldn't brush his. Elly did brush her teeth every morning and before bed, but Elly laughed and said Danny still got a mouthful of cavities. As far as Elly could tell, all her sisterly love and advice hadn't added up to much. Sort of like a cool breeze on a hot summer eve.

"You're like a visitor might be at some fine country inn, Daddy," said Elly, watching me rock gently on the porch seemingly removed from our house. She and Danny were seated in the old metal glider that Elly had loved as a child and then as a teenager—gliding with her various beaus. Those teenage years were the most contentious times for Elly and me, especially when she and her steady would arrive past her curfew. She would ask her boyfriend to turn off his head-lights and engine and coast down the street to our house. One late night too many, they were surprised to find me seated on the dark-ened porch, as I was on this night when Elly and Danny arrived home.

We sat in silence. Elly was fanning herself with a newspaper. There was the crack of far off thunder announcing the promise of a soothing night rain.

"Well, this is fun," said Danny. There was another long silence. "Gene's fell to the wrecking ball. Another piece of America lost."

"Nothing's lost, just can't be what it was," said Elly.

"We're well rid of certain things," I said, gently rocking.

"I liked what it was. I like having to look at a menu," said Danny. "I know it's unreasonable but I like to taste what I eat."

"I say good riddance." I just could not help myself as Elly had told me on occasion.

"Gene's was the last thread of sanity in this arm pit. Everyone hangs out at Walmart now. Damn big ugly blue box."

"Lower your voice, boy. Don't want to wake your mother." Danny got up from the glider and went inside.

"Your brother had the world on a string. Can you tell me why some people let go?"

Elly didn't know the answer, but she knew that if you're given wealth, warmth, enlightenment, and background, you have to "reach a little higher"- like the Kennedys. She had found the expectations frustrating, but she went ahead for she knew that failing to take advantage of certain opportunities would be a serious mistake. Joe Kennedy was more my persuasion than Sam Walton. A Kennedy can't be the manager of a drug store. Elly knew Danny was a failure in my eyes. You have to reach a little higher—the burden was great, the price was high. Ideally, Danny would realize what he needed to do in his own self-interest, but people in this part of the country seldom do. As Elmira says, they will vote against their self-interest every time.

"Danny lets things swallow him up. Just like my dad."

"What about your dad?" Elly asked, having hardly ever heard me talk about my father.

"I'm thankful to God you're doing so well, Elly," I said, changing the subject.

"You didn't answer me, Daddy. What about your father?"

"I'll give you a flu shot while you're here. We got an early supply of the new vaccine. Don't want to take a chance. Take care of your health and it will take care of you. Salubrious."

"Daddy."

"You're a wonderful teacher, Elly. You are molding young lives. Be nice but firm, let them know you're the doctor. Your students won't even know they're learning. Push them to do that little extra. After they leave school, they'll continue to strive for the best. They'll remember you for the rest of their lives!"

"I'm not looking for immortality, just some students who want to learn."

"They wouldn't be at Harvard if they didn't wish to learn."

"Not all students are at Harvard for the right reasons. Harvard does not like to give up on a student but some students give up on Harvard. We need to be a little more flexible in the courses we offer. Harvard was too restrictive for Danny. He wasn't prepared to pick a field of study because he had had no idea of what he wanted to do."

"Like my dad. Danny's got his head down looking for potholes. Maybe my father was right…I've been afflicted with too much pride."

"He was wrong."

"You think so?"

"You're a wonderful doctor, Daddy, a surgeon, and a husband and father, a community leader. People love you. You should be proud."

"Well, sometimes you think you're right, Elly, but you still don't win. You can't win them all, I know. You can't learn everything. But you don't give up. Like this new intern Sister told me about today. Apparently he couldn't find the patient's vein. But Dee said he didn't quit. He was poking the patient all over. She said the patient had more needles in him than a porcupine He finally hit pay dirt only to lose hold of the vial. Dee said the blood squirted up out of the man's arm…." Elly and I shared a good laugh. "You keep going forward. Why can't your brother see that? 'Early bird gets the worm. But you have to be educated to know what to do with it.' It was a concept Danny never seemed to comprehend—he won all the science awards in junior high…graduated with honors from military school. He's still young…. he's smart… I keep telling myself to let it be, but I don't…. So glad you're home, honey, so proud of you. Hope you'll be able to get some rest."

"I want to clean out my room. It looks like a teenager's museum, a snapshot of the 1960's. I think Douglas will get a kick out of my old scrapbooks."

"You have papers to grade?"

"The life of a teacher, too many students."

"And too many papers."

"Yes, and sometimes I feel, 'What's the use?' But by the time I finish grading all of them, I feel refreshed, ready to tackle the next batch… You have your charts to catch up on?"

"The life of a doctor."

Elly kissed me goodnight. I knew she had come home on request in order to have a heart-to-heart talk with me. It could wait. I turned the radio on and closed my eyes, wondering if Elmira was asleep. I wanted to snuggle up.

"Sometimes I wonder where your head is," said Elmira, walking out onto the porch.

"Believe I was dreaming, Mama. Were you saying something?"

"Christ on a bicycle, Daniel," she said, turning off the radio blaring a Jerry Lee Lewis number. "This is not the operating room."

"I play Beethoven in the operating room."

"I'm going up."

"I'll be right there."

"I'm going to read for awhile."

29

Elly and Danny were raised in that generation when children were expected to marry well, be financially secure, and live happily ever after, with their doors forever unlocked.

Other than the new pale yellow paint and the rose print rug, Elly's bedroom had been untouched since she had lived at home. Her room was a collection of memories, of how impossibly busy and full her life had been as a high school student. Not that Harvard was any less busy. Several high school and college pictures decorated the walls. There were honor-roll certificates, trophies, girl-scout patches. Framed was her birth certificate. She weighed in at eight pounds, six ounces. The bookshelves were full of her old dolls and stuffed animals, yearbooks and textbooks among the many novels and biographies. The next morning, I noticed that the scrapbooks I had placed just outside her bedroom door were gone. When I went downstairs, the scrapbooks were spread across the dining table and Elly was looking through them.

The scrapbooks documented Elly's every activity from the time she was born. She realized the inscriptions were in my handwriting. I had taken it upon myself to fill in Elly's first scrapbooks. There was the University of Alabama pennant that had hung in her room from the time I took her to Homecoming Day when she was seven years old. Years later, though I had fond memories of my alma mater, I would not allow Elly to apply there.

Included in the scrapbooks I had compiled for Elly were various newspaper clippings about my being appointed to some board or being elected president of some organization. Looking through the scrapbooks, Elly was reminded that I had been a very vital member of the community, heading up efforts to build a YMCA, establishing a scholarship fund, serving a stewardship for my church, and not only holding for many years the presidency of the Rotary believing in it's motto "Service Above Self," but serving as physician for local and state companies. I was, reported one article, "a man of many talents." There was an article detailing my delivering of triplets on two occasions—with a picture of me and the triplets. I related to Elly that I was asked to choose names for one set of triplets. I had considered names from American and Roman literature and Greek mythology before deciding upon the first name of then president Franklin Delano Roosevelt, and the first names of two World War II hero's; Dwight David Eisenhower, and John Fitzgerald Kennedy.

"Of course," Elly smiled and said, "John Kennedy would be one."

There were scrapbooks of all the yearly family trips to my medical meetings: New York City, Washington, D.C., Boston, Chicago, New Orleans, Philadelphia, Richmond, so many places I wanted my children to see, to touch. I had compiled the scrapbooks in some attempt to validate my life, to justify my life.

"These scrapbooks ….I love you, Daddy."

"I wanted you to see them."

"You and I need to have a face-to-face talk, Daddy. It is another one of those times when… as a teacher, sister, or daughter, I feel a little helpless."

"I doubt that," I said, a little nervous at what was to come. "Persistence is what separates you from the crowd, Elly." She laughed.

"You told me never to give up."

"And I know you won't."

"I couldn't if I tried."

"Morning," said Danny.

"Come in." I said.

"I was just looking at some of my old scrapbooks," Elly said, pushing them aside.

"Little young, aren't you," said Danny, "to be sifting through memories, Sis? You remember when we would both be home on school breaks, and we would watch the Late Show and then go outside to sneak a cigarette and talk till the wee hours?"

"You children were smoking?" I asked. Don't know why their smoking came as a surprise. *Undoubtedly, there were many things I didn't know and that was probably just as well*, I thought.

"I couldn't wait to get home, Daddy, and tell Danny all about school and boys and complain about how smart all my classmates were and how many papers I had to write and talks to give. You were so good. You patiently let me vent."

"I would be worn out just listening to your typical week that you delivered non-stop. It's funny, isn't it? All I wanted was out of that school, all I dreamed about. When Joan got pregnant, I thought, *great—at least that would get me out of Harvard.* Yeah, well…She got pregnant on our one and only time. That's like winning the daily double. I thought that only happened in the movies. When she had the miscarriage, I don't know whether I cracked up because I was sad or just upset because I no longer had an excuse to leave Harvard. I had to demolish my car and break my leg to get out of there. You can't say I didn't leave my mark on that school."

At one time, I had meant to tell Danny that it was an abortion that Joan had had, but I was conflicted because I would be betraying a confidence, and it wasn't my responsibility. Obviously, Joan did not want Danny to know. She, as I understood, was not sure how Danny would handle it.

Elly had a survival instinct allowing her to see things as they were. If things were not going her way, she would make adjustments, whatever it took. Her gospel was the idea that life changes, and one's reaction to these changes will have an upshot one day. She expressed this thought to Danny.

"Now where have I heard that before?" Donny laughed. "Sis sounds like you, Daddy. I'm glad you're here, Sis."

"Good," Elly said and smiled.

"I really do appreciate it," said Danny.

Elly, I sensed, did not want to get into the big sister—little brother routine. Elmira and I had expected her to lead the way, and she had tried her best.

"I can run the store," Danny now said to me. I nodded. "Talk to him, Sis. Daddy gets out of his car to tell the guy pumping gas about his daughter the Harvard professor."

"You just don't trust the man, Daddy. You should pump your own gas."

"A surgeon can't be too careful with his hands," I said.

"A couple of doctors, both prominent men, want to build a clinic out by the drugstore, Sis. They're going to put up all the money. Tell you the truth, I was surprised because doctors around here are getting so greedy you can hardly stand them." It struck me how much Danny's "prominent men" sounded like something I might say. "We'll be the clinic's sole source of drugs and supplies—you know beds and walkers, health care stuff. That means expanding the store. I just hope the store can hold out until the clinic is built. Got to move fast before Walmart gets into the doctoring business. 'We cure for less.' They're looking to drive us out. We can do things Walmart can't, do some high-end stuff. Hope to get the ball rolling before the end of summer. It's hard. We gotta bend, hound, pester, bug people, swallow some pride in order to get things done. Guess I'm kind of looking for a bad time." Again, Danny looked straight at me. "You get used to it after a while."

There was some desperation in Danny's voice.

"What do you do?" asked Danny. "You make the best of it, I know. If I was smart, I'd open a completely automated store, no druggist, no sales people, no fights, no smiling 'How are you today, Mrs. Wilson'. The beautiful part, Sis, is we can really have something."

Danny wasn't happy with the hard truth of the world, and he wanted to do something about it. Elly wanted to help her brother, but was afraid, despite how beautiful Danny had made it, that a nostalgic drugstore that was losing money every month was not going to be the answer. She had voiced her concern to her mother and me. I felt responsible, having not done due diligence on the complexities of opening a family drugstore in this day and age. Danny was trying hard to make it work, but he was not going to wake up and be a different person, the person I wanted him to be. And who was that person? I don't know. I think when my mother died, something in me died. And I had to start over from scratch. It is a process.

30

That evening the family sat on the porch. Elly was finishing up leading a cheer.

"Give me an "T.""

"T," Danny and Sonny responded.

"Give me an "I.""

"I," shouted Danny and Sonny

"Give me a "A"."

"A"

"And what does that spell, boys?"

"NOVA SCOTIA!"

"Not bad for an old cheerleader," said Danny, as we all applauded Elly for her cheers. Danny began singing.

"Nova Scotia here we come, right back where we started from."

Sonny cheered, for he would be leaving for camp again in Nova Scotia in a month or so. Danny told Sonny he would freeze his butt off. Sonny thought that was funny.

"It's warm, Danny. Swimming."

"I don't think so, Sonny. You don't go to Nova Scotia to get a tan."

"Stars," said Sonny, "big stars in Nova Scotia." He suddenly looked up to the heavens.

"Yeah, the stars are wide and alive tonight," said a reflective Danny.

"Can we walk to heaven?" Sonny asked.

"Not in a thousand years. We'll have to wait for angels and hope we're not too heavy," said Danny.

"Maybe we'll be a shooting star," said Sonny. "A falling star," he continued, showing Danny a map. "Star of the East."

"What about it, boyscout?" Danny put his arm around Sonny. Sonny didn't answer.

"It led three wise men to Bethlehem, Sonny," said Elly.

"Yes," said Sonny eagerly.

"Wish it would lead 'em here," said Danny.

"Where are they?" asked Sonny.

"Who?"

"Wise men," said Sonny.

"Good question, Sonny. They're out there somewhere," Danny nodded toward the dark sky.

"Nova Scotia," said Sonny excitedly. "The boys, too."

"What boys?" Danny asked.

"Butch, Eddie…Walt."

"Christ, what made you think of them?"

"Not home," said Sonny.

"They haven't been home forever."

The "boys" had been school friends of Danny's. And since Sonny was always with Danny, they were his friends too. To my knowledge, they had never brought attention to Sonny's halting speech or the awkward gait of his walk that slowed him down.

"Boys coming home?"

"Hell, no. Never see any of the guys anymore," answered Danny, immediately regretting his tone. "Everybody comes home eventually. Right, Sis?"

"Sure they're coming back, Sonny," Elly said.

"Where are… they?"

"I don't know, Sonny. Maybe nowhere, maybe they're lost, lost among the ruins," lamented Danny "All the old places are gone.

We're still here, Sonny, but we go out, and we're strangers. Easier that way, I guess. Living in a story land, strangers in our own county. Get lost driving around the town anymore. I missed the turnoff one morning and was 5 exits down the by-pass before I realized it. Wasn't sure where I was. Lost."

Sonny's face was sad.

"Can I see one of your maps," I asked Sonny. He pulled out several maps from his back pocket.

"I need one of these," I said and pointed to a spot on a map. "Here's where they are, those boys. Here's Nova Scotia, and they're way beyond."

"Far?"

"Yes, Sonny, I suspect far. But they're coming back," said Danny.

"Oh boy. When?" Sonny was looking up at the stars.

"Too many questions, Sonny," said Danny.

Watching Danny with his arm resting easy around Sonny's shoulders and the way he tasseled Sonny's hair and straightened his collar, I was taken by how protective of Sonny, Danny was. Danny had promised Sonny's mother that he would always look out for Sonny. It occurred to me that she would never have to worry about her boy when he was with Danny. *This was love*, I thought, *at its purest.* Danny would make a good father, I thought, watching him—my son, thinking he was never more himself than when he was with Sonny.

"Danny, what's on other side of the stars?" Sonny asked.

"Walmart, probably," said Danny. That brought a round of laughter.

There was a bird whistling in the dark. *That's what I'm doing,* I thought, hoping against hope, telling myself that things were going to work out, telling myself to keep going, whistling in the dark. But still, this night was so good that I wanted to hold on to it like Elmira did with a good book she didn't want to end. But then, there always seemed to be another good book on her eagerly awaited horizon of literature. There is always hope for another good journey

Watching Danny's pure easy enjoyment of Sonny as they contemplated the heavens, I was struck by how at peace Sonny was, how he seemed to understand where he was, what he was given, and that he was accepted—an enviable place to be.

31

It was Sunday, and Dee and I had come in from the early church service. Elly was enjoying the sun porch with a cup of coffee.

"The weather is just grand, Elly," announced Dee. "Isn't it, Daniel?"

"Yes, it certainly is. Missed a good sermon, Mama."

"Tore the rafters off, I bet," said Elmira, entering the kitchen, still in her housecoat.

"Huge crowd. It was rousing, Mama. Rousing."

"The man's a bore, a sour, dour Presbyterian," she replied, taking her morning coffee and paper into the den.

Dee and I walked out onto the sun porch to join Elly. Dee looked out the windows into the expansive back yard leading down to her house that was undergoing remodeling.

"I worry about Elmira," said Dee, lowering her voice. "It's sad to see someone spend time in bed when they don't have to."

Elmira had lost interest in her various clubs—the Women's Club, the Garden Club. They bored her, she said, saying she had done her time. I was concerned that she was becoming a bit of a recluse.

"Your father bought all the land back here as far as you can see," said Dee, "didn't you Daniel?"

"Yes. Was going to build houses for you and Danny, Elly, when you came back here after college." I laughed. "All the memories this yard has. I like the yard."

"You're never in it," Daddy," said Elly. "You just like knowing it's here."

"Sometimes that's enough."

"I was surprised to see you, Elly. Are you home long?" Dee asked this with a guarded casualness.

"No, I'm leaving tomorrow." Dee, I knew, suspected the reason Elly showed up unexpectedly had to do with the drugstore and Danny.

"The property and house, they help take my mind off the hospital and any pressing problems," I said.

"Like the drugstore," said Dee.

Neither Elly nor I said anything.

"You never know," said Dee.

"What?" asked Elly.

"Oh," said Dee, "what people are thinking, what they are going through, what they feel is their duty." Dee sat down beside Elly, looked out on her remodeling project. "After you married the first time, your father needed a project. Elmira put her foot down on expansion, didn't she, Daniel?"

"Yes, said if I built a guesthouse—I could live in it."

"When I got married the first time, Aunt Dee, you said you were afraid Daddy would have a heart attack."

"I did?"

"Yes. You told me you knew how much I loved Daddy and said you didn't understand why I hadn't postponed my marriage—delayed it a few years, I think is what you said—because my whole life was ahead of me. That marriage did not survive, but Daddy has." Elly wrapped her arm around my waist.

"He didn't want to lose you to a husband, did you Daniel? Not since our mother died had I seen your father so distressed."

Dee's mention of our mother was surprising. Elly had asked me about my mother, but I told her that I really knew very little. I looked out at the yard and made the observation that you could really see things as they are in the morning light.

"What do you think, Elly, of Dee's renovation?"

"It's going to be nice."

"Yes, I think so."

"You need more room, Aunt Dee?"

"The extra bedroom will be handy for relatives."

"Half of them will be dead before it's finished," said Elmira, coming back into the kitchen, throwing her voice toward the open portal over the sink to the sun porch. Elmira poured herself another cup of coffee and joined us.

"The gardeners said they would move that God-awful pool table out to the garage for me tomorrow. I figure someone will take it like they have taken everything else out of there. You never had doors put on so everything's been stolen. One day they're going to steal the cars. Did you get my pills?" I made a show of fumbling in my pocket and brought out a vial and handed it to Elmira. She held the vial up to the morning light.

"Two pills! Thank you kindly. You double your dosage for a sore throat."

"Two pills are enough."

"You never suffer, so sanctimonious."

There was a knock at the door, and Elly was only too glad to answer it. It was Janice. Elly welcomed her in. Janice preferred to wait for Danny in the foyer with General Robert E. Lee, thinking, I mused, she might need his protection. Janice was surprised to see Elly, who complimented her on her earrings.

"Walmart—cheapest prices in town," I heard Janice say, with a slight laugh. "Did Danny tell you I did a commercial for Walmart?"

"Yes."

"It was a good while ago but they're still using it. I thought Danny would have a hemorrhage, but he didn't."

"No."

"He called me a traitor—not in a mean way. I was forgiven," she said and laughed. "Is he here?"

"Yes."

"I need to talk to him. I wouldn't have come, believe me, if it wasn't necessary." She could see me standing in the sunroom. She waved. I nodded.

"I'll get him," Elly said, excusing herself. "Be nice," she mouthed to me.

I whispered, "Does she have a gun?"

"Daddy, stop it," warned Elly.

"She's dangerous."

Elly gave me a scolding look and went to find her brother. The family 'confidant' and intermediary was on the job, persisting on, standing by—again. Elly's husband, Darren, had only half-jokingly told her that she had the makings of an ambassador. I suspected her talk with me would not be put off much longer. She appeared with Danny in tow.

"You changed the lock?" Janice asked him, not smiling.

"What lock?"

"I just tried to open the store, and my key won't work. I felt like a jackass standing out there trying to figure out why my key won't work. Then I thought, wait a minute, you dummy. Danny changed the lock because he's afraid to tell me face up that I'm fired again! So I came here to tell you to take your store and stuff it. I quit." She turned and headed for the door.

"Your resignation is accepted," I said, entering the foyer. Elly gave me a dart of a look.

"I didn't change the lock," said Danny.

"Somebody did, my key doesn't work. The lock must have been changed after closing last night," said Janice, looking straight at me.

"Who has a key to the new lock?" Elly asked.

"Phil-the-pill would be my guess," said Janice. "Unless he's loaned it to a druggie."

"He is an accredited pharmacist, and I would appreciate it…"

Danny interrupted me with, "I'll have to force the son-of-a-bitch to give me a key."

"I'll get the key," announced Janice and was out the door.

"The lock was changed?" asked Danny looking at me.

"Well... not by me. The pharmacist told me," I stammered, "there had been some break-ins in the area."

"So he had the lock changed!?" Danny's voice was now nearly a roar. "Without telling me? Why didn't you tell me? You think I'm going to break into my own store?"

"Boy, don't be ridiculous. Of course I don't."

"I've been locked out of my own damn store?"

"It's not your store, it's a family business."

"Am I missing something here, Sis?"

"Calm yourself, son."

"Calm myself, shit."

"Watch your language, son."

Elmira entered the foyer, which was becoming crowded

"What's wrong now?" she asked.

"Stay out of it," Danny told his mother.

"I'll be glad to."

"Watch how you talk to your mother."

"I can take up for myself," shot back Elmira.

"This is just too damn funny," said Danny, returning to his room.

"There's been an epidemic of these break-ins," I said. "We had no choice. A gun-toting blackmailer is capable of anything."

"Jesus," said Elmira. "I wish to God that store would burn."

"You don't mean it," I tried to soothe the situation, but, as usual, wound up making things worse.

"I'll light the match myself."

"Elmira."

"I blame every bit of this on you, Daniel."

"It's all going to work out," I assured her.

"Yes, I know. Most things get better by morning."

"They do."

"This is not going to get better! Sometimes I wonder if you even like Danny."

"Please, Elmira."

Elly then told me that she would like to talk with me suggesting we go into the library.

"Of course, Elly."

"I need to get down to my place," said Dee, taking Elly's hand. "This drugstore business has been very trying for your father. He won't tell you but he keeps things in, doesn't let you know what's bothering him."

"I'll be fine, Dee."

"You've always shied away from confrontations, Daniel, especially those of a family nature."

"Don't worry Aunt Dee, he'll survive this little crisis."

"I hope you're right," said Dee, as she opened the door to leave.

Elly and I entered the library. There was a long silence. I stood very straight.

"You look like you are before the firing squad, Daddy."

32

The library was dark despite being mid-afternoon, due to the dark redwood paneling and the shuttered two windows on each side of the stone fireplace. I had the habit of not entering a room—just standing in the doorway making conversation, leaning against the door frame in my green scrubs while munching on an apple—a casual action belied by the distant look I felt in my eyes. Now I was standing in the middle of the room with my arms folded across my chest, and my head bowed as though in meditation.

"Daddy?"

Turning to Elly, I smiled and took out my handkerchief, using it to cover my fingers, as I turned on a lamp.

"You should just wear gloves all the time, Daddy."

"A surgeon can't be too careful with his hands—like a pianist." Elly could not help a small smile at my familiar words. My reason for never changing a diaper was because of the fear of disease. But it worked both ways. I didn't like to hold my children unless I had scrubbed my hands. I still had my suit coat on from church with my tie pulled snug at the collar.

"Take off your jacket, Daddy, and stay a while."

I did so, laying it over the back of Elmira's thick cushioned reading chair. Timmy, the calico cat, wandered in and jumped up to what he saw was a soft pad, my coat. Timmy broke the ice. We laughed.

"Timmy's up in years. He's entitled to a little comfort."

"Like you, Daddy?"

I picked up a photo from a side table. It was a picture of six-year old Elly standing beside a boy's bicycle.

"Your first two-wheeler."

"I couldn't even push it, let alone ride it."

"You managed. Never liked any of the girl's bikes. No selection," I said continuing to look at the photo for a moment before setting it aside. "Sorry you couldn't bring Douglas."

"He and Darren are having a good time."

"I imagine."

"When is the last good time you had, Daddy?"

"You've given me many good times, Elly. I'm glad you're here; you are good therapy for your mother. Better than any medicine she takes."

"She's worried about Danny. So am I."

"Hope you have time to play your piano while you're here. I keep it tuned. It's still good, gets better with age."

"Like you?"

"Still doing what I was doing twenty—thirty years ago. Just like a Steinway, Elly, holding my value. I want to get the Steinway appraised."

"What you ought to appraise is your relationship with your son," Elly said, determined not to let me detour around what she wanted to talk about.

"Your brother doesn't have our stamina and will. He lets himself go, doesn't have your discipline."

"Danny has many faults, none of which have proved fatal yet."

"He'll be fine."

"When did you stop expecting anything out of him?"

"I haven't."

"You never trusted us, Daddy."

"I trusted you."

"Not enough to let me write my own college essay."

"I was wrong."

"It's funny. I never knew you could apply to Harvard. I thought you had to be invited."

"But you made your way. You're in the club."

"You haven't missed anything, Daddy. We never summered in Nice or skied in the Swiss Alps. But we were lucky. We got our refinement and learning from the southern Appalachian Mountains."

"There are many ways to raise children, I imagine. Your mother and I tried our best to give you both some order. Danny's talent may yet be called forth. He's young."

"I go away," Elly mused, "and everybody here stays young. Then I come home."

"Don't you love it here, the mountains?"

"Yes, but sometimes the aesthetic is better from a distance." She walked across the room and took a framed photo from the top of the wall-to-wall bookcase. "See this picture," she said handing it to me. "Look at it closely, Daddy."

"Believe Danny had just gotten a promotion," I said, looking at the photo of Danny in uniform at military school. "He was a patriot."

"He still is, just a disillusioned one."

"Glad you and Danny can spend some time together, Elly."

"Danny was 17 in this picture, Daddy. He's 34 now. I'll tell you what you don't see—the children Danny used to play with. Because they've all grown up, except Sonny, and disappeared into the adult world, while Danny's grown up and disappeared into this nice, big, safe house."

"That's why I built this house, for our family. It is our protective membrane, Elly. Danny won't have to struggle. He'll have a good life."

"Yes, it just won't be his, Daddy. You're the one who always told me not to let other people's voices drown out mine. Danny has been looking for something, and everyone wants to tell him what it is—'the good life.' He can sit here and drown himself in the 'good life.' Mother cooks his meals, washes his clothes."

"She enjoys it. That's what family is all about, Elly."

"A man who cannot wash his own socks is not a real man. I read that somewhere."

"Your mother washes all my socks. What would Danny do? Live alone?"

"How is he ever going to take care of himself?" Elly asked.

"He has his family. Gives us pleasure to help him, help you both."

"I just hope you'll be able to support him for the rest of his life."

"He won't have to struggle."

"What are you afraid of, Daddy? I think you gave up on Danny a long time ago. Why don't you let him run the store? Afraid he'll fail? Or are you afraid he'll succeed? What would happen, Daddy, if Danny succeeds—if he turns out to be a good businessman?"

"I hope he will."

"If he does make the store a success and gets out of this house, you and mother are going to have to deal with each other. Does that scare you?"

"No," I said, and then gave a small nervous laugh. "Danny doesn't concentrate…makes rash decisions."

"Making me part owner of the drugstore was a rash decision."

"No, Elly. That's the best decision I could make…..That girl…"

"What girl? Janice?"

"No."

"Are you talking about Joan?"

"No, no….nothing," I said as I reached for another photo. "Here you are with your first car, good car, safe."

"So are tanks."

"I want to get you a new car."

"I don't need a new car. Daddy…"

"I want to give you what you want so…"

"No, Daddy, you want to give me what you want, and I've always given you what you wanted."

"Yes. But you are a professor at Harvard because you worked hard. You wanted it more."

"I'm Harvard crimson through and through."

"Not a bad thing."

"No. You are a successful surgeon. You've worked hard. You wanted it more. At Harvard, Daddy, the trick was to work hard but never show it. It gives you away when you try too hard. It took me awhile to learn that little trick. I was naïve."

Walking over to the window, I opened the shutters, and there was the maple tree gracing the front yard. "Your mother planted that tree after you left for Harvard. It has grown, like you, Elly. I just wanted you to climb the tree, because the more branches you reach, the more you have to choose from."

"It seemed at times during those years I was too far out on a limb, hanging on for dear life fearing it would break off any moment. That's why I was in analysis."

"Elly, I…"

"I know how you feel about head doctors," she said, joining me at the window. "But I needed help because the only living I was doing was in my head. Every time I stepped a little ahead, I would slip back here. I've worked hard for your love, Daddy. I'm not sorry at all, but your love is indomitable, like the Appalachian Mountains. Sometimes your love is best appreciated from a little distance. I've been so bound to you, but sometimes… I guess, I thought fathers were always right. It was part of their mystique. I've spoiled you, Daddy. And it's come back to haunt me. God knows what it's done to Danny."

"Elly, forgive me. I'm so sorry. I'm to blame. You're the last person I ever wanted to hurt. I never wanted you to be disappointed in me. You are everything to me. It's my fault for not giving Danny more confidence. He's good with his cars."

"Is that supposed to be a compliment? Danny can see through that at a hundred yards with his glasses off."

Elly then went on to tell me that she had consulted with her lawyer who had drawn up the necessary papers, signing over her interest in the drugstore to Danny, giving him majority ownership and final say over who works there, what kind of music is played, whatever. It was now Danny's responsibility. He was now free to work things out for himself at the store.

"I don't want you to be burdened with this," I said.

"You should have thought of that a long time ago. Maybe I want to be burdened."

33

It was dinner time before Janice returned. She had gone back to the store to see if the Phil-the-Pill had opened yet. He hadn't...

"So I went straight to that junkie's house. He was hung over. He threw the key at me and slammed the door in my face. I laughed. Oh yeah, he told me he was quitting to go to work at Walmart."

"Three cheers," said Danny, coming down the stairs into the foyer with Elly who had retrieved him. "Saves me the trouble of firing him," he said, looking at me.

"Here's the key," said Janice, tossing Danny the key.

"What took you so long?"

"I opened the store. I thought you would eventually show up."

"I was tired," shrugged Danny.

"I wouldn't exactly call what you've been doing hard labor."

"That's... not what I mean."

"You're not going to let that asshole pharmacist get you down," said Janice.

"Please, if you could refrain from that kind of language," I said wearily getting up from the table, trying hard to maintain my demeanor. "I think I would know if our pharmacist, whom you so unkindly referred to, was planning to pursue other opportunities."

"Good riddance to him," Janice said. "All you have to do with those people is tell them how things are going to be. Simple as salt."

"How presumptuous." The words grunted out of me.

"Don't know what that means," said Janice.

"Not surprised."

"Daniel! Please!" Elmira said in exasperation.

"I may not have any degrees, but I'm smart enough to know opening a drugstore down the road from the largest company in the world wasn't too swift, unless, of course, you wanted it to fail." Janice looked at me as she said this.

"Walmart said they'd work with Daniel," said Dee firmly, seated at the dining table.

"Hello, honey." Janice gave a little wave. "You forget where you live? This ain't America, this is Appalachia, dear. Getting fucked is the motto around here."

Dee's eyes opened wide.

"That kind of language will not be spoken in my home," I said.

"Change or die, baby," said Janice to Danny. "We can do it, Danny. We can make that store work. Come on, baby. I'll take care of you. We can have something good…..Danny… maybe our families don't go together, but we do."

"What do you know about family?" I asked.

"Daddy, please," said Elly.

"Enough to know that I got more of a chance of finding one at Walmart than here."

"How dare you," said Dee, getting up from her chair and coming to my defense.

"And enough to know that nobody around here, Danny, will give you what I have."

"And what may I ask is that?" My impervious nature had given way once again, on being confronted by Janice. I felt sick to my stomach and did not dare look at Elly.

"The chance to be a man, honey!" Janice's eyes went to Danny. "I'll see you in the morning?"

Danny did not answer her. Janice turned to leave, then turned back to Danny. "Christ, don't know what I've been waiting for all these years! Guess my time's so cheap, it never mattered how much of it I wasted."

Elmira had remained seated at the table determined to finish her dessert while the rest of us stood in General Lee's foyer. I mused that the General had not overseen the proceedings in the foyer any better than he had the overseen the battle at Gettysburg. Janice and Danny stood in the shadow of the large redwood cathedral door.

"While I was doing my commercial at Walmart, I ran into Joan's mother. She works at Walmart," said Janice.

"Like everyone else," said Danny.

"She congratulated me and offered to buy me a drink when I finished. Later that night, after a few drinks, she told me Joan had been pregnant and that she had had an abortion."

"What?" Elly asked.

"Yes. She said it's a small world. 'It's a small town,' I told her. She said that your father delivered Joan, and that he had been very supportive during a very difficult time for their family."

"What does that mean, abortion?" asked Danny. "She had a miscarriage."

"Ask your father. Joan's mother said that he arranged it. Joan never really got over having an abortion, but, her mother said, she's found God and that's helped her with the guilt and depression."

We all stood, silent, as if at attention before General Lee. Janice looked at Danny for a long moment and then left. Danny closed the door and came back into the dining room.

"Did you know Joan had an abortion?"

"Yes," I said.

"Did you give her the abortion?" asked Danny.

"Your father doesn't do abortions," said Dee.

"I paid for her to have the procedure. The family had little money and as your father, I felt a responsibility."

"To kill my child?"

"Please, Danny," said Elly.

"They killed my baby."

"It's all right, Elly," I said.

"It's not all right," said Danny. "It was my child, too." I could hear my father's tortured scream. Danny's was more like a silent wail. "You paid for her abortion?"

"Yes. She did not want the baby."

"That's not true!"

"Her mother told me so, Danny. I wanted her to go to a reputable place and not chance having happen what... happened to my mother, your Aunt Dee's mother."

"Our grandmother?" asked Elly.

"Yes."

"What happened?" asked Danny.

I looked at Dee for help.

"Our mother died as a result of an ugly abortion. It was not a pretty sight."

"The girl's mother and I....were together about it, grieved together. I'm sorry, son. Joan's mother and I...we understood what the other was feeling."

"The only reason you paid for her abortion was so I would stay at Harvard," said Danny. "Isn't that so?"

"I wanted you to stay at Harvard, yes. But, as your father, I felt it was my responsibility to get Joan the best possible care. I...Forgive me, Lord, my insufficiency," I said, clasping my hands in prayer.

"He forgives you, Daniel," assured Dee, standing behind me now, her hands on my shoulders.

"I don't," said Danny, and started up the stairs before turning back. "Was it a boy or a girl?" I told Danny I didn't know.

No one moved. I tried to hear Mozart's peaceful and cheering, "Toy Symphony," trusting it would drown out the real-world pressure and make all things possible.

"I should have heeded your advice, Sister."

The sun was fading when I told them that I had given Joan's mother $2,000 to pay for her daughter's abortion.

"Told myself I was looking after the girl's welfare. Have seen too many women die when they did not have to. I told myself I was only doing what the mother wanted, but really, I was doing what I wanted. I led the discussion where I wanted it to go. I had an agenda. A man has to decide how far he is willing to go for success. I stepped over the line. The procedure was at a clinic in Washington, D.C., a legal abortion provider," I confessed through tears. "No matter how deep my faith, I feel my prayers have been in vain. God will not hear a man who has betrayed Him. I am not worthy. My transgressions cannot be forgiven. I don't know God," I said. "It would be better for your father, Elly, if a millstone had been hung around my neck, and I'd be drowned in the deepest sea."

"Daddy."

"You're being very melodramatic, Daniel," said Elmira.

"Don't worry, Elly, I'm not like my father. Will not go that far. He…."

"What?" asked Elly.

"…took his own life…..I never wanted you to know, Elly, or you, Elmira…. or Danny…I…. "

"Our father was not a pleasant man," Dee said, "especially after our mother… He kept yelling at her as if she was still there. He was very angry and the most defeated, pessimistic, frightening man I ever knew. He never could get over the pain, the bitterness. He could not move on. Afterward, he never had any faith in himself, and he never showed any faith in you, Daniel. You were not a child of encouragement. He would not have let you go, either of us. There wasn't a lot of family warmth," Dee continued to Elmira and Elly, neither of whom had moved a muscle. "It's awful to grow up in the shade of sadness. Your father would never admit it, Elly, and Lord forgive me for saying it, but Dad was the meanest son-of-a-bitch who ever lived."

34

Elmira and I were seated at the kitchen table. She was having a cocktail.

"Elly says Harvard girls today like their liquor hard, just maybe not in jelly jars," said Elmira with a half-smile.

"Not real sophisticated, Mama," I said, smiling. "

"Guess drinking out of a jelly glass makes me an authentic mountain woman. Mr. Turley was a drinker." Elmira always referred to her step-father by his surname. "He always said he was a 'responsible drinker,' but he drank up a lot of money. And in the end his drinking isolated him. He must have felt very alone. Did your dad drink?"

"Not that I know of."

"Maybe he should've."

"Maybe. We all have our burdens…. Dad hated anybody's thinking of him as a hillbilly."

"Dee said that he would have never let you go."

"He needed help on the land. But he said many times, 'It's a wasteland, a dirt poor crude, decent-less place, where you're not even human.' Dee was adamant about my not coming back."

"But you did."

"Yes, and I somehow convinced you to come with me. I am sorry, Elmira, for all the trouble. The people here needed a good doctor. You still don't see any Harvard doctors down here, not for love nor money. We're lucky if we can get some foreigner….I'm from these parts and will always be."

"Used to be a mildly charming town," mused Elmira, "just big enough to be spared everybody's dirty laundry. This is no one-horse town anymore, not the cow-pasture it was when we first came here. But some people's visions here go about as far as the next hill," said Elmira.

"When I was a boy, I would look across the way and wonder what was on the other side of the hill. One time I hiked up that hill—took me all day—and when I got to the top, I looked out—and there was another hill."

"People are still suspicious of outsiders, but I have no complaints that way. Folks here are pretty much like everywhere else, I suppose. It makes me mad when I read about hill people being too backward to help themselves. Hills are pretty… even when snow-covered, as they soon will be. They're not as exotic or dreadful or isolated or full of squalor as everybody seems to think. You do find a lot of fatalism here. The hills do make me claustrophobic. I don't fear them, but after living here for so long the hills seep in, the inevitability of it all."

"Elly called me at the hospital. We talked about this proposed clinic Danny mentioned. I promised her I would talk to Danny about it and would be sure to encourage him about the possibilities. The clinic is a good idea. It's got a real up-side to it," I told Elmira. "Danny and I need to talk."

"When are you going to do that? Even Danny is in bed by the time you have been getting home lately. You fell asleep in my office the other night in your hat and coat."

"I woke up and didn't know where I was."

"Why doesn't that surprise me? You get to the hospital and you lose all track of time."

I had been working ever-longer hours at the hospital, anxious over its possible sale, and, as usual, was overwhelmed with paper work.

"I'm a month behind on my charts," I said.

"You're always a month behind, Daniel."

My surgeries had been pushed later into the days because I was getting slower on my rounds. I had always felt a little guilty lingering with overly needy patients when I should be home spending time with Elmira. If I have been a bad husband and father, it wasn't, I told myself, for a lack of love.

"Danny has not been out of bed all day," said Elmira.

Danny had refused to go back to the drugstore. "Phil the Pill" was now distributing pills on behalf of Walmart's pharmacy. I had managed to hire a part-time "retired" pharmacist and a sales clerk— trying to keep up appearances about my plans for the drugstore and even mentioned to Elly the prospect of opening a couple of others. She told me the writing was on the wall.

"I'm just hoping this clinic idea will entice Danny to go back to work," I said.

"If there's any store to go back to," Elmira replied. "You have dillydallied so long, I'm at the end of my wits. You have never given up the idea that Danny would come around, see the light, and go back to school… Admit it, Daniel."

"No. I'm afraid I have given it up. I told Elly I wished she could spare some time to come home. She could cheer Danny up. He's fragile, down in the dumps."

"I think he is on the verge of a breakdown. So am I," said Elmira. "Danny and I can't help each other much, just stay out of each other's way. The extent of our dinner conversation, when we have dinner, doesn't go much beyond, 'Pass the salt.' Though the other day, out of the blue, Danny said, 'Joan didn't want the baby. She didn't want my baby.' I told him that was not the case, but he was not in the mood to listen to me. He mostly stays downstairs sitting in his rocker, ball cap on his head, drinking Cokes and smoking cigarettes, listening to his music and watching television while playing Chutes and Ladders with Sonny. He's stopped shaving. I clean up when he's out for something. The basement is usually in as much disarray as he is. But I must say I've gotten used to watching television without the sound. It's much better."

"We're feeling sorry for ourselves, Mama," I said, putting my hand on hers. "Danny can't just sit here. Elly says it's like he's in storage, like a long Saturday matinee, little popcorn, his rocker. There comes a point, she says, when Danny has to take responsibility for his life."

"She told me," said Elmira

"Any fool can throw his life away," I said. Judging from Elmira's look, whatever I said was, apparently, not the right thing to say.

"Whether or not Danny goes back to the store, he has got to get out of the basement! Obviously," said Elmira. "Elly said she asked Danny about going up there to stay a while. He laughed, she said. 'You live near Boston, don't you? Isn't that near Cambridge? I break out in hives when I get near that ivy.' ...I thought he would eventually move out," said Elmira. "When he and Janice got married, I had hopes. Sometimes you fool yourself. You tell yourself whatever you have to, don't you, so you can go on."

"It wasn't good the way she treated Danny."

"How do you mean?" asked Elmira.

"Running around," I said.

"Danny did the same," said Elmira. "It was his idea to separate from Janice. I don't think he'll ever go back with her."

Just then the doorbell rang. We could not imagine who would be making a house call so late. It was Sonny. His mother was waiting in the car. Sonny was looking for Danny, and Elmira explained that Danny had gone to bed early.

"Nova Scotia rock," said Sonny, holding out a football-sized rock.

Examining it, I concluded that it had once been a piece of wood. "It's petrified, Sonny," I said, rubbing my hand across it.

"Danny's rock."

"A petrified rock. It's heavy. Got to be a thousand years old, Sonny. Danny will appreciate this, I know."

"Do rocks grow?" asked Sonny.

"Now, that's a good question, Sonny. What do you think, Mama?"

"Don't think so. I've never seen one grow."

"Die?" Sonny asked.

"No," Elmira said.

"They just roll away," I said and gave a little laugh.

"Can I sit on Danny's rock?"

"I'm sure he wouldn't mind, Sonny," said Elmira.

"Can I build a wall with it?"

"Sure," she said.

"Roll it down the hill."

"How will it get back up?" I asked.

"Plant it in my garden." Sonny was smiling at his decision. He took the rock and held it close to his chest.

"Good idea, Sonny."

"Right," said Sonny, and he held up his palm. "High five."

Elmira and I slapped hands with Sonny and he left, taking the rock with him.

35

The inevitable happened the next night, Thanksgiving Eve. I had the television on while I was catching up on my charts, only paying half-attention to the news.

"Walmart was riddled with gunshots during the night.....A Walmart spokesman said the store suffered cosmetic damage only. The letters "l," "m," and the "a" in 'Walmart' were shot out so that the Walmart sign now reads "Wart." I'm sure they'll want to correct that as soon as possible. A Walmart spokesman said its annual holiday celebration would go on as scheduled. In other news, a man was killed in a single car accident when his car crashed through construction barriers on highway 79. Identification of the victim is being withheld until the family is notified."

Sleep did not come so easily as it once did. I use to be able to sleep on command. I was waiting for Danny to come home so we could discuss the clinic. I had lain down and was reading one of my medical journals. I always read until sleep can be denied no more.

Next thing I knew father's distant voice cried out from some deep bitter place. "God will have his revenge." It was 3:00 a.m. but the phone on my bedside table often rang in the middle of the night. Elmira had made me put in my own line so the late night ringing would not disturb her in her bedroom. Answering the phone, almost casually, for I knew it was the hospital calling about a patient, probably concerning medication of sorts. There had been many times I stayed overnight at the hospital when one of my patients needed careful monitoring. Occasionally I would be awakened at home and would make the long mountain road drive back to the hospital.

The phone dropped from my hand as if bitten by a snake. After a moment I managed to put the receiver back to my ear asking the caller about "vital signs." Holding the phone a few moments, then hanging up. I sat up in bed and pulled my legs over the side, noticing my tired aging face darkly profiled in the dresser mirror. Sitting on the edge of the bed, my head in my lap, I started to cry and then to bawl like a baby. Elmira heard me.

"What's the matter, Daniel?"

"Policeman. Our boy…"

There was only silence. Time stood still once again. Elmira did not need an answer. Through my tears, I asked her to get on her knees with me and pray. She didn't move. At times like this you are alone. I lowered myself to my knees beside the bed and started to pray.

"Dear Lord, please watch over our boy…he's a fine boy." The sobbing overtook me, bending my head to the floor. Elmira stood looking down at me, and the mysteries hidden away in my head. The maze was complicated, too many dead-end entrances and exits. There was no way for her to have ever deciphered me. I could not do it myself. I was still circling, looking for a way out of the maze that had its beginning long ago. I was still aching to believe in the goodness that my mother had talked about. There was no going back to knock on the door and ask for an answer. No one was home.

"Get hold of yourself, Daniel. All the tears in the world can't help Danny now," Elmira said, and left the room.

Maybe Elmira was right about the "futility" of looking to God for answers.

———————————

It was mercifully daylight. I had just returned from identifying Danny's body. There would be no autopsy. There was no need. It would not assuage my guilt. The rest of the day, I did not move from my bedroom.

When she arrived late that day, Elly made her brother's funeral arrangements and cooked dinner for Elmira, me, and Dee. The next day she chose a casket for her brother, wrote his obituary, and tried to contact as many of Danny's friends as possible, including his estranged wife, Janice. Yes, I knew she should be told.

That night, lying on my bed, the blankets pulled up over the chill, with my medical journals in hand, searching even now, despite being exhausted, to be the best doctor I could be. But I was back at the hard bottom hearing my father rage while mother lay dead in his arms.

"That's where she's left us, boy—the hard bottom."

Had Danny reached the hard bottom? The death certificate stated the cause of death was an aorta infarction. Actually the cause was whatever happens when you drive through a concrete barrier and plunge 200 feet to the bottom of Coal River. Danny's death was not ruled a suicide, though Elmira was sure it was. The hard bottom could possibly drive a man mad, I thought. It could drive a person to act irrationally. To have no purpose in life is to be lost.

"What you are as a person is what you do in life, what you accomplish," I had told Danny. Could I have had it all wrong, I wondered?

The thought of Danny's taking his own life was an unbearable thought. I had read where one of Gregory Peck's sons had committed suicide. This, I knew, must have been very troubling for Peck. As I was sure Peck had done, I went to the Bible for solace and guidance in the great mystery. My faith would rally me, "the substance of things hoped for, the evidence of things not seen." Would faith sustain me? Would God abandon me? I knew the real world. I had seized it before. I would do so again.

Standing at my bedroom window looking out at the streetlamp and at the children playing under it, I watched them throw little stones upward trying to hit the glowing lamp. *Don't be so anxious, children*, I thought, *dark will come soon enough*. Suddenly a stone hit the bulb and the light popped, flashed bright, and died.

All things ended. My mother and father were long gone, apparitions, ashes to ashes, dust to dust. Young as I was the night mother died, I became aware of my own mortality. Now, not a day goes by that I don't think of the grave.

Years later, I saw a new young nurse at the hospital and thought I recognized her, almost calling her by name but realized it was the name of my mother, Esther, I was about to utter. The young nurse looked strikingly more like my forever young mother than I remembered even Dee looking, who favored our father. Grandmother and grandson, I lamented, had never met. Perhaps in heaven, I mused. Mother would know her grandson for he was a carbon copy of her youngest son.

The same record kept playing. Danny was dead. What had gone wrong? Hadn't I provided my children with a sanctuary, smoothed and straightened their path? Elly had seemed to thrive. Danny had exhibited great possibilities, was very gifted, creative, but seemed to have no facility for bringing these things into being. Didn't I instill a desire in Danny for the best kind of life, a productive life? Certainly I had tried to make him aware of the possibilities of life.

"There is no need to be doomed by oblivion. Knowledge is there for the taking, but you must take it. You've got to see beyond the next hill. Don't give up, Danny, don't ever give up."

Not being in school, not being in pursuit of knowledge, meant a wasted life. I had tried to live the life I thought was best. I wanted my children to do no less. There could not be a worse fate than to just wander through this world, having not contributed to its betterment, having people not know you had lived, you had strived for the best.

What a miserable fate. Danny could not grasp this, could not understand.

"We're like oil and water, Daddy," Danny said sadly after one of my pep talks.

It was true, none of Danny's habits or interests or women or music or dreams had appealed to me with the exception of singing. I would sing tenor, Danny would sing bass, Elly would sing alto and play the Steinway grand piano on the occasional Sunday family sing-alongs. Elmira, with her sewing at hand, and Dee, sitting attentively—her hands folded in her lap—would enjoy the trio. I liked the old standards from the time I was courting Elmira or the old hymns Mother had sung. I was partial to the mountain gospels of the Carter family. Maybelle Carter was the queen of country music. The Carters and my family both lived on Clinch Mountain in southwestern Virginia. We had been to the Carter family house to hear them sing.

Elly's favorites, Elvis and Johnny Mathis, were easy on the ear. Danny wanted to sing a Phil Ochs anti-war song. Danny told me that Ochs was a fan of JFK's. That was enough for me. I gamely tried singing the Ochs song, but it was like a train wreck waiting to happen. Still the family would laugh, me the hardest. I loved the sing-along moments. These were the kind of family moments I liked to dream about—happy moments. Like the day Elmira said "yes" to my marriage proposal, and the birth of my children and grandson, or when Elly became a professor—my happiest moment.

Dee said I had been a force, a quiet torrent. If so, she was the encourager, the strong tailwind pushing my dreams, for the right kind of life, the ideal life. There would be no way to close my eyes against the night. How to make sense of what had happened? I did wish to be the ideal father, to keep my family healthy, wealthy, and wise. I had always made sure the family was up-to-date with their various "shots." When Jonas Salk came up with the polio vaccination, I made sure the family was vaccinated the first day it was available. I schooled them on nutrition, becoming a strict vegetarian as an example.

Danny had been a small baby, a sickly baby, but a pretty one with blue eyes, blond hair. His fair skin made his sister envious.

"Why, Lord? Why? It was all … for nothing … nothing …." I was talking to myself.

As a doctor I had managed death, holding it at arm's length. As a surgeon I had mended many bodies, saved many lives, brought patients back from the brink when there seemed to be no hope, when life or death was a question of a few minutes. But each one lost took its toll, and now the biggest toll had been taken.

36

Carefully folding the obit that Elly had dictated to the newspaper, I put it in my wallet. Dee straightened my tie and picked a piece of lint from my suit sleeve as we prepared to leave for Danny's funeral. It was Dee who had bought me my first suit, a dark brown suit. She made this purchase when I made the decision to forgo a career in music and take up medicine.

"Doctors need to have a good appearance," she reminded me again as she straightened my suit coat.

Elly drove our black Buick up the tree-lined driveway, curving its way through the manicured grounds of the cemetery to the mausoleum sitting on the hill overlooking the town below. The mausoleum was the only such burial site in the moderately small scenic mountain town. The site sat on a rolling plateau, giving a panorama of the surrounding Appalachian Highlands. Being on the board of the Ridgeview Cemetery, I had persuaded the members to pick this spot. Some had dropped off the board for lack of interest in their sunset. Many people in the town had no time or money to think about such things. Some could barely afford a doctor let alone an undertaker.

The Georgian marble of the exterior of the mausoleum added a bit of grace and panache to the cemetery grounds. The weather on the knoll was temperate and delightful especially in the summer. The winters were cold, and a chilling wind could howl across the mountains.

Reverend Parker, who would conduct Danny's service, was waiting in front of the large ornate iron doors of the mausoleum's entrance. Along side the doors were two etched windows of guardian angels holding torches.

"Look at him, the charlatan," Elmira hissed as we walked across the parking lot. Dee has more pictures of him than the Vatican has of Christ."

Dee did adore Reverend Parker and dismissed the rumors about his philandering. The preacher aspired an Elmer Gantry type of personality.

He charmed most people in the town, especially the women. Dee knew certain women were attracted to him. You would see women of all ages clamoring around him after every service. Some would practically throw themselves at his feet, wishing he would literally lay his hands on them.

With a warm smile and a glad hand, Reverend Parker had managed to build a thriving church. There were a number of churches in town, fifteen at least, but Parker's church drew crowds of people who had heard about the soaring, fiery sermons. The preacher was especially adroit at tapping the coffers of wealthy patrons, the coal barrens of the area who controlled the real money. But I was high on the list of the well enough off who could afford their name on a wall, or statue, or window.

"Keep your hand on your wallet, Daniel," said Elmira as we neared the entrance. "The only reason Daniel's giving less money has not tarnished his image or place in the hierarchy of the town is because he is the doctor Parker and the coal barrens as well as everyone else, want—if the need arises."

Reverend Parker held out the saving grace of God as a carrot. His healing was done in the name of the Lord. If it didn't work, "don't blame the Lord." The person simply hadn't given his total commitment to the Lord, or God was simply doing His work in His own time.

"You can't rush God."

You could not question the Lord, and you certainly could not question Reverend Parker. He had a direct line to God.

As a student in college, I had regularly attended church at Dee's urging. As a surgeon, I was quietly skeptical of "hands on healers" like Reverend Parker. Too many times when someone had been "healed" at church on a Saturday or Sunday in the name of God, they would soon find themselves in my hospital seeking treatment for the condition they supposedly had been cured of. I lamented that the preacher "healer" and his posse were long out of town with their coffers full motoring on in their Pontiac convertibles to the next town and the next victims where again a tent would be pitched with a portable generator providing minimal power for the bare light bulbs hung dimly over crying babies and murmurs of a fearful congregation, suddenly hushed by the booming voice from the pulpit echoing through the fields of parked cars and heathen beer-drinking, fornicating teenagers out into the dead-end hollows. The voice, the messenger of God, offered salvation or hell. The choice was the cowed worshippers to make. I kept my questions about the healing powers of ministers to myself.

Dee said she had never felt closer to God than when Oral Roberts had his "blessed hands" on her shoulders. She had bought a personally-blessed handkerchief from his array of merchandise. The handkerchief lay atop her chest of drawers, still in the box it came in. Dee was a "believer" who knew there was a greater power at work. I did not dismiss the power of suggestion, but I did not believe in magic. I did firmly believe modern medicine was the greater power, though I had seen people cured of maladies for no apparent medical reason. How the body puts itself back together at times is a mystery. As a surgeon, I knew I was not the be-all, end-all, but I also knew my powers as a doctor were better than any fly-by-night self-professed healing preacher, whose religion was a gift of gab—like Oral Roberts—even if the man had a university named after him.

This fact was a dilemma for me because a university bearing one's name was not easy to disregard. But I could not deny my disdain for such preachers, and my greeting to Reverend Parker in front of the mausoleum's majestic iron doors was brief and business-like. Give me Gregory Peck anytime.

As the Reverend led the family past the wall crypts, I noticed the brass plaques identifying the occupant of each crypt. Before purchasing my crypt, I questioned whether it was necessary to put the dates of birth and death. Didn't mind so much the date of death, but saw no need to list the date of birth. Why should anyone be interested? The mausoleum director had not had a big demand for the rather expensive crypts, so he agreed the date of birth was superfluous.

"How 'bout we just knock off ten or so years at the event," said the director.

He and I had a good laugh. This was after I had agreed to buy crypts for my whole family, including Dee, at a 10% discount.

"The family will like being up on the hill," the director had said, dryly. "The view is better."

It took me a moment to catch the humor.

As we passed by, I told Elly I had purchased one for her.

"Thank you, Daddy, but I have not made any such arrangements yet. Besides… I think I want to be cremated."

"Oh, ah…well, just in case you change your mind, I've put one on hold."

The organist went through her repertoire of sad songs. The hymns were some of my favorites from my boyhood. I had committed them to memory after hearing them so often at the old river church I attended with mother. First was "Hold To God's Unchanging Hand" followed by "I'll Go, Gladly I'll Go," then "Glory To Jesus, I'm Redeemed." I found it hard to feel "redeemed."

The Baptist hymns of my childhood took me back to those Sunday mornings when mother would sing full-throated with a voice like a blue bird.

On a hill far away stood an old rugged cross… Shall we gather at the river…the beautiful, the beautiful river… Mother's voice singing me to sleep. I was too old, Father said, "Boy can sing himself to sleep." But I couldn't. How can you be too old to be sung to? I could never sing as pretty as Mother.

I could sense Mother's presence as I raised my hands to God, feel her rough calloused farm hands wrapped snugly around mine, a child again, and the wind was having its way with my homemade kite, snapping its lifeline, taking it further and further into the wild yonder.

"Wait for me, wait for me," the boy cried. "Wait for me."

For weeks I would lay speechless and scared on the hard ground and cry for my mother.

Sitting before Danny's casket, my hands resting on my lap, palms down, as in a séance, trying to conjure the immoveable heavy past. I was transfixed by the petite organist, her feet barely reaching the organ's pedals forcing her to extend her leg straight exhaling an audible gasp of breath each time her foot thudded, emitting a jarring note out of the organ's pipes, reminding me of a fog horn on the Mississippi River. The heaviness of the organist's playing echoing off the dark purplish marble walls of the dimly lit mausoleum only accented the sadness of the service, which suited me just fine. The hymns I had selected to be sung at my own funeral were now being played at my son's funeral.

We were seated in the first row. Elmira was dressed in a dark purple two-piece suit she had bought especially for Danny's funeral. Danny had always complimented her when he thought she looked nice. She didn't want to disappoint him. She held her folded arms tightly across her chest, her head bowed.

"At Aunt Grace's funeral, they sang the saddest songs they could find," Elmira told Elly, shaking her bowed head.

After "the dirge" was over, Elmira lifted her head revealing a deeply creased tired face, like parched, hard earth. Her eyes though could still light up at the sight of her grandchild, Douglas—who had his hand in her lap—but mostly her eyes held a steady but forlorn gaze.

As a solitary young man, not on anyone's radar, I would have been described as non-descript, someone you might not pay attention to unless you saw me running to exhaustion in the rolling Alleghenies. I was still running, but now lost and forgetting any pretense of appearance, "I want a good casket for your brother," I had told Elly. *The casket looked nice, substantial, rich*, I thought. I leaned forward and rubbed my hand over the cherry wood, thinking it was the kind of casket I would like for myself. *Life's lessons*, I thought, *are hard*. We all have a cross to bear. The family had been forced to witness the slow torture of life's vice-like predicaments squeezing until Danny could resist no more. Elmira had insisted on a closed casket, but had consented to my wish that an enlarged photo of Danny adorned in his military school uniform be placed by the casket. It was in this uniform that Danny would be laid to rest. I insisted that he be buried in full military regalia. I had taken the photograph and managed to capture Danny's moment in the sun. I had kept the photo in my chest of drawers in the box with cufflinks and tie clasps. I had looked at the photo often over the years, the golden promise, the fulfillment of that promise I had hoped would soften the slippery, unsure, messy deeds of my father and mother. I had tried to explain this to Dee, how she had built me a bridge of love to span the "deep gorge of our mother's death." I had collected several photographs of Danny, photos of his cars, his cat,—little treasures. These pictures were put in Danny's casket.

"No one will see them unless they tear the mausoleum down," Elmira had said.

"God will see them."

Perhaps in time the photos would be found and someone would know Danny had lived. He had much more to do, a longer road to travel.

I stared at Danny's photo, remembering that moment, that special moment, when he had come home on break from the military academy proudly showing off his drill team uniform with its red sash wrapped around his waist and tailing down one side of the long double-breasted brass buttoned coat, his right-gloved hand holding erect a sword—the sword I had placed in the coffin by his side—and the gold embroidered rivulet decorating his left shoulder, and a white belt with its silver crest running diagonally from his right shoulder. Danny's white shirt and black tie, the dark striped gray trousers, the spit-shined black shoes and the first lieutenant officer's hat—that I had placed on his chest—sat high on his head, the bill resting just above his black horn-rimmed glasses giving him owl-like eyes completed my vision. It was too late to make sense of it all, to weave a tale with a satisfying ending.

"Self-examination results in the conviction of sin," Reverend Parker intoned. "We know how weak and undeserving all of us are of the love and grace of God."

"I know how weak and undeserving he is," Elmira, her eyes shut, said to Elly. Elmira covered her ears trying to wall out the minister's "over-cooked verbose emotional service" she had warned me to be prepared for. "It will be interminable."

"But God sent Christ to lift you, Daniel and Elmira, from de-spair as you, Daniel, have lifted many from the despair of sickness and disease and bodily injury. But it is only through Christ we can find forgiveness and immortality. You, Daniel and Elmira, Danny's parents, can never be fully reconciled to Danny's being so suddenly gone. You can only trust in The Almighty's wisdom that Danny's tak-ing has not been in vain. Danny was involved in the anti-war move-ment while a student at Harvard. The Vietnam War would not have ended without protests like Danny's. He made a difference. His life made our lives better, more noble." *If only I could believe that*, I thought.

Elmira's coughing caught the preacher's eye. She raised her hand in a circular motion, signaling for him to please wind it up. The minister discreetly nodded and simply continued on, expounding on the belief of the immortality of the soul.

"Your boy still lives. Death is only a change in form. His soul is now free. It will ascend into the land of true being where the greatest love is found. You should take comfort in knowing your son has given you immortality. We all want 'good' in our presence." Reverend Parker emphasized the word 'all.' "We also want immortality. That is one reason you have cared for your children. You gave your son your name Daniel. 'Daniel E. Friend Jr.' That was done out of love."

Yes, it had been. Out of Elmira's love for me, she had honored me by naming our son after me as I had honored her by insisting we name our daughter after her. One day our daughter came home from school and announced she wanted to be called "Elly." Years later, I told tell her how Gregory Peck's mother had picked his name, Eldred, out of a phone book.

"He never liked it, so he went by his middle name, Gregory."

"He was smart," said Elly. "Names help, nice names."

The minister made an unscheduled reference to a child fathered by Danny.

"I know how pleased, Daniel, you and Elmira must be." I looked at Elmira in wide-eyed confusion.

"Did he say a child?" Darren asked, leaning across Douglas.

"He assumes we know," Elly said.

As I turned to ask Elmira if she had any inkling of a child, I was surprised to see Janice sitting a few rows back. She smiled at me. I averted my eyes and took hold of Elly's arm.

"It's Janice," I said.

"My God, my God," Elmira gasped.

"It is this child who will continue the family line," the minister declaimed assuredly, having evidently forgotten, or never knew, that we had a daughter who had already provided us with a scrapping young grandson. Elly felt her mother's elbow jabbing at her side when the preacher weighed in on Danny's unborn child.

"The man is an idiot," Elmira hissed, yet again.

"He thinks we know," Elly whispered.

Elmira started to stand, but Elly pulled her back down into her seat.

"Is this true?" Elly asked.

"I have no idea," said Elmira.

"First I've heard of it," I said. "It's possible, I suppose."

"Oh, you never believed it back when Joan was pregnant with Danny's child," said Elmira.

I heard Elly remind Darren about Danny's past relationship—which had resulted in a void that over the years swelled into a silent deep pool of despair before flooding its poison. The minister was still talking as Douglas poked his mother asking if he was going to have a cousin.

"Could be."

"That would be neat," he said. Elly smiled, patting Douglas's hand.

Elmira had given up any pretense at politeness. "Will that ignoramus ever finish?"

The minister glanced our way, and I wondered if he had heard Elmira. *He must have*, I thought, for he abruptly concluded the service, noting the occasion was not sad, "…for the pregnant soul…is a higher form of procreation than the pregnant body."

There was another audible groan from Elmira.

"I can not listen to that wind bag another second. I think I am going to throw-up. This service is longer than Sherman's march to the sea." She held her stomach and thrusting her head toward the exit, stood up and made her way out of the mausoleum as though for an emergency bathroom visit. Elly looked at Darren.

"Go," he said.

Elly quickly got up, leaving Darren, Douglas, and me and hurried to catch Elmira. The service concluded, the mausoleum was emptying of the hundred or so people attending the service, many of whom were patients and colleagues and fellow Rotarians of mine who had stopped to pay their respects or just lay their hands on my shoulder. In the small community I could not avoid knowing my patients. I would see them on the street, at church, in the grocery store, in the neighborhood, at Wednesday Rotary luncheons, and at funerals. Reverend Parker and Dee stood on each side of me like sentinels on duty. I threw myself across Danny's casket and wrapped my arms around it. The cold dim room was quiet but for my sobbing. I could not bring myself to leave, a drowning, tired, man whose life was passing before him.

"It was God's will Danny is gone," Dee reminded me.

"God's will or my will?"

"Jesus has taken on your sins, Daniel," Dee was leaning over, whispering to my back. "You must trust Him. Do you?"

"Yes," I finally answered. "Yes, I do." I pulled out my little black pocket prayer book.

"Heavenly Father, you know the weakness and cowardliness of my heart. You know how much I care for the opinion of men. Help me, please help me...."

"You will see him again," said Dee, assuring me.

What if I did see Danny again? What would I say? Dee's faith was so unquestioning. She put her arm around my shoulder and leaned her head against mine, again whispering, "God will take you. Immortality is His to give. You need not be perfect. God loves you."

With Reverend Parker's help, I slowly raised my body from Danny's casket and shuffled toward the door. A youngish woman, noticeably pregnant suddenly emerged near the door. She stepped inside the door blocking my path. My eyes forced upward. There before me was Janice.

"You killed him," said Janice. Dee tried to hurry me along.

"No, no, Dee. Wait."

"Janice, please," said Dee.

"The dead body in that casket is my husband and the father of my child."

The minister looked at us. Still Janice remained, blocking our path and staring at me as though awaiting some answer. The eerie silence of the mausoleum was punctuated with my labored breathing. The chaotic world of my making was closing in.

"I guess now that my husband is dead, you can't call me an adulteress, isn't that right, preacher?"

Reverend Parker seemed confused.

"Isn't that right, preacher?"

The preacher looked at me and then smiled back at Janice who had earlier prevailed upon him to honor her husband by not forgetting the gift he had left behind, their child. The preacher nodded in the affirmative and then to a dark suited man hovering nervously at the door he said, "Kindly escort this young lady to her car."

"Janice, I want..." She did not let me finish.

"Don't worry," she said, "you will never see your son's child. He will never know you exist. My lawyer will be in touch."

"You won't need a lawyer. Danny's child will give me a second chance to do better. I will be thankful if you let me help you and your child in any way I can, no strings attached, I promise. It is the least I can do for Danny."

Janice looked at me for a moment and then smiled, turned and walked away. The black-suited hovering man hurried to keep pace. The sound of Janice's black-booted hard heels on the marble floor echoed. I felt a jab with every click of her heels. Turning back to Danny's casket, I saw the funeral director and three of his employees dressed alike in black, shifting their weight waiting to lift the casket onto a gurney to be wheeled to its slotted crypt. Dee took my arm and slowly walked me out of the mausoleum.

––––––––––––

Elmira and Elly were waiting in the welcoming setting sun.

"Are you all right, Daddy?"

"Yes," I said, seeing the maple trees bow to the unseasonable warm wind, their leaves hanging on despite being late November. Elmira was grateful for winter's delay and grateful for the care and attention she always received from her daughter. She squeezed Elly's hand, as they enjoyed the soft breeze. Elmira unbuttoned her coat and took a deep breath.

"Never a dull moment," she said. "Those hymns!" She shook her head. "They were so sad, the saddest ones Daniel knows. I've had to go around with my defenses up. If I had let down the least bit, you would have collapsed."

"You're right, Elmira. In fact, I did. Thought I might have to be carried out."

"Well, you can stop beating your chest in grief. There's no one left to impress." I supposed I deserved that. "I felt numb during the whole service," said Elmira.

The parking lot had nearly emptied. A car stopped in the driveway across from us. The passenger window rolled down.

"Hi," said a sprightly voice, if a frog-like voice can be called sprightly. Sonny was a sky-full of birds. Sonny greeted each day with unbridled elation. Spirited was the word to describe him. He stuck his hand out the window and smiled, giving Elly a vigorous hand-shaking.

"Hi, I'm Sonny."

"Hello, Sonny," replied Elly.

"Danny's home."

"No, Sonny."

"He probably thinks Danny was just asleep," said Elmira turning away.

"No, Danny's home," repeated Sonny. He had been at the service with his parents, who had sent the most beautiful flowers with a lovely letter telling Elmira and me how much they had appreciated Danny's friendship with Sonny. They were convinced the friendship was responsible for Sonny's well-being these many years. Elly said she noticed Sonny had spent most of his time looking at all the flowers.

"Danny's in my garden. Oh boy, oh boy." Sonny clapped his hands several times.

"Danny loved you, Sonny," I said and leaned in and patted his hand.

"I love Danny. Love is real," said Sonny, his head now sticking out the car window looking back as the car pulled away. Elly returned Sonny's wave. She was crying, touched, as we all were, by Sonny's unselfish love.

"Danny helped Sonny plant his garden every spring," said Elmira. "He'd laugh. Said there was no rhyme, nor reason to the garden, but it was fun. Danny enjoyed it."

I thought that like Sonny's garden, Danny's life had no shape.

Dee's hands clutched a small pocket Bible. Her deep serenity was her faith in knowing her nephew was going to a better place. He was going home to Jesus, which is where she too would go one day.

Slowly, I made my way to the car. Elly was in the driver's seat already, Elmira not liking to drive anymore, and I was in no condition to drive.

"Traffic is such a mess," Elmira said, "it would take your father forever. The other day we were coming back from the shopping center, and he wanted to stop and get some gas. He had to cut across traffic. We nearly got hit three times. It's a self-service station. They didn't have any paper towels to cover his hand while pumping the gas so he had to use his handkerchief which didn't please him. Then he didn't want to cut back across traffic so we had to go all the way around town. I thought we'd never get home. And he only got ten gallons. Mercy. It takes that much to get that Buick down to the hospital and back."

Dee and Reverend Parker were making their trek toward the car.

"Dee has a pacemaker and other problems," said Elmira to Elly. "At times she can hardly lift her purse, and still she's the head nurse. Lord, help the patients. It's a real comedy. She's come close to dying twice. We went down to her house one morning, and we both thought she was dead."

"We did indeed," I concurred. "We didn't think she was going to make it. I insisted on taking her to the hospital. Dee was adamant about not going to the hospital, but when push came to shove, and she couldn't talk or move to stop me, she had no choice."

"She had been going to a Chinese woman, an engineer who also practices holistic medicine, prescribing various herbal remedies. Dee said the woman was quite capable, smart. She tried to persuade Daniel to try it, didn't she?"

"Yes. I thought it was voo-doo. Everybody has their way of doing things."

"You'll be the same. If anything happens to you, I'll have to drag you, kicking and screaming, to the hospital, too. I guess the close calls got Dee thinking about arrangements. Dee wants to be buried in her uniform, cap and all, with her diploma in her hand."

"Good for her," said Elly.

"She said she would like you to read something. You can just scatter my ashes over the rhododendron in the back yard."

"You're not serious, Elmira."

"I am serious, Daniel." Just then a familiar face caught Elmira's attention. "Oh, there's Janice, isn't it?"

"Yes, it is," said Elly, watching Janice, who was across the parking lot. "She looks like she's ready to pop. Danny never knew about the baby?"

"Apparently not," said Elmira.

"I thought she moved away," said Elly.

"She did. Nashville, I think. Some fellow down there saw her Walmart commercial and told her he thought he could help her find more of that kind of work."

My eyes drifted across the rolling hills of time. I wondered if the true meaning of family lay in the valleys of these hills, buried deep in the hollows. Time was precious, and you had to learn how to be judicious with it and learn when to put it aside.

37

It was another beautiful autumn in New England. Elmira and I made our annual fall pilgrimage to Elly and Darren's. We again had the privilege of sitting in on one of Elly's classes. When she had finally told me of her full professorship status, I could not stop crying, telling Elly my tears were tears of joy over her accomplishments. The words 'tears of joy' brought back my mother's face when she spoke those words in church that long ago morning when I asked her why she was so sad. Darren reminded Elly of the time when his first advertising campaign was announced to the world. He said she had cried like a baby.

"I was happy for you. I come from an emotional family," said Elly.

"You ever feel overwhelmed, Elly?" I asked.

"When I have a hundred essays to read," she answered. "That is an overpowering and helpless feeling. Push here, rush there—rush, rush everywhere. No time for anything special because so many things need to be done. But I'm not complaining."

"You are a wonderful teacher, Elly."

"Sometimes I think I'm not suited for it, but I'm a pretty good teacher, I think. Besides, someone has to do it."

"Is that what you tell your students, Elly?"

"I tell them the best stories are about people who overcome adversities. My problem," said Elly, "has always been that I do not know how to do nothing. Darren says that doing nothing is an art. You've got to cultivate it. You got to learn how to do nothing. But they don't teach that at Harvard."

That's true, I thought. It was also true that Harvard promoted very few to a full professorship.

———————————

Some weeks later, Elly, Darren, and Douglas were back in Appalachia for Christmas. Elly had accompanied Dee and me to church. Walking down the street was almost impossible for all the people offering sympathetic words and handshakes. Walking back to the car, I told Elly that we weren't going to observe Christmas any more.

"You never cared about Christmas anyway," Elly said, smiling.

"Please don't get us any more gifts."

"You won't have to open them. You can give them away, Daddy. Douglas will be disappointed not to receive any presents from his grandparents not to mention your daughter, who I remind you loves to get presents."

"You and Douglas can send us a list anytime."

Back home, Elmira took Douglas out to help her feed the birds. From the sunroom, Dee, Elly, and I saw Elmira hand her slingshot to Douglas. He put a marble in the pouch and pulled back hard and took aim at a flock of pigeons.

"Every life is precious, even a pigeon's," said Dee.

The pigeons safely scattered, and Elly laughed, watching Douglas reload.

"Your father's not a well man, Elly."

"I'm fine."

"You have been deliberately overworking yourself. As a doctor," Dee said to Elly, "he can cope, but as a father...I think your father wants to kill himself."

"I'm not going to worry, Aunt Dee, unless Daddy makes a sudden gift to me of his stethoscope. Besides," Elly said, putting her arm around me, "I like people who die in harness."

"You're right, I suppose," agreed Dee. "None of us accept the fact of death. Even as old as I am. 'He that shall endure unto the end, shall be saved.'" Dee sat in the Kennedy rocker. "One day the pain will be gone; it won't be anything. Your father's had a hole in his heart. All boys want their mother no matter how old they are."

After dinner that night, Douglas helped his grandmother sort out Danny's things. They found a set of Match-Box Cars Danny had collected. Elmira asked Douglas if he would like to have them. Douglas was delighted and took them downstairs to the library to play with. After a while he came into the kitchen with my old violin. He asked Elmira if he could play it.

"Someone ought to get some use out of it. Remember Danny's teacher telling me he didn't think the lessons were worth our money," Elmira said to Elly. "By the time Danny finished his popsicle and went to the bathroom, the lesson was over."

"You and Daddy are going to be grandparents again," said Elly.

"When?" Elmira's spirits lifted.

"I mean Janice and Danny's baby."

"Oh, yes," I said. "Afraid the baby is going to have a poor environment to grow and develop in. I have heard Janice is living back in the mobile home, and some guys have been seen going in and out. I do think Danny would have been a good father."

"I can forgive lots of his actions, even suicide," said Elmira

"It wasn't suicide," I said.

"He drove off the side of a mountain."

"Maybe we should take a trip," I said.

"I've had my fill of your trips, even short ones. Every vacation, you looked for a Rotary sign in every town. If there happened to be a meeting, you'd go, wouldn't know a soul."

"You did, Daddy."

"You either stopped for a Rotary meeting or a haircut," complained Elmira. "Haircut's about as exciting as a Rotary meeting, I bet. Else you'd have the car greased and oil changed— always in some dumpy little burned-up place with no shade."

"You may be right, Mama."

"Dee tells me you have a new office nurse. Your dressing up so dapper lately wouldn't have anything to do with her, would it?"

"What?"

"You heard me, your new nurse," said Elmira.

"What about her?"

"Is she attractive?"

"Who?"

"Your new nurse!"

"She's nice," said Dee, referring to my new nurse.

"I'm so glad, but I didn't ask you, Dee," replied Elmira. "So, is she attractive?"

"She's efficient," I allowed. "Conscientious."

"Is she attractive, Daniel?"

"She's handsome," I said.

"Men are handsome, Daddy."

"You might call her attractive"

"You might?" Elmira asked, laughing.

"Where's Nova Scotia?" asked Dee, looking up from the two-day old newspaper she was reading.

"It's on the east coast of Canada. It's beautiful up there," said Darren, who, having been driven out of the living room by the screeching violin, arrived on the scene in time to get a chuckle about the handsome office nurse.

"It says here that Walmart is expanding there," said Dee.

––––––––––

Sitting on the porch, my medical charts on my lap, I suddenly flinched and realized I had been asleep and had dreamed about my father. The day before his death, I had hiked up Goat Hill to check on him. He was standing at the edge of the hill looking out across the mountains.

"My past is gone, boy, with the trees, the woodpeckers 'n streams. I'm still lonely 'n scared 'n so hurtin' sad…. I was addicted to yer mother, the promise of her love kept me on edge. After she…I just sat there filthy with coal dust from the awfulness I had witness'd. I've never been able to leave the sadness of it all—a terrible sinkin' from which I've never recovered. Son, it breaks my heart to know how I've treated ya. I'm no good, poison. I'm sorry, son, fer ever layin' a hand to ya. Fergive me."

"I forgive you, Dad." It was the last time I saw him alive. I got up from the rocker and walked out to the sidewalk. Elly stepped out onto the porch and walked down the steps, joining me.

"I know it has not been easy for your mother being married to a doctor, Elly. Mine is a selfish game. But now the lights are flashing, the gate is down, and the train is coming. I am witnessing the deterioration of something I cherish and that is the quality of what I do. Put me out on the garbage heap. The mind is willing, Elly, but the body will have its way." I held my hand out. "I don't know how much longer I will be able to control my little tremor. I will be forced to give up operating, but I will try to meet my fate with grace and dignity."

"I know you will."

"If I were a superstitious man, I'd say I'd been cursed… like the Kennedys."

"You've been blessed to do something you've loved, with all your heart."

"Yes, I have, Elly. I have indeed. And I've been blessed with you."

My eyes searched the hills, contemplating what only a hill person can. "Family, Elly, is what binds these hills together."

"There was a time when I flirted with the idea of coming back to the hills to live because, try as you might, you can't fully get away."

"Suppose not. I could never leave this place. People do, and some come home to the hills. My heart has soared watching you on your chosen path. You are genius, Elly. You deserve your success. Your ancestors came out of debtor's prison, no earls or dukes. Guess you are not surprised. Landed about 1760, came over the mountains a few years later and ended up near here at the mouth of Coal River miles from anywhere. The water was clear and cool, fed by mountain streams surrounded with oak and elm and paw paw trees, everything green. You could fall asleep naked on the rocks, and things of wonder and delight filled your dreams. It's odd because I never really knew my ancestors. I would have liked to. I didn't have a whole lot behind me, a lot of loneliness and sadness. But I had dreams."

"It's okay, Dad." She took my arm.

"I wanted to do it all for you and Danny, cover all the bases, keep you healthy, wealthy, and wise. But you can't. The world is complicated. You recall that word Danny used neither of us knew?"

"Adscititious. I looked it up."

"I knew you would. But no matter how tough, how painful, how unessential you feel, you keep going forward. My father had no way to ease the hurt. Anger didn't do it, and he did not have the words to say it. Perhaps he did, but I could not share his pain because I had my own to deal with. As hard as it is to say, I don't think there was love enough between us to allow us to connect. Father's pain had little to do with me. It was Mother and his feeling he had been wronged, not just by her but by the coal and timber companies."

"Like Danny felt about Walmart," said Elly.

"Yes. ...My Father and Mother could not resolve their hurt so your Aunt Dee and I were left to somehow continue on, and we did, thanks to her. I know I'm sentimental." The tears ran down my cheek. Elly wiped them with her hand. "At heart, your daddy is a hardcore realist. As a doctor, I have seen miracles. Talking of miracles, I am going to resume my dancing. I have signed up for some dance classes taught here in town by a man and his wife. I delivered their baby."

"One of the things I've always loved about you, Daddy, is you've never stopped going forward. I love you for that."

"When I can't, will you still...love me?"

Now Elly was crying too. She held her arms out wide like she did when she was a very little girl and I would ask, "How much do you love me?"

"This much, Daddy and so much more."

"And how much do I love you?"

Again little Elly would hold her arms wide and say, "This much, Daddy, and so much more."

"Well, I've run a few red lights.… I always tried to fill the empty space, the void, like coloring the whitening of my hair so I couldn't see what was there. I've never worn a watch, so I wouldn't be so aware of time passing. But it surely does and whatever moments were there are gone, lost, and there are no words to bring to bring them back. This doctor doesn't have many answers. I can easily recognize malnutrition, but a lack of knowledge is sometimes harder to see. The one thing I know for sure though: without knowledge part of you dies." I looked to our house.

"Where are we, Elly? Look up there," I said, pointing to the second floor.

Elmira's bedroom light was on, and we could see the last trace of the hall light bleeding through the empty rooms out into the street. We couldn't see the faint blue glow of the television because it's in the basement where dragons reside but have been put to rest with the civility of redwood paneling. The nocturnal owls were in the attic watching over us, and all our memories.

"It's a nice house, isn't it?"

"It's a very nice house, Daddy," said Elly, squeezing my hand.

"I thank God for you, Elly, everyday. I love you."

"I love you, Daddy."

"Are you hungry?"

"Famished."

"Let's go inside, and see what we can dig up."

The End

Excerpt from *Stairway To Heaven* by *David Selby*

Deadend, though fairly dark – even in mid-afternoon, was a
place of solitude with a Vegas motto of what plays here, stays here,
an oasis for stressed-out, watchful men, men slumped around a long
table – no pressure of having to be anywhere anytime soon or even
desiring to be – mid-fifties, regulars, laid-back, deliberate, resignation in their eyes, bleak at times, no surprises left, no more boasting,
just enjoying a smoke and a beer as they commiserate over another
lost football game or a bad weed crop.

"War on weed's failing just like prohibition," said Doc.

"Gangs get all the money," said Desperado, as his cell phone
rang.

"I agree," said the mayor. "Country's starving for money and
we spend what little we got to fight weed – idiotic, defies description."

"Junior?" Desperado barked. "Where the hell are you?!... I'll
say it again, real slow. Where… the hell… are you… Junior! Better
have your shit wired tight. You wash your car? You trash those Grateful
Dead stickers?.. You little shit... Junior?!.... 'Cause cops like to stop
and search and seize! You get a hair cut?... Short? …. Wear a suit
and tie to the hydro store… . Suit and tie freaks the customers out,
that's why…No! I told you, don't text about bud, growin,' or smokin'.
Understood? And don't drive around with wet or freshly dried bud…
Sheriff's no good. He hates Dewey. He'll haul your ass in for a gram.
You're pulled over, he'd search your home…if you had a home! Did

you hide the gun?...You're in denial my friend. You get busted then they'll be on my ass…and I won't be happy. What?.....Junior!" The line goes dead. "Damnit!"

"You put that tower on the mountain, Mayor," said Coach. "Now we gotta listen to Desperado's bullshit."

"Everybody's bullshit," said Doc.

"It's an eyesore," said the coach.

"You can't see it, looks like an evergreen tree," said the mayor.

"Bull turkey," laughed Coach. "It looks like a cheap artificial Christmas tree. How much they put in your pocket? It's all right if Big Brother sticks his nose up your ass as long as he pays for the privilege. Right?"

"Verizon's lettin' the Feds listen to everybody," said Doc.

"Wonder if they give the Feds a rate break?" said Coach.

"The Feds ain't doing nothing they ain't been doing for a hundred years," said the mayor, checking his cell. "NSA's going to bring the antenna down over in Sugar Grove, put a bigger one couple of mountains down. Don't bother me none – got nothing to hide, like some I know. They filter millions of calls in no time flat. You gotta get with the program, Coach. Technology could make even you a winner. Besides, this is a designated quiet zone."

"Tell that to Dewey," said Mary Ellen.

"Don't have to. It's a federal and state law."

"Hey Desperado," Doc said, "put this lady on the wall." Doc unfurled a poster of a pin-up girl.

Mary Ellen looked at the poster and said, "In your dreams, boys."

"I dream in 3-D, honey," said Doc.

"Lather me up, Romeo," said Mary Ellen.

"I would love that, Juliet," replied Doc.

"What?" asked the mayor.

"Romeo and Juliet," said Doc.

"What?"

"You wearing your hearing aid, Mayor?" asked Mary Ellen.

"Don't need a hearing aid. I hear what I wanna hear."

Looking at the pin-up poster that Desperado was hanging – next to a mounted deer head – Mary Ellen asked Desperado if he remembered what a pin-up looked like.

"Oh yes, I saw one once. That last bit of pleasure has been excised. Where have you been?"

"Why is that mangy thing still here?" Mary Ellen asked, referring to the deer head, ignoring his question.

"To annoy you," said Desperado.

"I found a tick on me from it."

"Poor thing must have starved. No warm blood there," he said. The intercom buzzed.

"Desperado doesn't deserve you."

"Mayor's right," said Doc.

"I love you men and I agree. This place can't run without me," she said.

"Some people will go against their own best interest every time," said Doc to his companions. Intercom buzzed again.

"All right, I'm coming!" yelled Desperado.

"You got three men here, Mary Ellen, who know how to appreciate you," said Doc. "Even though the mayor's interests lie elsewhere."

"I still appreciate her."

"Ah, that's so nice," said Mary Ellen.

"She's not that desperate," laughed Coach.

"She's working for Dewey, isn't she?" said the mayor.

Desperado opened the drive-thru window. "What can I do for you?"

"Just leave, honey," said the mayor.

"You're all sweet," said Mary Ellen. "Dewey wants me to leave."

"Yes, he wants you to leave!" said Desperado from the drive-thru window.

"I know too much, don't I? I'm in the way."

"Just keep your mouth shut. Please…a customer."

"You're obstructing justice, Desperado," said the mayor. "If Mary Ellen leaves town, that would prevent her from giving information to the sheriff about Dewey's drug business, past or present. If I were you, I'd let Dewey worry about Mary Ellen."

"What is it with you people?" Desperado took a few steps away from the window "Take a vacation till the heat from the sheriff cools off."

"I'll go to Maui," said Mary Ellen.

"Where?" hissed Desperado.

"Hawaii, you ignoramus."

"Ohio… bitch. Dewey gave me money so you can go to Ohio."

"Ohio?! That's rich. He'll put me up at Motel Six."

"He doesn't want you talking."

"I'm going to Hollywood."

"I ain't got all day, Ricky," said an exasperated Desperado, walking back to the drive-thru. Ricky was about twenty and a regular.

"You'll be a star," said Doc.

"Why not?" asked Mary Ellen.

"Hurrah for you," said the mayor. "But we need to make this a place where young people want to stay."

"She's America's Idol. She'll be a hero around here," said Doc.

"True," said the coach.

"Whole-wheat pizza with pineapple. No cheese," said Ricky.

"How hard could that be punker?" Desperado said and turned back to Mary Ellen. "All you have to do is be on television, and people think you know it all. You're famous."

"You can be my manager. We could sell our 'guns for drugs' story."

"Damnit, Mary Ellen."

"We could go undercover."

"Stop it!"

"You nervous, Despo?"

"I got a rash on my stomach!" Desperado walked away.

"Think of all we know, the stories we could tell!..You got a better idea?"

"Hard to find opportunity in these woods," said the mayor.

"I'm not walking away from a bountiful harvest," said Desperado.

"This year's could be our biggest cash crop. We put in new irrigation, moved a lot indoors."

"I think there's more Mexican weed here than's grown locally," said Doc.

"Whoosh!" With that, Mary Ellen shot her hand past Desperado's face.

"What's whoosh?"

"Your life."

"I got a plan," said Desperado with bravado, while making the pizza.

"A scheme you mean," she said, laughing.

Just then Desperado's cell phone rang. "Yeah? …Who is this?" Whoever it was – they were gone. "Retard."

"What's he on," asked Coach, nodding his head toward Desperado.

"High-fructose corn syrup," Mary Ellen replied.

"He's inhaling what he cooks," said the mayor.

"The wind's right, you can smell the cooking when you pull up – like dry rot," said the coach.

"Dry rot's what Despo has for a brain," said Mary Ellen, cleaning the tables.

"I thought crack was bad, then meth came along," said Doc.

"Desperado's teeth don't look good," said Coach.

"The sheriff campaigned on getting rid of all of it," said Doc.

"Made good press," said Coach.

Mary Ellen wondered if the sheriff, who had shared a few joints with her, really was all he was made out to be. She had no guilt delivering a little weed to folks who needed to feel better about their lives or just feel better. She couldn't understand why people in pain couldn't get marijuana without risking arrest or going to jail or having to pay lawyers to defend them if arrested. Mary Ellen wasn't worried about the sheriff or the Feds – or any man for that matter taking away her rights. At 18, she discovered she was all woman, more woman than most men would know what to do with. "Feds got these planes that can see the color of your underwear," said Mary Ellen, casually.

"FedEx don't come up here, let alone Feds," said the mayor. They're like the old-time census-takers who wouldn't come into these southern Appalachians for fear of what they'd come upon."

"Or fear they wouldn't come out," said Doc.

"Feds couldn't find this place if you gave 'em a map," said the mayor. "This place spooks them out."

"Feds don't need a map, Mayor," said Mary Ellen.

"How do you know?" asked Desperado.

"I read. You oughta try it."

"'Sides Dewey's strung fish hooks at eye level all around the place," said Doc.

"He's even put up surveillance cameras to watch the property," said the coach.

"You mean we're on TV?"

"Yeah, Doc," said the mayor. "When the exhaust fans are on, I think we're taking off."

"They clear the air," said Doc. "Blow that pungent weed smell into Virginia."

"And those damn dobermans bark at the drop of a leaf," said Coach.

"Dewey's paranoid," said the mayor.

"Only the paranoid survive," said Desperado.

"He oughta get a couple of pit bulls," laughed Coach. "Their reputation alone would scare off intruders."

"I do a lot of my work at night," said Desperado.

"Don't matter, Despo," said Mary Ellen, "all the old people up hollow, they're watching your every move."

"Mary Ellen has a point," said Doc. "Old folks can't chance losing the Fed's benefits just because they have to grow weed in order to make ends meet."

"You're expendable, Despo," said Mary Ellen.

"People got to do what they got to do," said Desperado. "I don't give a shit. All the dogs and barbed wire don't matter. That's for the poachers'cause the law doesn't care."

"That's what you say," said Mary Ellen.

"That's what I say! Feds are at a loss. It's a joke. A merry-go-round. Feds confiscated eighty bales of weed and uprooted a half-million plants – Dewey still didn't have to raise prices," said Desperado. "That was just a diversion crop, give the Feds something to brag about."

"They could be listenin'," said Mary Ellen.

"Who?" asked Desperado.

"Feds!" said Mary Ellen. "Every time you go online, the Feds are watching. You can't hide, Despo."

Desperado's face got paler. "It's all show."

"True, to a point," nodded the mayor. "Doc's right. All the retirees up hollow need their Social Security. And folks would lose their food stamps or housing supplements should they'd be arrested for cultivation. The law knows this, the sheriff does. He's sympathetic. Not to Dewey…too much history there."

"What the mayor's saying, Despo is that you better be careful whom you confide in unless you don't care everyone knows you're a guns for drugs trader," said a straight-faced Mary Ellen.

"This is a low-risk county. I haven't heard many choppers lately," said Doc.

"Just a few drones. Feds got night cameras that can see up your ass, Despo. You know growers here, in Kentucky, Tennessee, have had their crops decimated, poisoned," said Mary Ellen.

"Pills and booze are more dangerous," said Doc.

"They should stop wasting their time and tax dollars and go after the hard stuff…pills, crack, go after the real crime," said Coach.

"It's a joke," agreed Mary Ellen.

"State could use the money that would flow in if weed were legal – millions and millions," said Doc.

"We could save 42 million just by cutting arrests. And more and more people are using," added the mayor.

"Marijuana, like aspirin, like statins, is being found to treat all kinds of ailments," said Doc, "including seizures of various sorts. I'll tell you how stupid it is – how threatening weed is to some. The Fed copters around these thick woods – they only show at harvest time – have to get treetop 'fore they can make out what's what."

"Give me a strong black boy who can catch and run like the wind – and like a bear to honey, every football pimp in the country will smell this place out – I guarantee you," said Coach.

"Win some games, Coach, and you can rape and pillage," smiled Doc.

"That's Dewey's domain," replied Doc.

"Feds could be listening and watching, just can't see them, Despo," said Mary Ellen, tauntingly. "Got those special cameras. Satellites. See the pimples on your face."

"Shut up. You make me nervous."

"Oh…I make you nervous?"

"Yes. I got pimples. My mistake was comin' back here and havin' to listen to the likes of you and all the other do-nothin's. Nothing for me here," said Desperado, quietly, as he went about filling the order.

"Never will be nothing," she said.

"Thanks for the encouragement."

"And beware of outsiders bearing gifts," said Coach.

Hearing the word "outsiders" gave Mary Ellen a pause. "Outsiders don't know shit about this place," she said. "It's not fun here, but nobody knows what's real here, what's not possible." She felt like an outsider. But weren't the Detroit and Columbus gangs outsiders – offering gifts – pills and crack, and whatever else was on their menu? She wondered about all the guns that Despo and Dewey were trading in return. The guns ended up God knows where, she thought. She didn't want to know, but it was haunting her. She knew that Dewey kept a record of how many guns went out but nothing of where they went and whom they killed. But where did he keep the record, she wondered – probably in a safe in his hilltop house.

Books by David Selby

Happenstance

My Mother's Autumn

In and Out of the Shadows

My Shadowed Past

A Better Place

Lincoln's Better Angel

The Blue Door

Light and Shadows